# THE LAST BOY AND GIRL IN THE WORLD

# THE LAST BOY AND GIRL IN THE WORLD

SIOBHAN VIVIAN

SIMON & SCHUSTER BFYR

NEW YORK • LONDON • TORONTO • SYDNEY • NEW DELHI

An imprint of Simon & Schuster Children's Publishing Division
1230 Avenue of the Americas, New York, New York 10020
This book is a work of fiction. Any references to historical events, real people, or real places are used fictitiously. Other names, characters, places, and events are products of the author's imagination, and any resemblance to actual events or places or persons, living or dead, is entirely coincidental.
Text copyright © 2016 by Siobhan Vivian
Jacket illustration and design by Lucy Ruth Cummins
All rights reserved, including the right of reproduction in whole or in part in any form.
SIMON & SCHUSTER BFYR is a trademark of Simon & Schuster, Inc.
For information about special discounts for bulk purchases, please contact Simon & Schuster Special Sales at 1-866-506-1949 or business@simonandschuster.com.
Also available in a SIMON & SCHUSTER BFYR hardcover edition
The Simon & Schuster Speakers Bureau can bring authors to your live event. For more information or to book an event, contact the Simon & Schuster Speakers Bureau at 1-866-248-3049 or visit our website at www.simonspeakers.com.
Interior design by Hilary Zarycky
The text for this book is set in Adobe Garamond Pro.
Manufactured in the United States of America
First Edition
First SIMON & SCHUSTER BFYR export edition April 2016
2  4  6  8  10  9  7  5  3  1
CIP data for this book is available from the Library of Congress.
ISBN 978-1-4814-5229-8 (hardcover)
ISBN 978-1-4814-5231-1 (eBook)
ISBN 978-1-4814-7547-1 (export pbk)

*For Vivi*

**INSPIRED
BY
TRUE
EVENTS**

# THE LAST BOY AND GIRL IN THE WORLD

It's impossible to tell what's underneath me, exactly which part of Aberdeen I'm floating over right now, but I still lean over the side of the boat and try to see something down there. Maybe the white gazebo across from City Hall where my parents were married. Or the seesaw Morgan and I sat on for hours at a time during the summer after eighth grade, dreaming about what high school would be like, the board steady as a park bench because we both weighed exactly one hundred and two pounds. One of the mangy tinsel snowflakes that hung on the Main Street light posts year-round but somehow still managed to sparkle when lit up for the holidays. I'd even be happy with a freaking parking meter. I'm that desperate for something real, one last concrete thing from my hometown where I can project the good-bye-forever feelings clogging up my arteries. But I have no idea where I'm at exactly. I can't see deeper than my own reflection in the murky water.

"Congratulations, Keeley."

The man driving the rescue boat, Sheriff Hamrick—I forgot he was here.

He has one hand on the tiller of the trolling motor and tosses me a windbreaker with the other. I'm shivering pretty bad, so I put it on. There's a big National Guard emblem stitched on the chest, because, right, he's not sheriff anymore.

I guess because I don't say anything back, he snaps, "You're officially the last girl in Aberdeen."

I twist around and look for the rescue boat that was ahead of ours, the one carrying the last boy, but it's disappeared into the fog.

When I turn back, Sheriff Hamrick is staring at me. "Was it worth it?" It's clear, by the earnest way he asks, that he truly wants to know. He doesn't understand.

Before I can answer, his CB radio crackles with stern conversation. Officers talking to each other in police code. I can't make out much beyond that there are two cruisers waiting to take us away. Sheriff Hamrick turns down the volume. I watch him try to release some of what has him so tight. He rolls his neck, cracks his knuckles. "It doesn't matter. Aberdeen's officially gone now. Everyone can move on with their lives."

My shivers change into something different, something harder than when I was just cold. "Some of us don't want to move on."

Earlier this week, I typed in my address and nothing came up. Nothing for the zip code, either. I had to go to the next town over, Hillsdale, and drag my cursor to where our town should have been. The roads where my friends lived, the baseball field, the movie theater. Even the stuff that wasn't underwater yet was colored blue.

"You'll think differently when you're older," he says, defensive and so sure of himself. Then a grinding noise steals his attention. He cuts the power to the motor and lifts the propeller out of the water. Someone's discarded T-shirt has gotten twisted up in the blades, a cotton jellyfish.

While he untangles it, I stare into the distance, hoping he'll take the hint and stop talking already. A breeze blows away some of the mist and I'm able to see a few triangles spiking out of the water, the roofs of the tallest houses in the valley. They won't be there for much longer now that the dam is finished. I focus on the house that's closest to us. Scalloped white shingles, shimmery slate roof. Something about it is familiar. And then, as we putter past, the puzzle piece suddenly clicks into place with the part I can't see, what is sunken.

I'm not too late.

I stand up quickly. The boat rocks and the sheriff nearly tumbles out the back. "I need to go over there! To that house!"

"Sit down!" He barks it so sternly that I immediately obey. "You're in enough trouble, don't you think?" He takes off his cap and, exhaling, wipes his sleeve across his brow. "Look, I don't have the pull I once did, Keeley. I'm in a new position now. If anyone asks me, and they very well might, I'll tell them that you're a nice girl, that you just got caught up—"

My heart speeds up so fast that the individual beats blur into a hum. "Sheriff, please. Please. They'll never let me back here. And even if they did, it'd be gone." I plaster on a jokey grin, hoping to charm him. "Doesn't the last girl in Aberdeen deserve one last favor?" I used to be good at this. But it doesn't take long for my smile to slip. One crack and the whole thing gives way. My bottom lip trembles. My eyes fill with tears. "Someone very important to me lived in that house, and this the last time I'm ever going to see it." I force a swallow. "I know I have to let go. I know it's over. It's just so impossibly hard." I wipe my eyes. "You, more than anyone, have to understand that."

The sheriff suddenly can't look at me. He lets out a deep

sigh. After glancing over both of his shoulders to make sure we're alone, he turns his CB radio completely off. "Not a word to anyone about this, you hear? I mean it."

I rub my eyes with the back of my hand and nod hard and fast.

He changes our course, angling the boat toward where I'm pointing, carefully steering us around random floating crap. Couch cushions, sealed Tupperware bubbles, dining room chairs, mailboxes. The flotsam and jetsam of abandoned lives.

When we get close enough to the house, I press my hand to the round window and look into Morgan's attic bedroom for the very last time. Where we used to sleep in every Saturday morning is a glass half full of dark water.

Sheriff Hamrick clicks on a flashlight and hands it to me. "You after something in particular?"

I'm shaking so hard now that the flashlight beam touches everywhere in the room except the one spot I want it to land. I don't answer him, but I am. I'm looking for a letter that was left for me, sealed carefully inside a Ziploc bag and duct-taped to a blade of my best friend's ceiling fan.

Senior year was supposed to be when I said good-bye to Aberdeen, but it wouldn't have been forever. I had my heart set on Baird, the least expensive in-state college option, barely thirty miles away. I'd come home for holidays and semester breaks, and probably a random weekend here and there to do laundry and see Morgan and whoever else was around. Of course, that was only if I got a scholarship to cover my dorm expenses. If not, I'd be commuting there, sleeping in my old bedroom every night.

So maybe I shouldn't be surprised how bad I miss it. Even the things that drove me crazy. Like the flashing red light that went up on Main Street, our first and only traffic signal. It seemed so completely unnecessary. Most people in town ran it. But I bet if I end up living on the other side of the earth one day, that traffic light will blink red behind my eyes when I close them and make me warm.

Although that spring was the end of Aberdeen, I'll always remember it as full of beginnings. And not just for me. For all of us. Things around us were changing, sure, but we were changing too, and we couldn't pretend we weren't any longer. Maybe that's what happens when you're suddenly living your life on a warp speed setting, trying to make the most of it before everything you know slides underneath the water.

But when the rain first began to fall, we didn't see the bigger picture. We didn't even want to. The bigger picture was for our parents to worry about. We were sixteen, seventeen, eighteen, and focused on more exciting things, like how many days were left before school let out. And Spring Formal and our dresses.

When it started, the only thing I cared about was kissing Jesse Ford.

## 1

## Sunday, May 8
Mostly cloudy, with steady afternoon showers, 49°F

I used to love rainy days. The coziness of hiding inside a baggy sweater. Of thick socks and galoshes. Curling up against your best friend to share her too-small umbrella. The drowsy, dreamy way a day can pass when there's not a single ray of sunshine.

That was before Aberdeen had its wettest spring ever recorded. After three weeks straight of precipitation, I was ready to blow off finals and move to the Sahara. The weather hadn't reached biblical levels. We'd had a couple of big storms, not one long and endless monsoon. Some days it just sprinkled, some days it only misted. But the air always felt damp and unseasonably chilly. I was sick of layering. Thermals under jeans, T-shirts under button-ups under hoodies, tights or leggings under dresses under cardigans. All of it thickening me like a full-body callus, while my dresser drawers were full of neatly folded spring clothes that I was dying to wear. In fact, most kids still wore winter coats to school even though it was the beginning of May. In those early days, I remember that, more than anything else, feeling wrong.

So it was really nice to wake up to the sun the morning our high school's Key Club went to help shore up the riverbank with sandbags. Especially since the forecasters were already predicting a band of severe storms later in the week, supposedly the worst to hit us yet.

Actually, the first thing I saw when I opened my eyes was a rainbow. Not a real one, but a rainbow sticker I had put on the underside of Morgan's bedside lampshade a million years ago. Everything in Morgan's room used to be covered in stickers—her walls, her mirror, her closet door. Over time, she'd peeled them away, though their sticky gum outlines were left behind, like permanent shadows. But she never found this one, and I liked that it was still there.

I lifted my head off the pillow. Morgan was already in the shower. I waited until I heard the water shut off before climbing out of her bed. It was too cold and too early to bother changing clothes, so I threaded my bra back through the armholes of the T-shirt I'd slept in and checked to make sure my leggings weren't too baggy in the butt to wear in public. Then I reached across Morgan's side of the bed, picked one of my socks off her radiator, and squeezed it. It still wasn't completely dry, not even after a night spent baking on the coils.

Morgan hurried into her bedroom in her bra and underwear, a towel twisted around her hair. Ever since her parents divorced and her dad moved out, she'd quit wearing her bathrobe. Or maybe it was ever since she'd started hooking up with guys. I wasn't sure.

"I'm borrowing dry socks, okay?" I knelt in front of her laundry basket.

She shivered as she pulled on her jeans. "You want an extra shirt, too?" she asked, pulling a white thermal with a tiny yellow rosebud print out of her dresser and offering it to me.

I shook my head. "I have my hoodie. And once we start

working, I bet we get sweaty." I looked forward to that, to being outside and not feeling cold.

Morgan put on the thermal and plopped down at her desk, a place more for makeup and hair stuff than for studying or homework. She unwrapped the towel. Her hair was such a dark shade of brown, it looked black when it was wet, and she barely ran her comb through it before twisting it up in a topknot. It was so thick that she used three hairbands to hold it, and I knew the center of that knot wouldn't ever dry, not even by the next morning. Then Morgan sat back in her chair and stared at her reflection for a few quiet seconds. When she noticed me noticing, she said with a chuckle, "I guess one good thing about having a long-distance ex is that I don't have to worry about randomly running into him in Aberdeen."

I crawled over to her on my knees and put my head in her lap. Sweetly, I said, "Hopefully he'll die soon, and then you'll never have to worry about seeing him at all! You should try praying for that the next time you go to church."

Morgan gasped and pushed me on the shoulders, sending me backward onto the carpet. "Oh my God, Keeley! That's so wrong! How could you even say that?" But she was laughing, because she knew I was joking. I was always saying crazy stuff like that, taking it too far. *Too far* was my default setting.

I flailed my arms and legs like a turtle stuck on her back. "Because that's what best friends are for!"

Morgan wore the tiniest hint of a smile as she reached to pull me up. "I'll text Elise and tell her we'll be over soon."

While she did, I pulled a peach sock with lavender stripes from her laundry basket but couldn't find its match. I went over to her dresser and opened the top drawer.

I had to dig a little to find it. It was underneath a plush stuffed chick with his wings glued around a plastic egg. There'd been a chocolate heart inside that egg. Morgan had given me half on our drive home from hanging out with Wes during Easter weekend. It was milk chocolate with Rice Krispies, my favorite. We ate the chocolate and drove home with the chick propped up on her dashboard, its googly eyes googling with every bump in the road.

Wes gave Morgan tons of little presents like that all the time—cheesy greeting cards, silk roses, key chains, perfume, candy. Elise said that showed what good boyfriend material he was, though I doubt he paid for any of it since his parents owned a drugstore. Before their breakup, Morgan prominently displayed the gifts around her room. When they disappeared, I assumed she'd thrown them away. But they were all there, crammed in the drawer. I lingered over them until Morgan chucked her phone aside. Then I quickly pushed the drawer shut.

"Don't you think this is a huge overreaction?" Morgan said, half underneath her bed, reaching for her galoshes. I wasn't sure if she knew what I'd seen or not. I certainly wasn't going to say anything about it. "I mean . . . I get that it's supposed to be a crazy storm, but Levi asking Key Club to come out on a Sunday morning to stack sandbags seems crazy."

I'd had the same thought myself. The river flooded at least a few times each spring, and even with the rain that had already fallen, it hadn't added up to anything disastrous. The people in town who lived closest to it knew to take certain precautions when it was supposed to storm, like parking their cars on higher ground and moving their patio furniture indoors. It was more annoying than dangerous.

"Yup," I said. "And also, Levi didn't *ask*. He basically *demanded*. I would have told him to screw off if I wasn't sure he'd kick me out for insubordination or whatever."

Our high school didn't have a ton of clubs, and so I needed to list Key Club on my college apps. I was even considering running for president next year, because my guidance counselor said admissions tended to favor candidates who held leadership positions over kids who just listed a bunch of activities.

"I wouldn't put it past him," Morgan said, her lip curling. "He's the total worst."

"Well, I'm choosing to think of it this way. If the river *does* flood, we'll have done our part to protect our soon-to-be-inherited beachfront property."

Morgan grinned at that, spinning around to face me. "Thirty-two more days until we're officially seniors."

"Thirty-two more days," I echoed, just as excited. At that moment, Wes was the only obstacle I saw between me and Morgan having another terrific summer together. And whether or not she kept his crappy trinkets hidden away in her drawer, he was still, thankfully, her ex.

Back in the old days, Aberdeen was primarily a countryside vacation destination for the rich residents of Waterford City, thirty miles downriver. It was cabins and summer cottages and pine groves. People swam in the summer, skied and ice-skated in the winter. My dad even has a vintage postcard showing people in old-fashioned bathing suits, striped umbrellas, and canvas beach chairs, enjoying our beautiful riverfront.

A hundred years later, the seniors of Aberdeen High School

still swam in the exact spot the tourists once flocked to, where the bank stretched as wide and flat as an ocean beach, complete with sand that glittered in the sunshine. This wasn't the only swim spot in Aberdeen, but it was the best. Except it wasn't as perfect as the old postcard because of the long-abandoned lumber mill that anchored the end of the beach.

The spot designated for juniors, where I spent nearly every day last summer, was a quarter mile upstream from the senior spot. The beach there wasn't pure sand like the seniors had, more a mixture of sand and dirt and pine needles. You always had to have a blanket down, but it was still nice. A rope swing looped around a fat branch of a tree that grew sideways out over the water. I'm not sure who put it up. It had been around forever.

Last summer, hardly any of the other girls tried it. They were scared the rope would break or their bikini tops would fly off when they hit the water. But after a couple of swings on the first sunny day, I had it down. Which knot to anchor my hands on, exactly when to let go so I'd hit the deepest part of the river, where the water was the coolest. I even took to screaming out something dumb to make everyone laugh whenever I'd make the plunge. Like this one time, I shouted "Super-absorbency!" because Elise had just admitted that she'd once worn a tampon *and* a pad while swimming at a church retreat, because she feared leaking in the water. The other girls there that day had no idea what I was talking about, but they laughed just the same. The boys shook their heads or groaned. They never knew what to make of me.

The sophomores and freshmen were relegated to a swim spot even farther upstream, near the highway overpass. They had to pull weeds to clear a place for their towels and pick up the trash tossed out of passing cars. The location sucked for those reasons, plus there were tons of plants, slimy reeds, and other crap you didn't want touching you when you swam.

Anyway, that's where we were told to show up for sand-bagging duty.

Morgan parked her car near the overpass and we followed the flow of students toward two dump trucks full of sandbags and a rapidly growing group of volunteers. Obviously, other school groups besides Key Club had been summoned to help. Adults came, too. People's parents, off-duty policemen, my second-grade teacher, Mr. Gunther. Even Mayor Aversano showed up, dressed like a complete tool in a suit shirt and dress slacks, with his slicked-back hair. He did have enough sense to swap his dress shoes for a pair of work boots, but I still rolled my eyes.

At exactly seven thirty, Sheriff Hamrick climbed up on one of the dump truck beds, clicked on his bullhorn, and asked everyone to gather around. Then he extended a hand to the mayor and Aversano's dress pants stretched dangerously tight over his butt as he lunged up. Aversano took the bullhorn and started talking but no one could hear him. Sheriff Hamrick had to lean over and show him the trigger to press to make the thing work.

I laughed. Hard. Morgan clapped her hand over my mouth.

"Thanks, everyone, for coming out today. Obviously, we're hoping that the weather forecasters are wrong, the way they tend to be about ninety-eight percent of the time."

A few adults chuckled at that lameness. I remember think-ing, hoping, that I would never turn into the kind of person who thought weather jokes were funny.

As Mayor Aversano went on, his voice took on a totally fake somber tone. My dad had been the one to first alert me to his penchant for doing this, after the mayor announced his most recent budget for Aberdeen, where he was "forced" to cut anything considered "nonessential" (quotations used to highlight his bullcrap). Since then, I always noticed it, a performance about as believable as our high school drama productions.

". . . but we must be ready in case they aren't, and do our part to protect our citizens from harm. I'm going to turn things over to Sheriff Hamrick to explain how today's going to work."

Morgan and Elise leaned their heads together.

Elise whispered, "I seriously can't believe he hasn't called you yet. It's been two weeks, right?"

"Almost," Morgan whispered back.

"It must be a pride thing. Maybe he's waiting to hear from you first?" Then Elise gave Morgan's topknot an encouraging little squeeze.

I burst in between them and grabbed each by the hand. "Let's go down to the senior spot. It's almost ours, anyway. And this place is giving me freshman-year flashbacks of those pink bikini bottoms that always gave me a wedgie."

"But Sheriff Hamrick hasn't finished his instructions yet," Elise said. "How will we know what to do?"

"What's to know?" I said, pulling her along. "Take sandbag, pass sandbag, repeat." It blew my mind how often Elise brought Wes up after the breakup. I knew she meant well, but why poke a bruise as it's trying to heal?

I think Morgan probably picked up on my Wes interference, because she walked a little bit ahead of Elise and me and changed the subject. "Eww," she said, pointing as we neared the bank of the junior swim spot. "It looks like chocolate milk."

The river normally ran clear. Not crystal, but close. But the previous storms had churned the water up big-time and it was so high, you couldn't see the tail end of the rope swing in the murky water. The current pulled it taut, like a fishing line had hooked a dolphin.

"Okay, so maybe sandbags are a good idea after all." I zipped my hoodie up to my chin, lifted the hood over my head, and stuffed my hands in my pockets to keep them warm. The morning sun was gone now, and the clouds hung low and oppressive, like someone's basement ceiling.

We walked to the senior spot. Another group of volunteers came from the opposite direction. Then everyone fanned out. I sat down on a rock in the sand and let out a big fat yawn.

"Keeley," Morgan whispered.

I ignored what I thought was her cue for me to stand up, even though I probably should have stood up if I wanted to look like someone who should be elected Key Club president next year. But I was tired. Normally, Morgan and I slept in on Sundays until lunch. And the dreary weather wasn't helping.

Morgan then knelt down in front of me and practically inserted her entire head inside my hood.

"Can I help you?"

The tip of her nose pressing into mine, she said, "Look left."

I turned my head.

And there was Jesse Ford.

His back was to me, but I still recognized him because Jesse had the cutest mop of wavy blond hair that was always the perfect mess. The pieces in front were long, almost chin-length, and he used their natural curl to keep them tucked behind his ears. That's how he usually wore it, except when he played soccer. Then he'd steal a rubber band off some teacher's desk and pull all his hair up into a little tuft at the top of his head, a man bun I guess you could call it. I know this is truly a look that only very cute and/or confident guys can successfully get away with. Put Jesse Ford in that slim minority. In fact, I weirdly liked it up in the man bun, because it showed off the million different shades of blond over his head. My hair is also blond, but it's all the same color—pale yellow, like a stick of butter. Jesse's is an entire box of Crayola crayons devoted to the shade. For example, some strands are as golden as the tops of the cafeteria corn muffins, some darker like pine sap, some as bright white as the sand that poured out of the splits in our sandbags that day.

Morgan quickly pushed my hood off my head and mussed my hair, pulling out a few stray pieces from the little nubby ponytail I had at the nape of my neck so they wisped around my face. She unzipped my hoodie ever so slightly, and pushed up my sleeves so they were at my elbows. She took a step back and smiled, pleased, and then beckoned to me to stand up.

I did, but only for a second, because as soon as I got to my feet, I pretended to faint dead away from happiness, flopping trust-fall style into Morgan's arms when I knew for sure that Jesse's back was still turned. Morgan barely managed to keep me upright. We both busted up laughing.

"What's so funny?" Elise called out from Morgan's other side.

Morgan pushed me off her and her cheeks turned rose-petal pink. It didn't matter that I was the one embarrassing myself.

Morgan always blushed by proxy. She leaned over and said quietly to Elise, "Nothing. Just Keeley being Keeley."

I watched nonchalantly as Jesse and some of the other guys on the soccer team kicked an empty Gatorade bottle across the ground. I guess they'd been asked to volunteer too. After fifteen minutes or so, the chitchat hushed and the sandbags started to come down the human chain.

Jesse shot me a quick smile as he turned to pass me the first one. Aberdeen High was small, with only about fifty kids in each grade. I'd had a class with him last year, Spanish II, but we'd never had an actual conversation before. Not in English, anyway. Still, I couldn't tell if he recognized me, or if he smiled because everyone knew who *he* was.

All the volunteers worked in painful silence for the first half hour.

"Do you think we're almost done?" I joke-whispered to Morgan as I heaped the next sandbag into her arms. The first few hadn't been so bad, but I swore they were getting heavier and heavier.

"Don't make me laugh, Keeley!" Morgan panted as she twisted toward Elise and passed the sandbag on. "My abs already hurt."

I gasped. "Oh my God, what if we're both so out of shape that we end up getting totally ripped from doing this, like two professional—"

"Hey! Watch out!"

I whipped around to Jesse lobbing his sandbag into my not-waiting, not-ready arms. I screeched and jumped out of the way because if that thing had hit my toes, it would have killed. Everyone around us turned to look.

But his sandbag didn't land on my feet.

It was never going to. Jesse had a hold on it the whole time, and he pulled it back at the last second, a perfect fake-out.

He doubled over laughing at how I spazzed, and I felt queasy as I stepped back into line. But then, when Jesse looked up at me, he winked. I realized he wasn't making fun of me, he was teasing me.

There is a difference.

"Hardy har har" was the first thing I thought to say. I groaned the words like an annoyed older sister, but really, inside I was all fireworks.

I let the next few sandbags come down the line, still sort of stunned that Jesse and I'd even had that much of an interaction. At some point, Morgan gave me a raised eyebrow and mouthed, *Talk to him!*

I ran through a hundred flirty conversation starters I'd over-heard Elise coach Morgan to say to Wes or the boys before Wes, but imagining them coming from me, out of my dumb mouth, each one sounded like a nauseatingly transparent cover for *Hello, Jesse Ford, please talk to me, boy I've loved forever.*

But a few minutes later, as Jesse turned to pass another bag into my arms, I had an idea. I pulled out my phone from my hoodie pocket and pretended to text someone. "Sorry," I sing-songed, holding up a hand to Jesse. "This'll just take a sec." This forced Jesse to hold on to his sandbag until I finished. He knew I was joking, of course, and he played right along without missing a beat. He grunted like it was killing him to keep holding the sandbag, but I think he liked showing off how strong he was.

The other guys on the soccer team were freakishly skinny. Like, skinnier than most girls. Not Jesse. I knew for a fact that he had actual six-pack muscles because he had this terrific habit of peeling off his sweaty soccer jersey after games and slinging it over one shoulder. For that reason, I never, ever, ever missed a home game.

Our little comedy routine got the attention of Levi Hamrick, son of Sheriff Hamrick and president of Key Club. He walked by us, glaring over the megaphone he'd taken from his dad, and said, "Pick up the pace."

I took great offense at this, because, okay, sure I was joking and probably slowing things up a little bit, but I was also working extremely hard, and if not for the adrenaline that my proximity to Jesse Ford afforded me, my arms would have functioned about as well as cooked spaghetti.

Jesse leaned in close. Close enough that I smelled the pancakes he'd had for breakfast on his breath. Close enough that I spotted three freckles in a perfectly straight line across his earlobe. "I think Levi Hamrick has a crush on you."

"Gross."

"No, seriously. This is like the third time he's walked over here to check on you. You should go for it. He's a catch. He's . . ." Jesse cleared his throat and switched into a corny announcer's voice. "*A Guy Who's Going Places!*"

*A Guy Who's Going Places!* was the headline of the local newspaper article that had run the week before, along with a picture of Levi holding up two handfuls of thick envelopes spread out like an oversize deck of cards. He'd received acceptances from every single college he'd applied to, which surprised a grand total of no one. Levi ate his lunch in the library. He won the science fair four years straight. His name always topped the honor roll. He scored the highest on the SATs out of the entire senior class. He clearly did nothing but study. He didn't seem to have any real friends, just nerdy acquaintances, because I never saw him at the movie theater on the weekend, or in the stands for home games. The one place he'd hang out was outside the police station with the officers, folding metal chairs circled up around an open garage bay while they waited for a call or a shift change. He was like a little cop-in-training.

The article was only interesting because of a dumb thing Levi said. The reporter asked him which of the schools he was leaning toward, and he answered, "Probably the one that's farthest away."

Obviously, that kind of snobbery rubbed a lot of kids the wrong way. Aberdeen was not a town of privilege, where people regularly got opportunities to seek bigger and better things. I heard someone giving Levi hell for it in the hall, and he looked baffled as to why. I bet he thought that because he was being honest, no one could be offended. Actually, I don't think anyone *was* offended. More like they had proof of what they'd secretly suspected, Levi Hamrick was a pompous jerk. I, on the other hand, already knew that for a fact, because Levi Hamrick was the reason I'd quit Mock Congress my freshman year. The only black mark on my high school transcripts.

I leaned in to Jesse and cupped my hands around my mouth. "Levi Hamrick isn't hot for me." I was already second-guessing the joke that popped into my head, but it came tumbling out of my mouth anyway. "He has such a hard-on for rules, I bet he jerks off to the school handbook."

Jesse backed away, a shocked-yet-delighted look lighting up his face. Like even though we'd been chatting for the last few minutes, he actually saw me now for the first time, like I'd materialized before his eyes.

It sent a surge through me.

A pop of thunder cracked just as the last sandbag came off the dump truck. Everyone scattered. I wondered if Jesse might say good-bye to me, but I couldn't find him in the melee and I didn't want to linger like a stalker. Well, I did, but Elise and Morgan were hungry, so the three of us hustled, sore and limp, back up the river toward Morgan's car.

I had her passenger door handle half-open when a pair of hands squeezed my hips. I buckled because I'm super-ticklish and also because of the sheer surprise of Jesse Ford touching me. He snatched my phone away. I tried wrestling it back from him . . . but not with enough force to actually take it, because even though I'd only ever kissed two boys in my lifetime, I wasn't a total dummy.

Fending me off with one hand, Jesse plugged in his phone number with the other and then sent himself a text from my phone so he'd have mine. Then he returned my phone with a wink and shuffled off to catch up with his friends.

I checked my sent messages. He'd written, Jesse, you are hands down the hottest senior guy. Also charming, funny, and kind to small animals. Can I pretty pretty please have all of your babies?

I steadied myself against Morgan's car and tried to catch my breath.

"What was that about?" Elise asked, one eyebrow curiously raised, as she climbed in.

"Nothing," I said, playing it cool. "Jesse just wanted to ask me something."

Morgan flipped down her visor and adjusted it so she could see into the backseat. "Hey, Elise, did I ever tell you how"—and this was where I started trying to cover Morgan's mouth with my hand, because I knew what she was about to say—"Keeley would make me pretend to be Jesse when we were in middle school? She had a whole scene worked out—dialogue, costumes, and everything."

Elise leaned forward so her head was in the front seat with us. "Umm, why am I only hearing this now?"

Morgan looked at me, her lips pressed together like she was about to burst. Though she wanted to, she wouldn't tell Elise unless I gave her permission. She was that good of a friend.

I wasn't embarrassed for Elise to know. My crush on Jesse Ford wasn't something burning and constant and tortured. Okay, maybe it had been when I was in middle school, but I blame that on the introduction of hormones into my bloodstream. Once I got to high school, it turned into something much quieter, something I hardly thought about beyond silently acknowledging how hot Jesse looked on whatever day, or momentarily wishing I was whichever pretty girl he'd be kissing in the hallway as I walked past them. Because by that time, I had matured enough to understand that Jesse and I would never happen.

As soon as I gave Morgan a nod, she couldn't get the words out fast enough. "Keeley would make me draw on a moustache and get down on one knee with a Ring Pop and beg her to marry me!"

I quickly clarified, "Just remember, Elise, this was middle school. Like, long before either of us had boobs." Because Elise sometimes made little comments about how *fun-loving* or *free-spirited* I was, which were all polite versions of *immature*. Part of me could actually imagine her thinking I still acted this way.

Then I swatted Morgan. "You kind of sucked at it."

"How could you say that?"

Turning to Elise, I explained, "There was no artistry to her performance. I'd have to keep reminding her to talk in a deep voice and—"

"Sorry I'm not as big of a ham as you are!"

"Whatever. I made the best of it. My love of Jesse transcended your awful acting."

Morgan was laughing so hard she could barely get the next question out. "Wait a second! What were the names of your three kids again?"

"Jesse Jr., Jamie, and"—the last name we said together—"baby Juliette."

Elise settled back in her seat and pinned the swoop of her hair with a bobby pin. She'd been growing out her bangs since Christmas. She laughed too, but more out of politeness, respect for a friendship that predated her.

Elise grew up in Hillsdale, where Saint Ann's Church was. Morgan knew her from Sunday school and then teen youth group.

I remember the first time I met her at a church picnic Morgan had dragged me to when we were in seventh grade. Morgan kept telling me how alike Elise and I were, how much we had in common. I took this as a compliment about our friendship, that if Morgan had to make a new friend, she'd pick the most Keeley person she could find. I pictured Elise as a sweeter, churchier version of me.

And she was, at first glance. Elise was thin and delicate with a brown bob that fell just past her chin and a silver cross pendant that hung in the hollow of her collarbone. I'm not sure if she was surprised that I was coming with Morgan to the picnic, because she'd only saved one extra chair. She stood up and offered both chairs to Morgan and me, and sat in the grass by our feet. I appreciated the show of respect.

But it might have been because Elise was afraid of me. I remember saying all kinds of borderline inappropriate things to her to be funny, like stringing together a bunch of curse words or making dirty jokes or whatever. Morgan kept laughing nervously and telling Elise, "She's kidding, she's kidding," to which Elise quickly forced a smile and replied lightly, "Oh, totally, I knew that."

We were in line for hot dogs when Elise pointed out a boy with flippy hair and mirrored sunglasses playing his guitar to accompany a pastor singing a Jesus song. She leaned in and said to me, "I used to be so hot for that guy, but it turns out he's the absolute worst kisser on the planet." And she stuck out her tongue and rolled it around like someone having a seizure, and then made a gag face. "I can't even see his cuteness anymore. He's, like, tainted."

Neither Morgan nor I had ever French-kissed anyone. We were still playing those pretend games at her house.

"She's not boy crazy or anything," Morgan whispered to me later on the ride home, as if she could read my mind. "She's just . . . uh . . . not shy." And then she threw in, "Like you!" to put me at ease.

Of course, after Elise's dad lost his job and they moved to Aberdeen, I saw plenty of Elise's sweet and churchy side, and I think that's ultimately what I liked best about her, those two identities mashed up together. She was super-sweet with her little brothers, and if we came over when she was babysitting, she'd be playing with them just as much as hanging out with us. And she never talked shit about anyone, even people who completely deserved it, like Wes. Meanwhile, her phone was full of numbers, boys we'd meet at the mall or the movie theater or who went to her church. Elise wasn't so much interested in having a boyfriend as she was in having someone to crush on.

I think, at first anyway, having a boy to obsess about kept Elise from feeling jealous of what Morgan and I had together. Because as close as the three of us were, every so often there were moments where our threesome was eclipsed by the previous two-some. I say this with no offense to Elise, of course. But you can only have one best friend. My friendship with Morgan went all the way to the cradle, because our moms were best friends too. She couldn't compete with that.

Later on, though, when it was both Morgan and Elise getting that kind of attention together, I became the odd girl out.

"Anyway, Jesse and I weren't flirting," I corrected her. "We were joking around."

Again, there is a difference. One I knew all too well.

Morgan cleared her throat. "Keeley, he checked out your butt as you grabbed us bottles of water from the cooler."

I couldn't play off my shock. I spun toward her. "He did not. Shut up."

"He totally did! He watched you walk the entire way!"

I wanted so badly to believe her. And maybe it was the truth. But we'd both heard what her ex-boyfriend Wes had said about me, the kind of girl I was, and I knew Morgan wanted to undo that damage. It was why she broke up with him in the first place.

So there was that possibility too. And for me, it was the possibility that seemed more likely.

Because like I said before, I had only kissed two boys in my lifetime. Neither one was from Aberdeen. They were both friends of boys that Elise and Morgan were interested in.

We'd get dressed up cute and make the drive to Hillsdale, or some other town, to meet them. At first, it was more Elise's thing, but then boys started asking Morgan for her number.

Over the past year, I lost count of how many times Morgan or Elise would stand off a little ways with the boys they liked, whispering to them or showing them something on their phones, leaving me with whoever else had tagged along. Unlike my friends, I never knew how to act. I'd either completely clam up, afraid I'd say something dumb, or I'd swing too far the other way and say, like, many many many dumb things.

In the last three years, I'd met lots of boys, obviously. But I'd only ever kissed two.

By the time Morgan dropped me off, it had started to rain yet again. Lightly, but the way the wind whipped through the trees, it was clearly the beginning of another big storm. The weathermen were right after all.

Mom's car was long gone. I knew she'd be working. The only patch of driveway that wasn't getting slick was underneath Dad's old work truck. It sat in our driveway like a clunker because Dad didn't drive anymore, but it still ran fine. We'd been trying to sell it forever but there were no takers. Mom said Dad was asking too much. Dad defended his price by listing off the truck's attributes—how dependable it was, the low mileage, how he'd splurged on new brakes right before his accident.

Before I went in the house, I climbed inside it and started it up, letting the engine run for a few minutes as I looked at Jesse's text again. I did it to make sure that the battery wouldn't die. I was hoping it wouldn't sell and then I'd get to drive it when I turned seventeen next March.

I jogged the path to our house, a clapboard cottage with shingles the color of buttercream and the front door painted robin's-egg blue. There were three bedrooms and a bathroom on the second floor, a living room, dining room, and kitchen on the first floor, plus a small attic with a pull-down ladder and a musty root cellar, which had always scared the crap out of me. We had a front porch just big enough for a swing, and the moss-covered roof came out from directly under my bedroom window.

I crept inside, knowing Dad would be sleeping.

Dad had become nocturnal ever since his accident. He'd spend every night on his computer, and then sleep pretty much the whole day away. It was easier for him, I think, to be asleep while everyone else in town was out doing the things he couldn't anymore. So I wasn't surprised to find his computer on. He used two chairs, one to sit in and one with a couch pillow on it where he could prop up his leg. I cleared away a coffee cup and a dirty plate, turned off the monitor, pushed the chairs back in, picked up his cane, and set it next to the stairs so it would be waiting for him when he woke up and came down again.

I went into the kitchen and made myself a grilled cheese. My sandwich in one hand and my phone in the other, I reread Jesse's text a few more times before I forced myself to delete it.

It wasn't even hard, because I was 99 percent sure I'd never hear from Jesse again. I didn't even blame Wes for making me think so pessimistically. It was just my reality, to never have a boy be interested in me romantically for more than one random moment. Like a TV show you don't like but you end up watching anyway, because there's nothing else on.

And remember, this was Jesse Ford. Not some less-cute friend of the boys Elise and Morgan were interested in. Jesse could get any girl in school he wanted. He was so charming and funny and disarming that it didn't matter if he wasn't the most traditionally handsome guy. It didn't even matter if the girl he was after had a boyfriend. The year before, some meathead football player found out that his cheerleader girlfriend had secretly kissed Jesse, and he punched Jesse square in the jaw in the middle of the cafeteria. The picture of the aftermath, Jesse proudly grinning with a bloody lip and a purple cheek, was still his profile picture.

I couldn't imagine a single scenario where he'd want to be with me.

# 2

Jesse texted me on my way to first period the next day.

Not a message, but a video he'd taken of the jacked-up speaker in his homeroom during morning announcements. That thing was so crackly, you couldn't make out one single word. Jesse spun the camera from the speaker to his confused face, back to the speaker, back to his confused face, and then cupped a hand to his ear like an old man hard of hearing, saying, "What? I'm sorry, what? Could you say that one more time?"

Jesse regularly posted videos of himself online. They were mostly funny, sometimes stupid, usually ridiculous. Our entire school watched them. But this video was only for me, one he made just to make me laugh. He never put it up.

It sounds weird, but I consider that my very first love letter.

I agonized over how to respond for the next two periods, but then, a gift from heaven, I spotted a mistake on the bulletin board outside the cafeteria.

PLACE AN ORDER FOR YOU'RE YEARBOOKS TODAY!

The *Guy Who's Going Places!* aside, our school didn't have the best reputation. Kids from nearby towns made fun of our tattered jerseys, our saggy, shedding pom-poms, our basketball hoops without nets. Only a handful of Aberdeen seniors went on to college each year. The others took jobs at the Walmart, joined the army, worked for their parents. Morgan's plan was to go to beauty school, though I guess that's a kind of college.

I get that college isn't for everyone, but the bulletin board was an embarrassment, so I stopped to snap a picture with one hand, framing the shot so you could see me giving a thumbs-down with the other. The letters had been individually hung, so I used my fingernail to ease out the staples and let both the apostrophe and the unnecessary *E* fall on the floor, and took another picture, this time with a thumbs-up.

When I turned around, Levi Hamrick was glaring at me with his arms folded. I think he was trying to guilt me into picking up the papers from the floor. Or maybe he was pissed because I was blatantly using my phone. He probably considered himself an unofficial hall monitor; he was that big of a geek. I pretended I didn't see him and disappeared into the crush of students heading to fourth period.

After that, it was on. Jesse and I texted each other on the regular, different funny observations and pictures all day long. Once, he sent me a picture of the janitor's ass crack. I replied with a covert video of Mr. Kirk digging in his ear with his pinky and then smelling it. That sort of thing. A couple of times I'd send Jesse a joke between periods and hear him laugh at whatever I'd written from somewhere down the hall, and I'd be soaring on cloud nine.

Entertaining Jesse became my one and only focus. I totally

slacked on my history quiz, I blew off grabbing pizza at Mineo's with Morgan and Elise when they scored an off-campus pass for lunch. The only thing I cared about was making sure I sent him something funny or clever enough to make him want to write me back one more time. I probably took a hundred selfies before I got one pretty enough to send, and forced myself to wait at least one class period before responding to whatever text he'd sent me, so he wouldn't think I was too eager. But whenever my phone buzzed with a new message from him, I'd feel absolutely euphoric.

When they'd returned from church camp the summer before our sophomore year, I'd immediately suspected Elise was no longer a virgin. Morgan would neither confirm nor deny it for me when I straight-up asked her, which I took as confirmation that Elise had, indeed, lost it. Elise would never tell me herself.

Morgan promised me she was definitely still a virgin, but admitted doing "stuff" with a boy named Douglas Bardugo she had also met at camp. Thankfully, she was much more forthcoming with info, and she stayed up an entire night answering even my most insanely personal questions—"Okay, but what if a guy tries to go to third base with you after you just peed?"—shyly but also with a level of clinical maturity reserved for teaching toddlers the actual names of their private parts. I remember leaving her house the next morning feeling exactly that way, like an inexperienced kid. And nearly two years later, I still basically was.

That's why, I initially kept Jesse's texts a secret from my friends. I was ashamed of how much each one meant to me.

Also, as amazing as it felt to have Jesse's attention, I knew every text could be the last.

He'd been driving a sophomore girl with insanely large boobs to and from school up until a few weeks ago, but I'd noticed that she was back to riding the bus. I still couldn't assume he was single, because Jesse also had a long-standing thing with another senior named Victoria Dunkle. They were on and off, on and off, but it wasn't drama. It was easy between them. When she wasn't with anyone, and he wasn't either, they'd find their way back together.

I tried forcing myself to face the reality of my situation. Maybe I'd caught Jesse in a sweet spot, but half a week of texting was barely anything. If I added up the actual number of texts sent and received, it felt a lot longer, but that kind of crazy girl math just made me seem, well, crazy. And it wasn't like Jesse was actually pursuing me in public. We were secret pen pals, that was it.

I even made myself remember the crappy things Wes had said about me to Morgan to kill any last bit of lingering hope left in my heart. Although that backfired big-time, because I ended up fantasizing that Jesse and I would run into Wes one day, our hands in each other's back pockets. I'd point him out, whisper to Jesse the awful things Wes had said about me, and Jesse—in all his hotness—would stare Wes down and laugh at what a spineless little turd he was.

I didn't beat myself up too badly for that daydream. Even if it was the longest of long shots, it still felt therapeutic.

# 3

Morgan and Elise were planning what outfits to wear to some youth group thing during lunch when they saw Jesse's picture pop up on my phone.

"Wait up. You once filled an entire notebook practicing your hyphenated signature if you married Jesse Ford, and now you two have been texting it up and you never bothered to tell us?" Morgan said *us*, and she even glanced incredulously over at Elise, but I knew she was really only talking about herself.

"There's nothing to tell! We're just joking around with each other!" I wished it were more than that, obviously, but it wasn't.

"I'll be the judge of that," Morgan said, grabbing my phone. She and Elise leaned in to each other to look at the picture.

Jesse had gone into town for lunch. Or maybe he'd taken the picture on his way to school; I wasn't sure. Either way, it was a shot of him making a very sweet and angelic face, eyes looking up and to the right, a hint of a smile, in front of some caution tape and a service truck from the power company.

"I don't get it," Elise said. "What's the joke?"

"Look closer," I said.

There'd been lots of electrical glitches with the recent rain-fall, little sizzling power outages here and there, and there was always a van from the electric company around to patch something up or pump water out of a manhole. Anyway, the men had cordoned off the middle of the street with bright orange cones and posted a sign that Jesse made sure was in focus just over his shoulder. It read DANGER: ELECTRIC MANHOLE.

I expected the girls to both make gross-out faces, because I was acutely aware that the way Jesse and I were talking was nothing like the way they talked to boys. But Morgan put a hand on my back and said, "Yup. This is flirty. No doubt about it."

Elise looked less convinced. "I mean, maybe? I'm not sure. It's kind of too weird to say." She tapped her finger to her lips. "Though I guess any reference a boy makes to his *hole* could be considered flirty."

I got a rush of good feelings from Elise saying that. She was the boy expert.

I'd only wanted them to look at the one picture, but they insisted on scrolling through all our correspondence. They examined every one of Jesse's messages to decipher hidden clues or hookup potential. They also critiqued every one of my responses.

Elise tapped the screen. "Now wait. Okay, see? What he sent you here is definitely flirty." She looked up at me with genuine surprise. I would have been insulted, if it hadn't been Jesse Ford we were talking about. Because of all the Saint Ann's boys Elise had in her orbit, there wasn't one of Jesse's caliber among them.

"Why?"

Morgan and Elise shared a look. "Because he used the doggy

smiley, not just a *smiley* smiley," Elise said. "And you kind of blew it by just writing *LOL*. I mean, Keeley, come on. You're not that basic."

"Yes, I am. I am that basic and you both know it!" I tried to wrestle my phone away.

Elise held it out of my reach. "What are you going to write back to that manhole picture? You need to have a flirty response. Otherwise he's going to think you're not interested!"

That seemed completely impossible. But suddenly our entire text history was recast in my mind. Was Jesse actually real-deal flirting with me this whole time?

"I don't know," I said, suddenly panicked. "Maybe I should send him a doggy smiley back."

"No!" they both screamed.

"Wait! Two seconds ago you both agreed doggy smiley was flirty!" I wrestled my phone back. "How about I send a banana? Banana is code for penis, right?"

Even though I was totally joking, Morgan held my arms while Elise pried my phone free again. Together they worked out a response for me. I made a big deal about it, sighing like they were cramping my style, but honestly, it was a relief. Usually when Morgan and Elise talked about boys, I had to occupy myself with finding a better song on the radio or getting us snacks. I was glad to have their help. I really didn't know what I was doing.

They went all emoji for the first text—a lightning bolt, a scared smiley face, and then the one with the girl crossing her arms like *hell no.* They followed that up with a second text. You should probably see a doctor about that ASAP.

"How is that going to make him think I'm interested?"

"Trust us," Elise said.

Jesse wrote back before the end of the period. So that wasn't cute? #flirtingfail

And then, Don't worry. I'll do better next time.

I couldn't believe it. I almost didn't believe it.

And then Jesse made good on his promise.

# 4

Spring Formal tickets went on sale the next morning, and Morgan and Elise and I put our coats and hats and scarves into our lockers and headed to the folding table set up outside the gym. We were about to round the corner when we heard music. There was Jesse, positioned next to the ticket table, dancing to songs coming out of his phone speaker. He had on a button-up that was open like a vest to his bare chest. A stripe of his boxer shorts—polka dot—lifted slightly above the waist of his jeans. He had a white sweatband across his forehead, and matching ones on each wrist. His friend Zito was holding a key-chain-size disco ball over Jesse's head.

A pop song, one that was always on the radio, was finishing up when we got in line. It was the kind of song a boy would pretend not to know or would say was stupid girl music. But Jesse shamelessly lip-synched along to the words, and he even knew the choreography from the video.

Morgan leaned in. "Elise, is Jesse on Dance Committee?"

"Umm, I don't think so. If he is, he hasn't come to a single meeting all year."

"Then what the heck is he doing?"

Even if I'd had an answer for that, I couldn't have said it. I was laughing too hard.

The pop song ended and a heavy metal song started up, chugging bass guitar and throaty screams. Jesse dramatically swatted the disco ball out of Zito's hands, and it rolled down the hall. Then he alternated between moshing and thrashing and bouncing like a pogo stick. There also may have been a jump kick and an air guitar solo, but I was trying not to stare.

When we reached the front of the line, his eyes went wide and he lunged at me. "Keeley!" I barely had a chance to hand over my ten dollars before he pulled me toward him.

"Is this your jam, Keeley?" He kept the whole dancing routine up, not missing a beat.

"Not exactly."

"Oh? Okay. No worries." He tapped his phone and skipped to a hip-hop song. "Well, how are you at break dancing?" he asked, threading his fingers through mine and snapping our arms to make a wave.

"I'm terrible. Terrible at break dancing," I said, shaking free. Everyone was looking at us, but it wasn't embarrassing so much as exciting. It was like our texts were becoming public.

"Okay then, how about the robot?" He switched up his movements to make them jerky and stiff. "I've been programmed to cut rugs," he said, this time in a metallic computer voice.

"You're crazy," I told him, backing up before he could grab me again, which he tried to do. I hustled over to the table, grabbed my ticket for the dance, and pulled Morgan and Elise in front of me as human shields. I was so aware of where Jesse had touched me moments before, how that hand was ever so slightly hotter than the rest of my body.

"There's no way I'm letting you off that easy at Spring Formal!" he called out over the crowd. "You can't hide from me all night!"

We ran off and ducked into the nearest bathroom.

"See!" Morgan said. "He clearly likes you, Keeley!"

"Seconded," said Elise. "You guys are totally, totally hooking up at the dance."

I pulled my hair up into a ponytail and fanned the back of my neck. Instead of talking myself down with some Debbie Downer version of *Keeley, this isn't happening, stop being crazy,* the words "Maybe I should buy a new dress" blurted out. My plan had been to wear something I already owned to save money, but now that seemed like a terrible idea.

Elise and Morgan shared a pleased look.

"We'll go shopping tonight!" Elise said. "I'll drive."

Except it started raining hard around dinner, and Elise's mom didn't want her driving in the dark to the big mall over in Ridgewood—a wealthy town exactly between Aberdeen and Waterford City—especially since she only had her learner's permit. They ended up getting into a big fight about it and then she couldn't go at all.

Morgan's mom needed their car, but Mrs. Dorsey called my mom and must have given her a serious guilt trip, because to my surprise, Mom put aside her paperwork for the night—something she hardly ever did—and offered to take Morgan and me shopping.

If she hadn't been with us, I would have never gotten that beautiful, beautiful dress. Though I'm still not sure if that would have been a good thing or not.

• • •

My mom ultimately decided to splurge on my dress because Spring Formal would be my very first dance (Aberdeen High only had two—Spring Formal for juniors and seniors, and senior prom, to which, surprise, surprise, I had never been invited), and also because I was supposed to pick something special for my sixteenth birthday, like maybe a locket or whatever, but I hadn't found anything I liked and two months had already gone by.

This was after we'd both blinked at the price tag. I didn't think to check how much the dress was before falling in love with it. I still feel crappy about that.

But she must have known what we were in for. Mom was the one to wander into Pearson's because she recognized the song being played on the shiny black piano by a real live pianist. I'd never been inside before. Morgan, either, even though we'd heard that the bathrooms there were so much nicer than the ones at Macy's. But Pearson's was the kind of department store where you felt the salespeople looking at you when you walked past them. They'd smile friendly, but you knew they were quietly judging whether you had the money to shop there. We definitely didn't.

When the song ended, Mom nudged Morgan and me onto the escalator with a hand on each of our backs, suggesting we check out what dresses they had here, since I hadn't had much luck in the other stores. Morgan and I gave each other a look like *Umm, okay, sure.*

Pearson's carried about half the clothes of Macy's. The racks looked almost empty. So it didn't take me long to spot it. A short shift, practically a minidress. It had an exposed silk lining that was the same shade as how my mom took her tea—with the cup almost half full of cream—or as tan as I got after the first solid summer day of lying out by the river. Over it was a shell of ivory lace, a pattern made up of daisies with their petal edges knit together. The sleeves were also lace, but bare underneath, no lining, and three-quarter length. A thin gold zipper ran up the back.

I never imagined myself wearing something so sophisticated to Spring Formal. I was thinking maybe a dress with a fun pouffy skirt that would lift up when I twirled on the dance floor. Or maybe one with hidden pockets for my lipstick and my phone so I wouldn't need a purse. I'd tried on a few of those dresses already, and while they looked okay, none of them made me feel particularly pretty. I didn't wear fancy dresses often, but that seemed like an essential criterion.

"Oh yes, please!" Morgan begged when she saw me pausing over it. "Please try that one on, Keeley!"

I wanted to before she said it. Though if Elise had been with us, I'm not sure I would have. Or if I did, it would have been more for the joke, a not-fancy girl clowning her way into a fancy dress. Since it was just Morgan with me, I didn't have to hide my wanting that dress inside a laugh. I carefully lifted the hanger from the rack and carried it in front of me like a waiter delivering a hot plate.

I came out of the dressing room and Mom's eyes went big. She said it looked like the kind of dress girls in California wore in the 1960s. Though I don't know how she could have known that, since my mom had lived in Aberdeen her whole life. Morgan said, "Keeley," then covered her mouth with her hand. She did that a couple of times. "You look like . . . a *woman*."

"And you sound like a tampon commercial," I said. But as I turned and twisted in front of the three-way mirror, I understood what she meant.

There'd already been a few times that year when I was out with Morgan and Elise and the people we were with thought I was younger than them by a year, sometimes two.

I'd been wearing my hair the same way since I was twelve—all the same length, cut straight across, though thankfully I had given up on bright-colored plastic barrettes. My hair was superfine, practically baby hair, and it never seemed to grow any longer than my shoulders. Morgan was always trying to get me to cut in some layers or maybe try a bob or bangs, but I didn't dare, sure that having a cooler, more daring haircut would make the rest of me look even more babyish.

The dress was snug in the right places and it fit me perfectly. It was the sort of dress where you didn't want to have boobs, which was lucky for me. Boobs would've made it look weird. It was more about clean lines and showing off your legs. Morgan always said I was the skinniest nonathletic person she knew, and I never wore short-shorts because I worried that my legs looked too spindly and sticklike. They didn't in that dress. Everything about it was working.

I'd been hoping to feel pretty. In that dress, I was beautiful. I didn't know before that moment that there was such a huge difference between the two. It was so lovely that I actually felt ashamed as I changed back into my jeans and baggy cardigan and my galoshes in front of it.

When we reached the register, the three of us couldn't stop touching the fabric. It looked delicate, but the lace had weight and stiffness and the tiniest bit of shimmer to it. Morgan pointed out how the zipper had a little gold heart charm attached to the pull.

That's when I first noticed the price.

I glanced up at Mom, not sure what to do, but she immediately waved me off like it was no big deal. Which . . . okay. I could maybe play along with that. But instead of opening her wallet, I saw her pay the salesman at the register with wrinkled twenties and fives and ones she tried to discreetly pull from an old greeting card envelope inside her purse. A secret place where she'd been saving up. I shouldn't have been embarrassed, because money is money, but I was. I pretended not to see the old envelope and instead chatted with the salesman and with Morgan about the rain, hoping they wouldn't notice it either.

But as Mom handed over that thick stack of bills, I did freak for a second. There's no way a dress can be as special and forever as a sweet-sixteen locket, but this one was just as expensive. Mom had clearly been squirreling away money for a while. Things were tight at home. Since Dad was no longer working, Mom took on the lion's share of duties, financial and otherwise. She worked all the time. I mean that literally. If she wasn't seeing patients, then she was cleaning the house, cooking for us, grocery shopping. I barely ever saw her sitting down.

She picked up any extra hours she could, and after bills were paid, anything left over went into my college fund. Affording college was Mom's number one priority. She wouldn't have taken any money from there. She would have sacrificed something herself. A lunch skipped, a coffee, maybe a new sweater. Probably all of those things, multiplied several times over.

I bet the salesman saw the second-guessing on my face,

because he smiled and cooed, "Your boyfriend is going to die when he sees you in this."

The word *boyfriend* echoed inside me so loud, I was afraid everyone might hear the emptiness.

Morgan gave me a hopeful squeeze, which was, thankfully, discreet. My mom knocked into me and teasingly said, "I remember when you used to be so disgusted whenever I kissed your dad, even just a quick peck on the cheek. Ahh, how times have changed."

I made a gag face. "Hate to break it to you, Mom, but those times have not changed. They will never, ever, ever change." Mom pulled out the elastic of my ponytail, like she was affronted, even though we both knew the truth, that my parents never kissed anymore.

I stayed quiet as the salesman zipped the dress up in a white garment bag with PEARSON's embroidered on it in gold script, instead of a normal paper shopping bag. I couldn't remember the eye color of the first boy I ever kissed. Or if the second was an Erik or an Eric. But for the possibility that Jesse Ford might be the third, the dress was worth the money. That memory would last way longer than any locket.

When we dropped Morgan off, her mom ran out in her bathrobe and with an umbrella. It was raining hard, but she wanted me to unzip the garment bag so she could see the dress. Even though Morgan and I were the ones who'd spotted it, she said, "Oh, Jill! It's absolutely gorgeous. It must have cost a fortune."

Mom bit her lip. "It wasn't that much."

Mrs. Dorsey smirked. "Everything at Pearson's is expensive." And then she reached across the car and swatted my mom. "But you know what I think. Every girl should have one expensive dress."

"When can I get one?" Morgan said.

"When you bring me home a report card without Cs on it, we can talk." Back to my mother, she said, "Remember how I begged my mom to let me spend my confirmation money on this . . . ?"

Mrs. Dorsey opened her robe. She was in a clingy red lace dress.

"Annie! I can't believe you can fit into that!" After her divorce, Mrs. Dorsey lost about forty pounds, and she and Morgan sometimes wore the same clothes. Mom sighed. "I wish I had the time to exercise."

I turned to her. "Mom, what are you talking about? You look great."

"It's not about weight loss. It's about health. Physical and mental," Mrs. Dorsey said. "And you won't find time unless you *make* time," she told Mom.

Morgan groaned. "Mom, please quit quoting your self-help books."

On our way home, Mom opened my garment bag up again, carefully removed the price tags, and threw them into a trash can, along with our receipt, when we stopped at the blinking red light along Main Street. On the rest of the drive, we came up with a hundred and one future events where I might wear the dress again to help justify the expense and also decided on a reduced price we would tell Dad if he asked.

Mom was not someone who lied, but in this case, she made an exception. First off, men don't understand how expensive clothes can be, especially not a guy like Dad. But also, for Dad's protection.

"He wants the best for you, Keeley," she assured me. "He hates that he can't contribute. You know how proud the Hewitts are. I think it's in their DNA. I don't want him to feel bad for something out of his control."

I nodded.

It was a little more than two years ago that Dad fell through the floor of a rotten hayloft while repairing someone's barn. Dropped twenty feet onto a cement floor, shattered his hip, and snapped his left femur in half. He had multiple surgeries and steel rods and plates screwed in. He could still walk, but not without a limp, because his leg could no longer bend. That was the last carpenter job he'd taken.

Anyway, none of our conspiring even mattered. When we walked in, Dad was on his computer, and he barely looked up from the screen as he asked, "Dress success?"

"Dress success," I confirmed, already halfway up the stairs.

## 5

## Saturday, May 14
Heavy rainfall, possible flood conditions, high of 43°F

On the morning of Spring Formal, I woke up early at Morgan's house, as if we had school. Except I wasn't groggy or begging for another five minutes of sleep, like on a school day. As soon as I opened my eyes, possible texts that I might send to Jesse Ford burst inside my brain like popcorn, hundreds of different funny-yet-flirty ways to say good morning.

I settled on taking a "before" picture with my hair extra mussed up and wild, my eyes half open and heavy-lidded, mouth open in a lion-size pretend yawn. Right as I took it, Morgan lifted her head off the pillow and squinted away from the glow of my phone screen. It was still dark out because of the storm. Actually, I don't think the sun ever came out that day.

She sleepily said, "Let him text you first, Keeley."

I laughed dryly, like Morgan had it wrong. "I'm just sending him a stupid joke. No declarations of love or anything like that." Even though, in my own weird language, that was exactly what every text I sent to Jesse was.

Morgan tried to take my phone away, but her arms were heavy and floppy and I easily outmaneuvered her. She eventually rolled back over to the wall. "Okay, but remember," she said through a yawn, "you don't want to make Jesse laugh tonight. You want him to kiss you."

She was right, of course.

I looked at the picture again. I didn't look cute. I looked crazy.

I quickly deleted it. Then I lay in Morgan's bed and watched the plastic blinds get sucked in and out of her half-open window, watched her ceiling fan spin from the wind outside. I listened to the rain. I went over the instructions I'd found in a beauty magazine on how I should do my eyes. I dreamed about kissing Jesse Ford on my tiptoes, hopefully with his blazer draped over my shoulders to stave off the chill from the rain they were predicting, because in my mind there was no more romantic gesture than when a boy does that for a girl. I silently willed Jesse to text me. To give me a sign that he was thinking about me, too. Or even that he was awake. I would have gladly settled for that.

My phone finally buzzed in the afternoon, while I was sitting in the Dorseys' dining room–turned–salon, Morgan's mom loading my hair up with bobby pins.

Mrs. Dorsey used to have her own salon on Main Street, but after Mr. Dorsey left, she broke the lease to save money and started working from home. She put a hair-washing sink next to the washer and dryer in the mudroom. And she transformed her dining room into a beauty parlor, selling her dining set at a big garage sale and replacing it with a salon chair and mirror.

Morgan pulled up a chair close to me. One hand held a sleeve of Chips Ahoy! for us to share, the other a photo I'd printed off the computer of how I wanted my hair to look so her mom could reference it. I'd figured Morgan would do my hair herself, but she didn't want to take the chance that she'd mess up. The stakes were too high.

Morgan's hair was already finished. Her curls had looked more pageant-y when her mom first unwrapped them from the big barrel curling iron, ribbons of dark chocolate, but they'd already begun to fall out the way Mrs. Dorsey had told us they would, turning looser and beachier by the minute.

Mrs. Dorsey sprayed me with hairspray and turned me around to face the mirror. Mrs. Dorsey mostly did old people's hair around town, and I wasn't sure she'd be able to pull this look off for me, but it came out perfect. She'd parted my hair off to the side, then braided a few pieces and pinned everything into a bun set low and off-center. It was pretty and special, but hopefully not so much so that Jesse would realize how less pretty and un-special my hair normally looked.

Right then, my phone buzzed in my hand. Two texts from Jesse, back to back.

The first was a picture he'd taken of an old photograph. There was a bit of glare from the plastic sleeve, so it must have been inside a photo album. The picture was of a little Jesse, maybe nine or ten, probably taken at some family wedding. Sweaty-headed, surrounded by adults, in the middle of busting a serious move on the dance floor. His arms in a V shape over his head, one foot lifted off the floor, chin jutted forward, eyes closed, mouth open wide enough to see his bottom molars. His hair was white, the center of the sun. Also, little Jesse was wearing a freaking mini-tuxedo.

My heart liquefied, hot wax dripping over my ribs.

His second text said Warning: This is my body's automatic response to hearing Cupid Shuffle. Just so you'll be ready for me tonight.

I was ready, Jesse Ford. Oh God, was I ready.

My mom was supposed to make it over for pictures, but she got behind seeing patients, so Mrs. Dorsey took some with her phone and texted them to Mom. Mrs. Dorsey also pulled out an old photo album of when she, my mom, and my dad were all in high school together. Spring Formal was called Spring Fling then. My mom looked beautiful. And so young, her hair the color of ginger ale. I'd never seen it that color in real life, only in pictures. This might sound gross, but my dad was a total fox, tall and lean and tan with dark hair and even darker eyebrows. He had his arms folded, his chin lifted, his legs spread apart just slightly. He oozed confidence. In a couple of the shots, I saw my grandparents, and great-grandparents too, all Hewitts, Dad's side. Mom had lost her parents when she was young, and the Hewitts basically adopted her once she and my dad started dating.

Just for kicks, Morgan and I tried to duplicate one of the poses together, where our moms were both doing some kind of weird curtsey to each other. Then Mrs. Dorsey sprinted outside and pulled the car inside their garage so Morgan and I wouldn't get wet climbing in.

At that point, the storm was more annoying than scary, even though it was the one we'd stacked sandbags to prepare for.

Our preparations were different. We were thinking of the dash from her car into the gym. Morgan had on her pea coat, plus a rain poncho on top of that, plus rain boots and matching umbrella. Her silver heels were tucked inside a plastic bag. She also had the genius idea of gathering up her long skirt with rubber bands so it wouldn't drag in the puddles. I had my winter coat on, my umbrella, and my rain boots. I tucked the shoes I was borrowing from Morgan, a pair of gold sandals, into my coat pockets.

As we pulled out of the garage, I couldn't have been more excited. I'd looked forward to Spring Formal since I started high school. But it was about going with my two closest friends, dancing all night long, having a great time, taking a million pictures.

I still wanted those things, but now there was something else. A huge thing that had seemed completely unimaginable one week ago but now appeared within reach. And even though I couldn't see the stars through the rain clouds, I had this feeling that they'd magically aligned for me.

Spring Formal was supposed to kick off at seven o'clock, but by a quarter to eight, Morgan and I and most of the other juniors and seniors from our high school were still stuck in our cars, engines running and headlights shining through the gray, waiting for the rain to let up enough to make a run for the gym. I'd never seen it come down so hard in my life. The rain made talking difficult, the sound of it thundering on the roof of Morgan's car. Which was fine. I was honestly too nervous to talk.

So far there'd been no sign of Jesse. When would he get here? What would happen between us tonight? His two texts from earlier were my asthma inhaler. They kept me breathing. I must have reread them a hundred times.

"Keeley."

"What?"

Morgan gently guided my hand away from my mouth. I hadn't realized it was there. "Your nail polish is going to chip before we even get inside."

At eight o'clock, the janitor propped the doors open, as if

that were the thing keeping us out. I saw inside the gym in brief but steady flashes each time Morgan's wipers crossed the windshield. Coach Dean spread some towels from the locker room across the wood floor. The other chaperones—Mr. Landau, Ms. Kay, Principal Bundy—stood in a circle and talked for a while, but then opened up some folding chairs and sat in bored silence. Only a handful of students were inside, the ones on Dance Committee like Elise, or kids who'd had their parents drop them off right at the doors. Someone had built a soda can pyramid on the food table. A few guys tossed a Nerf football across the empty dance floor. Two girls swayed to music we couldn't hear.

The rest of us were trapped.

It sucked for everyone, but way worse for us girls, I think, because the guys were in khakis and button-ups, nothing special. The girls were the ones who were dressed up. And we'd dressed for how May weather was supposed to be, not what it actually was. That meant we had the heating vents pointed at our bare legs, legs that had been bronzed with either lotions or light bulbs, but not the sun. Even though our fingers and toes were painted juicy watermelon pinks and strawberry reds, they were numb from the cold. We had spritzed on too much perfume, blooming flowers and freshly baked angel food cake, because our whole school still had that dry, overcooked radiator smell left over from winter.

Worst of all, we were smothering the prettiest spring dresses with our winter coats.

My down parka definitely showed the extra two months of wear and tear. I'd lost the belt that kept it from looking like a sleeping bag with sleeves. It needed to be washed, but I was too afraid it wouldn't survive the spin cycle. Already, every time I sat down, a few stray feathers poked free, as if I were not a sixteen-year-old girl, but a molting goose.

We would all soon learn that the cold temperatures were partly to blame for what happened later on. The ground hadn't ever fully thawed from winter. It was still frozen five inches down, the dirt as hard as concrete. There was nowhere for the rain to go, nothing to soak it up. I didn't know that at the time. And even if I had, I doubt I would have cared. I was just annoyed that I had to cover up my dress in the first place.

Morgan let her head tip forward until it was resting on the steering wheel. "What if it doesn't stop? Do you think they'll cancel it and send us home?"

I feared that too, but I shook my head like the idea was crazy. "They'd better not! Bundy can see everyone out here waiting. Plus, we don't need the rain to stop. Just slow down a little."

Although I'd gotten more and more excited as the night passed, Morgan drifted in the opposite direction. I was a bottle of soda shook up, while she defizzed on her way to flat.

Morgan had planned to wear her Spring Formal dress to Wes's prom. It was strapless, mint green, with a pleated sweetheart bodice that snugly wrapped around her and a long skirt that flowed loosely to the ground. I worried it looked too much like a prom dress, but she accessorized it differently, swapping out the sparkly rhinestone jewelry for her everyday silver horseshoe pendant and a pair of tiny hoop earrings. She did her makeup dewy and fresh, just shimmery shadow, mascara, and a strawberry-colored lip. She'd been so proud of her frugality, though I bet it felt in that moment like a missed opportunity.

I hoped that was all it was.

"You look so beautiful, I'm thinking I might just ditch Jesse and try to score with you tonight."

She smiled a thin, brokenhearted smile.

As soon as we got in the gym, I'd make sure Morgan had a good time. Maybe I'd have the DJ dedicate some terrible song to her, like the chicken dance or the hokey-pokey, just to embarrass her. I'd come up with something to lift her spirits, to help her forget about Wes. It was the least I could do, all things considered.

Her phone dinged in her lap. "It's Elise. Someone in the gym heard that a huge tree fell across Basin Street and people had to be diverted."

I unrolled the passenger window the littlest bit for some air, but the rain blew in sideways, so I rolled it back up. Then I texted Elise myself and asked if any cars were trapped underneath that fallen tree. I was specifically concerned about a black hatchback like the one Jesse drove, but I phrased it in more general terms.

Not that I heard, Elise texted back. But apparently it took a bunch of power lines down. The news guys were already there with their stupid cameras.

Ever since the sandbag day, the news channels had begun showing up in their trucks in anticipation of tonight's storm. They'd park half in the ditch and film themselves on our riverbanks in the kind of gear you'd expect a fisherman to wear, watching as the river crept closer and closer to sandbags we'd stacked. It became a game for me. Whenever we'd drive past them, I'd reach over and beep Morgan's horn or yell out her window to mess up their shots.

I imagined Jesse Ford blocks away, his car stuck in traffic on Basin Street. It was practically guaranteed that he'd dress up for Spring Formal wearing something cool, something that would set him apart from the other guys. Like flip-flops and a bow tie. Or maybe he'd go full-on tuxedo, rented, or even some weird retro number from a thrift store. That would be so Jesse.

The rain began to come down hard enough that Morgan's wipers could barely keep up. She turned them off to save gas or her battery or whatever. After that, we could barely see anything. Morgan reclined her seat as far back as it would go. The navy fabric ceiling had begun to sag away from the roof. The airy pockets looked like an upside-down circus tent. She dragged her fingertips across them and made them flutter like sea waves. The car was old. It was her father's. It was the one thing he'd left for them after taking off last year.

Morgan wasn't having fun. That much was clear from the way she'd keep sighing or checking the radar app on her phone. She wasn't the only one. My phone lit up with whiny, complain-y texts from girls in our homeroom about how bad this whole situation sucked. How over it they were. By that point, we'd been waiting for more than an hour.

So I took it upon myself to keep things fun. Keep everyone's energy up, keep us excited and primed for a good time. I took a bunch of pictures of Morgan and me and traded them with Elise and other school friends stuck in other cars in other rows of the parking lot. You really couldn't see anyone's dresses, so it was mainly us showing off our hair and makeup to each other, but it was something. There weren't many chances for people to get dressed up in Aberdeen. Basically just church, which my family didn't go to.

Next, I got everyone to tune their car stereos to the same station so we could pretend we were in the gym together. We seat-danced as best as we could for a couple of songs, but the commercials and breaking weather reports got annoying, so we eventually turned it off.

Then I spotted a feather from my down parka stuck in the daisy lace of my dress. I got Morgan to blow it back and forth across her car with me like a game of Ping-Pong. We got to six passes, but seven seemed impossible, so we quit without trying. I pulled my hands into my coat sleeves to warm them back up and tried to think of some other way to pass the time.

A big crack of lightning lit up the parking lot. Everything glistened for a second.

"I hope we'll be able to get home," Morgan said nervously. "Also, touch up your lipstick. It's fading."

I'd never worn something so bright, but Morgan had insisted I borrow it. I loved the color. It reminded me of the pink azalea bushes that bordered my house. There should have been blooms by then, but there weren't even any buds on the branches. The cold and rain did weird things to our spring that year. It basically never happened.

I was carefully tracing the corners of my lips when my phone dinged. Before I could check it, Morgan took it and said, "Finish what you're doing first."

I quickly smeared the rest on. "Is it him?"

"Mmm-hmm," she said, but handed me a tissue instead of my phone. "Now blot."

I snatched the tissue and the phone from her, laid the tissue across my bottom lip, where it stuck, and checked the text.

`Ahoy matey.`

Morgan carefully peeled the tissue away while I typed back, `Arrrrrgh. Where ye be?` I pressed Send before Morgan could veto it, because I knew she'd forbid any sort of flirting done in pirate-speak.

`Look out yerrrr window.`

I used my hand to wipe away a porthole in the condensation from the glass. Jesse's car occupied the next parking spot over, full of other senior guys on the soccer team. I think he had five crammed in the backseat. I couldn't tell for sure because the windows were steamed up, all except for his, which looked freshly wiped. Someone made the car rock and shake like sex. Jesse rolled his eyes like they were idiots.

I smiled sympathetically and tried not to look nervous.

He wiped the glass free of encroaching steam with his sleeve and then blinked a few times, taking me in.

Would he think the makeup looked good on me? Would he see how hard I was trying for him? A different type of trying than how I'd acted down at the river, before I'd dared to have any expectations, when I would have said anything to make him laugh. This kind of trying felt way more obvious, way more embarrassing.

Jesse smiled a crooked smile. Then he pressed his pink tongue against the glass and gave a big fat sloppy lick of the window, aimed right at me, like he was a damn golden retriever.

Before I could stop myself, I pressed my tongue to the glass too, fake-licked Jesse back, but just for a second, because Morgan pulled me away from the window, shrieking, "Eww! Keeley!"

My heart was pounding.

Morgan pulled more tissues out of her pocket pack. "Please wipe your cooties off the window!"

I was about to when Jesse texted me, Hey, was that our first kiss?

And then :P

I felt prickly all over. It was the flirtiest thing he'd ever said to me. I didn't need Morgan or Elise to spell it out for me.

BRB in big trouble, I managed to write back, because Morgan was swatting me with the tissues, telling me I owed her a car wash.

He answered back, Me too. Zito just farted.

I laughed out loud. Eww! Kick him out of your car!

"Keeley, what's he saying?"

And let him drown in the school parking lot? What kind of crap friend do you think I am?

"Crap" is the right word, I wrote back. You guys are going to smell like Zito's ass smog. Keep away!

So you're not going to dance with me tonight? :(

Morgan shook me. "Don't ignore me," she pouted.

"Okay, I'm sorry! Just give me a second!"

I was trying to work on a cool response when he texted, Yo. I think we're gonna head back to Zito's. Send me a video of your best running man if you ever make it inside.

"Wait. What just happened?" Morgan asked. "Why are you making that face?"

I turned to her, tried to contort my mouth out of the frown. "Jesse's leaving," I said, stunned.

She shook her head back and forth, faster than her windshield wipers on high. "No! No, no, no! Keeley! Make him stay!"

Encouraged by her confidence that this was possible, I wiped my clammy hands on my bare legs and quickly typed back, Seriously? When Jesse didn't reply right away, I added, desperate, You losers just got here.

I ain't about to die in this gas chamber waiting to get into a school dance.

Thunder tumbled through the air. We were already almost an hour and a half into Spring Formal. Jesse was going to leave, and if he did, Morgan would definitely want to bail too, because she was here mostly for me tonight. We couldn't wait out here forever. Eventually they would cancel the dance.

I happened then to catch my reflection in the visor mirror. I knew there wouldn't be another chance like tonight. Jesse was a senior about to graduate and go off to who knows where. I'd heard a bunch of rumors, everything from a soccer scholarship to him moving out to California to become an actor. Our friends didn't mix with each other, and toward the end of the school year, the seniors mainly stuck together.

But mostly I felt I wouldn't ever look as beautiful as I did right then. This was my best night. Some people might be depressed by a revelation like that, but not me. I was glad I was self-aware enough to know it. That's what gave me the courage to do what I did next. The storm, and everything that happened after to Aberdeen, forced us all to be brave in different ways, over and over again.

This was the first time.

"I've got an idea." I pounded out a text to Jesse, a few friends, and Morgan.

Her phone dinged in her hand. She read my text aloud.

Making a run for the gym at exactly 8:26 p.m. Who's in?!?

She turned to me, wide-eyed. "Okay, wait. That's not what I had in mind."

"I think the rain's slowing up!" As I said it, another rumble of thunder cracked overhead.

"Are you crazy? If anything, it's raining harder now than before! You heard Elise. Trees are falling! People are losing power. Plus the thunder and the lightning and the water on the ground. We could be killed!"

I squeezed Morgan's leg. "Wouldn't that be a cool way to go, though?"

"Electrocuted in a puddle? That would be a terrible way to go. Like, maybe the worst, Keeley."

We both glanced at the dashboard. The clock read 8:25 p.m. before the screen went dark, because I shut off the engine and pulled Morgan's keys out of the ignition.

She sighed. "Why are you always getting me into these situations?"

I sucked in a breath and glanced over at Morgan, wondering if that was a dig, a jab for my part in what had happened between her and Wes. But it wasn't. She was smiling as she flipped the hood of her rain poncho up and set her hands on her umbrella.

We were all good.

I pulled my hood up too and tried to tuck up the bit of dress that hung past my parka, in the hopes of keeping it protected.

"On three," I said, and then grinned. "Three."

"You are the worst!"

I swung out the passenger door and opened my umbrella over

the frame to make an awning. But the rain was wild. It blew sideways into the car. Morgan screamed, and so did I, but it was too late for us to do anything other than get out, shut the door, and run as fast as we could for the gym.

We took off like two deer across the parking lot. The wind made my down parka ripple tight against my chest. Morgan's poncho lifted and snapped behind her like a plastic flag. I kept looking back, trying to see if Jesse and his friends had gotten out of his car, but I'd have had better luck trying to see through a waterfall.

Maybe he'd already left for Zito's.

I gripped my umbrella tight, wrestling as the wind tried to rip it out of my hands, and took careful but quick steps. Even still, there was no avoiding the puddles. I sank into a few that were ankle deep. My rain boots leaked water, rain blasted my parka from every angle.

Then, finally, I heard Jesse and his friends whooping and hollering behind us, and a couple of them chanted my name. Jesse's voice was the loudest and it sizzled inside me like a downed power line falling into one of the big fat puddles.

Teachers positioned themselves at the gym doors, flabbergasted by our stunt, shouting at us to be careful. The cars we ran past were full of people staring out of their windshields like we were crazy. It did feel crazy. We were all screaming and laughing at how absolutely crazy it was.

And then someone pulled me to a stop.

"Dance with me, Keeley!" Jesse screamed into the wind, a steady stream of water dripping off the tip of his nose. The dummy didn't have an umbrella or a coat. His white button-up was already see-through and clinging to his chest, his gray pants darkened to black up to his knees, his brown boat shoes squishing like sponges.

There was nothing goofy or comedic about his outfit. He'd dressed up for real, just like me.

I tried to pull him forward, angling my umbrella so it would cover both of us. "Come on, you lunatic! We're so close to the doors!"

But he grabbed me under the arms and lifted me up off the ground and began twirling me. The water splashed around us in hundreds of drops, liquid fireworks, because he stomped his feet so hard. A gust of wind caught my umbrella and blew it straight out of my hands. It tumbled across the parking lot until it hit the chain link fence of the athletic field.

"Keeley!" Morgan shouted from a few feet away. The wind flipped her umbrella inside out but she was still smiling, as happy as I was, before she turned and ran into the gym.

Everyone who'd made it inside filled up the doorway to watch me and Jesse, pointing and clapping as he twirled me. Cars in the parking lot honked their horns and flicked their high beams on and off.

Jesse dipped me backward like a rag doll and the rain pounded my face.

Needless to say, I was completely soaked. And I almost screamed at him to stop, to put me the hell down. But when he pulled me up from the dip, when we were nose to nose, his eyes bright and his smile so freaking big and his skin slippery and sparkling, I threw my arms around him and told him to spin me again, faster, faster, faster.

It was really happening, me and Jesse, no joke.

## 6

**Saturday, May 14**
⚠ **EMERGENCY BROADCAST SYSTEM ALERT:** A Severe Thunderstorm
Watch is now in effect, through midnight, for the following areas: Aberdeen County
and the entire Waterford City Metro Area. Heavy rainfall is expected to continue
through the night, with possible wind gusts up to 20 mph.

---

Everyone stepped aside as Jesse and I walked into the gym, applauding us as if it were our wedding reception. He and I were holding hands and laughing our asses off. The DJ immediately cranked up the volume of the music and a few girls bounded out on the floor to dance.

We had started the party. Officially.

I turned to tell Jesse that, but I slipped. Coach Dean grabbed me and saved me from falling. "Easy there, Keeley. The whole floor is wet."

I saw Jesse disappear into the guys' locker room. I figured he wanted to dry off. Poor thing was soaked completely through. I reached into my pockets for the gold heels but I only found one of them. Rushing back to the open gym door, I almost slipped twice more. The other shoe had probably fallen out, I bet while Jesse was spinning me. I scanned the parking lot for it but I saw only glistening water, a shallow lake growing deeper by the second.

"Can't let you back out there, Keeley," Coach Dean cautioned. I tried pleading with him, but he guided me aside and called out, "Slow down!" to more kids who were now following our lead and running through the rain toward the gym. Shaking his head, he hurried over to speak with Principal Bundy, but she had her phone pressed to one ear and her hand covering the other.

And then I was surrounded by girls, chorusing how insanely romantic it was, me dancing in the rain with Jesse, like we were the stars of a movie. Emma from Algebra II, Trish from my study hall, June whose locker was next to mine. They applauded me, called me the MVP of Spring Formal.

"Hey, Keeley! Smile for yearbook!"

Even though I was soaking wet, I grinned as best I could with my teeth chattering, and gave a goofy thumbs-up to David, the boy holding the camera. Luckily, the adrenaline running through me kept me from feeling the cold.

Morgan slid through to my side. She was wet too, but not as wet as me. She had a wad of napkins in her hand. Shivering, I took half the stack and told her, "I'm sorry but I think I lost one of your shoes in the parking lot." People laughed as if that were a joke.

The briefest flash of disappointment crossed her face before she touched my arm and said, "It's fine. We'll come back tomorrow morning and look for it."

I glanced around. "Where's Elise?"

"She went to get us some paper towels from the cafeteria." Morgan put her hand on my back and said, "I'm going to take off my jacket. I'll meet you in the bathroom."

"Got it." I hurried to the bathroom, slapping five with a few more people before I pushed open the door.

It was empty.

Maybe it was because I was suddenly quiet that I finally noticed the pitter-patter sounds of water dripping off me and onto the floor. My jacket hung heavy, the wet down feathers like lead, and I felt the rain that had collected in my crappy rain boots sloshing around my feet.

I leaned in to the mirror. My hair was a straight-up mess. The bun had uncoiled, leaving a soggy puff behind my left ear, and my braids had started to come undone. I quickly pulled out the bobby pins and ran my fingers through my hair. It was sticky from the hairspray. Then I turned to the paper towel dispenser and spun the crank fast, sending a spool of thin brown paper unfurling to the floor. I ripped it off and wiped my face clean, the paper immediately disintegrating into ropy bits. I started reapplying eyeliner, but my hands were shaking too badly, so I shoved it back into my purse and figured I'd just do a touch-up of lipstick and some blush.

Elise came in with two rolls of paper towels. Actual paper towels, the white kind that people have in their kitchens. They felt as absorbent as beach towels compared to that brown paper crap.

"Thank God for you," I said. "I think this stuff is actually just really thin pieces of cardboard."

"You don't look bad. You look wet, but not bad."

"I'll take it," I said, laughing.

Then a song we knew, the one we'd likely be blasting all summer long, came pulsing through the tile walls. We screamed and hurried up, desperate to dance.

"Bundy better let us stay late," I said, pulling out my lipstick.

"Yes! Yes! Keeley, you should ask her!" Elise said, leaning against one of the sinks.

"Yeah, right. Bundy hates me almost as much as I hate her."

"I don't get it. You're on honor roll every semester."

Even now, I still find that crazy. I'd been a very good student, mostly As and Bs, always on honor roll. And I'd been a solid member of the Mock Congress team, at least before the whole thing with Levi Hamrick.

I unzipped my wet parka with the thought of laying it on a radiator to dry, but then I changed my mind and dropped it on the floor with a slap. "You," I announced, pointing down at it, "are officially retired as of this moment. Viva la Spring Formal!"

Elise turned toward me and her face fell.

"Keeley, come here and I'll dry . . ." Morgan bit her lip as she pushed in. She'd already peeled off her outer layers, taken the rubber bands out of her skirt, and changed into her silver sandals. She wasn't nearly as soaked as I was. Barely damp. "Oh, shoot, Kee."

Even though there was a mirror a few feet away mounted on the bathroom door, I didn't turn to look. I didn't need to. I could already tell by how wet I still felt that my dress was in bad shape. My hair was one thing. Everyone's hair was likely a little messed up. But my dress . . . ?

"Come on," I said, rushing for the bathroom door. "I don't want to miss another song." I just wanted out of there. Back to the gym, back to Jesse.

Morgan eased me to a stop. "At least sit under the dryer for a few minutes. You can't go out there soaking wet."

I didn't want to, but I knew I probably should, if only to not look completely ridiculous. "Then you two go dance! I'll be there in a sec." Morgan and Elise looked so terribly sad for me, it was hard to stay smiling.

"Well, maybe I'll get us a table," Elise said. I nudged Morgan to go with her, but she ignored me and pressed the silver button on the hand dryer.

I held my dress taut like a sail in the lukewarm wind.

Trying to stay positive, I said, "That was the most romantic thing that's ever happened to me. Probably that will ever happen to me."

Morgan nodded. She raked her fingers through my hair and it clung to her in clumps. "I should do a quick French braid. It's not going to dry good with all the product in there."

"Okay. Thanks."

When the dryer stopped, Morgan hit the button again, and I turned to dry a new part of my dress. I felt my hair pulled in ropes. Even though I was trying not to look, my eyes caught my reflection in that big silver button. The silk shell was beginning to ripple, and parts of it had turned a different shade of tan than the rest. It didn't sit underneath the lace the way it should. And the lace wasn't creamy white anymore. It was drying a weird, tea-stained color. Jesse hadn't even seen me in it yet.

"Don't worry," Morgan said. "We'll find a dry cleaner who can fix it. Even if we have to go all the way into Waterford City."

I bit my lip and nodded. The upset feelings crept up and squeezed me, but I shook myself out like a rag doll.

I knew that the only way to salvage the dress, the money my mom had spent, was to have the time of my life. So that was what I was going to do. For me, it's always been as simple as that.

. . .

I hadn't noticed when I first came in, but walking back, the gym looked pretty amazing. I mean, it still looked like a gym, obviously, but the Dance Committee had done a great job and I knew they didn't have much of a budget. I made a mental note to compliment Elise.

White crepe paper twists were taped everywhere, wrapped around the railings of the bleachers, twirling in long strips inside a door frame to mask the ugly school hallway. The overhead cage lights were turned down, and strings of tiny globe lights were threaded around the basketball hoops and fanned out to the opposite wall. They had lots of food on the food table, two huge submarine sandwiches, chips, bowls of Hershey's Kisses, and plenty of sodas, too. Off-brand sodas, but no one cared, especially not the guys. They'd drink anything.

I was happy to see that our running through the rain had inspired other juniors and seniors to leave their cars, because the gym was now way more crowded than it had been when we first came through the doors. Elise claimed us one of the last open café tables set up along the sidelines of the gym. I slipped off my rain boots and rubbed my bare feet back and forth against the wood floor to try and warm them up. I had a pair of sneakers in my locker that I thought about changing into, but I figured other girls would take off their shoes eventually, once people started dancing.

I looked around for Jesse, finally spotting him along the wall where the wrestling mats were folded in a tall stack. He had changed out of his button-up shirt and pants and into an Aberdeen High hunter green and gold wrestling singlet with his argyle dress socks and loafers. I guess that was his only option. I saw the lines of his tighty whities through the spandex. Any other boy would have looked gross, but Jesse, well . . . of course he looked handsome. Handsome and hilarious, which was my favorite combination. And it felt good that, just like me, Jesse was down to keep having fun tonight, wet clothes be damned. I tried to catch his eye so he'd see me laughing, appreciating his new outfit, but he was either talking with the guys or posing with random girls who came over to take pictures with him with their phones.

The DJ put on a fast song. I wanted to sit and wait for Jesse to notice that I'd come back, but that would have been lame. It would be better if he saw me having a blast out on the dance floor. So I said to my friends, "Come on. Let's get some blisters."

Elise stood right up with me, but Morgan scrunched up her face. "Maybe in another song or—"

I grabbed her hand and dragged her out to the center of the basketball court.

After a few songs, if it was still raining, I had no idea. I was too busy dancing. Elise mostly swayed to the beat, but Morgan and I used to dance in her basement when we were little, and we had a few routine moves down pat that I eventually forced her into doing with me. I'd always been jealous that she got to take real-deal dance lessons, but she let me wear her costumes, and she'd teach me the moves she learned and it ended up feeling like I'd taken the classes too. We'd even put on performances for her grandmother.

As much as I was there in the moment, every time a song ended, I'd wonder if Jesse would come find me. When he didn't, I'd think about going to grab him. Could I be that brave?

But then a new song would come on and we'd scream,

because it would be absolutely the one song we needed to hear right then. I guess because we'd started late, the DJ was focusing on keeping us dancing and not trying to mix in slow songs, which I was grateful for. A bunch of junior girls eventually made a circle and I kept being pushed into the center. I'd try to make Morgan dance there with me, but she always found a way to shimmy back to the edges. I hoped Jesse was watching.

A slow song finally came on. I pulled Morgan close, but she wriggled free from my arms. "Keeley!" she whispered suddenly. "Here he comes!" And this time, she hurried to the table before I could grab her again.

Jesse popped up in front of me. Still in that wrestling singlet.

"You look ridiculous," I told him, but of course I was smiling.

"Ridiculously . . . hot?" He took my hand and led me to the center of the dance floor.

The crazy thing was, he did. Because he was handsome and confident and funny and God, could he freaking rock a singlet.

He put his hands on my waist, finding the little divots in my hips so fast and sure that it took my breath away. I lifted my arms up around his shoulders. And we began to slowly tip our weight from side to side.

We had a good bit of space between us at first, but as Jesse swayed, he inched closer to me and I to him, until we were pressed together. He'd recently gotten a haircut. The skin around his hairline was pink and the hairs there sparkled like tiny bits of gold thread.

He leaned close to my ear and said, "Kinda boring compared to our rain dance, huh?"

I shook my head. I thought it was more romantic than the

dance we'd had outside. It was my first real-deal slow dance with the boy I'd adored forever. I hoped he couldn't feel me shaking.

"You're staring at me," he said.

"Am not," I said. But I was. And he stared at me, too. Intensely. I almost couldn't take it. I wanted him to kiss me so badly, right then and there, in the middle of the dance, with everyone watching, even though Principal Bundy would probably have tossed us both back out into the storm.

"Do you know this song?"

I shook my head. I could pick up his cologne underneath the rain smell, coconut but with a little bit of spice.

"Me either. I think it's old. Maybe even from before we were born." Jesse cleared his throat. "All the old slow songs have a saxophone solo in them. Have you ever noticed that? Like it was a mandatory thing." You could have knocked me over with a feather because Jesse was nervous too. I heard it in his voice, the tiniest barely perceptible quiver that I picked up only because I was that close to him. It thrilled me. He kept nervous-talking, words bumbling out of his mouth. "You know, slow dancing is an oxymoron. I mean, can this even be called dancing? Really? It's more like walking in place. Or like we're—"

"Please shut up," I whispered. "You're going to make me not like you anymore." And then I laughed, because it was a ridiculous thing to say, because I knew right then that a part of me would love Jesse forever. This was my locket moment, a memory I'd keep until the day I died.

"Wait up. You only *like* me? That's it?" Jesse asked, peeling back from me the littlest bit, mock offended.

I bit my bottom lip and rolled my eyes. "Fine. I'll admit it."

I turned my head slightly to the side and rested it on Jesse's chest. "I'm in love with you, Jesse Ford."

I'd meant it to come out 100 percent sarcastic, but there was something very clear and quiet and undeniably earnest in my voice. I heard it. Jesse must have too. I felt him stiffen. Even if he didn't, my cheeks warmed against his cool skin, giving me away for sure.

I didn't even have enough time to regret it. Out of nowhere, my neck snapped back hard and the lights overhead streaked fast like shooting stars. It wasn't a slow, romantic dip. It was more like whiplash.

Once I was upright again, Jesse's hands let me go. It took me a second to figure out what was happening. Jesse and I were no longer slow dancing, even though the slow song poured out of the speakers. That he'd hip-checked me, and it popped me a few steps to the side. Off-balance, I tried to steady myself, but Jesse spread his legs and thrust his crotch at me, grinding himself on my bare leg to a nonexistent beat. Hard, almost like I was a soccer player on an opposing team and he was trying to steal the ball from me. I wish I had been ready for it, I wish Jesse had given me a heads-up, because if he had, there's no way I would have fallen.

There were gasps from the people watching us as I hit the floor, I definitely heard them. And then laughter. Shocked, I stared up at Jesse, but he was all smiles, giving me a come-hither look and crooking his finger, beckoning me to stand back up. He opened his mouth and said something, but I couldn't hear it because of the screams of everyone rushing close to watch us. I turned and saw Morgan. Even she was clapping. And Victoria too, with a bemused look on her face.

So I did it. I did what Jesse wanted, what the entire gym wanted, the only thing I really could do in the situation. I hopped back up to my feet and grinded on him as hard as he'd grinded on me. I did the running man in a circle around him while everyone clapped to the beat. I forced him to turn around and spanked his butt over and over again while he bit down on his finger and made groaning sounds.

That's when Bundy raced over and got between us. Jesse held up his hands in mock shock, pretending not to understand what she was upset about. The crowd booed. Then Bundy looked at me. Glared at me.

"Three years later and you're still hell-bent on embarrassing yourself."

My mouth plopped open. It was a sucker punch, as mean as or maybe even meaner than the way she came at me right before I quit Mock Congress. Even though I was older now, practically a senior, I shrank and shriveled inside like I was still a freshman. And just like she had then, Bundy turned on her heel and walked away from me before I could defend myself.

Unfortunately, she wasn't the only one to walk away from me.

I looked for Jesse to see if he'd heard, but he was already strutting back toward his friends, who either had their hands up for high fives or shook their heads with amused disbelief.

Left alone, I smoothed my dress. It was even dirtier now, the lace smudged muddy, having picked up the dirt from the gym floor on the spots that were still damp. I walked over to the food table, hoping they might have club soda or something, but of course they didn't. High school dances were club soda–free zones.

"Keeley!"

Elise and Morgan waved me over to our table.

I got myself a can of soda and headed toward them, trying to hold on to the good feelings I'd had earlier in the night.

"This is honestly the craziest courtship I've ever seen," Elise said as she scrolled through pictures on her phone she'd taken of Jesse and me. "I don't even know how to advise you."

Morgan rested her chin on her hand. "But it's so perfectly them, don't you think?"

"Oh, totally! Whatever you're doing, Keeley, keep doing it. It's clearly working!" Elise held up a photo of me and Jesse dancing and beaming million-dollar smiles.

"Keeley, what's wrong?" Morgan asked. Even though she said it quietly, Elise looked up from her phone.

"Nothing," I said quickly, and I rolled my wrist to be extra convincing. "Just Bundy being a beeyotch. Whatever."

Morgan twisted her head around until she saw Bundy, and then curled her lip. "Ugh. Forget it." It was the second time in two weeks that my best friend had said those words.

*Wes didn't know Morgan had him on speaker when he asked her not to bring me to his friend's party because I was obnoxious and not funny and none of his friends wanted to hook up with me anyway.*

*Morgan and I looked at each other, and then at the phone on her bed. Morgan dove for it, but she wasn't quick enough.*

*"Not even Beeker," Wes said. Which was probably another insult, though I didn't know Beeker, so I couldn't say for sure. "Come on. Can't you tell her you and Elise are doing something else this time?"*

*The way he asked it, whiny, I knew he'd asked her not to bring me before.*

*Morgan finally turned the speaker off and put the phone up to her ear.*

*I sat down on the floor and for whatever reason, started folding random clothes that Morgan had strewn around her room. I probably shouldn't have been surprised Wes would say such shitty things about me, especially considering what had happened a few days before, but I still was.*

*After that, I only heard half the conversation.*

*"Screw you, Wes, she's my best friend." And then, "I told you she didn't mean it. She was just kidding around." There was a long pause. "No." And then a longer one. "Yeah, well, if you can't take a joke"—at this point, she looked at me and made a stupid face, like Wes was being annoying—"then, yeah, I guess we are breaking up." She hung up her phone and threw it across the room.*

*"You and Elise can go without me," I said after a few minutes of stunned silence. "I don't care. You're not going to hurt my feelings." That wasn't even a lie. I couldn't be any more hurt than I already was.*

*"Forget it," Morgan said. Then she hugged me very, very tightly, as if she wanted to make sure that this was really happening, that her dumping Wes wasn't just a bad dream.*

Even though it hadn't worked the first time, I tried again to do exactly what Morgan said. Forget it. I sat quietly in the gym for the next few songs, while Elise sent texts and Morgan danced in her seat.

And then, lo and behold, "Cupid Shuffle" came on.

A rush of people headed to the dance floor, boys as well as girls. Maybe because the song lyrics were instructions? I'm not sure. The three of us went out too. Of course I looked for Jesse, but didn't see him.

I went through the motions, twisting and turning, but I kept scanning the gym. Where had Jesse gone? Maybe back to the locker room? I knew he wouldn't miss this opportunity to put on a show in front of everyone.

About halfway through the song, I figured I should go look for him.

I'd be lying if I said I didn't also have a sense of dread. I already knew that the night had slipped away from me somehow.

I walked quickly down the hallway, past the girls' bathroom, past the guidance offices and the library, "Cupid Shuffle" melting away underneath the rain the farther I got from the gym. My feet were still bare, the bottoms black, and I moved silently. No one would hear me coming. I rounded the corner and peered down at the science wing.

And there, at the end of the hallway, was Jesse Ford.

With Victoria Dunkle.

She sat on top of the hall monitor desk where Mrs. Treasman handed out demotions. Victoria's legs were crossed and angled to the side. She wore a lemon-yellow halter dress, a plain cotton one, nothing special. Jesse had both hands on the corners of the desk and he leaned in to her, whispering something. She tipped her head back and giggled.

I whipped back around the corner and steadied myself against a set of lockers, listening. I couldn't make out what they were saying. It was Jesse talking, mostly. Victoria, all she did was giggle.

I almost, almost laughed. But then I looked down at my dirty dress and everything got blurry.

I quickly wiped my face.

I did not cry at school. Ever.

I felt a hand on my shoulder. Morgan's hand, I thought. I hoped. I remembered her warning earlier in the morning. *You don't want to make Jesse laugh tonight. You want him to kiss you.* God, I screwed that up.

Or maybe it was Jesse?

I didn't want him to see me crying. But maybe it would be a good thing if he did. He'd know that I really did like him.

But how could he not know that already?

I looked up. Levi Hamrick, in wet jeans, running sneakers, and a black rain slicker. "Keeley."

I had never heard my name spoken so gently.

Then the lights flickered out.

# 7

**Saturday, May 14**
⚠ **EMERGENCY BROADCAST SYSTEM ALERT:** Intermittent power outages due to high winds are being reported across Aberdeen County and Waterford City Metro. Residents are being advised to avoid unnecessary travel.

We stood in the dark for a few seconds. Then the emergency lights flicked on and woke everything up.

"Don't sneak up on people like that!" I hissed.

Levi made a sour face and drew his hand away from me quickly, as if I were suddenly hot to the touch. "I wasn't trying to sneak up on you," he said, an edge to his voice, the same way he'd spoken to me at the Key Club sandbagging when he'd caught me joking around with Jesse. Like an annoyed older brother. Or a dad. "I found you crying in the middle of the hallway."

"Oh my God, *shhh!*" I glanced to where the science wing began and prayed Jesse and Victoria hadn't heard that. Levi hadn't come to Spring Formal, or rather, I didn't remember seeing him, not that I would look. "What are you doing here?"

"The power outages. Now, just stay where you are a second," Levi said sternly, holding his palm to me as if he were directing traffic. He looked up at the emergency lights, counting the beams of weak spotlight after weak spotlight. They were mounted over every other classroom door and barely made a dent in the darkness, a total joke compared to the bright pops of lightning outside. Some didn't even turn on.

Levi was only a couple of inches taller than me, still a good size for a guy but not nearly as tall as Jesse. He unzipped his rain slicker and underneath was a white polo shirt, two points jutting down like arrows. His hair was buzzed to peach fuzz. He'd worn it that way as long as I could remember. I had no idea what Levi looked like with hair, if it was curly or wavy or straight. His eyes were plain brown like mine, or so I thought.

It wouldn't be until a few weeks later that I'd notice the yellow flecks.

While Levi was preoccupied, I began walking backward the way I'd come, hoping to disappear to the gym without anyone noticing. But Jesse and Victoria rounded the corner.

"Oh," Jesse said, his eyes meeting mine. He didn't say it surprised. Or apologetic. It came out straightforward and plain, like the fifteenth letter of the alphabet.

I said "Hey!" as cheerily as I could. Which, looking back, I bet didn't sound cheery. But I tried.

"Hi, Keeley," Victoria said sheepishly. Had Jesse told her what I'd said to him? Had they both been laughing at me?

Levi groaned and shook his head. "Everyone needs to get back to the gym now," he announced. "The hallways are off-limits."

Jesse looked at me and rolled his eyes toward Levi before walking back to the gym.

Maybe Jesse thought he'd caught me with Levi?

If he did think that, would it make him jealous?

I quickly decided no. Because of what Jesse already thought

about Levi, and also knowing all the mean things I'd said about Levi that day we were sandbagging the river.

*He has such a hard-on for rules, I bet he jerks off to the school handbook.*

That one had really landed. Jesse was shocked to hear a girl make a jerk-off joke. Wasn't that the start of everything? The moment when Jesse really noticed me? It sure felt that way. And we'd had so much fun over the last week, drawing lines in the sand and daring each other to jump over them.

Had Jesse ever planned to kiss me tonight? Or was that a joke too?

I convinced myself that the reason I had never been loved by a boy was because I hadn't met a boy who *got* me. Jesse was supposed to be that person. I was so sure he was. Except Jesse was with the beautiful girl who I bet never once took a purposefully ugly picture of herself or did a stupid dance.

I used to think Morgan and Elise had some secret special knowledge of how to get boys to like them. And I felt lucky that they were there to help me get it right. But it suddenly seemed far simpler. I just had to do the opposite of my natural impulses. Because something was obviously wrong with me if I thought licking a car window was an acceptable way to flirt with anyone. Or making masturbation jokes. Or admitting my love for someone I'd really only known for a week.

As we reached the doorway to the gym, I saw flashing bright red and blue lights through the streamers. Four police cars were parked outside the gym doors and more were pulling into the parking lot. But I wasn't nervous or scared. I felt sick to my stomach over what had happened with me and Jesse.

Principal Bundy pushed through the streamers. She was already frowning, but when she laid eyes on me, it doubled. "What are you kids doing? The hallways are off-limits."

Levi, flummoxed, tried to explain. "I know. I was going after them to bring them back."

I seized the opportunity and hurried over to the café table where my friends were. People lit the room with their cell phone screens, waving them around like they were sparklers.

Morgan elbowed me. "Where'd you disappear to? Did you and Jesse . . ." I wanted to make a joke but couldn't. So I shook my head. "Don't worry," she said. "The night is young!"

My phone buzzed. It was a text from my mom. I knew by the length. She always wrote the longest texts.

Kee, so sorry I missed pictures. Annie sent me some and you looked beautiful. Are you having fun? If so, DO NOT WASTE YOUR GOOD TIME WRITING BACK TO YOUR POOR OLD MOTHER. But please text when you get to Morgan's house tonight so I know you made it safe. Be careful out there! The roads are really bad. Looks like this "storm of the century" is living up to the hype.

Jesse was now sitting two tables over from ours, tossing kernels of popcorn into the air and catching them in his mouth. He caught every single one. There were a couple of senior girls with him, keeping count. But not Victoria.

More red and blue lights danced off the walls as additional cop cars pulled up to the gym. Levi pushed open the door and let in his father. Really, the only difference between them was that Sheriff Hamrick was in a uniform and Levi was not. Levi held the door open for the other officers as they filed in too, and each one regarded Levi in some knowing way—a pat on the shoulder, a nod of the head. Those officers brought in emergency lights, battery-powered I guess, and placed them in the center circle of the basketball court, pointed up to the ceiling. Other officers positioned themselves at every doorway, preventing students from either wandering the hallways or going outside.

Principal Bundy set down her phone and headed directly over to Sheriff Hamrick. A heated discussion ensued.

"What do you think's happening?" Morgan asked.

Even though Levi had told me, I said nothing.

"I bet another tree fell somewhere," Elise said. "Probably took out the power lines." She leaned forward giddily. "You guys, maybe we'll have to spend the night here! Like a huge coed sleepover!"

I smiled, but really, the idea made my head hurt, the thought of Jesse and Victoria sneaking off again together, or maybe spooning together on a shared gym mat. What would Elise and Morgan say then?

A few minutes later, the electricity came back on. We squinted at the sudden brightness. The DJ's music blasted out of the speakers after an ear-deafening pop. The students cheered and Morgan gasped and put a hand on my back, like maybe we'd have another song to dance to, but Principal Bundy quickly shut that down by giving the DJ the kill sign. She walked to the center of the gym floor, cupped her hands around her mouth, and called out, "Because of safety concerns, we've decided to end tonight's Spring Formal early." The whole room erupted, boos and hisses and whines, which Bundy tried to quell by holding up her hands. "For those students who drove themselves here tonight, we are going to have a caravan of officers leading you out through the flooded roads." Levi appeared by her side and lifted a clipboard high over his head. "The rest of you, please see Levi Hamrick, add your names to this call list, and we will get in touch with your parents and provide you rides home in one of our school buses."

Everyone began to murmur. No one was concerned about the danger or the weather. They were annoyed that Spring Formal was officially over. They didn't want the night to end.

Morgan reacted to something over my shoulder. "*Shhh.* Here he comes." And then I felt something under the table. It was Morgan, slipping me a piece of gum. She winked.

I didn't know how to play it. I couldn't tell them the truth, especially when I wasn't sure what the truth was. Even my possible misunderstanding of everything was too humiliating. So I put the gum in my mouth, picked up my phone, and stared at it.

Jesse leaned over our table. "Party at Zito's house. You guys know where he lives, right?"

Without being too obvious, I watched his eyes scan our table. Morgan and Elise both nodded, looking excited to go. Zito was a senior and we were being invited over. I'd heard there were two trailers on his property. One for his family, and one just for him. Finally, Jesse's attention landed on me. His gaze did not linger on me any longer than it had on anyone else.

I was trying to come up with an excuse for Morgan and Elise as to why I needed to go home, while Jesse went around the rest of the gym and invited other people to Zito's house, but in the time it took for the caravan to be ready, we lost electricity in the gym twice more. After that, it seemed like everyone was resigned to calling it a night. I was so glad of that.

Principal Bundy made an announcement for everyone to get into their cars. Elise tried to get Levi to allow her to ride home with us, but he told her rules were rules and she'd have to go on the bus. I put on my rain boots again, found my coat in the bathroom where I'd left it. The rain was still coming down in sheets. It was far less fun and exciting to step back outside than it had been on our way inside. Not just for me. For everyone.

Jesse was still in his wrestling singlet. He had his wet clothes tied up in a knot and he was holding them by a pant leg. The doors were open now and he shivered. I felt compelled to go to him. To at least say good-bye. To lie and tell him I hadn't meant what I'd said on the dance floor, that it was obviously a joke, come on. But I was such a mess of sad and embarrassed and confused that I didn't dare. And it wasn't like he was looking for me, either. Instead I started talking about who the hell knows what really loudly to Morgan as we walked past him.

Levi, wearing a thick black policeman's poncho, helped direct cars out of the parking lot. As we drove passed him, he definitely gave me the stink eye for what happened in the hallway. I gave it right back.

Our ride home was like a weird and meandering funeral procession, with everyone following Sheriff Hamrick's squad car in a slow line. Officers were positioned along the way to keep us away from streets with fallen trees and power lines. It took us almost thirty minutes to go one measly mile.

At Morgan's house, we changed into dry clothes, made some nachos in the microwave, and brought them up to her room. As we talked about the dance, I kept glancing at my phone to see if Jesse had texted me to check that I'd gotten home safe.

He hadn't.

I'd thought Morgan was already asleep, but after a while of being quiet, she rolled over and hugged me tight. "You were right," she said. "Tonight is exactly what I needed. I don't think I thought about Wes one single time."

I hugged her back.

At least they were still broken up. At least Wes would never have to hear the story of tonight from Morgan. How it basically validated all the terrible things he'd said about me.

She went on. "And I don't want you to feel bad about not kissing Jesse tonight. It's totally the storm's fault. It screwed everything up. Seriously. There will be other chances."

I sighed. "I'm not sure about that."

"What? Why?"

"Something weird happened tonight. Between me and Jesse." The truth lingered just underneath my tongue.

"Keeley, what happened? Everything was going so well!" I hated how disappointed she sounded.

I realized in that moment that had Morgan and Elise never found out about my texts with Jesse, I wouldn't have allowed myself to think he might like me on my own. They both egged me on, but Morgan especially. Why? Did she actually believe it could happen? Or was she just trying to pump me up in the wake of the Wes stuff?

I blurted out, "He got a boner when he was grinding on me and it totally freaked me out."

She squealed and hit me with her pillow. "Oh, gross!"

"I'm kidding! I'm kidding!"

I wanted her to ask me again, press me for the truth. If she had, I bet I would have told her what really happened. She was my best friend, after all. But my joke was enough, I guess, to convince her everything was okay, because then she was snoring tiny little whispery snores. I wish it was enough for me, because I stayed awake the whole night.

## 8

**Sunday, May 15**
⚠ **EMERGENCY BROADCAST SYSTEM ALERT**: A Flood Warning is now in effect for Aberdeen County and the Waterford City Metro Area. A Severe Thunderstorm Warning is also in effect. Gale-force winds are expected this afternoon and continuing overnight. The heaviest rainfall will arrive Sunday evening. We anticipate the threat of flooding in low-lying areas near the river to continue into Monday afternoon.

---

With the morning came my worst nightmare: Jesse hadn't texted me once. Not an explanation, not an olive branch. Not even a single joke or picture or video of him doing something funny, like the ten-second clip he'd sent me on Thursday, where he stuffed an entire slice of Mineo's pizza in his mouth at once and then smiled with big chipmunk cheeks into his camera and waved hi. Clearly, I had blown the chance—if I'd ever really had one—to kiss him. And apparently I'd wrecked our whole friendship, too.

I watched that pizza video underneath the blankets with the sound off while Morgan was asleep, and again with the sound on when she got up to pee. I sat on the side of the tub and watched it three times in a row before I got into the shower. Each time Jesse waved at me on the screen, I wanted to cry.

Morgan wasn't in her room when I got out of the shower. That wasn't unusual. Sundays were always busy at her house because of Mrs. Dorsey's hair appointments. Women from town would come in and out all day long. Around every hour, we'd pop downstairs to help out. Morgan would sweep up and make fresh coffee while I put a load of towels in the washing machine and made sure the shampoo bottles were filled.

That morning, though, it was strangely quiet when I came downstairs. There were no women sitting in the living room, gossiping or flipping through magazines while they waited for their turn in Mrs. Dorsey's styling chair. The lights in the dining room were off, the brushes and combs laid out untouched, capes hanging on their wall hooks, laundry basket empty.

I heard laughing coming from the kitchen.

Morgan and her mother were at the table. Morgan was still in her pajamas, and she was picking at a bagel with cream cheese. Mrs. Dorsey wore black jeans and a tight black sweater, but she had her house slippers on instead of the flats she wore when she was working. She wasn't eating breakfast, just sipping coffee.

Lowering her mug, Mrs. Dorsey said, "Morning, Keeley. I'm just getting the recap on last night. You want a frozen bagel?"

"Yes, please." I sat down at the table. "Are you closed today or something?"

Mrs. Dorsey put a bagel in the toaster for me. As soon as she pushed the lever down, the lights flickered out. "Not again," she groaned. "This is the fourth time this morning! I canceled all my morning appointments because of the power cutting in and out."

"Here," Morgan said, passing me the uneaten half of bagel on her plate.

"Morgan, can you get me my appointment book? I'm just going to reschedule everyone else." Morgan got up, and to me

Mrs. Dorsey said, "I haven't had a Sunday off in Lord knows how long! I'll call your mother, see what she's up to." Her face lit up. "We can have a girls' day together. Jammies, maybe even a movie, if the electricity holds up." She winked. "We can't let our kids have all the fun."

"I think she's working."

"Again? But she worked yesterday. That's why she missed out on taking Spring Formal pictures. When's the last time she had a day off?"

I shrugged. "It's been a while." There was an awkward silence then, which I tried to fill. "She was so glad you texted her those pictures," I said. "Did you send her the one of us posing like the shot in your photo album? Did she recognize it?"

Mrs. Dorsey nodded, her smile slightly faded. "Of course she did. Right away."

The next time we lost power, Morgan said we should probably eat the ice cream in the freezer before it melted. Which was my cue to go downstairs and get us some. Morgan had no vision when it came to snack foods. If left in charge, she'd grab whatever random crackers or half-empty bag of chips she could find, no bowl, no napkins. I liked making a presentation of it . . . perfectly cut cubes of Cracker Barrel cheddar, onion dip scooped out of the plastic tub and into a big mug, actual melted butter poured over the microwave popcorn, our glasses of soda filled tall with ice cubes. A little extra showmanship went a long way.

Morgan was in charge of picking our entertainment. She was the one to control the remote, channel, volume, content. My favorite was when she'd create some kind of theme for the day, like Movies with Hot Guys Who Play Guitar or Ladies Who Time-Travel.

This used to be how we always spent our sleepovers before boys and before Elise. But that afternoon, maybe because of the rain and the fact that we weren't supposed to be on the roads, that's what we did. We were halfway through the second film in a Witches block, and Morgan's laptop was low on battery, so I hurried downstairs and got two matching bowls.

The ice cream had begun to soften, so it was easy to scoop. I added a thick drizzle of Hershey's chocolate syrup and some crushed-up peanuts, and then sprayed a dollop of Reddi-wip on top. In the fridge door, I spotted a glass jar of maraschino cherries. There was only one inside, so I cut it in half and nestled a piece on the very top for each of us.

I thought about doing a video for Jesse, me filling my mouth with Reddi-wip and licking my lips. Funny but a little bit flirty, too. But that couldn't be the way to reach out to him, not after his silence. Not if he didn't like me the way I'd convinced myself he did. Then I'd just look pathetic. I imagined him and Victoria watching the video and laughing at how clueless I was.

The power came back on again as I was passing through the living room. Mrs. Dorsey was asleep on the couch and she didn't wake up when the television flickered on to The Weather Channel. I stood there with the cold bowls chilling the palms of my hands and watched the bottom of the screen, where there was a running clock with urgent red numbers tracking how many hours, minutes, seconds it had been raining.

Above that were loops of Waterford City footage. Waterfront real estate flooded up to the doorman lobbies, the doors of beautiful glass office buildings sandbagged shut, people dressed in suits and ties and fancy dresses trying to wade through flooded streets. Caution tape roping off the train stations and the wharf. An airport full of stranded travelers.

Then they switched to Aberdeen, cut to a live shot of the river. The sandbags had seemed almost stupidly far from the banks when we'd stacked them last week, but now there was river water splashing over the tops in waves.

My phone was upstairs. I felt the pull to check in with my mom and dad, to make sure they were okay. But mostly, I left the room because the news was depressing me even more than I already was and our ice cream was turning to soup.

Saint Ann's offered a Sunday Mass at 4:30 p.m., and they held a dinner and youth group meeting after it. I usually stayed at Morgan's house all day and then got dropped off on their way out of town. We'd be lounging around pretty casually, but sometime around three, Morgan would start getting ready. I knew she took the church aspect of it seriously, a thing I always reminded myself of when she'd ignore me to be on the phone with Elise while she got ready, doing her makeup or her hair. She got more dressed up for church than she did for school. If I had my book bag with me, I tried to catch up on homework or whatever. But I didn't that day, so I just packed up my things.

I decided to leave my Spring Formal dress at Morgan's house, because I knew my mom would be upset that it'd been ruined. If I couldn't find a dry cleaner to fix it, I would buy myself another dress so Mom would never know this one was ruined. I'd use the money I earned from my summer job. It was supposed to be college money, but I had to do that for her or the guilt would eat me alive.

Then, because Morgan was still on the phone, I wandered downstairs.

Mrs. Dorsey stared out her kitchen window at a huge oak tree. "I keep telling myself I should take that thing down. Do you think it's swaying more than it should?"

I went up beside her. "No, I don't think so."

Even though dinner would be served at the church, Mrs. Dorsey was fixing my mom's favorite dish, baked ziti. Aside from two scoops for her and Morgan that went into her fridge, she told me to take the rest home. "This will give your mom the night off," she said. "But don't let her have a single bite unless she promises to do nothing but lie on the couch with her feet up."

Morgan finally came down. She had on a cap-sleeve blouse under a navy jumper, paired with her green galoshes with cream knee socks. Her hair was bouncy, she'd tried hot rollers. I felt like a kid sister next to her, still in my pajamas, no makeup. I tucked my sweats into my rain boots.

Then the three of us got in the car and Mrs. Dorsey drove me home.

Though it was still raining, a few people dressed in rain gear were prepping their houses, laying down their own sandbags. The water rushed down the edges of the streets like rivers, so we drove in the very center of the street. There were bits of broken branches and bark sprinkled over the ground, like tree confetti.

I leaned forward to Morgan. "We never went to look for your shoe in the parking lot."

"Don't worry about it. I never wear them anyway."

"Oh. Okay." But I didn't like the thought of that shoe out

there. I didn't want to see it on Monday morning when we got to school. It was just a reminder of Jesse and how things had gone so off the rails.

She looked at me out of the corner of her eye. "What's with the sad face? Have you not heard from him today?"

I avoided the question. "I don't even know if I like him anymore." This, I thought, would be a great plan. To extricate myself from Jesse. Make Morgan think it was my decision, not his.

"What? Shut up! You do too!"

"He's honestly not that cute or that funny now that I've gotten to know him."

Morgan turned around to face me. "Are you talking like this because of what Wes said about you? Because if you are, then I want you to cut it out right now."

Mrs. Dorsey's eyes found me in the rearview mirror.

I knew Morgan and her mom talked about everything, but somehow I thought this might be off-limits. And if Mrs. Dorsey knew what Wes had said about me, did she also know what I had done to Wes to make him so angry? My stomach twisted into a big fat knot. "No. I'm just saying . . ."

"Good. Because I couldn't imagine a more perfect boy for you."

Me either, which really sucked.

When I came up our walkway, the curtain in our front window was pulled aside. My mom met my eyes and smiled. She was going to want to talk with me about the dance, how crazy everyone went for my dress. She'd want to see pictures. I realized the only ones I'd taken were when I was in Morgan's car. After my rain dance with Jesse, I'd looked like total crap. I didn't want to lie to her, so my plan was to get up to my bedroom as fast as I possibly could.

I started peeling off my wet layers as soon as I walked in.

Mom was on the couch, typing on her laptop with two fingers. That was just the weird and inefficient way she typed. "Just give me one second to finish this last chart!" Mom works as a nurse, the kind who travels to people's homes and cares for them there. She loves her job, loves being there for her patients, but she sucks at the paperwork part.

Dad was on his computer too, a small off-brand laptop he'd gotten at a Black Friday sale. Since he could no longer work as a carpenter, my dad had taken a liking to politics, even though he thought most of the people in charge were a bunch of liars. Local, national, international . . . he was a junkie for all of it. He also didn't trust news reports, preferring instead to get information through message boards. If there was something shady going on with the government of Ireland, he'd find a message board and talk to the people who were there, living through it. Israel, South Korea, Mexico—you name it. My dad liked to say he had friends all over the world. Probably because he didn't have many left in Aberdeen.

It wasn't always that way.

My dad had been relatively successful before the accident. If people didn't know him personally, they at least recognized the Hewitt name, and they trusted it. My family went back a long way in Aberdeen. Grandpa and Great-Grandpa had both worked at the mill. Dad, too, right out of high school, until it closed eight years later. Then he became a carpenter. Dad was strong then. Muscular and always tan from working outside. Now he barely left the house except for town meetings.

"Hey, Keeley," he said to me, without looking up from his screen.

"Mrs. Dorsey sent food over. Ziti." Mom's eyes lit up, which made me laugh. I set the baking tin on the counter. "But she says Mom can't have any unless she doesn't work tonight."

Mom smiled to herself. She shut her laptop.

"How come I can't ever get you to do that?" Dad said with a smirk.

Mom picked up her phone, presumably to text Mrs. Dorsey a thank-you, and asked me, "Is your phone working, Keeley?"

"Yeah, why?"

"Some people are saying service is being affected by the constant cloud cover. Satellites can't pick up the signals."

"Oh," I said, cheery now. Maybe that was why I hadn't heard from Jesse. "Did you guys lose power?"

"Our lights flickered a few times," Mom said. "But we've been lucky. How was it down in the valley?"

"Lots of flooding and downed trees and stuff," I told them. "And it's supposed to rain more tonight, you know."

"We know," Mom said, pausing to rub her tired eyes. "It's the only thing on the news. This storm is actually starting to scare me."

Dad laughed. "That's what they want to do. Scare you into watching." Mom slid her glasses down from the top of her head and pointed knowingly at the newspaper next to him on the desk. Grumbling, he flipped it over to hide the headline, IS ABERDEEN SINKING? in big bold type.

# 9

---

**Sunday, May 15**

⚠ **EMERGENCY BROADCAST SYSTEM ALERT**: As of 11:00 PM, Governor Ward has issued a mandatory evacuation for Aberdeen County, as well as those residing in Zone A of Waterford City. Emergency shelters are open and operating, and local police and fire are working to inform residents and provide transport as necessary. This order is scheduled to expire by 6:00 AM, but may be extended as needed.

---

Just before midnight, a loud knock at the front door jolted me out of sleep. I sat straight up in my bed. No one ever came to our house, and definitely not this late.

I heard my mom get out of bed and race across the room for her robe. My dad got up too, slower and with a little more effort, from his seat downstairs in the living room.

I hurried to my window and looked for any cars parked in our driveway or on the road, but I saw nothing but darkness and rain. I grabbed a sweatshirt from the back of my chair, crept out to the top of our stairs, and leaned over the railing.

Mom still managed to beat Dad to the door. She pulled it open and there stood Sheriff Hamrick. He was in uniform, with the same rain slicker Levi had shown up wearing to Spring Formal and a wide-brim hat covered in plastic wrapping, like a shower cap. He was glistening.

"Is everything okay, Matt?" Mom asked, breathless.

"I'm sorry to disturb you, Jill, but the river breached the sand-bags a few hours ago." He pressed his lips together and shook his head sadly. "A good portion of the lower valley is completely flooded. We've even had a few homes washed clear off their foundations on the south end of town."

My mom gasped. I did too. We were on the north end, near the top of town. I tiptoed back into my room and tried to find my cell phone in my covers to see if anyone had texted me, but it was dead. I had it plugged in, but the power was out, so it never charged.

I heard my dad say, "We're fine here. Appreciate you check-ing in."

I went back out to the stairs. Dad hadn't opened the door any wider for Sheriff Hamrick.

"Do you have water in your basement, Jim?" he asked my dad, craning his neck to try and see into our house.

"We're fine here," Dad said again, but colder, and that time, he closed the front door ever so slightly. Behind him were boxes Mom and I had carried up before bed. After ziti, Mom and I had spent the rest of the evening on chore duty, trying to divert the water that had begun to pool around the basement window wells with old boards and bricks.

"This is a mandatory evacuation, Jim. You don't really have a choice in the matter."

"Mandatory? According to who? Mayor Aversano?" Dad folded his arms.

Sheriff Hamrick shook his head, incredulous. He couldn't have been surprised, though. He looked at my mother. "It's an order from the governor," he continued.

"Where are we supposed to go?"

"We've set up temporary shelter at the high school and—"

"The high school?" Dad scoffed. "That's on lower ground than we are here. How is that safer than us staying in our home?"

Looking back, the things my dad was saying, they did make sense. But in the moment, I was just annoyed with him. I was used to my dad being argumentative with people in town, speaking his mind, but not fighting our sheriff during a mandatory evacuation.

"Trust me. I know it's a hassle and that, but look. Things aren't safe right now. Anyone who lives in the valley is in imminent danger. And we've got to assume that the rest of the hill isn't much safer. We may have even lost some lives tonight."

Who, I wondered. Jesse? Could Jesse have lost his home? Or worse? I had no idea where he lived.

I took a step forward and the floorboards creaked. Everyone looked up at me.

"Keeley, sweetie, get dressed," Mom said, pressing a hand to Dad's back.

My mother had a way with my dad. She let him bluster, she never tried to shut him up. But when she wanted something, when she needed to take control, she did. I knew my parents' marriage wasn't perfect. Far from it. Especially after Dad's accident. But we'd slipped into a comfortable routine that pretty much worked.

"Fine. We'll pack up the car and drive down there within the hour."

"Roads are flooded. I can't have the accessible streets blocked up with abandoned cars. We've got a transpo spot down on Main. I'll drive you all over there and then another officer will bring you over to the school in one of the rescue boats. Do you think you'll be physically able to climb in a boat? Or should I make sure we've got enough hands down there to lift you?"

My dad stiffened.

It was honestly the worst thing Sheriff Hamrick could have said. And I wonder now if he didn't do it on purpose, because of the hard time my dad was giving him and all the other hard times he'd given him at town meetings.

"How long will we be there?" my father asked.

"Until we get the official order that it's safe to return. The river will crest in the morning. If everything stays status quo, and we get the A-OK from the governor's office, we could start sending some folks back by lunchtime tomorrow."

Mom asked, "What should we bring with us?"

"Some clothes, enough for a day or two should suffice. Toiletries. We have plenty of food there, Jill. And bedding."

She nodded. "Do you want to wait inside?"

Before he could answer her, Dad closed the door on him.

I heard my parents talking in hushed tones while I raced around my room, putting things in my book bag. If our whole town was headed to the gym, that meant everyone I knew from school would be there. I wish I hadn't put my hair up right after showering at Morgan's, because now it was dented, and so it would have to stay in a bun. I changed out of my pajamas and into a pair of leggings, a tank top, and a more fitted hoodie.

I feel terrible about this now, but even knowing that bad things had happened to some people in town, there was a part of me that felt excited. Mainly because I would have another chance to see Jesse and, hopefully, undo whatever damage I'd done at Spring Formal, if it wasn't too late.

# 10

A few sorry-looking crepe paper streamers from Spring Formal were still hanging when my family walked through the gym doors around 1 a.m. You could see where the others had been quickly ripped down because of the white bits still taped to the walls.

Aberdeen was a small town, with only about 500 families, but it didn't look the part with every one of them crammed into the same place. The heat was cranked and the air was muggy. It was loud, too, dogs in cages barking at cats in cages, kids playing tag and screaming with the kind of frazzled crazy from being up way past their bedtimes. The adults were clustered in little groups, wringing their hands or patting each other on the back.

Rows and rows of cots were set up in straight lines like a big army barrack, each one half the size of a twin bed and tightly made with a white pancake of a pillow and a moss-green blanket. Most had already been claimed, either by a body or with bags of crap.

My book bag suddenly felt way too light. What if we were here more than one night? It seemed like most people were prepared for that possibility. I'd stupidly packed only one change of clothes. The rest of the space I'd filled with fun stuff like a little set of speakers that hooked up to my phone to play music and a couple of different bottles of nail polish, so Elise and Morgan and I could give each other manicures if we got bored.

There was one random thing that I did not regret bringing. A pad of Mad Libs that had been in my Christmas stocking when I was a kid. I'd filled out some of the pages, but plenty were still blank.

I pulled it out from the front pocket and scanned the room for Jesse.

Jesse had a little sister named Julia. I knew that because she sometimes starred in his videos. She was either seven or maybe eight, and she was just as hilarious as Jesse. Her hair had all the same shades of blond as his, but her curls were tighter, like tiny springs. One time, he made a video of her sneaking into the bath-room when he was in the shower to flush the toilet so he'd get hit with a blast of hot water. Apparently, she did it all the time, so he was ready for her. He actually brought his phone into the shower and filmed her from a small gap between the curtain and the wall. Even though Jesse had seen her coming, after she hit the flush, he screamed like he was surprised and Julia ran out of the bath-room cackling. She had an unexpectedly deep laugh for a little girl, throaty and raw. I liked her immediately. He was hoping it would go viral, he said so in his own comments. "Let's make Julia go viral!" The video did get a lot of hits, but not that many. I bet almost half were from me.

I figured the Mad Libs would be a good thing to give her, to keep her entertained or calm in case she might be scared. And, more than anything, it would be a way back into talking to Jesse. Even though I hadn't heard from him, I didn't want to believe that hope was lost.

I didn't see him, or any of my friends, either. There was no way they'd be sleeping, since we obviously weren't going to have school tomorrow. Morgan and Elise had probably found a classroom to hang out in. Maybe Jesse had too.

Mom unzipped her navy raincoat and pulled back the hood. She'd carried her briefcase with her nursing files and her laptop inside the raincoat to make sure it stayed dry. Her jeans were rolled up to her calves and her nightshirt was tucked into the waistband like it was an actual *shirt* shirt. On her feet were the muck boots that she only wore when she was working in the yard. While she walked, she looked up at the banners in the rafters, searching for the year she and my dad had graduated, I guess.

I put the Mad Libs away and then tried again to take the rolling suitcase she was pulling along, but she smiled and said, "I've got it, Keeley." It was full of nursing supplies that she'd gathered before we left. Her stethoscope, some rolls of gauze, alcohol pads, things like that. Sheriff Hamrick had told her it wasn't necessary, that a first-aid station had already been set up, but Mom insisted. "Several of my patients live in Aberdeen," she'd explained. When she had trouble fitting everything she wanted to bring, she left behind her toiletry bag and just packed a toothbrush so there'd be enough room.

Dad lagged a few steps behind us, in a flannel and jeans, one hand stuffed in his pocket, the other gripping the head of his cane. He had his laptop wrapped in a plastic bag from Viola's Market and tucked under one arm. Before we got in the boat, Mom knelt down to roll up Dad's pants for him. He waved her off, I'm sure because he was embarrassed for her to do that in front of the police officers. My mom pretty much waited on Dad in our house, but he didn't seem to want to let other people see it. Even if that meant spending the night in jeans that were soaking wet up to his knees.

A volunteer approached us looking apologetic. "If you can't find three empty beds together, don't worry. They're in the process of setting up overflow cots inside the classrooms." He pointed down a hall, where I saw Levi Hamrick lifting folded cots off a stack and opening them up for another volunteer who was ready to carry them away.

Mom nodded and then switched her laptop bag from one shoulder to the other. "I guess we should find a spot," she said. "Preferably near an outlet, so I can get some work done. I doubt I'll be sleeping much tonight."

Dad pointed at a stack of cots being unfolded by another volunteer near the sports equipment closet. "You two head that way, I'll get us some coffees." And then, loudly, to no one in particular, he announced, "I hope someone's planning to give us regular updates. You can't keep us locked up and not tell us what's going on out there."

I know why he said it. On the ride over to the gym, things hadn't looked that bad in town. Granted, we hadn't been anywhere close to the river and there was clearly a lot of flooding. But when we were in the boat, there'd been a couple of places where there was barely enough water to be floating. Every time the boat scraped against the ground, Dad would huff and puff, all pissed off. It was the same way he spoke at town meetings—a righteous know-it-all. People tolerated him for two reasons, because he was a Hewitt, and because my mother was beloved.

A few people nearby turned to see what the volunteer might

say to Dad's request. But one freshman girl I recognized from school lifted her head off her cot and begged my dad with her eyes to be quiet. She was spooning her younger sister, running her hands through the little girl's hair, trying to soothe her to sleep. I met her gaze as we walked past and made an apologetic face. That's when the reality of the situation hit me. Not that we were in danger, but that everyone I knew would be in the same room as my father tonight.

There were times when I was deeply embarrassed by my dad, in a way that went far beyond anything my friends experienced with their fathers. Maybe their dads would sing too loud at church, or beep the horn too many times when they'd pick them up from school. But since his accident, Dad was well known in Aberdeen. Another word would be *infamous*. Thankfully, it was mostly adults in town who were familiar with his antics. Not anyone my age.

The monthly Aberdeen town meetings were well attended and also broadcast live on the local cable channel. At first, during his recuperation, Dad would watch from the bedroom television. I'm not sure if he ever watched a meeting before his accident, but after, he wouldn't miss one. And when he was well enough, he started to attend them in person. Without fail, there'd be an issue where he'd take the stance of opposition, of defiance. Raising the price of parking on Main Street, the budget for pothole repair, a variance on the building code. Sometimes he'd prepare an actual speech beforehand, and because of the rules in place for public discourse, the mayor and his cabinet would have to listen to him drone on and on and on. But Mom and I mostly encouraged it, because that became the only time he'd leave our house.

I felt my mom come up behind me. As if she could sense my anxiety, she gave my shoulder a little squeeze.

It was weird to see people shuffling around in their pajamas and slippers in public. I mostly kept my eyes on the floor. I did not want to see any of our teachers half dressed, or worse, Principal Bundy. My mom was greeted warmly by a few people. It was like she was the exact opposite of my father. We couldn't go anywhere in Aberdeen without some old person falling over themselves to say what a wonderful, caring nurse my mom had been to them.

"Jill!"

Mrs. Dorsey ran over. She hugged my mom so hard, she practically tackled her. "I've been calling you nonstop!"

"Sorry. My phone must be buried at the bottom of my bag."

Mrs. Dorsey let out a deep breath of relief. "I figured you guys were safe . . . but you never know."

"And your house is okay?"

She nodded. "So far. The basement is flooded, but that's about it." They hugged again. This time, more tenderly. And then she took my mom by the hand. "Come on. I saved three cots next to ours. We're by the bleachers."

"Where's Morgan?"

"She went looking for Elise."

Dad came shuffling back over with two coffees and a huge handful of baked goods. Like, enough for five people. My mom and Mrs. Dorsey noticed that too and gave Dad a look.

Dad ignored us all, or else he wasn't paying attention. "Did either of you notice those Army Corps of Engineers vans outside?"

"I must have missed them," Mrs. Dorsey said.

"Jim, Annie saved us cots next to hers."

Instead of saying "thank you," my dad was looking around the gym. "Something funny's going on."

Ignoring him, Mrs. Dorsey spotted my mom's briefcase and said, "Jill, don't even tell me you're planning to do paperwork. Can't you take tonight, of all nights, off?"

"I won't be able to sleep," Mom said sheepishly. "Better I stay productive than lie awake counting sheep, right?"

Meanwhile, Dad surveyed the room skeptically. "I'd love to corner one of those engineers. I bet I could get some information out of them. Unless they've been told not to talk to us . . ."

I had to get away. "I'm going to go look for Morgan."

I walked the halls, peering into classrooms, clutching my dead cell phone. I kept passing other kids from our high school, running down the halls or sitting in the stairwells. It felt bizarre to be here so late. It didn't even feel like a school. Maybe because the normal rules of daytime didn't apply. There'd be no bells, no attendance, you could walk in and out of any classroom you wanted.

I eventually found a bunch of girls from my grade—Emma, Sarah, Frances, June, Lisa, and Morgan—inside an English classroom. They'd pushed the desks into a circle and each girl was sitting on top of one, swinging her legs. Some were in normal clothes, some had changed into their pajamas.

I pushed open the door and did a little rain dance by hopping on one foot and patting my open mouth. What was happening was definitely scary, but at the very least, we wouldn't have to go to school tomorrow. I wanted to remind them of that, the good stuff.

Everyone looked up, startled. Morgan hopped down and

came rushing over. In a whisper, she said, "Where've you been? I've been calling you!"

I held up my dead phone. "What's going on?"

Lisa put a finger to her lips and *shhh*ed me.

"Are you guys still there?" said a very small, shaky voice.

Someone was on speaker.

Morgan took my hand and pulled me over to where a phone had been placed on a desk. "We're here, Elise."

I looked around. Elise wasn't there in the room.

Shit.

"We're honestly so lucky," Elise said, sniffling. "I mean, we left church the same time as Morgan did, but my dad had the idea to hit up the Walmart for groceries and stuff because it wouldn't be crowded. If we'd gone straight home . . . we probably would have died."

I forced a swallow.

"Don't even say that," Morgan said, gripping my hand.

"Our house flooded, and then . . . then the ground started to shift, to give way underneath it. Everything's gone. Like, everything."

Something popped into my head. A joke, about how Elise's mom was going to love shopping for new furniture. She was obsessed with those decorator-on-a-budget shows. It seemed like something good to say, something to brighten the mood. But I swallowed it down.

"Where are you right now?" I asked, and plugged in my phone.

"We're at a really nice hotel in Ridgewood," Elise said, her voice lifting into a register that sounded more normal. "You know, the one near the mall? They have a rooftop pool. An indoor one. It's closed for the night, but they let my brothers in to swim in their boxer shorts because of what happened to us."

I nudged Morgan. "She sounds good!" I whispered.

Morgan shook her head, like I was an idiot. "She's in shock, Keeley."

Then Emma leaned close to the phone and asked, "When are you coming back?"

The silence crackled between us, and I was about to repeat the question when Elise broke apart. Between heaving sobs, she managed to say, "I'm not sure if we are. We don't really have anything to come back to."

Morgan and I hit the bathroom together. I wanted to talk about Elise, maybe call her again now that it was just Morgan and me, but there were a bunch of women already in there. One was old, like a grandmother's age, the other two were younger than my mom. They had one of the windows cracked and raindrops were spraying the floor at their feet. The women blew the smoke from their lit cigarettes into the night.

It dawned on me that they probably went to our high school years ago.

Morgan and I quietly set up at the sink with our toothbrushes.

The older woman kept touching the back of her hair gently. "Governor Ward is planning to do something big. Why else would he be coming here tomorrow to make an announcement?"

The other two silently considered this as they puffed.

And then the one with long brown hair said, "Funny that

he didn't come once during his campaign, but now he wants a photo op."

The third woman rolled the tip of her cigarette along the wall, clearing the glowing tip of ash. "Some photo op. Look at this school. Practically falling down. Ridgewood gets all the funding, they have a damn television studio in that high school, and meanwhile our kids get the old computers they were going to throw out." She peeled a piece of cracked paint off the wall and tossed it carelessly onto the floor, where it shattered into tinier pieces, like glass. I glanced over at Morgan, but she kept her eyes on the sink. "We're even worse than the schools in the city, and that's saying something."

The older woman nodded. "It's the land that's worth something to them, controlling the river. They're going to try and squeeze us out." Then she gestured at me and said, "Ask Jim Hewitt. He'll tell you. He's the one that just tricked Sheriff Hamrick into admitting that the governor is coming to address us personally in the morning. Why would they be keeping secrets like that from us if there weren't something shady going on?"

I quick spit into the sink and dried off my toothbrush, even though I'd only brushed my bottom teeth. "I'm going to check in on my parents." I was already pushing open the bathroom door.

"I'm just going to wash my face and I'll be right there!" Morgan called after me.

I walked quickly over to our cots in the gym. My mom was asleep, her laptop open on her chest, light glowing on her face. Mrs. Dorsey was next to her, awake, with a book open. But she wasn't looking at the pages. She was watching my dad.

He was over by the coffee table talking to some people. He

was pointing his finger through the air. I thought he was just doing that to illustrate a point, but then I realized he was looking right at Sheriff Hamrick. The sheriff had his arms folded, and he was a few feet away from Dad, so they weren't having a conversation. It was clear my dad was openly talking shit about him. And Sheriff Hamrick was not happy about it. Levi stood next to him and glared at me the same way his dad was glaring at my dad.

I spun around and bumped right into Jesse Ford. He was holding two Styrofoam cups, and both sloshed about half their liquid onto his sneakers.

"I'm so sorry!"

Jesse peered into the cups. He poured one into the other to make it full and slid that cup into the empty. "No, it's cool. I was just complaining that I wasn't wet enough."

I laughed too hard. Jesse gave a tight-lipped smile and tried to step around me, but someone was walking past us and made it so he couldn't. "I can get you another drink and bring it to your cot."

"No big deal. Don't worry about it."

"I . . . I'm sorry," I repeated, that time for what I'd said to him at the dance, or whatever it was that had suddenly put the chill on us.

Again, Jesse looked as if he was going to walk away, but then seemed to decide against it. Maybe because I looked so desperate. Whatever the reason, he leaned down close to me and whispered, "Cots are for suckers anyway. I scored a cave."

"A cave?"

Jesse pointed to a blanket draped over the space between two chest-high stacks of gym mats. Light glowed out from the seams. He nudged his chin toward it. I tentatively walked over and peeled back the blanket. Julia was asleep inside, curled up on a gym mat. Jesse had his laptop open on the floor, facing her. I knew it must be his, because he had a soccer ball sticker on it.

"It took her twenty-three videos of pigs cuddling with other animals before she fell asleep," he whispered.

"Is that all?" I whispered back. "Amateur."

Jesse laughed. It felt good to make him laugh again. I knelt down, unzipped my book bag, and handed him the Mad Libs. "This is for when Julia wakes up. Or when your battery runs out. Whichever comes first."

He looked surprised. Genuinely surprised and also a little embarrassed. He mumbled, "Thanks. That's really cool of you." Then Julia twisted, groaned. We both held our breath as she settled back down, her breathing turning heavy again.

I couldn't tell if I'd just managed to fix whatever was broken or not. I don't think Jesse knew either. But before either of us said anything more, Dad shouted out, "Keeley!" He was walking away from the people, toward my mom and Mrs. Dorsey. "We're going home."

His words seemed to echo throughout the gym. A lot of people were asleep, but the ones who were still awake lifted their heads and turned to see what was going on.

"Holy shit," Jesse said. "Is that your dad?"

I didn't answer him. I was hustling over. Mom sat up. She'd been asleep. "Jim, what . . ."

Mrs. Dorsey said, "Come on, Jim. Just relax."

If Dad heard Mrs. Dorsey, he didn't show it. He handed me my raincoat.

Sheriff Hamrick came up. A few of the other officers were behind him. "Jim, put your things down."

"I know my rights," Dad said.

"This is a mandatory evacuation," one of the other officers said, puffing up and stepping forward.

Dad wasn't intimidated. He stayed focused on putting his laptop back into the Viola's plastic bag and calmly said, "Just because it's mandatory doesn't mean you can forcibly detain me here. That's the law."

Sheriff Hamrick put his hand up to settle his officer. To my dad, he pleaded, "It's just a couple more hours. You'll be allowed back by morning."

Dad folded his arms. "I don't trust that you're being honest with me, or with anyone in this gym for that matter." I didn't know what trusting them had to do with anything. It wasn't like the flood was some elaborate fake-out. My friend's home was gone. This was clearly, undeniably real. "Tell you what. I'll put my things down if you answer this honestly. Does the governor coming here tomorrow have anything to do with those surveyors that were down by the river, taking measurements earlier this spring?"

I vaguely remembered my dad being worked up about that. He'd brought it up at a town meeting. Mom usually took Dad to them, but that time I was allowed to do the driving with my brand-new learner's permit. I sat in the back row, doing my homework. Dad wanted to know who they were and what they were up to, but no one had much of an answer for him. Honestly, I was barely listening, it was all so boring.

I swear, you could have knocked Sheriff Hamrick over with a feather. He looked at my father for a few seconds, blinking, and red tinged his cheeks. "Jim, come on. Be reasonable."

"That's what I thought," Dad said. He turned to Mom and said, softly, "Okay, Jill?" When she didn't answer, he reached out his hand to her. "You know I would never put you or Keeley in danger." His eyes were big and bright.

"I know that," Mom said.

And I knew it too. But still . . .

Mrs. Dorsey let out an uncomfortable laugh. "Jill! Please talk some sense into him!"

Mom shrugged. "Keep your phone on, Annie." To me, she said, "Kee, get your things."

Morgan appeared just then, her face pink and freshly washed. "What's happening?"

"Umm, I think we're leaving." It came out sounding like a joke, but it clearly wasn't because Dad was already walking across the gym, his head held high, the tip of his cane tapping the hardwood floor.

Morgan was aghast. She looked at her mom, but Mrs. Dorsey had sat back down on her cot, making the metal springs squeak.

Following Mom, I walked past Jesse, who watched me with his mouth hanging open. I gave him a little wave good-bye.

Levi Hamrick peeled off from the other officers and hustled over to the gym doors. My gut squeezed, wondering if he was going to try and stop us, even though the other officers weren't. He beat us to the door but he just stood there, watching, as Dad pulled it open. I even waited for him to say my name again, like he had in the hallway at Spring Formal, but he just looked down at his shoes as my family stepped into the rain.

I shrugged off my book bag and balanced it on my head as

the water climbed higher and higher up my legs. Each step forward was slick and muddy, and I couldn't see where my feet were landing. It was significantly deeper than it had been when we first arrived at the gym. And it was still pouring. A few times I nearly bit it going over the curb or one of those slabs of concrete that mark a parking space. Still, I tried to be quick about it because . . . we were on the run.

Dad stopped when he reached the boats tethered to the school's bike rack. Neighbors had brought their own rowboats, dinghies, and kayaks. But Dad chose to untie one of the police boats, a long canoe, and he guided it away from the others.

"We're stealing a police boat?"

He tipped the canoe on its side to drain the water that had collected in the well. "Borrowing. We're borrowing it."

Mom scrambled into the canoe and carefully sat down on the wooden plank seat at the very front, in the hopes of steadying it. "Here," she said, "pass me your bag." I did, then climbed in after her and took the plank in the middle. My leggings were caked with grit, my sneakers, too.

Dad tossed in his cane. Mom reached out to help him, but he climbed into the boat on his own—a little too eagerly, considering his physical state—and nearly tipped us over. He had to sit with one leg stretched out, as stiff as the paddle next to him. After the wobbles settled, Dad untied the rope and began to use the paddle like the pole of an Italian gondolier, plunging it into the parking lot lake until it hit pavement, and then leaning against it to drive us out into even deeper water.

He was already soaked.

I craned my neck to see past him to the gym doors. I figured any second the cops would find us with their flashlights in the misty dark and shout for us to stop. But they never did. Instead, my high school shrank farther and farther away, until I couldn't see the building through the dark, just the glow from the parking lot lights through the rain. Those got smaller too, fuzzier, like stars.

By then my dad was paddling us down Main Street.

There were two distinct parts of Aberdeen—the valley and the hill—and the shape of our town always reminded me of a skateboard ramp. Most of the hill was still densely forested, from the tippy top until about three-quarters of the way down. That's when you began to see a few houses pop up, linked by winding country roads.

But the majority of people in town lived in the valley, on a mile-long grid of residential streets that went from the bottom of the hill to the river. At the very center of the grid was Main Street, with its shops and stores and the movie theater. In all the years of flooding we'd had in Aberdeen, I never remembered the water reaching Main Street. But now Main Street looked like a stream.

Which meant at least half our town was flooded.

We paddled up to Main Street's one traffic light, that red blinker, but the light was out. Dad stopped paddling for a second and let us drift. We all looked at the bright floodlights shining up through the trees on the hillside, likely set up by emergency workers near where the slide had taken place.

I wondered if that would be enough for Dad to turn the boat around and bring us back to the gym.

But no, he went back to paddling, puffing out air in thick blasts from his cheeks. Even in the dark, I could see his face was flushed.

"Jim, give me the paddle," Mom pleaded. "I'll take over for a while."

Dad shook his head. I was about to offer too, but he drove the paddle into the water and pulled it through super-hard, pushing us forward even faster than before, as if to prove to us that he could do it just fine.

Mom couldn't take her eyes off him, her lips slightly parted in surprise. I'm pretty sure I was making the same face. Here was the man we hadn't seen for more than two years.

As we neared the north end of town, the water finally became shallower. When the bottom of our canoe scraped against the street, Dad tied it to a stop sign, saying the cops would have an easier time finding it that way.

There was at least another mile uphill until we reached our house.

It was still raining.

Halfway through the walk, and despite Mom's pleas that she was managing fine on her own, Dad took her rolling suitcase and pulled it along with one hand, pushing himself forward with his cane in the other. His pace was crazy quick, determined, a man on a mission, and he led the way up our street about fifteen feet ahead of us, his cane tapping the road in an even, steady beat. Mom held her laptop bag underneath her rain jacket to make sure it didn't get wet. I was soaked straight through to my shirt, my bra.

We didn't walk through our front door until almost dawn. Dad promised to keep watch, but he said he didn't think the water would reach us. We didn't have power, but Dad set up his laptop and turned it on with what little battery juice he had left.

I went upstairs, peeled off my wet clothes, changed into a nightshirt, and went to the window of my bedroom. Usually, I could see down to the river. The view reminded me of a Christmas village, like the kind people set up under their trees, miniature houses with twinkling lights. But that night there was only darkness.

# 11

With all that rain, I'd almost forgotten how warm the sun could feel. But I woke up that next day with rays shooting straight through my comforter, turning my white sheets a honeyed shade, like yellow cake batter baking in the oven.

I kicked the covers off and sat up, cross-legged, in my striped nightshirt. I used to have matching pajama pants that went with it, but they split open while I was doing an impression of the weird way that Wes fast-walked through the movie theater parking lot—exaggerated lunges and leg splits—the one time I went to the movies with them and we were late for the show. It honestly was more embarrassing than those weird old people who speed-walk through the mall for exercise. Morgan didn't want to laugh at first. She actually seemed a little mad, but eventually she gave in, and I had her cracking up so hard she was in tears.

The sun was everywhere in my room. I clicked on my bedside lamp, just to see if we had power, and thankfully, we did. The combination made me so hopeful that things would be okay.

I returned to my window.

Our front lawn looked more like a bog, pools of water collecting wherever the ground sloped. Tree branches were splintered, snapped. But it was minor damage. At most, a day of yard work.

Down the hill, into the valley, was like nothing I'd ever seen before.

The river had poured into the first few streets, filling them up like little streams and tributaries, transforming the houses into islands. You couldn't see any blacktop. Just water. It gave the neighborhood a creepy, surreal look. The water cut everything in half and then doubled it, like a rippling fun house mirror. Houses with two roofs, trees with trunks that sprouted two sets of leaves, cars with two tops and no tires. When the wind picked up, everything shimmered, and it reminded me of the moment right before you wake up from a dream.

But it was no dream. Things were not good for a lot of people. The flooding had never, ever been this bad. Elise and her family had lost everything, and it hardly felt like the rest of town was much better off.

I patted around for my cell in the sheets, but it had fallen onto the carpet sometime during the night. The screen was full of missed calls and texts. One text was from Jesse, the other nine were from Morgan.

I sat on the edge of my bed and scrolled through Morgan's in reverse order, newest to oldest.

OMG KEELEY CALL ME!!!!!

Can they even do this? Like, legally?

I think I'm going to puke.

This is so not right.

Okay. That did it.

I'm honestly five seconds away from crying.

Kee?

Wait up. Kee, are you hearing this?

Last chance for speaker phone.

Our old middle school crossing guard (remember him? Bert?) offered my mom his chair. So sweet! Too bad he's eighty years old.

If you want, I can call you and hold the phone up so you can hear what's happening.

The women in the bathroom had said some kind of presentation with the governor was supposed to go down this morning. And from Morgan's texts, it was clearly not good news. Maybe the emergency order was extended and they were forcing people to stay in the gym. Or maybe they weren't telling people which houses had been flooded, or worse, destroyed. Morgan and her mom lived about six blocks from the river. I hoped their home was safe.

I felt like the worst friend in the world as I dialed her number. My call went right to her voice mail without a single ring. I sent a text to her right after. Though I knew she was upset, I tried to keep things light until I knew more about what exactly was going on.

Hey! Are you still at the gym? Did you hear anything about your house? Sorry I missed your msgs. Call me!!!! Let me know you're okay!!!

Then I opened the text from Jesse.

He'd sent it at six in the morning.

I hope you made it home ADVERB. That was completely ADJECTIVE the way your dad stormed out of the PLACE like that. What a ADJECTIVE + BODY PART. So Julia is ADJECTIVE for Mad Libs. Meanwhile, I'm ADJECTIVE because I only VERB—PAST TENSE for PAINFULLY MINUSCULE AMOUNT OF TIME.

Okay, I'm going to VERB some BREAKFAST FOOD ITEM. Thanks again.

I leaned backward and let my head sink into my pillow. Even though his text didn't necessarily require a response, I wanted to send one anyway, to try and keep the ball rolling. I thought about asking him if he knew whether his house was okay, but that felt too serious. So I decided instead to send back some funny answers to his fake Mad Libs.

The strange reality is that just because your town is almost washed away doesn't mean you stop being in love with a boy.

While I paused to consider which breakfast food item was funnier—either Belgian waffles or eggs Benedict, because I figured sausage would come across as too racy—my phone went to the lock screen and flashed the time.

1:13 p.m.

Jeez. I'd been sleeping forever. Definitely later than I would have on a crappy cot in the middle of the gymnasium.

I opened the draft back up, went with Belgian waffle for my breakfast food item, and hit Send. Then I closed my eyes and imagined the text soaring through the warm sky and hitting his phone, imagined him opening it up and laughing, and it blew the sadness and fear from the night before away, so my heart felt as clear as the bright blue sky outside my window.

I went to pee but only made it a few creaky steps across my room before I heard my parents in the living room below me. Talking about the night before, I assumed, though I only heard Dad speaking. He didn't sound angry, exactly, but his voice was definitely raised and agitated.

I tiptoed down the stairs and leaned over a few steps, straining to hear what exactly Dad was saying. My phone buzzed in my hand. I hoped it was Morgan, but it was Jesse.

Nope, sorry, but thanks for playing. The correct answer is: stale ass Danish. BTW, where are you?

I typed, Just getting out of bed. Where are you?

I hit Send as another man's voice drowned out whatever my father had been saying. I swear my heart stopped beating.

The cops.

The cops were here.

I hurried down the rest of the stairs and turned toward the living room, but I couldn't enter it. It was too crowded. Only not with cops. There were about fifteen or maybe twenty families filling it up, crammed five deep on our couch, in each of our kitchen chairs, leaning against our walls. I recognized a woman perched on our radiator as one of the smoking ladies from the high school bathroom the night before. Her eyes were red and puffy.

Everyone faced my dad as he held court in a chair he'd pulled up in front of our fireplace. I couldn't see my mom.

"Listen, Russell," Dad said, gesturing to an older man in dirty coveralls who was seated on our coffee table, hunched forward, shaking his head sadly, eyes on the floor. I recognized him from the gas station. "I appreciate that you've come here. But—"

"You're the only one who saw this coming, Jim. And you were brave enough to say so. So we're hoping you'll also know how we can stop this."

Looking back, I can see how much that simple statement must have meant to my dad. To go from the town crier at those stupid meetings to someone respected. And, even more than that . . . needed.

Dad shyly lowered his head. "Well, there is plenty of precedent. In fact, about a month ago, there was a land grab on Block Island. The mayor there was trying to say certain beachfront homes were blighted, so they could condemn them, kick the people out, and build mansions to bring in more tax revenue."

A shocked silence settled over the whole living room. They'd never heard the story. I had, but only because Dad had been railing about it for a whole week when it happened.

A female voice piped up from a part of the living room I couldn't see. "That might be what they're going to do to us! The first floor of my house was full of water last night, but it's mostly gone down now. Only damage is a few broken windows, really. But they're telling me not to bother repairing any damage. I'm just supposed to sleep in the gym until I can have it assessed. They said that'll be my best chance at getting a good payday."

Dad turned his chair so he was facing the woman. His fingers found the back of his neck and he rubbed the skin there so hard it left white streaks where the blood had been pushed away. I squeezed my way into the room. She had long white hair and clothes that looked dated, but were in good condition. She was trembling. Another neighbor had an arm around her.

"I can't say one way or the other," Dad said. "Block Island wasn't dealing with the flooding we've got on our plates here. My guess is that they'll try to use that against us. But, Bess, it's still your home. You own it, they don't. And you can do whatever the hell you want with it and no one should tell you any different." His voice was rising. A few people nodded, but Bess started to cry. "I know how upsetting this is. Luckily, there's no more rain in the forecast, at least not for the next few days. I've got some old plywood we can get up over those windows today so you can sleep at home tonight."

A few men in the room offered to help too. They also had tools, and trucks, and materials. "Put us to work, Jim," one man said. "We'll do whatever you say."

Dad stood up. He seemed to be drawing energy from everyone in the room. "You all found your way here because something about this doesn't feel right. And believe me, I hear you. Until we get more information, we have to stick together and take care of each other." He reached for one of my school notebooks that I'd left on the coffee table and opened it to the back pages. "Here, I want everyone to put their names and addresses down on this sheet and let me know what damage we need to take care of to get you back into your homes. And reach out to your neighbors, find out what they need. We can help them, too."

My phone buzzed again.

Nice jammies.

I searched the room but didn't have to look hard. There, on the arm of our couch, sat Jesse Ford. As soon as we locked eyes, a toothy grin spread across his face.

I immediately ducked into the hallway and pressed my back against the wall.

Jesse Ford was in my living room.

The first boy to ever be inside my house.

I glanced around, panicked, and saw every flaw.

There were fevered scratch marks dug into the wood of our back door from our old dog Donut begging to be let outside, even though he'd died years ago. Outlets that had no plastic covers. A big pile of old newspapers on the floor. An even bigger pile of dirty laundry waiting to be taken to the basement. A collection of embarrassing school pictures that Mom insisted on framing and displaying. Eyeglasses that were too big for my face in sixth grade, bucktoothed and banged in fifth, rocking a boy's bowl haircut in fourth, and in third, one of those weird reflection things where it's two of your faces, one looking straight on, one in profile, with a backdrop of the cosmos. That one, unfortunately, was my idea. I went through a huge NASA phase that year.

Jesse came through the doorway. I tugged down the hem of my nightshirt to make sure my underwear was covered. Underwear and the nightshirt were all I had on. I folded my arms across my chest because I wasn't wearing a bra.

His eyes traveled up and down the length of me and it sent me on a woozy roller-coaster dip.

"What are you doing here? What are these people doing here?"

He leaned against the wall next to me. "It's Monday."

"I know it's Monday."

He grinned. "Then why does your underwear say *Thursday?*"

I felt like I was having a stroke. Or an aneurysm. Something medically epic and potentially debilitating. It took me a second to get ahold of myself. "I'm serious. What did the governor say?"

Jesse started laughing. Which confused me, because it was pretty clear that something terrible was going on. Finally, he composed himself enough to tell me, "I want to be the first one to welcome you to the future home of Lake Aberdeen."

My face squinched up. "What are you talking about?"

"They've decided to dam the river and sink this place for good. It's for a flood protection thing. Apparently, they never should have built up this land in the first place. Something about the elevation is screwed up. Oh, and the logging from back in the mill days likely made things unstable. Whatever. There was a very informative-slash-boring presentation given by a guy from the Army Corps of Engineers this morning, but I fell asleep. The point is that everyone in town will supposedly get a chunk of relocation money from the government. But we've all got to bounce."

It was hard to make sense of what Jesse was saying, mainly because of how he was saying it. Bored. Unemotional.

"Can they do that?" I said, echoing Morgan's text.

"Probably." Jesse shrugged. "Look, we're small, we're poor, and a bunch of houses in town are completely wrecked. It's kind of the best scenario for a fuck-over."

Just then, my mom passed us on her way from the kitchen into the living room. She looked like she hadn't slept a minute, and I felt guilty for being so rested. But she was still smiling. Not a happy smile, exactly, but more dazed shock. She had a pot of coffee in one hand and as many of our coffee cups as she could loop through her fingers in the other. Her head whipped around as she passed us, giving me a stern look that basically said, *Clothes, now,* before disappearing into the living room.

Jesse lifted his hand in this shy little boy way. And I swear his cheeks turned the littlest bit pink.

"I should—" I felt someone tug at the hem of my nightshirt. Julia, Jesse's little sister, was still in her nightgown, one that had a pattern of horses with pink hair; a hooded sweatshirt; and a pair of jeans and rain boots that had ladybug spots on them.

"Can I have something to drink, please?" she asked, rubbing her eyes.

"Umm, sure. But I don't think we have juice or anything. Maybe milk?"

"Julia, this is Keeley. She's the one who gave you the Mad Libs." I was expecting a smile or a thank-you, considering how Jesse had implied with his text that she loved them so much, but Julia barely looked at me. Jesse lifted her into his arms and she immediately dropped her head on his shoulder, like a baby about to fall asleep. Except she was long, like him. "Sorry. She hardly slept last night. Anyway, she doesn't drink milk, but could she have some water, if it's not too much trouble?" He rubbed his sister's back and then patted it a few times.

It made my heart break wide open.

I remembered that I had one of those plastic loop-di-loo straws in our junk drawer that Julia might like, and I was about to grab it, but then the meeting broke up and Jesse's mom poked her head around the corner. I don't know that I would have recognized her if not for her curly blond hair, because she looked way too young to have two kids. Her jeans pockets had rhinestones on them. "Let's go," she sighed, lifting Julia out of Jesse's arms and walking out the back door. I was happy that she didn't notice my near nakedness.

"Wait. So is your house okay?" I asked Jesse.

"Yeah. Piece of crap was barely touched, unfortunately. I bet they offer us five dollars for it."

Another joke, obviously, because what else could we say?

I suddenly had the overwhelming urge to hug him. Because our town was apparently being condemned. Because I had no idea what tomorrow would bring. Because I loved him and I didn't want him to leave, not yet.

Jesse nudged his chin at one of my photos across the hall.

"I didn't know you used to wear glasses." Teasingly, he pushed an invisible pair up on my nose. Then he ran his hand slowly through my hair before he followed his family out our back door.

Every inch of me tingled.

Whatever I saw in the hallway at Spring Formal between Jesse and Victoria, it couldn't have been anything. It must have been the dark, my eyes playing tricks on me. Or, even more believable, my own insecurities getting the best of me, casting shadows where there should only be sunshine. Because something was clearly still sparking between Jesse and me.

I was sure of it.

After the last person left, I expected Dad to flop on the couch. Instead, he zoomed around the house, digging for tools in the basement boxes we had carried up the night before. Stuff that hadn't seen the light of day for two years.

Mom, too, sped around, though she was focused on cleaning and tidying up.

I was the one who couch-flopped.

"I still can't believe it," Dad said to me, bewildered, as he passed through the room. I thought he was talking about the plans to flood Aberdeen, but he wasn't. "Some of these folks didn't even stop home first. They came straight over and knocked on our front door."

Finally he sat down. He lifted his leg onto the coffee table, stiff as a long wooden board, and, wincing slightly, rolled his foot in a circle. "It's crazy. You read about these things happening to other places in the country. You just never imagine it coming to your doorstep."

Mom slid on her rain jacket. It still looked wet. "Jim, you

sure you can't rest for even an hour? You barely slept last night." She glanced around the room and then spotted her laptop bag propped up on our fireplace mantel.

"Can't," Dad said, and switched to a different stretch, twisting his torso to the left and to the right. "Charlie and Sy are going to meet me at Bess's house to get that plywood up." He picked up the notebook. "We've got a list a mile long."

Though it was great to see Dad so animated, I had the same worries Mom did. That it was too much too soon. "Dad, you should make those other guys your employees. Order them around." It sounded like a good idea to me, but Dad just frowned.

Mom set a hand on his shoulder. "Why don't you rest for an hour or two while I check on some of my patients and Annie. Then I can drop you off somewhere with your tools and—"

He looked at me. "Maybe Keeley—"

"I don't want her driving in these conditions with just a learner's permit. The roads sound like they're awful."

Dad shrugged. "Well, Charlie and Sy are already picking up some guys themselves, so . . . I guess I'll have to drive myself." I bet Mom and I looked equally stunned, because Dad started defending himself. "I mean, I do still have my license. I just don't *like* to drive. It hurts my leg. But I can do it if I absolutely have to." Dad reached out his hand. "Do you still have my key?"

I went to fish it out from my coat pocket, making eyes with Mom along the way, in case she was going to tell me not to. She didn't.

Dad got up and kissed her on the cheek. "I promise I won't go at it too hard. And I have my phone on me, if either of you need to get in touch."

Mom and I watched him disappear out the back door.

"This is crazy," I said.

"I know."

"I mean the flooding stuff, but also Dad."

"I know," Mom said again, this time her face blooming into a big smile. "But this is who he's always been, Keeley. He just forgot it for a while."

"I still don't get how he knew this was going to happen to Aberdeen."

Mom was still watching him through the back window. "He didn't. It was just a hunch." Finally she turned to me. "Apparently, he'd read an article about how some developer was considering a new high-rise on the water down in Waterford City, but the environmental studies said it would be too unstable and Governor Ward was very disappointed." She shook her head. "Maybe a month after that, one of the neighbors asked Dad if he knew anything about a group of engineers taking measurements down by the old mill."

"Oh. Wow."

"So at the next town meeting, Dad asked about it. The mayor gave him some line about a company being interested in buying the building, which didn't pass Dad's sniff test, especially when Mayor Aversano refused to say *which* company. After that Block Island story came out, I think Dad started putting two and two together. Of course, I told him he sounded paranoid."

I knew exactly what Mom was feeling because I felt it too. Like a jerk. Dad's interest in local politics were eye-roll fodder. I would have teased him about it more, probably, if not for the fact that it gave my dad a purpose. He couldn't take care of us, his family, but he could care for Aberdeen.

I ran outside. Dad was packing tools into the bed of his truck. He was breathing pretty hard. "I could kick my own ass for not taking that physical therapy more seriously."

"Just please take care of yourself, okay? I don't think Mom could survive being your nurse again."

"Yeah," he said with a chuckle. "I think you're right."

"And you're sure you're okay to drive? You want to flip through my driver's ed manual as a refresher?"

"Just don't make fun of me if I stall out. I'm rusty."

"You know I can't make that kind of promise."

"Right. Of course."

It took him a minute to figure out how to position his leg inside the truck cab. He stalled out twice in the driveway, and both times, I applauded and wolf-whistled. By the time he turned onto our road, he had it down. He pulled away extra fast, tires squealing, and gave me a thumbs-up.

# 12

I turned on the shower. While waiting for the water to get hot, I clicked on the TV in my parents' bedroom, thinking I'd watch for a second or two, see if we made the news.

It was weirdly comforting that the regular channels were showing normal programming—game shows and soap operas and reruns. If things were super-dangerous, if Aberdeen was really going under, wouldn't there be those emergency broadcast alerts blaring nonstop?

When I got to the twenty-four-hour news channels, I saw Aberdeen everywhere.

Mom sat down next to me on her bed. She didn't even complain about the water I was wasting.

We flipped through channel after channel. I don't know what we were hoping to hear, exactly, but we didn't linger on any one broadcast. The news flashed in snippets of talking heads, graphics, helicopter shots of waterlogged streets. The dramatic footage felt so foreign, even though I heard those helicopters in the distance.

It was too soon to know the full extent of the damage done, exactly how many homes were ruined, the number of cars swept away, injuries and accidents. For now, the focus was on the plans for the future. Evacuate the residents of Aberdeen and turn our town into a reservoir capable of holding and controlling ninety billion gallons. The government would purchase all 4,480 acres of our town to make a man-made fortress to prevent such a tragedy from ever happening again.

It was hard to make sense of what I was seeing. Honestly, I didn't even want to.

Mom took the remote from me when we landed on a clip of Governor Ward. He was in a suit, standing outside the gym doors of our school, cameras and microphones surrounding him. On his left, mindlessly nodding like a bobblehead, stood Mayor Aversano. And on his right, Sheriff Hamrick.

"This must have happened right after that presentation," Mom said, raising the volume.

"We are lucky that the events of the last forty-eight hours did not result in any fatalities. And it appears the imminent danger has passed. But because certain environmental issues are only now coming to light, we have no other choice but to take dramatic action. It's not safe for residents to stay here long-term, and it's not safe for those living downstream in Waterford City, either. And while the residents of Aberdeen will surely mourn the loss of their town, these proud working people who helped transform this valley so many years ago can take heart in the fact that their sacrifice will save future lives. This is quite the little town, believe me, and I have promised everyone here that we will not soon let anyone forget it."

I got a text from Morgan.

We finally got the okay to head home. On our way now.

I jumped up. "Mom! They're on their way home!" I didn't even need to say who.

I wrote back, Be there ASAP.

Mom and I drove through town in stunned silence. I'm not sure what she was feeling, but to me, there'd been something about seeing Aberdeen on television that made the whole thing feel less than real. But there was no denying the destruction when it was right on the other side of the windshield. There were heaved sidewalks, uprooted trees. The front doors of houses were pitched wide open, with people pushing mud out with snow shovels. Broken furniture was piled up, possessions set out to dry on the lawns. Cars had floated out of their garages and settled into the streets. Trash was everywhere.

But it was by no means a ghost town. Everyone was buzzing with activity. Police cars, vans from the electric and gas and telephone companies flashing emergency lights. Neighbors met out on their lawns and stared in awe. They comforted each other, or joked with each other, or told each other it would be okay.

I felt crappy to have a wonderful little thing to hold on to but I gripped it tightly anyway. Because despite everything going on around me, I still felt tingles from when Jesse had run his hands through my hair that morning.

"Oh no," Mom said. The car stopped fast, pulling me tight against my seat belt.

Morgan and Mrs. Dorsey were standing on the curb in yesterday's clothes, both staring at the huge elm tree that had smashed into their garage. The trunk had taken out the corner and broken through the shingled roof; the limbs and leaves completely blocked the garage door.

Mom jumped out and swept Mrs. Dorsey up in a hug.

Mrs. Dorsey had been crying before we got there, but once she saw my mother, she began to sob. I'd only ever seen her cry one other time, and it wasn't when she was divorcing her husband, because she was *that* ready to kick him to the curb. It was three summers ago, on the night before Morgan and I started high school, and that was because she and my mom had polished off two bottles of wine at their picnic table. Both of them practically tackled us on the front lawn when we came walking up after watching a Little League game, kissing us, wiping their faces dry across our cheeks, promising us they were happy tears. I wasn't sure I believed her then, but now, seeing the other kind, I understood the difference.

I came over to Morgan and knocked into her.

"We're okay," Morgan quickly assured me, sniffing back tears. "This is really the worst of it."

Mrs. Dorsey pulled her arm inside her sweatshirt sleeve and wiped her eyes. "It's my fault. I should have had that tree taken down months ago. I have the stupid estimate in the house. It was just so much money. And I didn't know if the guy was trying to take advantage of me because I'm a single woman, so I was going to get another guy to give me a price and—"

"Annie, stop."

"And now it's going to cost me so much more. If I can even get someone over here with all this mess. Not to mention I don't even know if my car is drivable. I definitely can't afford to get a new car right now!"

"Let me call Jim," my mom said. She pulled out her phone.

"He's out with some other guys working on a neighbor's place, but maybe they can swing by here next."

"What?" Mrs. Dorsey said, slowly turning away from the scene for the first time. "Jim is where?"

Mom couldn't help but grin. She covered her phone with her hand and whispered, "We've had a crazy morning," before my dad picked up. "Jim, it's me. I need your help."

As my mom stepped over toward her car to speak with my dad, both Morgan and Mrs. Dorsey looked at me to explain. I shrugged. "Crazy morning!" I said, like a bad sitcom.

My mom stayed for a cup of coffee, and by the time she left to check on her patients, Dad had arrived with three other pickup trucks and a team of guys, some old, some young, all carrying tools. They made quick work of the tree, sawing it up into logs, rolling them down to the street and stacking them curbside. Dad acted more like a foreman, directing the guys. For a while he set aside his cane and wielded a chain saw himself, but people on the street kept coming over, wanting to speak to him.

After the tree was cut down, the guys collected the broken bits of roof and secured a tarp over the gaping hole. It definitely wasn't fixed by any means. In fact, I assumed it would probably need to come down at some point. But the guys were able to use a crowbar to force the garage door open, because the track was off and the door dented. They started up Mrs. Dorsey's car to make sure it was running fine.

Mrs. Dorsey was outside, watching them, her arms wrapped around her. She kept bear-hugging Dad. He patted her stiffly on the back.

Morgan and I were up in her room, kneeling on her floor and sharing space at the window, watching it all. Behind us, her television was tuned to a news channel on mute.

I shouted "Bye!" to my dad before he got into his truck and drove off to the next house. When I turned back around, Morgan was on her bed, staring at me. Her face began to redden and her bottom lip trembled.

"No!" I said, and tackled her backward into a hug that made her bed creak. "No more crying!" I fought her for the remote and turned the TV off.

She shook her head, fat tears rolling down the sides of her face, falling into her ears. "Why aren't you crying?"

"Because nothing's for sure yet. I mean, who knows what's really going to happen? If they'll go through with it." And also, because of the Jesse thing, though it felt like the wrong time to say so.

She reached for a tissue. "Oh, it's happening," she said, her voice low. "They made that super-clear."

Of course I believed her. I'd seen the news reports, and also Morgan had heard what the governor had said firsthand. But it still seemed too weird to imagine. And our house had been full of people who weren't going to roll over and give up Aberdeen without a fight. There had to be more of them in town. This was a prideful place. If enough people made noise, maybe, just maybe, the governor would reevaluate. Come up with some other plan.

"I mean, where are we all supposed to go?" I asked.

Morgan shrugged.

"Seriously. Did they say anything about that?"

"Not really" was her answer. And then she opened her laptop and brought up the website of a newspaper. On the front page was an aerial shot, one I hadn't seen on television. It was almost unrecognizable. A green slope with jagged seams of broken dirt and debris where a cluster of houses had slid free, like a kid dragging each of their five fingers deep across different parts of a freshly iced chocolate cake.

"Jesus," I whispered.

"I think that's Elise's," she said, and moved her mouse so it pointed at a pile of debris in the picture.

"Have you heard from her?" I asked, realizing simultaneously that I hadn't. I clicked my phone screen on. Maybe she'd tried me when it was dead. Or maybe the call hadn't gone through.

I actually typed out a few possible texts in the car ride over to Morgan's house, but didn't send any because they just looked so awkward and stiff on the screen. How are you? How's your family? Sentiments that could have come from anyone. Elise was my friend. I needed to do better. Except I was dreading talking to her, because I didn't know what to say.

"We traded a few texts. She's going to try us later."

I didn't want to linger on feeling crappy, so I changed the subject. "Has anyone said anything about school? I mean, we still have a month left." It was odd to think of the end of the year with the same enthusiasm as the beginning, to suddenly be looking forward to every single day instead of counting them down, the way you normally would before summer officially begins.

"It's canceled at least through tomorrow."

Then Morgan was crying again. Sobbing this time.

"Morgan, come on," I play-whined. "Your house is fine, mine

is okay. We've got another day off from school! We're lucky. We should be celebrating." I said it even though I felt the good feelings about Jesse unspooling their grip on me.

She sucked in a deep breath, trying to calm herself, but it only made her shudder. "I can't imagine not living in this town, not living near you."

Her words hit me hard. I hadn't even considered that. The idea that someone from my family wouldn't always live in the cottage on Hewitt Road, that my best friend wouldn't be within walking distance from me.

I couldn't consider that.

"Then don't!" I said, cuddling next to her.

"But what if it happens?"

"It won't."

"Why won't it? What makes you so sure?"

I closed Morgan's laptop and leaned back in her bed, my hands behind my head. "The power of our friendship."

Morgan rolled on top of me. "Keeley! Be serious, will you?" She swatted me with a pillow.

"I am being serious," I said. "See? You're already feeling better. Am I right?"

She laughed and a snot bubble popped out of her nose. I'd released a pressure valve.

"Okay, yeah. I guess I am."

"Power of friendship," I said again, grinning. "Now say it with me."

Morgan rolled her eyes, but she lay down next to me and put her hands behind her head, just like me. "Power of friendship," she mimicked.

I leaned up on my elbow. "You've got to say it like you mean it," I cautioned. "Like you believe."

"Oh jeez, fine, you goofball." She wiped her eyes. And she did say it again, exactly how I asked.

Morgan had always been the most important person in my life, but I sometimes worried if the same still went for her. But here was our friendship, zipping up like a coat readying for a storm.

People say that it sometimes takes a tragedy to put your life into perspective, to show you what really matters.

It was amazing, really, my talent for finding silver linings in even the darkest clouds.

---

## 13

**Monday, May 16**
Clear skies in the evening, low of 42°F

---

Morgan hadn't slept much at the gym the night before. She was yawning like crazy and her eyes were puffy red from crying, but she couldn't fall asleep. I put on a movie that we'd both seen a hundred times before. *Aladdin* over *Little Mermaid*, for obvious reasons. She passed out cold about five minutes into it.

Morgan's phone was on the pillow next to her head. I kept glancing over at it, waiting for Elise to reach out, like Morgan had said she would, but she didn't.

Wes did.

He sent her a text.

`Trying you one more time to see if you're okay.`

One more time? I scrolled up. He'd sent several messages to her. Morgan hadn't responded to any of them, and it made my heart swell up like a big red balloon for her.

Then came another.

`Just wanted to make sure you are okay with this flood stuff.`

A minute later, another.

`Keeley too.`

I rolled my eyes.

He wrote again.

I know you're still mad, but just let me know you're safe and I promise I'll stop texting.

It took all my self-control not to write back, Yup, all good, now lose my number, asshole.

The movie ended. I switched to the news to distract myself.

The reporters were saying there was no rain in the forecast for the immediate future. And the water had begun to slip back into the river. The fact that our power lines were up in the air, and not underground like the more affluent areas, actually worked in our favor, and nearly all residents were back on the grid. It seemed like really good news. I almost woke Morgan up to see it.

But they kept showing the same clips of the governor's speech, applauding our town for making this great sacrifice, as if he'd given us any say in what was happening. And the talking heads repeated the same environmental mumbo jumbo, voiced over computer projections of future rainstorms causing future floods, wiping out more homes, extending beyond Aberdeen to towns downstream.

What wasn't being made clear was . . . how soon could something like that happen again? Would another rain shower do it? Or did it have to be a whopper of a storm, as bad as we'd already had?

I put on *Aladdin* again.

For the rest of the afternoon, both Morgan's and my phone kept blowing up, friends texting to check in on each other, sending pictures of themselves posed in the flood damage to their homes, their neighbor's homes, inside their church, on their street.

And then I saw Jesse's name pop up on my screen.

Are you getting any of this crap?

Any of what crap? I wrote back.

Disaster selfies.

Jesse sent a picture next, of him draped on a fallen tree, lips pursed and eyes downcast, trying to look tragic yet sexy. I laughed so loud, I had to quickly cover my mouth so I wouldn't wake Morgan. It probably sounds strange, but because this was our reality, that somehow gave us permission, I think, to laugh at things other people probably wouldn't find funny.

LOL

People are so stupid. Hey, make sure you check out my site later. Julia and I shot a fake Jaws reenactment. I'm gonna post it in a bit.

Which one of you plays the shark? I hope it's Julia.

No spoilers, but there's a celebrity cameo. You around tomorrow?

It was just enough of a something to completely push Wes's texts to Morgan out of my mind.

I wrote back, Yup, and hoped that was true. That I'd be around, and Jesse, and Aberdeen, too.


I came home and found our living room blanketed in paper. Dad was on the phone, excitedly gesturing and pacing back and forth.

I half expected a more pronounced limp, just because of the work he'd done that day, but if anything, there seemed to be an extra bounce to his step. I quietly hugged him, breathed in sawdust and sweat, two things I hadn't smelled on him in years. Then I sat down on the couch and listened. I had no idea what was going on, but it definitely sounded good.

"I think I've got something here, Dwight." He leaned over

a stack of papers and traced a paragraph with his finger. "There are rules in place for when and how the government can take privately owned land for things like highways and mass transit." He traced his finger along some of the lines. "But the law is very clear that the land may not be used 'for the purpose of advancing the economic interest of private parties.' The governor's waterfront development deal would definitely fall under that category." He made eye contact with me. "Right. Yes. Okay. I'll be over in a bit."

Dad hung up and eased down onto the armrest of the couch. He was breathing heavy, as if he'd just finished running a race.

"You're seriously going to make me ask?"

Grinning, he said, "Eminent domain. We've got rights, Keeley. And I think what the governor's trying to pull might be just enough out of bounds that we can make him put the brakes on this. But I'm hoping to hear back from a lawyer on that."

"You hired a lawyer?"

"Well . . . no. I made a few calls to ones who specialize in this sort of thing. So far, none of them are biting. Or they want some retainer money up front, which we obviously can't afford. But I'm not sure I'll need them." He reached over to another pile. "It's all pretty clearly spelled out. I've written up a protest letter, making a case against what the governor's trying to do. Legally and ethically. And I sent it off to every single news organization, elected official, our representative in Washington. Someone's got to listen." The phone rang again and I nodded for him to answer.

As Dad talked, I made us dinner, nothing fancy, just BLTs and macaroni salad. Then I went outside.

The sky looked like rainbow sherbet as the sun set, ribbons of oranges and red and yellows. The air was almost warm. I tied my sweatshirt around my waist, rolled my T-shirt sleeves up over my shoulders, and sloshed around our yard, picking up the sticks that had snapped off the trees and whipping them like boomerangs into the woods.

Mom pulled into the driveway and waved. By then, I'd finished that chore, and I was sitting on the porch steps, texting my friends.

I heard Dad hurry off the phone. Then the screen door slapped at he came out to greet her.

"I can't believe you're still standing," Mom said. She let her bag down and rubbed her temples.

"I can't believe it either. How did things go with your patients? Everyone okay?"

She sighed. "They're scared. They don't want to leave. Not only that, but most of them don't have any obvious place to go." She sat on the swing and her eyes wistfully wandered the front porch, as if she were trying to memorize it before someone snatched it away.

"Well, hopefully they won't have to figure that out." Dad kissed Mom on the forehead, then me. "I'm off to Charlie's."

"Are you sure you can't stay?"

Dad was already halfway down the stairs. "I need to get the word out that I'm onto something before anyone goes to speak with the adjusters. Apparently, they're supposed to arrive any day now."

"Okay."

I brought Mom's dinner out to her on the swing. I had another scoop of the macaroni salad in a mug so she wouldn't have to eat alone.

I watched Jesse's video and liked it, then showed it to my mom. She laughed hard at the part where he cut back and forth from a plastic shark to him and Julia standing in a big puddle, screaming in mock terror.

"Do you really think Dad has a shot?"

After a yawn, she said, "If he believes it, I think we have to, too. I think we owe him that chance."

Mom rocked until her eyelids closed, her empty dinner plate balanced on her lap. I watched Jesse's video a couple more times, but on mute, so I wouldn't wake her.

# 14

Elise called me the next morning.

"Hey! How are you?" I said brightly. Probably too brightly. But I was so glad to hear her voice. Elise answered with a long and heavy sigh. "Sorry," I said quickly. "That was a dumb question."

"I can't believe you didn't call me, Keeley."

"Morgan said you were going to call us! I figured you were busy!" Those two things were true, but I still felt bad about it.

"Fine, but you still could have reached out."

I knew by her tone that she was annoyed, but not super-annoyed, probably because I wasn't the one she talked to about serious stuff. That was Morgan. I didn't blame her. Morgan was the person I turned to, too.

"Hey, let's do something fun tonight."

"You and Morgan could come swimming at our hotel," Elise offered.

"Awesome," I said. "I'll let Morgan know."

"I already texted her about it. I thought she might be with you, that's why I called."

"Oh." I chewed the inside of my cheek. "No, she's not here. I think she's out with her mom."

I was starting to feel bad all over again when I heard Elise switch the phone from one ear to the other. "Keeley, I need you to help me with something."

"Sure," I said. "Absolutely. Anything. You name it."

"Help me convince Morgan to take us on a little . . . errand before we swim." I heard her wet her lips. "I want to go see my house. Or what's left of it, anyway."

I winced, remembering the newspaper picture Morgan had shown me. "Are you sure that's a good idea?"

"No. But I want to anyway."

I was pretty sure it was a terrible idea, but I felt backed into a corner. I'd been a shitty friend to Elise, so there was really no talking her out of it. "Okay, Elise. You got it."

I was sitting cross-legged on my bedroom floor, in a pair of cutoffs and a baggy navy sweater over last summer's bikini, blow-drying my hair. I thought I heard a knock, but I wasn't sure.

An endless stream of people had stopped by to chat with my dad. They reported in hushed voices that a team of government adjusters had arrived in rental cars and set up shop at City Hall. Or they asked Dad if he'd heard such-and-such rumor, or they shared memories with him of my grandfather, or they talked about their own family history in town.

Dad had only stopped home for a quick lunch, but he spent almost the whole afternoon on the front porch, counseling, being a shoulder to cry on, offering to help with home repairs or lend his tools. He gave out copies of the protest letter he'd sent to the mayor and the governor. He promised he would do whatever he could to stop this from happening.

And, unlike the reception he normally got at town meetings, people pledged to support Dad in whatever way they could. Who could blame them? The stakes were infinitely high this time. And the squabbles that had once branded my dad as a stubborn grouch now proved that he was their best, not to mention only, chance to save Aberdeen.

I liked listening to him from up in my room. It was incredible to see how he'd changed practically overnight, woken up as if he'd been in a coma. I'd forgotten how personable Dad could be. And kind, and sympathetic. It felt good to know change like that was possible. Mom was amped up, too. I saw her pride in Dad, and it made me realize what a funk we'd all been in for the last two years. Of course she was still worried about him. Still reminding him to take it easy, to rest, to ice his leg if it felt sore.

Everything in Aberdeen was turned upside down, except my house was weirdly right side up.

My mom came upstairs and cracked my door. I'd ordered her to take a nap an hour ago, but she insisted on putting in a load of laundry and washing the bathroom floor.

"There's someone downstairs asking for you." Then she slouched against the wall and asked wryly, "Is this the boyfriend you and Morgan were talking about when we bought your dress?"

My heart leapt. I quickly shut off the hair dryer. "You mean Jesse?" After all, now he knew where I lived. I stood up and went to my window. There was a BMX bike parked neatly alongside our bushes. Jesse drove a black hatchback. But maybe his mom had taken that car to work?

"Oh. I thought Jesse was the boy in that *Jaws* video." I nodded my head *yes*, and then she shook hers *no*. "Sorry, Kee. It's someone else. Looks like your Spring Formal dress made quite an impression."

I came downstairs slowly. I honestly had no idea who it could be, but my first guess was one of Jesse's friends, like Zito, and maybe Jesse was hiding outside. Maybe he'd jump out and scare me and film me looking surprised for one of his videos.

Dad was in the living room, pounding his computer keys furiously. He didn't even notice me coming down. He had his left leg propped up and wrapped in an Ace bandage, a bag of frozen peas hanging over his shin.

I opened the front door cautiously.

Levi Hamrick was sitting on our front porch, staring out at the road.

"Can I help you?" I asked. It came out equal parts surprised and annoyed.

He rose to his feet. He was in a hunter-green windbreaker and jeans, which he'd rolled up to his knees because of the flood-waters, and a pair of running sneakers. Curtly, he said, "We know your dad stole an officer's boat."

My cheeks burned. I wondered if Dad could hear him, if he'd come out and say something. I hoped he would. He'd make Levi Hamrick pee his pants.

"If you knew, why didn't you stop him?"

He leaned back against the railing. "Fine. We didn't know at the time it was happening," he conceded. "After the meeting, Officer Saft reported his boat missing. We put two and two together."

"We tied his boat up to the—"

"I know, I know. Another officer found where you left it." He knocked off the hood of his windbreaker and rubbed his sandy peach fuzz. It looked freshly cut and was the only part of him that was clean. Every other inch of him was flecked with mud.

And then there was quiet again.

I couldn't figure out what Levi was doing at my house, but I had a sneaking suspicion he was trying to get me to tell him something incriminating. I straight-up asked, "So are we going to be arrested or something?"

Levi shook his head. "No. I just wanted to make sure you were okay."

"Umm, yeah. I'm fine." I sarcastically gave him the okay sign with both my hands.

He frowned. "What your dad did was really dangerous, Keeley. You could have been hurt."

Hearing Levi say that made me second-guess Elise's plan for tonight. We planned to park someplace inconspicuous after dark, then head through the woods with flashlights to get there.

Putting my hands on my hips, I said, "My dad was upset. A lot of people are upset, Levi."

I was hoping he might get so annoyed with me that he'd leave, but instead, he leaned against the porch post.

I cleared my throat. "How did you even know where I lived? Did you look me up in some police database? I bet that's not legal either."

"Keeley, I once gave you a ride home from Mock Congress practice."

I didn't remember that. "Well . . . okay then."

"Also, your street is the same as your last name, so . . . it doesn't take a genius," he said, his voice slightly louder.

"I said *okay then*." I leaned against a different porch post. Levi wasn't going anywhere. "I just don't get it. I mean, my family's been living here since the very beginning of Aberdeen. But now suddenly we have to go? How does that make any sense?"

"It's not so sudden," he said darkly. Knowingly.

I realized that Levi probably knew more than any of us did because of who his father was. Maybe that could help my dad. I dialed back the bitchiness. "When did you find out?"

"Me? Not much before everyone else. I mean, there's definitely been talk for a while. Nothing official. Some environmental surveys and economic stuff. It really started to kick up when they began projecting that big storm." He stared hard at me. "But it's not like they told my dad anything when the governor decided to evacuate. My dad wasn't lying to people, like your dad was telling everyone in the gym. He was following orders, and he was making sure people were safe." Then Levi turned his head and lifted up slightly, trying to see into our living room window. "What's your dad up to in there anyway?"

"I have no idea." I really didn't, not specifically, and even if I did, the last person I'd tell was Levi Hamrick.

"I've heard he's telling people in town that maybe they won't have to leave Aberdeen."

I slid my hands into my back pockets. "That definitely sounds like him."

"Leaving isn't going to be a choice, Keeley. The adjusters are going to begin meeting with people tomorrow. Governor Ward wants construction on the dam to start ASAP. It's a done deal."

"Well, I guess there's nothing to worry about, then."

Levi stood up straight as an arrow. "I didn't come here to pick a fight with you. I don't care what your dad might be cooking up.

Like I said, I wanted to make sure you're okay. After you left the gym last night, and then when I found you crying in the hallway . . ."

It was obvious to me in that moment why Levi Hamrick was not a popular kid. On paper, you'd think he would be. He wasn't bad-looking, he was involved with plenty of school stuff, and he was *A Guy Going Places!* But he was also clueless. Maybe I'm wrong, but I think most boys inherently know not to continually bring up to a girl they found secretly crying in the hallway that she was secretly crying in the hallway.

"Okay, first off, I was barely crying at Spring Formal. I dropped, like, maybe five tears max. And secondly, can you please not mention that again? Like, to me or to anyone in the whole world, ever?"

He stood up. "Never mind."

And that was it. That was his good-bye.

I watched Levi get on his bike. He rode a circle in our driveway, looking at me one last time before he stood up and pedaled hard like a sprinter until he disappeared down the street, splatters of mud curling up from his tires.

# 15

Jesse posted another new video later that night. I watched it while riding shotgun in Morgan's car on our way to Elise's hotel.

It was of Julia in a one-piece bathing suit, red with little white stars. It looked too tight on her, like it was maybe even from two summers ago. She stood in a puddle with her hands dangling at her sides, her round belly pushed out, her blond curls tucked messily underneath a white rubber swimming cap. Off-screen, Jesse turned on some Beastie Boys, "Fight for Your Right to Party." After nodding a few times to find the beat, Julia dove forward toward the ground and did the fish across their front lawn, each of her belly flops sending up plumes of water from the soaked lawn. She went the entire length of their sidewalk while Jesse ran around her, shooting from all angles.

I watched it again, paying no attention to Julia. I was focused on the glimpses of Jesse's house in the background. It was small, a little box, even smaller than ours. It might even have been a trailer. Anyway, there was a naked laundry line stretching between a pole and a sickly-looking pine tree. A big empty flower box hanging underneath the front window. A spiderweb crack in the glass of their rusty storm door. There was also a lot of junk strewn around the lawn and the driveway, Julia's toys mostly. But also a ten-speed without a front wheel, a soccer ball, and a basketball hoop that wasn't hung up. It sat half sunk in the mud.

The third time I watched the video, I noticed how the sun had been setting when he'd filmed Julia, and the sky and the splashes of water took on the prettiest pinkish hue. I wondered if he'd done that on purpose.

Jesse must have been refreshing his window, because seconds after I'd clicked Like, he sent me a text.

Thanks. Julia says you rule.

Smiling, I wrote, Girl's got moves.

Of course she does. I'm her big brother.

"Ugh, what now!" Morgan said.

I looked up. On the opposite side of the road, a line of orange cones tapered the lane down to a parked police car, lights on and flashing. Two officers stood with a flashlight and a clipboard talking to a driver. There was a line of parked cars behind them, waiting to drive into Aberdeen.

We blew past them.

"Oh, wait," I said. "A neighbor was talking to my dad about this today. They're setting up roadblocks to make sure no nonresidents come into Aberdeen after dark. I guess the police were worried about people looting the houses that had been destroyed."

"Looting what? What could they take?"

"I don't know. Like, copper pipes?"

Morgan shook her head. "That's beyond depressing."

I put my phone back into my pocket and stared out of the window as we left Aberdeen and headed twenty-five minutes down the highway to Ridgewood. We played Ridgewood in high school sports, which was a total joke, because they were about five times the size of our school and totally, disgustingly rich. I bet every kid went to sports camp in the summer. They always kicked our asses. Anyway, you could tell they had money by the quality of the snacks they sold at the concession stands. I'm talking hot chocolate with real marshmallows, cookies made with butter instead of shortening, from an actual bakery, not bulk from Costco. They also had separate soccer, football, and baseball fields, while Aberdeen used the same rectangle of dying grass for all three. Their high school was enormous, like a college campus. Ours could have fit inside their junior high wing.

There weren't many old houses in Ridgewood like there were in Aberdeen, either. When my grandpa was a kid, it had been farmland, but now it was new construction, homes with big foyers and large front lawns and long driveways and in-ground pools. From a few places, you could even see the Waterford City skyline glowing off in the distance.

As we drove through the town center, it was strange to see no flooded streets, none of the wreckage that Aberdeen had endured. I mean, it had clearly rained here, probably the same amount as it had in Aberdeen. The blacktop was shiny but that was it. It wasn't anything close to the disaster area we'd just come from. Part of it was the elevation—it was on much higher ground and set a mile back from the river. But part of it felt like they were just luckier than us in about a hundred ways.

I was happy for the escape. I liked seeing people going about their normal, everyday business. Heading into the movie theater, or standing outside a restaurant waiting for a table, or waiting for a parking space at the mall. The entire world wasn't doomed to be underwater. Just our little corner of it. You couldn't drive on any block in Aberdeen without seeing neighbors huddled together in conversation, or people chatting in their cars, wondering what exactly they should be doing next. Everyone was still in shock.

The hotel where Elise's family was temporarily living was a silver high-rise near the mall where I'd bought my Spring Formal dress. The windows were reflective except for the very top floor, where the indoor pool and gym were. That part was plain glass, lit up with white lights.

Two men in navy suits and skinny black neckties stood attentively out in front, ready to assist guests with bags or getting taxis. We pulled up at the same time as a sleek black sedan with tinted windows. Morgan's crappy car stood out like a sore thumb.

Luckily, Elise was in the lobby waiting for us. Morgan barely put her car into park before Elise came running out through the doors. I don't know if this is completely accurate or if it's just my memory, but I remembered thinking Elise looked slightly more exotic, like the way you'd expect a girl who lives in a hotel to, if that makes any sense.

We got out and hugged and jumped around like we hadn't seen each other in years. It was joyous and I was glad. I was worried a bit that Elise would be cold to me over the phone thing. But she wasn't. She was just happy to see us. And then the three of us piled back into the car.

"You guys, can I just say that I am already so so so sick of hotel food," Elise told us. "I mean, we can order whatever we want. And Lord knows my brothers have been taking crazy advantage of it. They get two desserts every night, one with dinner and one before bed. The food is good, don't get me wrong. But it's not the same as something cooked at home."

"I like your top," I said. "Is it new?"

It was a light pink silk blouse with tiny red hearts embroidered all over it, and it was so very Elise. She smoothed it before buckling her seat belt. "Yeah. Someone from the governor's office showed up at the hotel this morning with a big FedEx envelope full of gift cards and a handwritten letter from the governor himself, telling us to go to the mall and get whatever we needed."

Morgan pouted. "All I did today was clean mud off of crap in our basement."

"Honestly, it was more stressful than fun. I have to replace my entire closet. I couldn't just buy whatever cute things I saw. I had to be strategic about it. I need underwear, socks, like, everyday stuff, a new coat. I knew it'd be cold tonight, but no stores are selling sweaters anymore. Just spring stuff. And there's so much that's gone that I'll never be able to replace. All my pictures, the quilt my grandma made me."

"So what's the latest?" Morgan asked gently. "Has your dad gone to the site yet?"

Elise shook her head. "No. An adjuster came to meet with him, though. He brought pictures of everything, but my dad wouldn't let me see them. He thought it would be too traumatic." I was about to cut in and tell Elise about what my dad was trying to do, thinking it would be good news, but she kept talking. "Anyway, they started going over numbers." Elise shook her head in disbelief. "Guess how much they're going to give us to move?"

I leaned forward so my head was almost in the front seat. I'd given Elise shotgun as a courtesy. "Wait. They've already made you a deal?" I remembered what Levi had said on my front porch. How quickly this was all going to go.

"Five hundred thousand dollars," she said shyly.

Both Morgan and I gasped. Half a million dollars? Even though I wasn't super clued in to salaries, that had to be way more than most people in our town earned in a lifetime. Elise's mom didn't work. And her father was a mechanic, but only after being out of work for more than a year.

Elise quickly added, "We're probably getting more because we lost everything. And please don't tell anyone. It's supposed to be a secret, I think."

"So are you guys taking the money?" I asked.

"We don't really have a choice," she said. "We're basically homeless."

"Not for long," Morgan said. "I mean, your family could buy any house in Ridgewood you wanted with that kind of money."

"Well . . . my uncle Rob is in real estate, and he's been sending us listings of condos near him and my aunt in Florida. There was one he forwarded today, you can almost see the ocean from what would be my bedroom window." She bit her bottom lip. "I think we're going to take it."

"Florida?" Morgan said, stunned. "You're not serious."

"Uncle Rob might have a job lined up for Dad, too."

It was quiet in the car for a few minutes, the three of us thinking about what this meant. Even though Elise and I weren't the closest, she was still part of all my visions of this summer, and then our senior year after that. Everything I had once seen clear as day was suddenly blurry.

"You know," Elise said, "my mom said flights are actually pretty cheap, if you buy them far enough ahead. We could plan a trip so you both can come and visit. Maybe at the end of summer, when you guys know where you'll be moving to. We can go to Harry Potter World!"

I didn't know if that thing about cheap flights was true. Neither Morgan nor I had ever even been on a plane, so it might as well have been a rocket ship ticket to Mars. Morgan's eyes returned to the road, but her mouth still hung open.

Meanwhile, Elise flipped down the visor and checked her makeup. I saw it on her face, her hope that this would come true trying to butt out the reality that it probably wouldn't.

On our way back into town, we hit the police roadblock, and all of us had to show photo IDs to get through. Every road that led to Elise's street had been cordoned off with lengths of yellow caution tape and unmanned construction equipment parked to make an impenetrable barrier. The closest we could get was a good quarter mile away, on a wooded stretch of road that wound up the hill without any houses or streetlights. We pulled off at a place Elise said would be good, and Morgan's car rocked to a lopsided stop half in the rain ditch. We got out and clicked on our flashlights.

Morgan and Elise were whispering quietly with each other. The vibe felt extra somber since the whole Florida thing. I ran ahead to try and scare them but ended up sinking pretty far in some mud. It took both of them to pull me free. I was laughing, and I admittedly made it a little tougher on them just to be funny, but the girls didn't really get into it. And they didn't laugh when I let myself flop on my butt, staining my entire backside with mud.

Elise led the way confidently, though she did get us turned around a few times. After about thirty minutes, I felt Morgan come up beside me. "Maybe we should go back," she whispered, but before I could say anything, Elise called out for us. She had found an open lane cut through the trees where a stretch of telephone poles and power lines snaked down the hill toward the valley.

"This leads right to my house," she said.

Another quarter mile and we veered left and ran smack into a mountain of fresh dirt, clearly man-made, that had to be as high as a house. It smelled so earthy and wet.

We scaled the dirt like we were in army training camp or something. Scrambling up like little kids. I think every one of us slipped at some point, and by the top, we were all streaked with dirt. No one was laughing.

We looked down into the canyon that had been carved away. What had once been a street at the bottom of the hill was nothing but a pit of mud.

"Jeez," Morgan whispered.

It was odd, because we'd already seen pictures in the newspaper and on the television. But there was something about seeing it live.

It was finally, undeniably real.

Elise scurried down first. She fell hard and smeared mud across the front of her pretty new blouse. And then once again. It didn't slow her. She took the stumbles and went with them.

At the bottom of the dirt mound, there were more bulldozers parked, and big Dumpsters filled with debris.

I had been on this street a hundred times, but there was no trace of pavement.

I had been inside Elise's house more times than I could count. I burned the inside of my forearm baking Christmas cookies in her kitchen in December. I streaked nude around her backyard with my hair in hot rollers on a sleepover dare. But there wasn't even a brick of foundation left, nothing even remotely in the shape of a house.

Morgan and I merged flashlight beams with Elise, hoping, I guess, that more light might help us find some kind of landmark. But Elise was wandering around aimlessly, spinning like a top that was running out of inertia.

"Is this it?" she said, breathless and impatient, finally coming to a stop in front of a spot that hadn't been cleared away yet. There was no house left to speak of, but plenty of broken bricks, some twisted pipes, and a bunch of wood half buried in the mud.

I shined my flashlight on a nearby tree. "That sort of looks familiar," I tried. "Couldn't you see that from your bedroom window?"

She started to cry.

Morgan rushed to her, held her. Then they were both crying, shaking.

I hung back, continuing to look around with my flashlight, a cramp tightening in my stomach. I didn't want Elise to be upset. I didn't want her to have to see her house destroyed. I wanted to reverse the whole night, this whole idea, and go back to when Elise first brought it up. I should have pushed way harder for hotel swimming.

I felt my phone buzz in my pocket. It was a text from Jesse to a huge list of phone numbers, including mine.

He'd sent a video of himself, in nothing but a pair of soccer shorts, careening down a Slip 'N Slide while holding a beer, and he managed not to spill a single drop. He was in front of the old mill, down near the river. The person taking the video was laughing so hard, a hearty boy laugh, probably Zito. When he reached the end of the Slip 'N Slide, Jesse pointed at the camera and shouted like a general rallying his troops, "School's canceled for the rest of the week! We can sink, or we can Slip 'N Slide! Who's with me?"

It struck me then, a thing Jesse and I had in common. We both would do whatever it took to make people happy, to keep them smiling. And everyone needed that now more than ever.

The girls looked up at the sound of his voice.

I was going to wait until Elise had finished crying, but I held up my phone. "Apparently there's a Slip 'N Slide party going on at the mill tonight."

Elise wiped her eyes. "Oh yeah?" She didn't sound that excited about it, but she and Morgan cuddled around me and I replayed the video. This time, they chuckled and sniffed back their tears.

"What do you say we drown our sorrows in cheap beer?"

Elise wrapped her arms around herself. "Is that even safe? To be that close to the river?"

"It's got to be. I mean, Jesse is crazy, but he's not *that* crazy. And it might be good to be around other people right now."

I made sure to say it gently, because it was up to Elise.

If it had been up to me . . . well, it really wasn't even a choice.

# 16

---

**Tuesday, May 17**
Clouds clearing in the late evening, dropping to a low of 50°F

---

The ride over to the mill was painfully quiet. Morgan had the radio going, but the volume was turned so low, you couldn't really hear what song was on. Elise stared out the window. She opted for the backseat.

"If it's not fun, we can totally leave," I said. I really wasn't being selfish. I wasn't even thinking about Jesse Ford. I turned around to face Elise. "Whenever you decide you're ready to go, we'll go." I meant it 1,000 percent.

"Okay," she said, and managed a smile. "Thanks, Keeley."

Morgan glanced across the car at me. "Are you excited to see Jesse?"

I didn't feel like I could say yes, not with what Elise was going through. But I was. "I'm more excited that we're finally going to a party at the mill."

The mill was our high school's backup party spot. By that, I mean it was a place people went to drink when they couldn't find another place.

You didn't have to be invited. Anyone could just show up, after a football game or on a random summer night. It was mostly upperclassmen, and of course, the rare freshman or sophomore who might be hooking up with someone older.

It wasn't our scene. We rarely went to parties in Aberdeen. In fact, the three of us had had our first drinks only a few months ago, when Elise invited Morgan and me to go to midnight Mass on Christmas Eve with some of her old friends from Saint Ann's. Turns out midnight Mass is the ultimate tailgating party for teenage Catholics. Everyone met up in the Saint Ann's parking lot. The church was a half-block away, but you could hear the choir singing hymns.

The kids who came had stolen some kind of alcohol from whatever family holiday party they'd been attending. It was the most random assortment of booze. I drank way too much Peppermint Schnapps and puked in the bushes underneath the kindergarten classroom windows. Not my finest moment.

That was also, coincidentally, the night Morgan first met Wes. He was a friend of a boy Elise knew.

Morgan liked him right away, I could tell. Of all the boys who were hanging out, throwing snowballs at each other, bouncing from car to car to car to keep warm, clinking beer bottles, she stayed focused on him, smiling like a goofball every time he'd say something. Which wasn't often. The kid was super-shy. He nursed one beer all night. I noticed that he had a habit of checking to make sure the tails of his scarf were of equal length and lying flat against his coat.

I knew Morgan wanted to talk to him, but she usually needed a push from Elise. And Elise was too busy catching up with her old friends to notice. So I grabbed Morgan's hand and walked over to Wes and started complimenting him on his ugly Christmas sweater, even though it wasn't an ugly Christmas sweater, it was just a normal sweater. By this point, I was already pretty buzzed.

It worked, though. I made the joke and Morgan immediately jumped to his defense. "I like his sweater!" she said, swatting me with her mitten. And Wes, blushing, groaned out a "Thank you," which I interpreted at the time to be said faux-indignantly, but I now understood was just indignantly.

Wes probably hated me from that first moment, even though there wouldn't have been a first moment if it hadn't been for me.

Morgan pulled into the mill parking lot, a crumbling pad of concrete where the parking lines had long faded away and tufts of grass and weeds sprouted between the cracks. There were tons of other cars already there, as if our whole high school was meeting up tonight.

"Cabin fever, I bet," I said as we climbed out. We snaked our way between parked cars and then along a chain-link fence until we found a rip to sneak through.

There were a couple of different ways to get inside the mill, but that night most people were using an old truck bay with a metal garage door that had been raised. Jesse had set up the Slip 'N Slide a few feet away in a patch of muddy grass, a bright yellow rectangle of plastic, but no one was taking a ride.

I imagined when people came to the mill they had to be quiet and inconspicuous, in case a cop drove by. I guess people already felt the end coming, because no one seemed to care about keeping it down. There was a fire going in a circle of bricks, people smoking and laughing and drinking beers right there in the open, legs swinging on the open loading dock. It looked like a beach party on a cool summer night.

The floodwater had mostly receded, but you could tell it had been pretty deep here at the worst of it because of the puddles and the debris and the mud it had left behind. The river was just across the parking lot. I saw what was left of our sandbag wall. It had been a perfectly constructed thing, but now the bags had toppled over, split open, and spilled out. The river was black, all except for the little whitecaps where it rushed over some sunken thing.

We climbed inside the truck bay and headed into a cavernous room. There was water on the floor, but people had thrown down old boards or ripped pieces of Sheetrock from the walls to make planks to walk on. I'd always wondered how it worked, since there was no electricity in the mill. But people had brought flashlights and lanterns and someone even had battery-powered floodlights like the police had used at Spring Formal when the power went out.

We walked in completely covered in mud, the three of us. People turned to look at us. Elise whimpered a few times, like she was about to break down. I grabbed her hand and gave it a squeeze and she nodded and said, "Don't worry. I'm okay."

A bunch of other juniors came over to say hello. Clearly word had spread that her family had lost everything. Elise gladly accepted their hugs, their pats on the back. Morgan turned to me and smiled, like I'd done something good.

I really loved that look.

"Keeley!"

Jesse walked toward us. He was now wearing a pair of brown cargo shorts, an Aberdeen soccer sweatshirt, and a pair of army-green galoshes. He had a cluster of beer bottles in his hands and offered me one.

"Thanks," I said, smiling graciously. Morgan gave me an

excited look, too excited, but she immediately ushered Elise away to give us a minute to talk.

Jesse reached out and scratched away some dried mud from my arm, as if we regularly touched each other. I probably should have been born in Victorian times, because these tiny touches were doing huge things inside me. "What have you been up to?"

"We went to check out Elise's house. It was crazy. Like, you couldn't even tell where it had been. It was just gone."

"Bummer," he said. Which did, I guess, cover it.

"So where did you come up with the idea to throw a Slip 'N Slide party?"

"Umm . . . when I dropped my mom off at Walmart this afternoon and saw they had Slip 'N Slides on sale." He spread his legs apart so he'd be less tall and could look me in the eyes. "Couldn't resist. Plus, I just needed to get out of my house."

"How's your sister doing?" I couldn't imagine how a kid Julia's age would process what was happening.

"She's good. We've been having a ton of fun together." His answer was so breezy, I figured he didn't get what I'd meant by the question. He scanned the room, tipped his beer bottle to his lips. "Where are your friends at?"

I pointed. Jesse walked over, me following closely behind. He passed out the rest of the beers he was carrying and the girls smiled. And then he kicked three boys off the milk crates they were sitting on so we could sit down. It was a glimpse at what having Jesse as a real-deal boyfriend might be like. He'd definitely be the kind your friends would be charmed by, who knew how to be cool and friendly and fun.

We *cheers*ed and took big fat sips.

And then a devious smile crossed his face. "All right. Let's get down to business. Which one of you is going to take a run on the Slip 'N Slide to pay for these beers?" My friends and I turned to each other. "It doesn't matter that our little corner of the world is sinking. You are still underclassmen, got it?"

The girls laughed nervously. Morgan asked, "How much are they?"

Jesse shook his head. "We usually accept money. But tonight, we're dealing only in Slip 'N Slide runs. That's our currency."

"Umm, it's kind of cold out," Elise said. It had been almost summery earlier in the day, but since the sun had gone down, it had turned downright chilly.

"Come on. One of you had better step up." When he said it, he was looking just at me, not at my friends, and I exploded in goose bumps.

"Don't they deserve a free round?" Victoria Dunkle shouted from across the room. "She does, at least," she said, pointing at Elise.

My heart sank. I'd sort of expected that Victoria would be at the mill too, but I'd hoped she might not, because Jesse had invited me.

Victoria had on a long-sleeved baby-doll dress, knee socks, and navy rain boots. She didn't look like a girl who'd been through a natural disaster. She looked like she was shooting the rainy day page of a spring catalog. And mud-covered me looked like a river rat.

But I was the one Jesse was talking to. That was probably why she was interjecting her way into our conversation. He was practically daring me to ride the Slip 'N Slide. Victoria would never take that dare.

I couldn't compete with Victoria on looks. But on this, I could take her any day.

"I'll do it." And then I lifted my sweater off and handed it to Morgan, who gave me this nervous, unsure look that I totally ignored. I took off my shorts, too, because they were muddy and gross. I stood there in my bikini and running sneakers, arms and legs streaked with mud like it was war paint. I pulled my hair into a little nubby ponytail.

"Wow," Jesse said, totally checking me out. "Someone came prepared."

"We were supposed to go swimming at Elise's hotel"—I tried explaining—"but—"

"Keeley! I'm definitely not complaining." Then he was two steps ahead, booking it toward the truck bay entrance, calling out to everyone at the party, "We've got our next Slip 'N Slider!"

We followed Jesse to where they'd set up the Slip 'N Slide. Jesse positioned me dead center at the start of it. People began to gather around, lining the yellow plastic edges like a gauntlet.

It was even colder than I thought outside. Or at least it felt colder, now that I had my sweater off. I looked down. There was no water running on the Slip 'N Slide. The plastic was mostly dry.

"How am I supposed to do this?" I asked Jesse.

His face lit up. "Right. Sorry. One second." He took a swig of his beer and then removed my nearly full bottle from my hand. Then, placing a thumb over the top of each bottle, he shook them both up and sprayed them out onto the plastic. The beer fizzed and foamed.

"Okay, wait! Don't slide yet!" he said, tossing the empty bottles across the yard. They smashed in the distance. "I want to film this!"

And he positioned himself at the end of the Slip 'N Slide, so he was facing me. "All right now, let's give Keeley some encouragement!" Jesse started clapping and whooping it up and it didn't take long for the others to join in. He clicked Record on his phone and then gave me a thumbs-up.

I counted to three inside my head and then dove down the yellow plastic runway. It was hard to stay straight, but I managed not to slide off the path. I did tumble a bit toward the end, though, and Jesse had to hop out of my way to keep from us getting tangled up.

The crowd roared. I sat up and gave a little wave.

Jesse clicked off the video and offered me a helping hand. "That was amazing, Keeley."

"Thanks."

"You wanna know a secret?"

"What?"

He put his face really close to mine. "You're the only girl to do a run tonight." He shook his head. "Actually, wait. Not even the only girl. The only other *person* to take a turn, aside from me."

"But I thought you said underclassmen had to do this to pay for our beers."

"I wasn't being entirely truthful. But I knew you'd be down." His eyes lit up. "Come watch the video."

He curled up next to me, held his phone for me to see. He was so close, I heard him breathing. Meanwhile, the cold beer was steaming off my body. Jesse didn't seem to care that I was getting him wet. He pressed Play, and I watched myself go swerving down the yellow ramp. The camera shook when I nearly crashed into his legs.

I wished I looked a little more graceful.

I wished I looked a little more hot.

I wished I didn't reek of beer.

"Is it cool if I post this on my site?"

I wanted to say no. I suddenly felt like such a dumbass. But Jesse's grin was so big. And I felt special. He'd never posted a video of any other girl besides his sister, Julia. "Yeah, sure."

Victoria walked over and put her arm around Jesse's shoulder. "Jesse, Zito's looking for your car keys."

"Okay. Keeley, I'll check you later."

I put my clothes back on and hung out with my friends. A couple of kids came up to me and told me what a badass my dad was, which felt pretty great. But it didn't take long for the same feeling I'd had at Spring Formal to return. That maybe Jesse was off somewhere with Victoria. Maybe *Zito's looking for your car keys* was code for *Ditch this girl already so we can go make out.*

I couldn't handle the rejection again.

I noticed Morgan and Elise sitting on a piece of machinery together, staring at Morgan's phone. And then I remembered those texts from Wes he'd sent the morning after the flood. Morgan had never mentioned to me that she'd received them. Maybe she was showing Elise. I feel guilty about this now, but I sort of snuck up next to them, trying to catch Morgan in the act. But she wasn't talking about Wes, she was showing Elise photos of us from Spring Formal.

"You doing okay?" I asked Elise, hoping she wanted to go.

She nodded pertly. "I'm having a great time."

"Great." I sat there, sipping another beer, waiting for Jesse to come back.

It hadn't been so long that Jesse and I had been flirting. I felt it should be easy to go backward to before we spoke down by the river, to erase the past two weeks. The problem was, of course, that I'd loved him for longer than that. Way longer.

On my way to throw my beer bottle out, I saw Victoria and Jesse hugging in a corner. I walked by fast, hoping he wouldn't see me, but he did. He reached out and tried to grab me. "What's the hurry?"

"I think we're leaving," I said, not because it was true but because I would make sure of it, and I tried not to sound heartbroken.

"Oh. So soon?"

"Yeah, well . . . you know how it goes." I ducked out from under him. "I'll let you get back to Victoria."

Jesse wrinkled his face, like that was a weird thing for me to have said, which I know it was. It was also cowardly, because I couldn't ask him directly what was going on. I was too afraid to hear the answer.

He stepped away from a frowning Victoria and took my hand, pulling me to a stop. "Don't go," he said, and let his head drop onto my shoulder. He whispered, "I suck at good-byes."

For a second, I thought he was talking about me. Saying good-bye to me. But then he looked over his shoulder at Victoria. She was watching us, but then one of her friends ushered her away. "She's leaving this weekend for good."

"What?"

"Her house was totally flooded. It wasn't destroyed like your friend's, but they definitely can't live there anymore. The adjusters are working on an offer. She's been holed up in the gym with her family ever since the evacuation, but it's driving them crazy. They're going to go stay with her aunt while things get settled. She's, like, three hours away."

"Oh. You must be sad to see her go. I know you two are . . . close."

He looked at me funny. "Keeley, I'm not with Victoria." I must have looked shocked, because then he said, "Wow. I thought I had skills, but I guess not if you didn't realize I've been flirting with you tonight."

I loved that it was all suddenly so simple.

But there was also the truth of what had happened. That something weird had gone down between us at Spring Formal that made what was hot suddenly run ice cold. I thought it was Victoria. Or what I'd said.

Maybe it wasn't anything.

Or if it was something, maybe that something didn't matter anymore.

"Seriously, though. I'm really glad you came. I feel like you're someone who gets the point of tonight."

"Am I?"

He nudged his chin toward two girls huddled in the corner. "See that girl over there? She's seriously been sobbing all night. I mean, I feel bad for her, but she's definitely making a choice to be the crying girl at the party." He shook his head, then looked back at me. "And then there's a girl like you, who doesn't hesitate one freaking second before stripping down to her bikini and taking a run on the Slip 'N Slide in front of everyone." He cleared his throat. "A very cute bikini, might I add."

I pinched the skin between my thumb and my pointer finger,

just to make sure I wasn't dreaming. Jesse was complimenting the very parts of me that I blamed for him *not* liking me.

"There aren't a lot of girls like you in the world, Keeley, which makes the fact that I found you here in Aberdeen so crazy awesome."

I felt deeply in that moment that Jesse and I were kindred spirits, one and the same. I think he felt it too. And for that reason, I leaned in and kissed him. I kissed Jesse Ford right on his beautiful mouth, and though I could tell he was surprised, he still kissed me back. He cupped the side of my face in his hand and kissed me back. I felt like every single crack inside me was sealed up with happiness. It didn't matter in those moments if Aberdeen flooded to the sky, because I was watertight.

He pulled away, but not too far. Enough to kiss the tip of my nose, then my forehead. Finally, he opened his eyes.

"Okay, wait. Now I really don't want you to leave tonight." He kissed me again. "If Aberdeen really ends up going under, let's make sure you and I are the last ones here, having a good time until the end, okay?"

"Keeley?"

It was Morgan. Her cheeks were hot pink, she must have seen us kissing. "Elise's mom just texted her and she wants her back at the hotel right away."

Because Jesse couldn't see, I mouthed *Oh my God!* before answering calmly, "Okay, no problem. I'll be right there."

Jesse gave me one last kiss. "I'll call you." And he sweetly waved bye to Morgan.

"Oh my God," I whispered again, gripping Morgan's arm tight as we walked away together.

"Looks like Jesse wasn't lying."

"What do you mean?"

She held up her phone. Jesse had posted the video of me doing the Slip 'N Slide to his site. He'd tagged it *#DreamGirl*.

I know a lot of people that night were worried about how their lives were going to change. But everything had already changed for me, and all for the better.

# 17

Elise sent a text at five the next morning. Turns out the reason her mom needed her back at the hotel was that one of the national morning news shows wanted to interview her family. An anchorperson from New York City had flown in last night while we were at the mill. Elise snapped us a few pictures of the chaos at the hotel. There were a hair and makeup team, men setting up lighting rigs, someone with a headset arranging a vase of fake flowers on a coffee table. The last picture she sent was one of herself getting done up for the appearance. The makeup looked heavy to me, her eyebrows almost Muppet-like, but I knew from magazines that it would look natural on television.

I knocked on my parents' bedroom door to tell them, expecting that only Mom would be inside. But Dad was there too, sleeping next to her, not downstairs at his computer like he would normally be. I blushed so hard, head to toe, as if I'd caught them doing something really gross. Like spooning or . . . worse.

That goes to show how far they'd drifted apart.

I quietly backed out of the room, but Mom shot up in bed. "Is everything okay?"

Dad rolled over and lifted his head. "Kee, what's up?"

"Sorry. I didn't mean to wake you. Elise's family is going to be on TV."

"No kidding!" Mom scooted over to the middle of the bed. I clicked on the television on top of their dresser and then climbed into her warm spot. I felt like a little kid again, when my parents let me watch cartoons in their bed so they wouldn't have to get up and take me downstairs.

I dozed off before the segment started, but Mom elbowed me awake to dramatic music and a lot of quick cuts. The river crashing over the sandbags, then creeping up the first few streets in town. Owen, the stock boy, wading through the aisles of Viola's Market. Inside the Presbyterian church, where the floorboards had buckled, the neat rows of pews all askew like a game of pickup sticks, Bibles covered in sludge.

I thought about texting Jesse to turn on his TV, but it was still crazy early and I had no idea if he liked to sleep in or if he was an early riser. I had memorized the facets of Jesse that were accessible to me from a distance at school—like, say, his love of orange Gatorade—but I couldn't wait to catalog the random, more intimate stuff. Like, did he wear pajamas or did he prefer to sleep in his boxers? Was he a late-night snacker, and if yes, did he typically go sweet or savory? Did he take showers at night or in the morning?

Meanwhile, the news anchor narrated the plans for damming the river. And there was a new interview with the governor, too. "Waterford City is the epicenter of the economy for the whole state. We can't allow it to be vulnerable because of Aberdeen's instability."

When the governor was elected, my dad had been so mad, he

went out in the middle of the night and started a fire on the brush pile and drank an entire six-pack of beer.

The last thing they showed was an aerial view of Elise's block, all the homes that had been washed away.

Then they cut to Elise and her two younger brothers on a hotel couch, her mother and father perched behind them on two director's chairs. It was weird to see Elise, someone I knew, on television. Anyone in the country could tune in and see her. Our little world of Aberdeen was so small, so incestuous. Everyone knew everyone. Everyone knew everyone's parents and their brothers and their sisters. I used to think that was kind of annoying, but now, suddenly, I didn't want to lose it.

A woman wearing a peachy dress, several chunky gold necklaces, and perfectly blown-out hair tossed softball questions, stuff like how it feels to lose your home and then your town. Elise's mom cried a little, the boys mainly fidgeted. Then the anchor brought up how the governor had given them a stack of gift cards to spend.

"See that?" Dad said, waving his hand dismissively at the screen. "I bet Governor Ward traded a favor to get that mentioned. He probably promised this lady an exclusive interview. He needs all the good press he can get right now, especially since I'm sure he's heard that a lot of folks aren't happy."

I didn't hear the newswoman's next question because of Dad's rant, but the camera was now on Elise. "My friends have been so incredibly supportive," she said. I chewed on my fingernail. Elise was definitely talking about Morgan, but I hoped she meant me, too. My mom ruffled my hair. She automatically assumed Elise did. "And it sort of makes it easier to cope, knowing everyone in Aberdeen is facing the same tragedy. We're just the first ones going through it."

Near the end of the interview, the reporter set her interview questions down on her knee and leaned forward. "There's been some suspicion among your neighbors about a very lucrative waterfront property deal gone sour in Waterford City, and that damming the river might now resurrect it."

"Oh my God, Dad! Your protest letter!"

Dad sat up. Mom laid her hand on his leg and gave him a gentle pat.

Back on the television, Elise's parents shrugged. "Yes, we've heard that."

The anchor nodded. "Then do you believe that Governor Ward's plan is about shoving aside the poor to protect the interests of the rich?"

It felt weird to hear someone refer to the people living in Aberdeen as poor. All my friends' parents had jobs, they worked hard, had nice homes with tidy front lawns. I think every single girl at Spring Formal was wearing a new dress. There were plenty of people who were way worse off than us in Aberdeen.

"That's exactly what it is," came an answer, my dad's voice. He sat up and reached for his cane. "Did you hear how that lady framed that question? Making anyone who's questioning this sound like we're a bunch of conspiracy loonies?" I wasn't sure I'd heard her do that, exactly, but I also wasn't listening super closely. Dad rose stiffly to his feet. "This is what happens. Ward has the media in his back pocket and he's using them to shut down the conversation before it even starts."

I felt bad. Here Dad was, practically going door to door to

help out his neighbors, trying his best to figure out a game plan and encourage them to fight alongside him. But that was nothing compared to the reach this news show was going to get.

Mom felt around the sheets for the remote. "Here, come back to bed. I'll turn this off and Kee and I can go watch downstairs. You should sleep."

"I'm fine," Dad said, crossing the room. "I got to get up anyway."

On the screen, Elise's dad cleared his throat. "It's not really our place to speculate on that. What I will say is that we feel we've been treated fairly."

"I doubt it," my dad muttered. He went over to his dresser.

I bit my lip. Elise had asked us not to blab about how much money her family had settled for, but I made the snap decision that telling my parents was okay. "Umm, Elise said they got five hundred thousand dollars," I said.

Mom's head whirled around. "You're kidding."

"Nope. I mean, they did lose everything. And their house was nice. But still. Isn't that a crazy amount of money?"

Dad's back was to me, so I couldn't see how my news landed. But he didn't miss a beat when he said, "That wouldn't be enough for us to leave. Not even close."

When he said that, Mom turned her eyes back to the television, blinking every few seconds, her face unfocused.

The forecast was up next.


Our Lady of the Angels, one of the churches in town, quickly organized a drive to donate supplies to the families who were most in need. I was glad of a chance to do something.

And I figured that donations would be a way to help out my

dad's cause. If people were comfortable, if they had the things they needed, they'd be more inclined to stay in Aberdeen and stand up to the governor with him.

I went into our attic and started grabbing blankets, old sheets that used to belong to my grandma and grandpa, and other useful stuff that people might need. I came upon a couple of boxes packed with my old toys and books and clothes. The clothes were easy to donate, but I weirdly had a harder time with the other stuff. Not that anyone was asking specifically for toys or books, but I figured that when you lose everything, you need everything. I pulled out a teddy bear I'd named Rosebud because her hands were sewn together and she was clasping a little rosebud. She was so soft and cute. Dad bought Rosebud for me when I was five and had my tonsils out. He picked her out at the hospital gift shop and I remember him coming into my hospital room in his dirty work clothes with her for me, looking so scared, wanting to make sure I was okay. He almost forgot to give the bear to me. Mom had to remind him. "Oh! Hey! What's that in Daddy's arms?" There was a rattle inside the nubby tail, but I didn't care if that made her babyish.

I gave Rosebud a hug. She felt weirdly small in my arms.

It was dumb to keep the bear now, especially when there were kids who didn't have toys anymore who might appreciate her. Rosebud had given me a lot of comfort, even more than the ice cream, and I liked the idea of giving her to another kid to comfort them. But it was still hard for me to put her into the bag. Same for some of my books, like the copy of *A Wrinkle in Time* that Mom read to me at bedtime. I sat on the floor of the attic and reread the first third of it before Morgan texted that she was on her way to pick me up.

Morgan and I baked chocolate cupcakes at her house, thinking they might cheer people up as well. Making them certainly cheered us up. We fought over licking the bowl. I flicked a little batter at her, and in retaliation, Morgan wiped the entire back of a batter-covered spoon across my face. We laughed so hard we nearly peed our pants. Once the cupcakes were cooled and iced, she drove us over to the church. I kept the plate steady on my lap, a toothpick in each cupcake so the plastic wrap wouldn't screw up our decorating job. We'd put the icing on extra thick and wrote ABERDEEN 4EVR with a red gel pen, one letter for each cupcake in the dozen. I was starting to get hungry for dinner, and I totally would have eaten one if we hadn't spelled something out.

And it was nice, not to talk about any of the bad things that were happening around us. We were so focused on each other and talking about the night before, about me and Jesse.

"I still can't believe you kissed him first, Kee."

"I know," I giggled. "Me either. But I did. I totally kissed the hell out of him."

Morgan could have been bummed. Her heart was still broken over Wes. I knew that. But she wasn't. She was one 1,000 percent happy for me. She was that terrific of a best friend. She said cheerfully, "I mean, who gets this? Who gets to kiss their first love?"

"Ahem. Who not only gets to kiss their first love, but has their first love basically tell you that they want to spend their last moments with you?" I clarified.

Morgan snorted. "That makes Jesse sound like he's dying. But seriously. You've wanted this forever."

I smiled. "Actually that's not true. I didn't let myself want Jesse, because I never thought I could get him."

Morgan swatted me. "And you're supposedly the smart one. You know, maybe *you* need to go to beauty school and *I* should be gunning for a scholarship."

On a surface level, our conversation was a duplicate of the car ride after we'd stacked sandbags, or all the conversations about what to text Jesse and what not to text Jesse that we'd had in the school parking lot. Except this one was me and Morgan, together like the old days, just the two of us.

I loved Elise. I really did. I missed her when she finally left Aberdeen, and I still miss her. But in that moment, I didn't. Not at all.

We were just about at the church when Morgan said, "Hey, so I think Elise is going to stay with me while her family's in the hotel. It's too far for her parents to drive there and back every day, especially when her brothers still go to Saint Ann's. This way, she'll get to spend more time here with all her friends."

"Oh. Cool." Though what struck me was not the practicality, which did make complete sense, but that there'd been conversations about those plans, probably a few, that I wasn't around for. "Do they know when they're leaving for Florida?" That I didn't already know this reinforced that feeling.

"They're not sure."

We pulled into the parking lot. I put the plate of cupcakes on the dash and got out with Morgan to start unloading her trunk. That's when a woman came walking out briskly through the rectory door to meet us. She shook her head and called out to us, "Don't bother, girls. We're not taking any more donations."

Morgan said, "But there are signs up everywhere."

"We've already gotten way too much stuff. Or should I say, junk," she explained curtly. "People beginning to clean out their houses, unloading their garbage on us. We were very specific with the kinds of things we were looking for, but now we're being treated as a dumping ground for things they aren't going to want to take with them when they leave." The church lady was grumbly, peering past us into our bags. She spotted Rosebud and rolled her eyes. "You know, the church is going to have to pay to dispose of this stuff now, which is really unfair and the opposite of the spirit intended when we organized this drive."

The stuff I was giving wasn't junk. I didn't want to give it up in the first place, but I thought it was a nice thing to do.

"Not to mention that the families we wanted to help, the ones who were in the most dire situations, will likely all take the relocation money. So . . ." She lifted her hands up only to let them drop like dead weight. "What's the use?"

I wondered exactly how many families had taken deals already. And if my dad knew.

Morgan closed her trunk and we climbed back into her car. The church lady wanted to take the cupcakes we'd baked, I knew by the way she was eyeing them, but I was like *hell no* and ignored her as I put them back on my lap. I figured we could bring them with us to school, whenever school started back up again. Even if they were a little stale, the kids would gobble them up.

At home, I found a list of things Mom wanted me to pick up from Viola's Market. It was mostly ingredients for dinner, but then she added a few other random things at the bottom, like batteries, bottled water, some nonperishables. The forecaster had said we were only expected to get an inch or two of rain, nothing that would trigger another flood, but I guessed Mom wanted to be ready just in case.

Viola's Market was our local grocery store. Most people did their big weekly shopping at the Walmart twenty minutes down the highway, but Viola's was perfect if you didn't want to drive far or needed something last-minute, like a roll of toilet paper, or if you had a craving for ice cream. It was family owned, a small and clean white box with a black-and-white linoleum floor, a couple of parking spaces in the rear, and hand-painted signs on butcher paper that told you the specials for the week.

I'd heard there'd been some damage to Viola's Market, and sure enough, there was a big sheet of plywood nailed over a broken window. You could see that the water had gotten in, because the bottom shelves in every aisle were empty. The freezer section was pretty bare too, probably because of the power outages. But otherwise, it looked good. The floor was mopped. They had plenty of milk and bread, veggies, eggs.

I bumped into Levi Hamrick in the cereal aisle. He was there with a big gallon jug of milk in the crook of his arm, deciding between a huge box of Lucky Charms and a huge box of Cheerios.

I would have been inclined to ignore him, but I needed a box of Lucky Charms myself. So I reached around him and casually said, "When picking a breakfast cereal, always go marshmallows. Always."

He shrugged and put his Lucky Charms back on the shelf. "It's for dinner, actually. I don't know how to cook, so . . ."

"You don't have to know how to cook to eat better than cereal for dinner, Levi. I mean, didn't anyone teach you how to make spaghetti?" As soon as the words came out, I remembered that Levi's mom had died a few years ago, when I was a freshman. It was just Levi and his father. So maybe no one had. "Umm, all you do is boil water, add noodles, cook for seven minutes, and boom. Dinner is served." I did a little flourish with my hand.

"Plain spaghetti. Sounds . . . appetizing. Think I'll stick with the Cheerios."

We tried to politely excuse ourselves, except we were both headed to the registers, so we had this awkward moment of racing to get away from each other in the same general direction. I stopped and flipped through a magazine so he'd go ahead of me, since he only had, like, two things.

"Keeley. I'll ring you up here."

Mr. Viola waved me over to the customer service counter. My mom had given me forty dollars. But some of it was in change. Her note said, *We can live without the orange juice and those cookies Daddy likes if this isn't enough. Just make sure you get batteries.* Even taking those items out, the total was getting close to that.

And though I'd talked to Mr. Viola before about him hiring me for the summer as a cashier, I thought I might be proactive. Why wait for summer? I could start tomorrow, work a few hours every day after school. Definitely on the weekends.

"Sorry to have to tell you this, Keeley, but I'm not going to be able to hire you."

"Wait, Mr. Viola. Are you serious?"

"I haven't told many people this yet, but . . ." He tossed his hands up in frustration. "We worked so hard to open back up, restock the shelves. Hardly anyone's coming in! They're cleaning out their pantries, eating what they've already got, in case we all do have to leave. Either that, or there's still too many roads closed and they can't park close enough to do a big shopping."

"I'm sure they'll get the roads open soon."

He gave a dismissive snort. "I wonder. If something underhanded is going on like your dad says, then they aren't going to hustle to make getting around town any easier for us." He tapped his head. "Think about it. Anyway, tomorrow wouldn't be soon enough for me. My insurance is already telling me they don't want to pay for the damage. The next flood, they won't give me anything. Every day I stay open, I'm risking everything. And for what? To sell a couple of gallons of milk a day?"

Mr. Viola was all fired up as if I were the insurance company, the governor, and everyone who hadn't come back to Viola's in the last week. I glanced over at the cashier. Her head was down and she was fiddling with the register. She probably got the brunt of this too.

"Are you saying you're going to close?"

He shot me a look. "Don't make me sound like a traitor! You know how long my family's owned this business? I was born in the back room!"

I started sweating. I wasn't trying to call him a traitor. Nervously, I joked, "That was only like twenty years ago, though. Right, Mr. Viola?"

He didn't even crack a smile.

I was acutely aware of Levi stepping through the doors so I chose my words carefully. "Things will hopefully go back to normal soon. There are a lot of people working to make that happen. We just have to stick together."

"I wish your dad luck, Keeley. I know he's working hard. I

saw him on my neighbor's roof yesterday evening, hammering shingles in the dark. Impressive, considering his injury. But he's going to need to do more than just get up on his ladder if he wants to save Aberdeen. Someone needs to do something big, and do it quick. Otherwise, we're all going under. I personally can't risk my livelihood to see how it turns out."

I walked out of there feeling whiplashed.

No one in their right mind would cry over a stupid grocery store job, but there I was, getting hot behind the eyeballs. I kept thinking of my mom's face that morning, when I told her how much Elise's family had received, like hearing your next-door neighbor won the Powerball lottery. I regretted saying anything.

Where was I going to work if everything was closing?

I felt for my dad, too, of course. He *was* working so hard. I hated to think it would all be for nothing.

Levi stood outside unlocking his bike. He had it chained to a parking meter.

I quickly turned my back to him and wiped away my tears with my hand. God, it was so embarrassing. I felt like I had to say something, because Levi was clearly aware that I was crying, again.

I forced a laugh. "Okay, this is going to seem like a regular thing for me, but I swear it isn't."

"Here," he said, gesturing for my two bags.

"I'm fine, Levi. They're not heavy."

But he took them from my hands and put them into the crate he'd attached to the back fender of his bike.

We walked for a while in silence. While I had to snake through blocked streets on my way into town, Levi just nodded to whichever cop was standing in front of the barriers. That cop would then nod back, and we'd be allowed to pass through.

I was thinking about what Mr. Viola had said. Was the town actually working to open up the streets so we could drive on them again? It didn't seem like it.

There was a lot of activity going on. At the houses that were empty, the front doors were open and workers were carrying out things like toilets and light fixtures and tossing them into Dumpsters.

"This is crazy. Are all the people on this block already gone?"

"I think so. The houses were in bad shape. I bet they made deals quickly."

I looked to the other side of the street. There was one house with cars in the driveway. A man and a woman sat on their front stoop, watching the chaos around them go down. Their house had suffered damage. A tarp was covering part of their roof and a pile of garbage furniture was mounded on their front lawn. Leaned against that pile was a dining table on its side. And on it were spray-painted the words HELL NO WE WON'T GO.

The woman saw me and pointed me out to her husband. They both waved.

They knew who I was because of my dad.

I waved back. I felt instantly lighter.

"Not everyone's going to make this easy, Levi," I said, feeling a surge of pride.

Levi shrugged. "What choice do they have?"

I didn't answer because I didn't know. I was just hoping there would be a choice, that my dad would figure something out, because people were counting on him.

"I heard your conversation with Mr. Viola. I might know of a job opening. Temporary work, but it pays well."

Skeptical, I asked, "Who? Where?"

"The town. They want the houses that are vacated to be inspected. Make sure all the possessions are cleared out, that the gas and electricity are turned off." He didn't look at me when he said, "They could probably use someone else, if you were interested."

"Levi, that sounds like the most depressing job ever. Right up there with gravedigger."

His lip curled. "It's actually an important job, okay? Because if the gas isn't turned off, and one of these guys rips out an oven, there could be an explosion. But forget it. Never mind."

"What do you need to work for? I thought you were . . . um . . . going places." It was too good, I couldn't help myself.

He groaned. "That stupid article. I wasn't asking to be portrayed like that. Anyway, a full ride isn't always a full ride. You'll see."

"Don't tell me that. Your grades were perfect, I'm sure."

He didn't dispute it. But after a few more steps, he said, "Well, there was one black mark . . . No Mock Congress championship."

I whipped around so hard, I had to pull strands of my hair out of my mouth. He had a grin on his face, but it only lasted a second, because he could see that I was fuming. "Is that supposed to be funny?"

Levi put a hand up. "Hey. Don't be mad at me. I was only kidding. And you were the one who quit on us."

*We had reached the semifinal round, which was way further than anyone thought we would get. But instead of it pumping us up, it scared the crap out of us.*

*Bundy ordered our team into one of the empty conference rooms at the hotel to go over our debate points. We'd been assigned to take the position against the passage of a proposed bill to eliminate advertising in schools.*

*It was a gift from God.*

*The Mock Congress bills before felt like playacting. Climate change or voter registration or mandatory jail sentences. None of that stuff affected our lives. But this one did. It was easy for a wealthy school to be all like, "No thank you, evil advertisers! We want to be pure!" But if Coca-Cola built us a new scoreboard so long as we sold their drinks? Or if Minute Maid offered to give our school a TV studio to broadcast morning announcements if we played ads for their orange juice?*

*We were the have-nothings up against the have-everythings.*

*We were really nervous, like puke nervous, because everything we were going to say was personal. And everyone would know it, because we were from the small town in the least-affluent district.*

*At some point, Bundy stepped out to get herself a coffee. We were supposed to continue practicing, but of course we didn't.*

*I think Dave Fallon was the first one to say, "Did you guys notice how the school we're up against are all in matching blazers and polo shirts? I didn't know we were supposed to do that."*

*We looked each other over. Some of us were dressed up—I'd worn black dress pants, a light gray sweater, and flats—but that was not the norm. Most of our team was in jeans. Every single boy was wearing sneakers.*

*"I bet they're the ones who came here in that air-conditioned bus."*

*"I saw two of them in the bathrooms. They were talking about how they were going to eviscerate us."*

*Ellen Botkin looked down at her note cards. "Do I have to make this point about our average salary in Aberdeen? It's embarrassing."*

*I watched my whole team losing confidence by the second. So I did what I do best. I started goofing off. I figured the best way for us to get over how we looked was to poke fun at us. Get it out on the table so we could move on. So I pretended to be a white trash hick, which is how those other schools saw us anyway. With a stupid-sounding drawl and hee-haw knee slaps, I read my note cards. Everyone started cracking up. I even stuffed Lisa Krawinski's sweatshirt underneath my shirt so I'd look like a pregnant teen.*

*Most of the kids were laughing, but Levi wiped his forehead with his sleeve and pleaded, "You guys, come on. We can win this, we just have to be better than them. And to be better than them, we have to practice." He was the only other one to dress up. He had on a green necktie.*

*I said, "Fine, Levi. You go."*

*He shuffled his index cards and started. But every other sentence, I cut him off. I was doing it to be funny. I mean, sure, I saw him getting mad, but I figured eventually he'd crack and have a good laugh, and then we'd get on with it. But that's not what happened. He stalked out.*

*When he came back in, I was in the middle of doing a square dance. Bundy was with him, and she was not happy. She made a big example out of me in front of everyone, yelling at me. Which I pretty much expected. But then she said, "Keeley, get on the bus. You are no longer on this team."*

*You could have heard a pin drop.*

*"Wait, what?" I said. I glanced around the room for support, but no one had the balls to look at me. Especially not Levi.*

*Bundy was so angry with me, she was shaking, so badly that she set her coffee down. "I'm not going to say it again. You aren't taking this seriously, so you are off the team. Go sit on the bus and wait for us to finish."*

*I laughed dryly. And then I walked out.*

*But I lingered just outside the door, thinking, hoping that maybe Bundy was all talk. Maybe it was a test, her wanting me to beg to be back on the team. I was so humiliated though, there was no way I was going to do that. So I did what I was told. I went out and sat on the bus for the next two hours and cried my eyes out.*

*I had hope that maybe we'd won. I thought about sneaking back in to see the awards presentation. But I didn't. I didn't want Bundy to think I cared.*

*When the kids came back on the bus, I greeted them with a smile. Actually, I put my arm around the bus driver and said, "You guys, I want you all to meet Larry, my new bestie."*

*I could tell right away that we'd lost. On the ride back to Aberdeen, most people were sympathetic toward me. They knew I wouldn't leave them high and dry. They blamed Bundy.*

*Not Levi. He'd given me no sympathy. I would have thought he'd felt worst of all, since he basically narc'ed me out. The one time we did make eye contact, he'd just glared at me.*

Now, as we got closer to my house, I knew Levi was going over that day in his mind too, the way his forehead crinkled up, shrinking the space between his hairline and his eyebrows.

I lifted my grocery bags out of his bike basket. I definitely wasn't going to give him the satisfaction of carrying them for me anymore. I'd rather my arms fell off. "I'm not too much farther," I said.

"Come on, Keeley," he said—annoyed! With me! "You live more than a mile from here. And uphill."

Just then, I spotted my mom's car pulling slowly down the street. The police officers made room for her to pass through. I waved her down. "I've got a ride," I said smugly.

Levi ducked his head in the window when Mom came to a stop. "Hello, Mrs. Hewitt. Sorry I didn't introduce myself to you yesterday. I'm Levi, Sheriff Hamrick's son."

Her eyes lit up. "Oh my gosh, Levi. I should have recognized you. You've grown so much. And my God, you look so much like your mother. You have her same eyes."

I glanced to see how he'd react to that, but Levi just stood there blankly, almost as if he hadn't heard her.

Then to me, she said, "Great. You made it to Viola's." She clicked open the trunk.

Levi let his bike fall to the ground to take the bags out of my arms again. "It's really sad that Viola's is closing. I know Keeley was planning to work there. But I was just telling her about a job she could take working for the town. It's temporary, but it pays well."

I glared at him. "What are you doing?" I said through my teeth.

"Oh, wow! Isn't that terrific, Keeley? Thank you, Levi."

"No problem," Levi said. He picked up his bike and rode away, not even looking at me.

As soon as I was in the car, I told her, "Mom, I don't want to take that job." I didn't understand why Levi had mentioned it in the first place, especially because I'd said I wasn't interested. I was already trying to view the whole Viola's Market thing as a blessing in disguise. If I didn't have to work, that meant more time hanging out with my friends and with Jesse and helping Dad.

"Why?"

I hated that she sounded disappointed with me. "Well . . . wouldn't it look weird to the other residents if they knew Dad's daughter was working with the sheriff's son?"

"It's a job, Keeley. We could use the money."

"College, I know, Mom, but—"

"It's not just that, Keeley." Mom's hands tightened around the steering wheel. "We just don't know what tomorrow will bring. These sorts of things can decimate people's savings if they don't have the proper insurance, and even then there are unexpected out-of-pocket costs. Everyone's talking about the next storm. We may need help simply making ends meet."

When we got home, Sheriff Hamrick's squad car was parked in our driveway.

"Shit," Mom said. She never cursed, not in front of me. She jumped out. "Is everything okay? Is Jim all right?"

My stomach dropped. What if Dad had gotten hurt again? Or, I don't know, arrested . . .

"Everything's fine, Jill, I just wanted to stop by and say there's no hard feelings about the other night in the gym, okay? If your family needs anything, I want you to call us right away."

I barely nodded. I knew it was nice of Sheriff Hamrick to say that. But right then I was so mad at Levi that I couldn't see it. I hated him as much as my father hated Sheriff Hamrick, and the mayor and the governor, too.

---

## 18

**Wednesday, May 18**
Rain tapering off after 7:00 PM, low of 58°F

---

After dinner, I got a text from Jesse that said, Playdate?

It had thankfully stopped raining, but even if it'd been pouring, I probably would still have gone out to meet him.

I wrote back, BYOJB? (Bring your own juice box?)

Pffft. You're my girl now. I got you covered.

I met Jesse and Julia at the playground behind Aberdeen's grade school thirty minutes later. He was wearing a pair of black Adidas track pants, and his gray sweatshirt was unzipped to reveal a red T-shirt that said SAVE EARTH! IT'S THE ONLY PLANET WITH PIZZA! His curls were pulled up into a bun at the top of his head.

"Whoa," I said when I walked through the gates. "I haven't been here forever. Everything looks so small."

This was not one of those newer playgrounds where everything was made of brightly colored plastic and the ground was that cushy foam that prevents kids from skinning their knees. It was a lot of weathered wood and rusting metal. The ground was supposed to be grass, but it was mostly scrubby plants and mud puddles.

"Crazy, right?" Jesse ducked underneath the monkey bars. He was so tall that when he stood flat-footed, his head popped up between the rungs. "I remember when this drop felt scary far."

I walked toward him and reached up for the bars myself. Little drops of rain from that afternoon clung to the underside of the rungs. On tiptoes, my fingertips just grazed them. "I could never do these. I have, like, zero upper-body strength."

"Try it now."

I gave him a warning face, but as soon as I reached up for the bar, he tried to tickle me. I smacked my arms back down to my sides. "Don't, Jesse!"

"Don't or you'll what?"

I smiled meekly. "Don't or . . . you'll be sorry?"

He took a big step toward me, closing up the space between us. "I think I could take you."

I wondered in that moment if being close to Jesse would ever be something I'd get used to or if I'd feel so tingly every single time.

Suddenly, Julia came zooming down a slide and ran straight over to Jesse. Her curly hair was pulled up into two tuffs at the very top of her head.

He moved a few steps away from me and I could suddenly breathe again. Julia jumped up and clung to him. He grabbed her hands and she did a twist, flipping over like a gymnast before falling back down to the ground. "You remember Keeley, right?"

Julia nodded, but she was looking around, distracted. "Where are all the other kids? You said there'd be other kids to play with." The seat of her pink polka-dot leggings was wet from the slide.

I'd figured there would be other kids here too. In fact, I'd come to the school at the same time that a woman and her two young daughters pulled up in their minivan. The driveway was roped off with caution tape, so they turned around for home. I would have done the same if I hadn't heard Jesse and Julia laughing in the distance. I ducked under the caution tape, which set her kids off screaming and pointing at me. The woman gave me a dirty look as she drove away.

Jesse shrugged. "You'll see them at school on Monday. And anyway, we don't need other kids. We've got enough for a race."

Julia grinned and pointed across the playground. "To the swings!"

Jesse crouched down like an Olympic sprinter waiting for the starting gun. He turned to me. "On your marks . . ."

I got down like a sprinter too. "Get set . . ."

Julia started running before he said, "Go!" and got a few steps ahead of us. But when she turned around to see how far behind we were, she tripped over her own feet and crashed hard onto the ground in a muddy tumble. She exploded in tears.

Jesse, who'd been fake-running before, clicked into a full-on soccer sprint and scooped her up in his arms. He didn't care that she was smearing mud all over his T-shirt. Julia was hysterical and flailing her arms. Jesse checked her all over to make sure she wasn't bleeding. He kept telling her, "It's okay, it's okay," but she wouldn't calm down. She was screaming, guttural and raw.

I felt completely helpless.

"Here, Julia! Check this out!" He set her down, and she was still crying pretty hard. I came up behind her and patted her back. Jesse shuffled backward to the monkey bars and quickly climbed up them so he was standing across the top. And though the monkey bars had seemed small before, they suddenly looked as tall as a house. "Want to see me do something crazy?"

"Jesse . . . ," I said nervously.

Julia didn't answer him, but she did stop screaming. Her chest shook with post-hysterical sobs.

He took off his hooded sweatshirt and tossed it aside. "Count to three for me, Julia, and I'll do a flip for you." He shifted his eyes onto me. "I've been practicing this on Zito's trampoline. I nail it about thirty percent of the time."

"Great," I said nervously.

"Come on, Julia. Count for me!"

Julia wiped her nose with the back of her hand. "One, two, three."

"Now in Spanish," he said.

That made Julia laugh. And me too. *"Uno, dos, tres!"* she said.

Jesse shouted something crazy, like a Tarzan noise, and leapt off the top of the monkey bars. He flung his head forward, tucking and rolling. He ended up spinning too much though, two rotations instead of just one, and it was clear he wasn't going to land on his feet.

I couldn't breathe.

He smacked the ground flat on his back with a thud. Julia and I both rushed over. I was afraid he'd be paralyzed or had maybe cracked open the back of his head. Julia was laughing like he was a stunt professional or a clown. Like there was no way he'd be hurt.

But when Jesse got up, I saw that he was. Maybe not hurt bad, but I think he'd gotten the wind knocked out of him at least.

"Pretty funny, huh?" he said to her, rolling onto his knees. He looked up at me and winked.

"You're bleeding," I whispered when I noticed the huge scrape on his forearm.

But by that point, Julia had taken off running again, shrieking with laughter.

"I'm fine," he said. I didn't completely believe him, but he pulled me close and gave me a kiss on the forehead. "Come on. I'll push you both on the swings."

We played like that until the sun went down. Jesse *had* brought me a juice box—fruit punch—and he pushed the straw in for me. He kissed me whenever we were sure Julia wasn't looking, our mouths sugary and warm.

I went home exhausted in that terrific mind-clearing way that only seems to happen when you're a little kid.

# 19

Our school reopened three days after the flood. I couldn't wait to go back.

I'm sure that sounds nuts, but it wasn't like those days off felt like an early start to summer. They were missing the freedom that summer would bring, the chance to spend your days how you wanted. There were too many chores to do. Too many places in Aberdeen that were still off-limits. Plus I just missed it, the routine of the bells ringing every forty-five minutes. I missed gossiping, I missed the assignments, I missed my SAT prep class.

Of course, I was also excited to be back in regular physical proximity to Jesse. Maybe we'd hold hands in the hallway, meet at my locker during breaks, have lunch dates.

In the morning, Jesse texted me a picture of him sitting on a huge bulldozer. From the way it was shot, kind of low to the ground, I had to think Julia was the one who took it. I smiled, until I noticed there were a line of bulldozers parked behind the one he was on.

You want a ride? I'll pick you up.

Not if that's what you're driving!

Come on! If we showed up to school on one of these together, it'd be so epic!!!

It would also be grand theft.

Okay, okay. Fine. I'll take the hatchback instead. How's quarter after seven?

It might seem like such a small thing, to have a boy offer to pick you up and take you to school. For me, it was as epic as a bulldozer ride. We were really doing this, being together for as long as we could. Of course, I hated that caveat, but I tried not to focus on it.

Can't. Dad's taking me. He wants to go to the meeting.

In the e-mail from Principal Bundy's office about returning to school, they told all students to report straight to the auditorium for an assembly instead of going to homeroom like normal. Parents were encouraged to attend.

"What do you think it could be?" Mom said. "I'm worried."

Dad frowned. "I'm not sure. But it can't be good."

"I'm trying to switch my patient schedule around," Mom said as she filled our sink with soapy water to do the breakfast dishes. "But I'm still waiting to hear back from one of the other nurses on my team."

"Don't worry." Dad lifted his coffee to his lips. "I said I can take her."

"No, no, it's fine. I'll just call my supervisor and—"

Dad picked up the newspaper. "You keep telling me to take a break, so now I'm taking a break."

Mom sighed like she was annoyed, but when she spun around from the sink, she had a smile on her face. "Okay, okay. Point taken."

Because it was my first day of school with a boyfriend, or whatever Jesse Ford and I were now, I decided to wear something nice. I'd borrowed an outfit from Morgan a few weeks ago, to wear to the party that Wes decided he didn't want me at. It was a light blue oxford shirtdress, almost too short for school, but very cute. It was still too cold for sandals, so I wore my red Keds and paired it with my jean jacket.

As I came downstairs, I sniffed the air. "Is that cologne?"

Turns out I wasn't the only one dressed up. Dad had put on slacks and a flannel. His hair was combed, not hiding under a ball cap, his face was shaved, and his fingernails were scrubbed clean.

He drove us over in his truck.

I hadn't seen the school parking lot since the night we escaped from the gym. The water had gone down quite a bit, but after yesterday's rain, it had risen back up again. Dad and I had heard on the radio that it was supposed to rain again later tonight. In fact, rain was in the forecast for the next few days. Would there be another flood? That's what I was wondering, anyway. And I'm sure everyone in town was too.

"Maybe that's what this is about," I remarked as Dad pulled into a spot. "Like, flood preparedness. Put a plan in place in case something does happen."

"Could be," Dad said. But he didn't sound like he believed it.

We parked and then joined the flow of everyone walking quickly toward the school in little whispery clusters, guessing what was going to happen, what would be said. No one seemed to have a clue.

One news van was parked in the no parking zone. Not many people paid it attention, I think because most of us were on news overload. I know I was. Anyway, we weren't the top story anymore, even with more rain supposedly coming this week. There'd been a car crash with some famous tennis player and he was in critical condition.

"Mr. Hewitt?"

Dad and I both stopped. A man in a suit and tie hopped out of the back of the news van. "Hey. Shawn Wilcox, KPBC. It's great to meet you, put a face to this." He held up Dad's protest letter. "People in town keep saying that you're the man to talk to."

"You read it?" Dad brightened. "No one at the governor's office will even acknowledge getting it. I haven't heard back from anyone on the town council. Mayor Aversano is ducking my calls."

"Well, to tell you the truth, Mr. Hewitt, things have cooled down on the Aberdeen story. But getting your message on air will definitely help pick attention back up. That, coupled with today's announcement."

"What are they going to announce?" I asked him, shifting my bag from one shoulder to the other.

He looked at me and swallowed. "We're not sure," he said, which was obviously a lie. An eager-looking cameraman came out of the back of the truck and started framing up my dad. The reporter angled himself away from me. "The problem is that your document is . . . well, it's not exactly *compelling*." He said the last part like a musical theater kid.

"Okay."

"You make a sound argument, and . . . off the record . . . I agree with you. I think there are other options the governor is choosing not to explore. Probably because he thinks you-all are going to be easy to railroad with a little"—and at this, the reporter raised his hand and rubbed his fingers together, the international sign for money. "But you need public opinion on your side. The best way to make that happen is a show of strength, like a rally at City Hall. Something visual to prove you've got people behind you. Popular support trumps facts, I'm afraid. We could get you on tape right now, a little interview where you hit the main points in your letter and announce the rally. And boom. You'll be back in business."

Dad looked at me, and then at the reporter. "I need a minute," he said, and pulled me around to the front of the news van. "What do you think?"

"I think he's right. You've got to do something big. A rally could be perfect."

Dad sighed. "I really thought that letter would make a bigger splash. But Governor Ward, he's big-time. He's controlling this story."

"You said yourself . . . people have won these kinds of fights, Dad. And look. This reporter thinks you have something."

"Right."

"Anyway, what's the worst that could happen? No one shows up? That's impossible. You have people supporting you. Charlie and Sy, and all the people you've done work for, Bess and Russell Dixon, and everyone who's come by the house. Not to mention Mom, and me . . ."

Dad nodded and then took a breath. "I guess I don't have much to lose. How do I look?" He cleared his throat. "Too slick?"

I almost laughed. Slick? "You look fine, Dad. Like yourself. Salt of the earth."

He crouched down to check his hair in the side mirror of a random parked car. Then we walked back over to the reporter.

"Okay, let's do this. But can we wait until after the meeting?"

The reporter shook his head. "We need to get you right now so we can edit a teaser for the lunchtime broadcast. The more we can get this out before the evening news, the more viewers you'll have tuning in."

Dad gave me an uneasy look.

"It's okay. I'll find you when it's over and tell you what they said in there."

As I walked away, I saw Levi and Sheriff Hamrick slowing down. They watched my father chatting with the reporter. I swear Sheriff Hamrick looked nervous. Levi's eyes moved on to me, and as soon as they did, I gave him a smug little wave hello.

Maybe the annoying man from the town meetings wasn't seen as a threat. But that wasn't who Dad was anymore.

They had no idea who they were dealing with.


I found Morgan in the middle of the auditorium. She'd saved seats on either side of her, one for me and one for Elise. Parents stood in the back of the auditorium or along the aisles on the side. I looked around for Jesse but didn't see him.

Mrs. Dorsey was there, and she gave me a warm hug hello. "Your mom said your dad was coming."

"He's outside talking to a reporter."

Her eyes went big. "Oh yeah?" she said, and I think she wanted it to sound casual, but it didn't. It sounded concerned. And as soon as I passed her and climbed into the row, I saw her take out her phone and I knew she was calling my mom.

Principal Bundy stood at a lectern in the center of the stage, waiting for everyone to quiet down. Most of the teachers and faculty were up there with her, and some were dabbing at their eyes. The red curtain was pulled back, exposing the gaping hole of a black stage. The props and sets from the musical a few weeks ago had been dismantled and thrown away.

Morgan took my hand and squeezed it, as if we were sharing a seat on a roller coaster and were about to take the first drop.

"Where's Elise?"

"She got stuck in traffic on her way from the hotel. She was going to sleep over last night, but her parents wanted to be here for this."

Bundy cleared her throat and launched into a very boring speech about the history of Aberdeen High School, how it had been around since the early 1900s and the first graduating class was only four students. She listed off a bunch of our notable former graduates, who didn't seem that noteworthy to me besides a dude who apparently worked on movies in Hollywood. And then, after a deep breath and a bunch of impatient mumbling from the crowd, she got to it.

"Officially, we have seventeen days left of this school year. Luckily, we had an easy winter, and we didn't have to utilize any of our five allowed emergency days. The state office of the Department of Education has reviewed protocol, and in light of current circumstances, they've decided that next Friday, a week from tomorrow, will be our last day."

I whipped my head around to Morgan.

We were supposed to have almost a month left.

Bundy continued. "Finals will be canceled." There was an uproar at this, mostly cheers. But I didn't cheer. I had a couple of zeros, and two crap test grades from the week spent chatting up Jesse before

Spring Formal. Finals were going to be my way to catch up.

"In lieu of exams, your grades will be calculated based on classwork that's been accomplished, and in certain circumstances, extra-credit opportunities will be provided and—"

"How is this legal?" shouted out an angry parent. Suddenly, there were a lot of rumbling whispers.

"I promise you, we've been in close contact with Governor Ward. What we have here is a safety issue. As I'm sure you are aware, there is more rain in the forecast, and we need to begin preparations for cleaning and maintenance and salvage of this building. Also, we want to be respectful to the families who will be departing Aberdeen in the coming days; we don't want them to feel as if they ought to be staying. We're going to be offering counseling services to any students who might—"

"What about graduation?" someone shouted.

"And prom?"

Both of those voices were students, not parents.

Bundy looked nervously at the teachers flanking her. I loved seeing her struggle up there.

"Prom is, unfortunately, also canceled. Our senior advisor will explain details about ticket refunds."

The boos were thunderous, and if I'd been a senior, I would have booed too. We'd already gotten cheated out of a Spring Formal.

"I hope you understand that this was a very hard choice. I started my teaching career here at Aberdeen thirty years ago, as did many of our other faculty. None of us wanted this to happen, but we have to do what's best. It's going to be a difficult week, but we will have each other to lean on."

Some parents began to shout, so Bundy dipped her face

closer to the microphone and spoke in a booming voice, meant to drown the other voices out. "As for graduation, there will be an abbreviated ceremony on the last day of school. To that end, seniors, please stay in your seats. We'll be having additional discussions regarding the modified graduation services. The rest of you are dismissed. Please make your way to homeroom."

Morgan looked totally blindsided. "I never thought they'd cancel school early. How quickly do they want us all out of town? Does your dad have any idea?"

I felt shaky. "I'm not sure."

We met up with Elise on the way out. She'd come in late and was listening in the back. She had a duffel bag with her, clothes I guess, to keep at Morgan's house. Mrs. Dorsey and Elise's parents were in a corner, speaking to each other. She whipped her head around and looked over my shoulder at some girls behind us, also juniors, chatting about how this whole experience was going to make for the best personal essay topic ever for college applications next year.

"Admissions loves these sorts of stories, people in turmoil," Rebecca said, yammering on. "This is, like, a golden opportunity for us."

Elise gave them both a fiery look, fists clenched at her side. "A golden opportunity? Are you serious? I lost my home!"

"Well, I'm losing my home too. And my school, so . . ."

Elise looked like a stray cat about to pounce. "Come on, Elise," I said, ushering her away.

But instead of relief, Elise was crying again. "We signed the lease and bought our plane tickets this morning. We leave on Monday."

"This coming Monday?" Morgan shook her head. "No! Can't your family wait until the end of next week?"

Elise lifted her arm and let it fall to her side with a slap. "We have to be out of the hotel by then. My dad's meeting with Bundy to work something out with my grades. Tomorrow's going to be my last day." She barely got the words out.

I gently patted her back, which was the only part of her not enveloped by Morgan's hug.

On our way out of the auditorium, I looked for Jesse. He wasn't hard to spot, standing up in his seat, waving his arms like a conductor, leading the seniors in a rowdy chant of *"PROM, PROM, WE WANT PROM."* It was ridiculous, of course, but something felt therapeutic about being so loud and letting our frustrations out. And none of the teachers, not even Principal Bundy, did anything to stop him.

The only senior not participating was, of course, Levi Hamrick. He sat quietly, looking at his phone. I guess what was happening didn't concern him much. Like Elise, he already knew that his future was beyond this place. Unlike Elise, he clearly didn't care.

# 20

The rest of that day was so strange. It was as if two simultaneous universes were beginning to exist inside Aberdeen High. Half of us, me included, kept to the schedule. We went to our classes when the bells rang, we handed in homework assigned before any of this happened and took notes on the lectures, we locked our lockers. Elise, Morgan, and I sat at our normal lunch table and had our usual, chicken fingers and fries. By then, Elise had mostly stopped crying.

The other half seemed immediately able to break through the artifice. For them, the rules, the structure, the hierarchy gave way like the sandbags we'd stacked to protect us. Those kids roamed the halls at will, used their cell phones blatantly. Or they went outside and sat in the bleachers and stared at the dim lights of the scoreboard, or they slept across pushed-together desks in class, or they spent the day in the library hanging out with friends on the beanbag chairs, or they went home. The teachers were too preoccupied to care. Actually, some of the teachers let go just as quickly, took attendance after the bell but then excused themselves to the teachers' lounge and didn't come back.

I ran into Levi talking to one of the guidance counselors in the hallway. Though he didn't pause their conversation, he held up a hand to me, asking me to wait a minute.

Mrs. Jergins said, "I know you want to stay and work, dear, but don't let it get in the way of any of your great opportunities. Precollege classes are an excellent way to get yourself oriented to your new surroundings."

Levi saw me waiting like he'd asked, but he still didn't try to hurry out of the conversation. "Well, the thing is that there's a lot of important work that needs to be done. And the guys at the station, they just don't have the manpower. I'd feel terrible if someone got hurt or injured because there wasn't enough time to put the safety precautions in place."

It was only when I was about to walk away that he glanced over at me and said, "Meet you after school near the bike rack."

"Wait. We start working today?"

Levi nodded like I was an idiot.

I realized then that he and I were on two different sides of this battle.

He looked me up and down. "Do you have anything else you can wear besides a dress?"

I did. In my gym locker. But because he was being such a jerk, I said, "Nope," and popped that *p* like a big old piece of Bubblicious.

He sighed and turned back to Mrs. Jergins.

After the last bell, I ran to my locker to grab my things. When I opened it, Jesse Ford came tumbling out like a zombie lying in wait. I screamed and pushed him off until I realized he wasn't trying to eat my brains so much as kiss me.

He closed his eyes and pursed his lips and waited for me to lean in. Which I did, happily yet nervously. There were other people in the hallways, teachers even, so I kept it quick. Just a peck. Also kissing on the regular was still a new thing for me.

His eyes fluttered open. "I've been waiting in here for like four periods and that's all I get?" He reached up for his neck like it was sore.

"You have not!"

"You're right. More like thirty seconds. But I have missed you." He wrapped his arms around me and it felt so good. And way different than girl hugs. Friend hugs are loose, airy. Jesse gripped me tight enough to lift me ever so slightly off the floor. "You feel good in my arms," he said, and he kept holding on to me long after I assumed he'd let go.

And just being touched, having someone's hands cling to me, want me, it felt like every single nerve ending inside me was amplified, turned up loud. I couldn't believe that I was now the girl I'd always watched jealously from afar, the girl in Jesse's arms.

"Me and Zito and a bunch of the guys have been collecting old toilets out of the Dumpsters in town."

I raised an eyebrow. It was not exactly the most romantic thing a boy has ever extended to a girl, but it was intriguing none-theless. "You don't say."

"Yeah, and we're going to bring them to the mill and drop them off the roof."

"Why would you do that?"

He recoiled in mock shock. "Haven't you ever wanted to throw a toilet off a four-story building? No?" He leaned against the wall. "Okay then. Well, at the very least, it's gonna make a badass video. Come with us!"

"I can't. I have to work."

"I didn't know you had a job. Wah," he said, and drooped his head. "I found a pink toilet just for you."

"Super wah," I said, and drooped my head too. Then we were forehead to forehead, nose to nose, toe to toe. My heartbeat quickened.

"Keeley!"

Elise and Morgan were coming slowly down the hall. Both of them were carrying plastic bags full of stuff, likely whatever Elise had in her locker. They both looked super-tired, and Elise's eyes were puffy and red. Morgan paused and waved shyly, I think because she wanted to make sure it was okay to approach. She didn't want to disturb us from our kiss. I had lived this same moment a hundred times before. So of course, I waved them right over.

Jesse propped himself up on his elbow against a locker. "Ladies! Care to come with us to the mill for a little video project? Blow off some steam?"

Morgan smiled. "Sounds good to me." Then she knocked into Elise and said, "But it's up to Elise. Whatever she wants to do."

"Come on, Elise. Turn that frown upside down with a little *destructive therapy*."

The corners of Elise's mouth turned up and she looked at Jesse, curious. "What does that mean, exactly?"

"Trust me. You'll love it." Elise was still debating, but Jesse cradled her chin in his hand and made her nod like a puppet.

I pouted, but inside I was beaming. It was nice to get to do the thing Elise did, knowing guys who invited us to hang out with them. Except Jesse was inclusive. Even though I couldn't go, he was happy to extend the invitation to my friends, the more the merrier.

"Text me when you're done," I told them.

"Wait. You're not coming?" Morgan said.

"She's working," Jesse said.

Morgan looked confused, because I hadn't mentioned anything about my job. "Where? Viola's?"

"No. It's a thing I'm doing with Levi Hamrick." The three of them looked at me, slack-jawed. "I know, I know. Believe me."

"I bet he hopes you'll give him some info so he can narc to his dad about what your dad is doing," Jesse said. "Like a good little kiss-ass."

The same thing had occurred to me, obviously, but it didn't matter because Jesse was jealous, and it made me so happy. Sometimes I wondered if we were an actual couple or just clinging to each other as we waited to see if this ship would sink. This was a moment where I felt, yes, we are real.

"Please don't talk about my coworker that way," I said.

"Sorry, but you dissing us for Levi Hamrick is not allowed," Jesse said, and picked me up and threw me over his shoulder.

"Come on! Put me down!" I squealed and kicked my legs until he did, even though I would have loved for him to carry me away.

Levi Hamrick was waiting for me outside school, sitting on the curb. He'd changed into work clothes, a pair of navy Dickies stained with streaks of black grease and dried mud, and a long-sleeved gray T-shirt. He wore brown work boots with rubber across the toes and camel-colored laces. A pair of black work gloves dangled out of his front pants pocket.

"You're late," he huffed.

"I am not." And then I pointed up to the old school clock above the main entrance, the clock whose hands never moved off 2:36 p.m., and grinned.

He raised his hand, palm up, and said, "That's what you're going to work in?"

I'd changed out of my dress, not to please Levi, but because I didn't want to ruin Morgan's clothes. I found a pair of jeans and a light pink Henley in the bottom of my locker that I'd left at Morgan's house that had ended up in her wash. "What's wrong with jeans? I bet jeans are actually thicker material than the pants you have on."

"Yeah, but my pants go all the way down to my ankles. Those are like, half-calf jeans."

I busted up laughing. "Oh my God, did you just call these 'half-calf jeans'? They're *capris*, Levi! Hello!"

"Sorry I'm not an expert in women's fashion."

I busted up even harder. "Okay, wait. Did you just say 'women's fashion'?"

Levi walked away from me over to the bike rack, which was fine. I was laughing too hard to say anything else.

Across the parking lot, Jesse and everyone jumped into cars. They were already laughing and having a good time. I wanted so badly to be with them and not with Levi. They drove past us on their way out of the parking lot, a caravan beeping and waving and screaming my name, ten or so toilets piled up in the back of Zito's truck bed. I waved wildly.

Levi didn't say anything but "Get on."

"Ride on your pegs? Are we twelve? Don't you have your driver's license?"

He ignored every one of my questions. "Fine. Walk."

Levi stood on the porch of the first home, between me and the door, the clipboard cradled in one arm. Slung over the other was a tote bag with a flashlight, a can of spray paint, and a big box of black trash bags. He dug around and pulled out a pair of work gloves for me. We were on Basin Street, the last street in town before the river, where the homes were hit hardest by the flood.

"Okay. So when someone officially leaves Aberdeen, they are supposed to report their address in to the police department. Once that happens, the home gets assigned to an inspection team." He eyed me. "That's what we are, in case you didn't know."

"Gee, thanks, Captain Obvious."

He cleared his throat. "Inspection teams have three main jobs. First . . . , Keeley?"

"Yeah?" I looked up from my phone, but only for a second. "Go on."

"First we go in and make sure electricity, water, and gas are shut off. If they aren't, then we call in to the police department, flag the house on our list, and move on." He sighed. "Keeley? Seriously?"

"What, Levi! I can listen to you and look at my phone at the same time. It's not rocket science."

"Do you not want this job?"

"No, I don't. I want to be with my friends right now. Having fun."

"So go."

"I can't. My mom says we need the money."

"All right then," he said, smugly clearing his throat. "Our second duty is to make sure the place isn't full of trash. If it is, that's a fire hazard. We bag up what we can, set the stuff on the curb, and page the sanitation team."

"Sounds disgusting."

He ignored me. "Then, if we've accomplished tasks one and two, we can move on to task three and spray-paint a red $X$ on the door." And then he actually pulled out the spray paint can, shook it up, and pretended to do just that. "The red $X$ means a house is ready to be torn down."

I rolled my eyes. "Can we go inside now?"

"I can, but you can't."

"Why not?"

"Because this house is too damaged, and you are wearing capri jeans, or whatever you call them, and, like, little girl sneakers."

"They're Keds."

"Whatever. Also I forgot to bring a hard hat for you."

"So what am I supposed to do while you're inside?"

"Sit and wait for me."

"I'll still get paid for this one, right?" Levi had told me we'd get twenty bucks a house, to split down the middle.

He pulled a face. "Do you think that's fair? What will you have done to earn that money?"

"I'm here lending moral support."

"Lucky me," he grumbled, and shut the front door harder than I felt necessary.

That was fine by me. I sat on the stoop and waited for Levi

to do his thing, while refreshing Jesse's video page, hoping to see some smashed toilets.

We went through a couple of houses like that and then moved deeper into town, where things weren't as bad. Maybe some damage to the roof or a busted window or two. A soggy carpet or a swampy basement. But totally repairable. Salvageable, so long as someone wanted to save it. Which, apparently, these families didn't. Levi allowed me to enter those houses.

The abandoned homes were like giant doll houses, without any furniture or appliances. Some of the people had taken care to leave their place clean. Some people had swept the floors. Some houses smelled like Windex and bleach. Other people had left piles of trash and weird belongings behind. Those were the kinds of houses where Levi handed me trash bags and put me to work.

Though it was gross to sift through that stuff, it was also kind of interesting. Every time I found something random, I'd hold it up. A pair of antlers. A bowling ball. A shoe box full of smudgy old reading glasses. I'd assign myself points out loud for every weird find, as if we were playing a game with each other.

We weren't. Sometimes Levi looked at whatever it was, sometimes he didn't bother.

"Levi! Come up here!"

He came bounding up the stairs. "What?"

I pointed across the bathroom. There was a completely decorated artificial Christmas tree in someone's shower stall. "Whoever put this here was clearly trying to mess with us. Right?" Levi barely smiled. "I mean, this has to be worth like a hundred and fifty points."

He sighed, completely exasperated. "Keeley, I don't care why it's there, but it has to go."

Then, out of nowhere, in the last house of the day, Levi came walking into the room I was in. "Umm, how many points do I get for this?" He lifted up a hand and presented a black tuft of fur.

"What the hell is that? A stuffed animal?"

"Nope."

"Dead cat?" I asked, wincing.

"It's . . . a toupee."

I gasped. "Eww!"

Levi turned it over in his hands. "I don't get it. So this guy wanted people in Aberdeen to think he had hair, but in his new life, he's okay with being bald?"

"Please put it on."

"What? No!"

"Please, Levi. Please. I've always wondered what you'd look like with hair."

He rubbed his hands over his peach fuzz like he was contemplating it.

"My uncle used to wear one," he said. "I had no idea when I was little. It was dark brown and really shiny. Anyway, one time when I was maybe four, he slapped it on my head when I was hugging him good-bye, just to be funny."

"That is funny."

"Well, he wasn't laughing after I peed on him." I must have made a gross-out face because Levi got all defensive. "What? It was very traumatic."

"Okay, here's a little tip from me to you. Next time you tell that story, leave the pee part out, especially if you're telling it to a girl."

"Thanks for the advice." He flung the hairpiece at me like a Frisbee.

Then Levi must have realized he was having fun. Because he immediately turned around and walked out.

Later that night, my parents and I watched the KPBC nightly news with our dinner on our laps. Mom had been too tired to cook, but Mineo's was still closed, so we couldn't order pizza. Luckily, she found a box of Bisquick in the cabinets and made us pancakes.

The reporter—Shawn Wilcox—introduced my dad as one of the leaders of what he called the Reservoir Resistance.

I laughed out loud. "Oh, Dad, seriously? That's so corny!"

Dad, his mouth full, said something like "I didn't say that! It was his idea!"

Mom scooted in from the kitchen with a fresh pancake balanced on a spatula. She dropped it on my plate and said, "Annie said you'd talked to a reporter, but she didn't tell me anything about this."

Dad turned in his seat and offered a goofy smile.

Corny moniker aside, Dad looked good on television. Handsome, even. But he was nervous. He wasn't sure where to look, at the reporter or at the camera, so he went back and forth between the two. He also kept squinting and running his hands through his hair. "It's crystal clear why Governor Ward wants to get rid of Aberdeen. He might think if he plays dumb about his waterfront deal, we won't put two and two together, but I'm here to assure him that we weren't born yesterday. We know what he's up to."

"You're referring to the Waterford City redevelopment project currently on hold."

"I am. And I also find it strange that our own mayor isn't advocating for us. Why? Where is he going to go after there's no more Aberdeen? Has Governor Ward offered him a new position, possibly in his cabinet? He's got to be getting something out of this."

I glanced over at Dad. He was throwing down some serious accusations. Stuff I knew he couldn't actually prove. I wondered if the reporter would question him on it, but instead, he moved on and asked, "Isn't this the chance of a lifetime? You and your family can start over someplace new with a payout lining your pockets. Set down new roots."

My dad shook his head, resolute. "This is not about money. This is about our identity. My family has been living in Aberdeen for over a hundred and fifty years, on a street named after my great-great-grandfather. We're not going to be able to find that in some other town. That's the kind of thing worth fighting for."

"Are you saying, then, that you won't be leaving Aberdeen?"

I set my fork down and leaned forward.

"I have to believe there are other options, other ways the government can think about addressing the flooding issue that won't require such a sacrifice from the people of this town. I'm encouraging my neighbors not to speak with the adjusters, to refuse to make deals until we know for sure that we've exhausted all other options. And I'd like to invite anyone who might support me in that idea to a protest this Sunday in front of Aberdeen City Hall, where we will call on Mayor Aversano to be accountable to the people who elected him. I want proof that he has our best interests at heart, that this is truly the only way forward. If he can show us that, then I'll sign whatever they want me to sign."

His last words hung in the air. Dad quickly turned to Mom and me and said, "Don't worry. I'm not signing anything. I said it to look reasonable."

I smelled a burning pancake in the kitchen.

Mom bit on her thumbnail. "I'm afraid of you making yourself a target. I mean . . . you said some pretty out-there things just now. And you're already disobeying orders by helping people repair their houses. I don't want you getting arrested."

"Who's going to arrest me? Sheriff Hamrick?" Our telephone rang. Dad lifted himself off the couch. "Trust me. I'm thinking about our future. That's the one thing I care about above everything else."

He held his hand on the receiver and let the phone ring and ring. Mom finally nodded. Only then did he answer it.

I jumped up and took the spatula from Mom's hand and walked quickly into the kitchen. The pancake was charred. I threw it into the trash, turned off the heat, and opened the window over the sink so the smoke detector wouldn't go off.

---

## 21

**Friday, May 20**
Sunny, 66°F

---

Though I had all the hope in the world for Dad's rally, especially after seeing the parental anger in the gym the day before, I knew it was way unlikely that our school year would be salvaged. Everyone must have felt the same way, because things immediately fast-forwarded to that End of Year feeling. There wasn't much learning going on, that's for sure. Lesson plans were replaced by movies. Hall passes were handed out liberally, for any and no reason. Teachers offered us extra credit for nonsense tasks like taking down a bulletin board in the back of their classroom or packing a box of books. I definitely wasn't complaining. In one day, I managed to raise my average in every single class.

Jesse sent me a text during third period. It was a picture of the art room full of supplies.

You should loot this for the rally. We can make signs and stuff.

It was such a sweet yet illegal idea. I curled up in my chair. Where are you?

I'm down in the gym grabbing stuff for Julia. Do you think she's too young for badminton?

I don't think so. Not if you hang the net low for her.

Follow-up question: by "grabbing" do you mean "stealing"?

You can't steal trash. Coach Dean tipped me off. There's a Dumpster already parked outside. Everything Must Go! So why can't it go to me?

I was not surprised to hear Coach Dean had given Jesse that heads-up. Jesse had that kind of chummy, lovable persona that made teachers treat him special. I did too, mostly. The only exception for me was Principal Bundy.

Also taking a couple of the floor scooters. Hey! Let's do an Aberdeen Gym Olympics. You and I can be the judges and we can award people trophies from the trophy case outside the main office.

Umm, you are crazy! I wrote, even though it did sound super-fun. They will totally notice if you steal the trophies!

No one's going to miss a 2nd place state bowling trophy from 1971. And no one will miss a couple sheets of poster board and a set of markers. Go get them! It's for a good cause!

I was happy to hear Jesse say that. I wondered if his mom would show up at the rally. And though I didn't want to infer too much, maybe if Aberdeen was saved, we'd be saved too. I'd take any possible extra time I could get with Jesse. A week, a day, a minute, a second.

It was as if he could see me hesitating.

Come on, girl. Be brave. All this crap is getting pitched. Plus, Ms. Scala left town already. I bet she's halfway to Paris by now. You know how she has those posters of the Louvre hanging all over her classroom.

No way! Ms. Scala is gone?

Yup. I heard some of the other teachers trying to guess how much she got for her house when I was grabbing my morning cup of coffee from the teachers' lounge.

OMG Jesse. Only you.

I didn't even ask to go to the bathroom. I just got up and slipped out. Mr. Zeilman had a movie on. I'm not sure what *Jurassic Park* had to do with social studies, but whatever. I had already ensured an A+ for the semester because I'd rolled up all his classroom maps and stuck them into cardboard tubes.

Jesse was right. Our school was getting cleared out fast. Every single trash can was overflowing with things that wouldn't normally be considered trash at all. Textbooks and supplies and even computers. It was grossly wasteful. We should have donated the stuff to another school, maybe even in another country. But that would have required someone in the administration caring. And it seemed like, for them anyway, caring was in short supply.

I walked through the halls and made my way to the art room. Through the window in Ms. Scala's door, I saw there wasn't anyone inside her classroom and the lights were off. It was full of supplies, just like Jesse had said. And Ms. Scala's desk was cleared off. I guess she really was gone.

I put my hand on the doorknob.

"Keeley? What do you think you're doing?"

I turned around and there was Principal Bundy, arms crossed, smug smile on her bitchy face.

"I . . . wanted to see Ms. Scala. I had a question for her. About art."

Bundy narrowed her eyes. "You're not a good liar, Keeley."

"I'm not lying," I said. "I really did have a question for her. A Picasso question."

Bundy was not amused. "There's such a thing as taking a joke too far, Keeley. Have you honestly not learned that yet?"

My heart was thundering in my chest.

Bundy stepped past me and reached for the doorknob. She seemed pleased to find it locked. "At some point, people stop laughing with you and begin laughing at you."

I know she wanted to provoke a reaction in me, just like she had at Mock Congress. I wasn't going to give it to her. I was going to walk away. But then I spotted Jesse Ford opening a door from an adjacent classroom and stepping into the art room. He grinned and held his finger up to his lips, like *shhhhhh*.

"Um, yeah, you're right. People have been laughing at you for a long time, Principal Bundy."

Bundy's eyes went wide. She was shocked and completely oblivious to what was happening behind her back. "How dare—"

"What's your problem with me, anyway?"

"I don't have a problem with you."

I grinned like a little shit. "You're not good at lying either."

The funny thing is, I wouldn't have done any of this, dared say any of this, if not for the circumstances of giving Jesse cover. But it still felt incredible to stand up to her for once.

"Things might be ending, but you still need to treat me with respect."

"But I don't respect you."

Her cheeks lost all their color. "Keeley, report to my office immediately."

I laughed. I actually laughed. "What are you going to do?

Expel me?" Right then, I watched Jesse, arms full of supplies, sneak back into the adjacent classroom.

"I'm going to go now," I announced in the bitchiest voice I could muster. And I didn't wait for an answer. I just started walking away.

When I rounded the corner and realized that Principal Bundy wasn't coming after me, I pressed my back up against one of the lockers and bit my fist to keep myself from whooping it up.

I was almost back to my classroom when Jesse texted me. That was beyond hot. Meet me under the bleachers?

What was my life? I walked straight past social studies and pushed out the door into the sunshine.

Though I'd suggested we go out for lunch that day, Elise actually wanted to eat in the cafeteria one last time.

Unfortunately, I lost track of time with Jesse, and about fifteen minutes into the period, I got a text from Morgan asking, Where are you?!? This is our last lunch period all together!

"Shit," I said, jumping up. We'd been working on signs and making out. "I'm late for lunch."

"Wait, don't go. I can't go out tonight because I have to watch Julia," he said, trying to cling to me. He grabbed my arm, and then one of the belt loops of my jeans, and then my back pocket.

I wriggled free and sprinted across the field back toward the cafeteria. "Text you later!"

I found them at our regular table. Elise had all her favorites— chicken fingers, pizza, French fries, the cookies with little broken bits of M&Ms in them—and spread it out, family style. She'd bought drinks, too: Sprite for me, raspberry iced tea for Morgan, water for herself.

"I'm so sorry I'm late!"

Elise gave me a knowing look. "She's been kissing Jesse," she said, cocking her head toward Morgan but keeping her eyes on me. "See how her lips are all bee-stung and pouty. And her face is sparkling." As soon as she said it, her forehead wrinkled up. "Wait a second. You're *actually* sparkling. Is that glitter on your face?"

I wiped my cheek with the back of my hand, which I then noticed was slashed in marker. "Jesse and I were under the bleachers, making signs for Dad's rally."

Elise's smile faded.

I'd been careful not to talk too much with Elise about what my dad was up to. I wanted to be sensitive. Her house was gone, she was moving to Florida regardless of how things would shake out. I shared a strained look with Morgan and then I noticed the notebook she had open in front of her. Quickly, I pointed to it and said, "Anyway, what are you guys up to? Tic-tac-toe wars?"

"We're working on the guest list for Elise's good-bye party."

Now that Elise's family had plane tickets, Monday loomed over us and lent an urgency to our remaining time together. Elise still wanted to be pouty, but honestly, I think we were all aware that there wasn't time for that. So she shook whatever annoyance she had with me away. "Okay. So the latest is"—and her face went excited again—"it's a two-pronged thing. I'm going to invite people to the hotel to swim. And then, afterward, I convinced my parents to rent us our own hotel room for the night. So we can spend my last night here together."

"Whoa. That's awesome!" I dropped into my seat and started chomping on a French fry.

Morgan readied her pen.

Elise started with friends from school. The girls in our homeroom, some of her friends from Dance Committee.

Elise looked up at me benevolently. "Jesse Ford, of course. And we should probably invite Zito, too, so he won't be lonely without him."

"Thanks," I said. It was nice, but I was also aware that having Jesse Ford at her party would only make Elise look cool in front of her other friends.

Then Elise and Morgan went over which friends from Saint Ann's to include.

Suddenly, Elise touched Morgan's arm, but she kept her eyes on me. "What do you think about inviting Wes?"

Morgan stiffened. It was clear this was an ambush. She was just as surprised as I was.

I shrugged. "I don't have a problem with it."

I honestly didn't. In fact, I'd love for Wes to see how a good boyfriend was supposed to behave. Jesse wouldn't insult anyone. He wouldn't try to make people feel bad about themselves. Jesse would be so funny and fun, he'd probably organize chicken fights in the pool or a cannonball contest. Maybe a synchronized swim to send Elise off. I imagined Wes standing on the pool's edge, arms folded, pouting, absolutely no fun at all. It might even help Morgan to see the contrast so clearly. If there was any part of her that still missed Wes, I bet that would erase it for good.

Also, it would likely be the last Wes land mine I'd ever have to navigate. With Elise gone, I certainly wasn't ever crossing paths with those guys again. And I doubted Morgan would either.

"I don't know," Morgan said. "Maybe that isn't such a great idea." She kept her head down, and she picked at the paper fringe inside the metal spiral of her notebook.

Elise blinked a few times. "Okay, no problem. I just thought I'd throw it out there."

I'm still not sure of Elise's intentions, if she really wanted Wes at her party, or if she was looking for a way to make trouble between Morgan and me. Whatever it was, though, it definitely worked out in my favor.

# 22

---

## Friday, May 20
Increasing clouds through the afternoon, turning to rain by early evening, low of 54°F

---

After school, I waited out front for Levi. But he didn't show. So I texted him, Yo. I'm here, where are you?

No. I'M here. Where are YOU?

I turned around in a circle. Are you pranking me?

I'm at the police station. I texted you earlier to meet me there.

You did not. And then I scrolled through my messages, just to make sure. I have no message like that from you.

I stood there, waiting for him to write back. It took a while. I glanced up at the school clock. Someone had removed the golden hands. It was now just a blank face. And it bummed me out.

Sorry. It was in my drafts folder.

Idiot. I angrily typed, Well, are you coming to pick me up?

I have to talk to my dad. Meet me here.

Luckily, the police station wasn't far from the high school. Just a few blocks away, the building next to City Hall. But it didn't make me any less annoyed. I hated this job. Hated it more than anything. Both the work, which was so boring, and the company, which was terrible.

The police station hummed with activity, people busily attending to phone calls or the copier or phones.

I didn't see Levi, so I took a seat to the side of the front counter. A few officers eyed me up as they passed, likely because of Dad.

Finally Levi walked out, followed by Sheriff Hamrick. Levi limply handed me some paperwork. "You need to fill this out to get paid."

I felt so dirty, working through the blank forms, signing up to help the enemy. Because every single house Levi and I would clear would be one less family who could join Dad in the fight to save Aberdeen. I was almost relieved that the third blank was something I couldn't answer. I looked up and announced, "I don't know my social security number."

Grinning, Levi glanced at his father, who was leaning across the counter. "Did you hear that, Dad?"

Sheriff Hamrick hadn't. He was speaking to a woman behind the desk. So Levi said, louder, "Keeley doesn't know her social security number either."

"No excuse. Get that residency paperwork in the mail tomorrow, Levi."

"Okay, okay." Levi pushed out the door, leaving me to follow a few steps behind.

"What was that about?"

"College stuff. He's worried I'm going to get shut out of the summer session dorms if I don't hand in some health form, but it doesn't work like that. Whatever. I don't care. Let's go."

I shrugged. "All right. So. How many houses are we going to do today?"

"Why, you have someplace else to be?" he huffed.

"Yes, as a matter of fact."

Levi dropped his head backward. "Are you always like this?"

"Like what?"

"Fucking impossible?"

I let my mouth fall wide open. I had never, ever heard Levi curse once.

"Sorry."

"Don't be. I'm actually kind of impressed."

He rolled his eyes. "Well, that says a lot."

We did seven houses, only three of which we were able to give an *X*. But seventy bucks was seventy bucks, and if I just thought of the work as a business transaction, I found it went much more painlessly.

Levi looked over his list. "I'm thinking we skip this last place."

I stood behind him on my tiptoes to see what he was pointing at, an address that we'd apparently skipped the last time we were out too. "You sure?" I tried not to sound too enthusiastic, but really, I did want to get over to Morgan's. And Levi didn't seem all that into the work today. I didn't know if it was the tiff with his dad or what, but he wasn't his normal taskmaster, anal-retentive self. It was like he was sleepwalking.

"Yeah. Better we get home before it starts to pour."

We closed up the front door and sprayed our red *X*. A big roll of thunder rumbled over our heads.

"I think we're too late for that," I said. We made it a few steps off the porch before a few pitter-patters quickly gave way to a downpour. We ran back inside the house for cover and stood at the windows.

With the stormy sky, it was suddenly very dark in the house, and there was no electricity to turn on.

"Don't be nervous. This isn't going to last long," he said.

"Okay."

"And this rain won't be enough to flood things."

"Okay."

"And if we got into trouble, we could always call in to my dad."

"I'm not scared, Levi, but you're starting to scare me."

"Sorry."

The next few minutes passed quietly.

And then, out of nowhere, Levi said, "I saw your dad on the news, talking about his rally. He sounded pretty confident."

"It's easy to be confident because he's right. What's happening to Aberdeen is a thousand percent fucked up. At least he has the courage to say so."

I expected him to defend his dad or the mayor. He didn't. Instead he said, "I read his manifesto thing. He made some interesting points."

"That's big of you to say." I sighed. "Did your dad read it?"

"Doubtful. He's busy, Keeley. He's working, like, twenty-four hours a day."

I thought about how my dad had said Mayor Aversano probably was getting something out of supporting the governor. If he was, I bet Sheriff Hamrick would too. It could be the smoking gun my dad needed. Proof that Governor Ward was giving kickbacks to all the people helping him clear Aberdeen out. So I straight-up asked Levi. "What's in it for your dad?" Levi looked like he didn't understand the question at first. "He obviously won't be the sheriff if this all goes down as planned."

Levi shrugged. "He's been thinking about leaving Aberdeen for a long time now. Especially after I got into college."

"Oh, so this has nothing to do with a cushy appointment somewhere else? Pretty convenient timing."

"A cushy appointment? Come on, Keeley. He might take another job. I don't know anything about it. But I know he's not staying here. Nobody's going to have that choice. Here is going to be gone."

"We'll see."

"Yeah, we will."

We stayed in the house a little while longer, both of us on our phones. Then the rain let up a little, and I think neither of us wanted to wait until it stopped completely. So I climbed on the back of Levi's bike and let him give me a ride to Morgan's.

Morgan and Elise were sitting on the bedroom floor surrounded by stuff. So much stuff, it was hard to push open the door.

I didn't realize my mouth was hanging open until Morgan teased, "Relax, Keeley. I'm not packing."

But even though that was what she said, it looked like packing to me. Or at least preliminary packing. And if it wasn't, why did Elise roll her eyes? I totally caught her doing it, and it instantly made my stomach feel sour. I'd thought whatever annoyance she'd felt at me had been squashed before the end of lunch. But maybe not.

Anyway, Morgan had clothes in piles on the floor. I could see how she sorted them based on what was where. The clothes that were newer, or that I knew she liked, were set neatly near her desk. A seersucker sundress. Her favorite jeans, with the rip in the knee. Her fall coat, a red wool one with a hood and wooden toggle buttons, which was only one season old.

The other clothes were rolled up into balls. Heaped into piles. A stretched-out T-shirt that was once her favorite but that now she only wore to bed. A bathing suit from two summers ago. A pair of denim overall shorts.

Elise opened a box and dug out a white leotard with a tutu made of feathers. "How cute is this?"

"My old dance recital costumes! I haven't looked at these in years!"

I changed out of my wet clothes and then sat on Morgan's bed, watching as they pulled things out of the box. Elise reacted to the cuteness, the tininess of every outfit. But I knew what every costume was, the recital Morgan had worn it in. At one point, I grabbed her strawberry outfit after Elise had tossed it aside. With a lot of wriggling, I managed to pull it on over my clothes, and did a few of the moves from the April Showers dance, which of course sent Morgan into hysterics. Elise went over and sat at Morgan's desk and began testing nail polish colors, painting stripes along her thumbnail, determined not to laugh.

After taking a bow, I sat down with my back against the wall and tried to catch my breath. That's when I noticed one small box in her keep pile. The flaps hadn't been closed and I saw all the Wes stuff she'd hidden in her top drawer.

I took out my phone and started scrolling through who knows what, just to have something else to stare at.

"Whoa," Morgan gasped. "Keeley! Check it out!"

She sank to the floor, cross-legged, next to me. In her lap was our sticker album.

I say *our*, even though it was a gift for Morgan from her grandmother the summer before we started high school.

Yes, high school.

Every holiday, every birthday, every possible gift-buying occasion that passed, we were reminded that Morgan's grandmother was under the delusion that Morgan was perpetually nine years old. The presents she got were always weird and completely off-base, like a dolly or a craft kit to puffy-paint a jean jacket. We'd always laugh so hard about them on the ride home, and they were honestly such bizarre picks that Mrs. Dorsey never scolded us for being rude.

But the sticker album truly blew our minds. There were collection pages with headings like *Rainbows Forever* and *My Favorite Animals* and *Funny.* When I saw that page in particular, I laughed so hard, I peed a little. What the eff kinds of stickers went on that page? There were blank pages too, in the back, with spaces to create your own categories.

For whatever reason, likely boyless boredom, we became obsessed with filling it up.

We were always looking for stickers. We'd buy them at the drugstore, we'd order them online, it was always the aisle we'd hit at the Walmart—just past the greeting cards and just before the art supplies.

And every single time we'd go to Viola's Market, we'd stop at the sticker machine near the exit doors. Two quarters and you could have a rubber moon bounce ball, a plastic egg with a fake gold necklace, or a sticker. The stickers would come out sandwiched between two pieces of stiff white cardboard. There were a couple Morgan always hoped to get. Two unicorns frolicking under one rainbow, a pink teddy bear with hearts for eyes that I found slightly creepy. Those were the ones advertised in the glass display right above where you put your quarters in. But they proved to be somewhat elusive, to the point where Morgan was convinced they weren't in the machine at all. Without fail, she'd get something weirdly masculine, like a reflective motorcycle or a skull and crossbones or a dagger dripping blood. We even dedicated a whole page in the book to *Biker Gangs*.

Our best page, though, was the very last one. Morgan knew it too. When she opened the book up, she flipped right to the back.

*The Story of Morgan and Keeley*

After we got bored with filling the assigned pages, we decided to use stickers like emojis or codes and tell our future life story. It was part of the challenge, using whatever you got to push the story further along, like those exercises you do in creative writing class. Morgan always said, though, that if we ever managed to score the double unicorn from Viola's, it was game over. There could be no happier ending than that.

It looked like hieroglyphics. A banana-seat bicycle, Strawberry Shortcake and her friends dancing around a mushroom, a reflective globe, a heart, a reflective unicorn, a dinosaur. All carefully, deliberately placed, left to right across the page.

Morgan pointed at a metallic Batman and Robin, racing off to fight, the lights of Gotham City twinkling behind them. "Was this supposed to represent our future husbands?"

"No. This was supposed to be us going on vacation to New York City once we graduated high school."

"I can't believe you remember that."

Elise spun around to face us, flapping her hands through the air so her fingernails would dry. She'd gone with a plum-colored polish. "Wait, when did you guys do this?"

"Eighth grade," I said. "Or, actually, the summer before ninth."

Elise laughed dryly. "That's a little babyish, no?"

I felt my face burn.

Like I said before, Elise always made little comments about how immature I was, but never as pointedly as this. I had an idea why. The space she'd carved out between me and Morgan was closing fast, both because of the move and because I was now with Jesse.

Morgan laid a hand on my shoulder and pushed herself up off the floor. Then she put the sticker book at the very top of her keep pile. "Shut up," she said to Elise. "You told me once that in eighth grade you were still sucking your thumb."

I snorted with laughter, even though it wasn't even that funny. And maybe I should have given Elise a pass, since she was going through a lot. But the chance to make her feel like the immature one for once was too good for me to pass up.

# 23

The morning of the City Hall protest, the coffee in Dad's cup got cold while he leaned over his speech and made adjustments with one of his stubby, knife-sharpened work pencils, the kind he normally used to make saw lines on two-by-fours. I'd only seen him more nervous one other time, when I walked into the hospital room right after his accident, before the X-rays came back and the surgeons discussed a plan and the pain medicine kicked in and we knew for sure that he'd walk again.

I have to admit, I was also nervous for him. My mom, too. A lot was riding on today. If there was going to be any chance of saving Aberdeen, then we'd need to stop people from meeting with the adjusters and taking deals.

At least the weather was nice. It felt like spring, like everything maybe still could be okay.

While Dad fiddled with his speech, we flew around the house, loading up the truck with the protest signs, filling a cooler with bottles of water, packing up the clear plastic drums of pretzel rods and cheese puffs we'd bought at Walmart, in case anyone got hungry.

We drove over to City Hall, all of us in Mom's car. The ride was super-quick, I think we got there in two minutes, but it felt like forever because it was so quiet, all except for some deep, chest-emptying exhales my dad would push out, as if he were blowing up a balloon.

I tried to make small talk to brighten the mood.

"Anyone want to hear some of the protest chants I've been working on?"

Mom chuckled nervously and nudged Dad. "Uh-oh."

I leaned forward. "Okay. So I think we open with the classic 'Hell no, we won't go!' It's got a lot of energy, everyone knows it."

Mom smirked. "She's really thought this through."

"Then we switch over to 'Power to the people!' to amp up the energy, keep the crowd excited, link those potential passive bystanders to our cause by their mere proximity."

Dad slowly turned his head, and I knew he hadn't been listening, but I kept going.

"I took the liberty of creating a new chant, something fresh and specific to our fight. Check this out." I cleared my throat. "Gov-er-nor, go away, let Aberdeen stand another day!" I sang, to the tune of "Rain, Rain, Go Away."

Dad reached back and ruffled my hair. "I love it."

We pulled around the corner of City Hall. There was a line of people wrapping around the sandstone building, each one occupying a square of sidewalk like in a human board game. And a couple of police officers standing guard. I guess they were called in to make sure things didn't get out of hand or that we didn't try to interfere with the people who were waiting to speak with the adjusters. But either way, their presence showed that Sheriff Hamrick was taking us seriously at the very least. I kept an eye out for Levi, wondering if he might show up, even if just to check things out, but he wasn't there and neither was his father.

"Look, Dad!" I said, pointing. "That's a lot of people!"

He leaned forward to the passenger window, but then just as quickly leaned back into his seat. "Those people are waiting to meet with the adjusters. We told our crowd to meet at the park across the street, near the gazebo where Mom and I got married."

"Oh." I felt terrible about my mistake, but not for long. Because as we turned into the park, we saw a crowd there, too. Maybe close to two hundred people total, way more than were in the line across the street.

"Okay," Dad said, a smile finally gracing his face. "I can breathe now. We aren't the only ones who showed up."

"Of course we aren't," Mom said, giddy. "Did you really think that?"

I reached forward and gave her shoulder a happy squeeze.

There were three news vans and reporters—Shawn Wilcox, the one my dad had spoken to outside school, and another man and a woman I recognized from other stations. All had their cameramen taking footage.

We parked, and as Dad opened the car door, the people in the park applauded him.

I pulled on his sleeve. "If you're able to pull this off, Dad, who knows? You could be the next mayor of Aberdeen!"

I'm not sure if my words inspired him or what, but when Dad walked through the crowd of supporters, he sure did play the part of a politician. He moved his cane to his left hand and shook hands with people with his right, thanking them for coming. Then he greeted the three reporters.

He looked young, strong, and handsome.

Morgan called out for us. She and Mrs. Dorsey raced over, waving excitedly. In that moment, I felt like I could see the future. Here Morgan was, supporting me, and standing just a few feet away was her mom supporting my mom. This was what I always felt our friendship would grow into. We would always be in each other's lives. Our mothers were proof that was possible. Or, not just possible, but our destiny.

Mrs. Dorsey hip-checked Mom. "This is really impressive, I have to say."

"Isn't it?" Mom was beaming. "He's worked so hard."

"Yes," Mrs. Dorsey said, and I caught her sharing a quick look with Morgan. "Yes, he certainly has. And we are all glad to see that." Then she hugged my mom, tight.

I saw Jesse's hatchback pull into the parking lot. I grabbed Morgan's hand. "Come on!" We ran through the crowd, which had the atmosphere of a festival. Everyone I saw was smiling. Upbeat.

Jesse popped out and hugged me, then Morgan. Julia bolted from the backseat and ran straight for the nearby playground. But there was someone notably missing.

"Is your mom coming?"

We'd talked about it underneath the bleachers. I'd asked Jesse what his mom was planning to do, if she'd heard anything about the rally. Jesse said he was keeping her completely filled in. And if she didn't have to work, she'd most likely come. I was looking forward to meeting her for real.

Jesse pouted. "She ended up getting called in this morning. Sorry." He slung an arm around me. "But we are here as her representatives. And Zito's on his way too, with a few of the soccer guys. I told them to wear their uniforms." He opened the backseat and there were all the posters we'd made together, plus a few other ones that Julia must have worked on, because the handwriting was very squiggly and shaky and unsure. Seeing me notice, he said, "She had no idea that Craft Time was actually forced child labor." Morgan and I laughed at that. "Hey, where's Elise?"

Morgan answered. "She went back to the hotel to get ready for her party tonight. Also . . ." She paused, choosing her words carefully, "I think this is tough for her, you know."

"Oh yeah. Right. Totally."

I noticed that Jesse was not in his uniform. He was in a pair of jeans and an old T-shirt with the sleeves cut away. "If you told Zito and those guys to wear uniforms, why aren't you wearing yours?" I asked, already knowing that his answer would be interesting.

Grinning, he said, "I thought you'd never ask." He raced around to the back of his car and popped the hatch. Inside was the furry suit of our high school's mascot, Hawkeye the River Hawk, like a deflated plush balloon. Brown body and wings, yellow socks, yellow plush claw feet that strapped over your shoes, big brown head with angry eyes and a snarling yellow beak. And of course, an Aberdeen High hunter green and gold athletic jersey.

I gasped. "Where did you get this?"

"That gym Dumpster I told you about. Can you believe it?"

Morgan reached in to pet the hawk head. "I haven't seen this in forever. Maybe since sophomore year?"

"You're right. I remember the kid who used to wear it. Max something? After he graduated, I don't think anyone else took it over. I should have asked about it. I totally would have played mascot in the off-season."

I said, "It's a little mangy-looking."

"Yes, yes. Hawkeye has seen better days. But I figured there's no better way to get the crowd pumped up than a little River Hawk pride. Also, this is going to make killer footage for the news guys."

I threw my arms around him. "You are the best." And I stood on tiptoes to kiss his cheek. "Here," I said. "Give me your phone. I'll film you getting changed in the backseat, and then, burst out of the car, okay? Like a superhero."

"You're perfect," he said, kissing me on the forehead.

My family and I watched ourselves on the news that night, before I left for Elise's good-bye party. Dad was on the couch, Mom nestled into the crook of his arm.

The rally was the top story of the evening. The studio anchor threw it live to Shawn Wilcox, still standing on the steps of the now-quiet City Hall. He lifted his microphone to his mouth.

"The showdown over Aberdeen's future hit a fevered pitch today with a rally at City Hall. Mr. Jim Hewitt, self-appointed leader of the Reservoir Resistance, said he came here looking for two things: answers and accountability."

They cut to their tape. Shots of our protesters as they paced the sidewalk, signs bobbing up and down against a darkening sky, chanting my rally cries. Of course, they showed Jesse in the mascot uniform, jumping around and fist-pumping.

The cameraman also videoed three policemen who stood stoic as some of the people from our side chanted, "Bring out Aversano! Let him speak to the people!"

Dad leaned forward and kissed the top of Mom's head. "Okay, good. I was hoping they'd show that."

They cut to a shot of my dad on the steps of City Hall, speaking to the crowds and to the people waiting in line for the adjusters. He read off a paper cupped in his hand. But his delivery, if a little stiff, was impassioned.

"Mayor Aversano and Governor Ward, we demand our due process. We want assurance that our politicians aren't trying to turn our tragedy into their opportunity, at the expense of us, the people who call Aberdeen home." Dad focused on the news camera. "We know you've been lowballing our friends and neighbors during your supposed 'good faith' negotiations. And we're not going to stand for it any longer."

He said that lowball part so confidently, I didn't question it, even though I knew Elise's family had gotten a crazy payday. After all, Dad was talking to people in town about this every day. He must know more about it than I did.

They cut back to Shawn and his microphone, live on the steps. "Though this appears to be something of a David and Goliath fight, there were several residents of Aberdeen who left their spots in the line for adjusters and wandered over to hear more from the Reservoir Resistance movement. We asked the offices of both Governor Ward and Mayor Aversano for direct comment but have yet to hear back."

I heard the beep of Morgan's car outside. "I'm leaving."

Dad waved without looking, but Mom turned her head. "Okay. And Morgan is taking you to school tomorrow?"

"Yup." After a hotel breakfast, Morgan and I would head straight to school and Elise would leave for the airport. This night might be the last time I ever saw her. But I wouldn't let myself feel sad. I didn't want to be a downer. My job tonight was to bring the fun. Make sure Elise had the time of her life. Give her a proper send-off. Because even though things were weird between us, I still cared about her. Deeply.

"Have a good time," Mom said. Dad started playing with her hair, picking up little strands of it and letting them fall. Mom curled even closer into him. Across the room, Dad's laptop was off. And Mom's work bag was zippered up.

I pulled the front door shut and ran to Morgan. "Uh, I'm pretty sure my parents are having sex tonight."

"Eww!" Morgan screamed.

I made gagging sounds. "I know. I know. Hurry up and drive!"

About halfway to the hotel, Morgan said, "I need to tell you something. I told Elise today she could invite Wes if she wanted to." She turned to me for a second and then looked back at the road. "I didn't think it was right to forbid her to see him on her last night here." She wet her lips.

"Okay," I said, and tried to make it sound like I wasn't anxious. I quickly pulled out my phone and texted Jesse.

You're still coming tonight, right?

As soon as my mom gets home from work.

"You know . . ." She let the words hang in the air. "I wouldn't be surprised if Wes isn't super-nice to you. I bet he feels really bad about what happened." And then, less confidently, she added, "And I know you do too."

The rest of the ride to the hotel was pretty quiet. I know what both Morgan and I were thinking about. The last time I saw Wes, almost a month ago, the moment everything went to shit.

. . .

*Because we had nothing better to do that day, Morgan and I went to visit Wes at his family pharmacy. She wanted to text him a heads-up that we were coming, but I told her surprising him would be more romantic. It was the first time I'd given Morgan any boy advice. I felt good. Like I had made a place for myself in this new part of her life.*

*The pharmacy was cute. Sort of old-timey and on a tree-lined street. Morgan thought we'd go in and say a quick hello. Though they'd been a couple since Christmas, she still got super shy and awkward around him. She liked him that much. But I was on a roll. I had a much better idea.*

*We walked into the store. I pretended to shop, like a regular customer. Except I filled my basket with the most embarrassing items I could—tampons, condoms, lube, douche, gas pills, wart remover, adult diapers, stool softener, upper lip wax, a cushion pad for bunions. With each item Morgan gasped. Or she whispered something like "Oh, no, Keeley!" Not in a* stop it *way. In a* you're hilarious *way.*

*Still, Morgan peeled off from me right before we reached the register.*

*So it was just me standing there with my head down, waiting as Wes made change for an old lady. When she walked away, I stepped forward and smiled. "Hello."*

*"Hey," he said. At first he didn't look at me. He was just staring at the stuff in the basket. But then he finally did, and it took him a couple of seconds to place me. Aberdeen was a half hour away so it wasn't like we ran into each other around town. Once he did, though, he wasn't exactly happy to see me.*

*I tried teasing him into that feeling by acting like a legit customer, asking him to tell me which vaginal cream he might recommend, stuff like that.*

*He turned purple. And he started looking around in the aisles for Morgan. Maybe he hoped she would rescue him, drag me away. But Morgan was hiding behind a rack of reading glasses.*

*I had no idea that his parents were behind him. Both were pharmacists, I guess. They started watching our exchange. Which, from their angle, looked like Wes not being a very helpful employee.*

*Eventually, his mother asked, "Wes? Do you need help with anything?"*

*"No!" he said. And then he whispered to me through clenched teeth, "What are you doing?"*

*But even though he'd said no, his mom came around to the counter anyway. "Is everything okay, dear?" she asked me. But her face went from friendly to confused to put off when she eyed my basket.*

*"Sorry," I said. "I'm a friend of Wes's. I wanted to stop by and visit."*

*His mother's eyes lingered on the condoms.*

*"Um . . ." I laughed sheepishly. "We're not friends like that."*

*Frowning deeply, she fiddled with the cross around her neck before I turned around and called for Morgan.*

# 24

The pool was on the roof of the hotel, in an atrium topped by a glass canopy. It was nice—I liked the little blue mosaic tiles they used to line it—but smaller than I'd expected. The deep end wasn't even deep, it was only five feet, so you couldn't really jump in. There was a big hot tub, though, big enough for eight or nine people to each have a jet. I loved the feeling of going from hot to cold to hot again, but I wrapped myself in a towel and shared a lounge chair with Morgan once Wes and his friends arrived in their swim trunks and began taking off their shirts and shoes.

I saw him stealing glances at her a few times. So I told her, "You can go talk to him if you want." She hadn't yet. He hadn't made a move to talk to her, either. Probably because I was sitting next to her.

"I know," she said, and patted my leg.

Elise's family ordered in a bunch of pizzas, and they had cans of soda in silver ice buckets brought up from the hotel restaurant, and a stack of cloth napkins. Every twenty minutes or so, one of the waiters would come clean our mess or make sure the lounge chairs had fresh white towels rolled into cylinders and placed at the crook between the seat and the back.

I kept checking and rechecking my phone for word from Jesse. I knew he'd be late, but I didn't think he'd be this late. The party had been going over an hour already.

About ten minutes later, Jesse came in through the sliding glass doors, Zito close behind him, looking down at his phone. I quickly leaned back in the lounge chair and closed my eyes, as if I were tanning. I felt him walk over.

I had on my second-favorite bikini, since Jesse had already seen me in my favorite one that night at his Slip 'N Slide party. This one was an underwire top with a bit of padding in the cups, which made it seem like I had a tiny bit more boob than I actually did. It was white and magenta stripes with highlighter-blue and pale pink flowers dotted on. It looked better on me late in the summer, when I'd have some color built up.

"Hello, ladies."

I opened my eyes. They were wearing their swim trunks and sweatshirts, which had been speckled by rain. Jesse set down a gym duffel bag and then pulled his sweatshirt off and tossed it on the lounge chair next to mine. Morgan discreetly squeezed my hand because he looked so freaking hot. Then he planked over me on the lounge chair and gave me a kiss on the lips. When he started pulling away, I wrapped my arms around his neck and pulled him back down to kiss me again, hoping Wes would be watching at that very moment.

"You're in a good mood," Jesse said, and then lifted me up, his hands locked under my butt. I shivered at how suddenly close we were. I was still wet from the last dip in the water, and also, it was like we were practically naked. I think Jesse could tell that it startled me, because he slowly let me slide back down to the chair.

Jesse opened up his duffel bag and looped a whistle around his neck.

"Are you on duty?"

"I figured this would come in handy for games." He took out a set of speakers to plug into his phone. "Where's Elise?"

I nudged my chin across the pool. She'd spent most of the good-bye party sitting at a table with her parents, a fluffy bathrobe cinched tight around her. I didn't get it. Elise was all about this party, the planning, carefully selecting who to spend her last hours with, but now she was being completely antisocial.

I said, "Morgan and I agreed that we shouldn't monopolize her time, since we're having a sleepover after, but now I'm wondering if that was a bad plan."

"Totally a bad plan. She needs to be rescued from herself. She's going to think back on this night and be completely bummed that she blew it." He picked up his duffel bag and then took my hand. "Come on."

We walked right past the hot tub where Wes was, and I knew he was watching me and Jesse. We stopped in front of Elise's table.

"Keeley and I wanted to give you this parting gift." Out of his duffel, Jesse lifted up a huge mesh bag of Florida oranges. It was so big and heavy and ridiculous, at least twenty pounds of oranges. Elise started laughing and then crying. I watched Jesse carefully unclip the snaps on the mesh bag so when he presented it to Elise, the oranges tumbled out and rolled into the pool.

Jesse blew his whistle. "Rescue! Rescue!" He jumped in feetfirst, dragging me along with him. And we dove to grab the oranges. Zito jumped in next, but not before he lifted Morgan up off the lounge chair and dropped her in the water. Suddenly the place was alive.

Jesse got out of the water and stalked over to the table. He was dripping wet, and Elise saw him coming for her. "No! No!" she started screaming, but you could tell she was loving it. Jesse lifted her up and carried her down the steps, bathrobe and all, into the water. Like a baptism or something. Smiling for the first time, Elise hugged Jesse and then he let her swim free.

I basically became Jesse's fun assistant for the rest of the night. Anything he suggested to make a good time, I seconded. Chicken fights? I climbed on his shoulders. We took second place, but only because we let Elise and one of her guy friends from church take us down in the championship. Marco Polo? I offered to be *it* first. We even got everyone to push around and around to make a whirlpool.

Wes and his friends lingered around the side of the pool. They were ready to leave. At some point, they'd changed out of their bathing suits and into dry clothes. Elise climbed out of the pool to say good-bye to them.

"I'm cold," Morgan said, passing me in the water. "I think I'm going to get out for a bit."

"You want to go in the hot tub? Now that Wes and his friends aren't hogging it?"

I meant it as a joke, but Morgan barely smiled. "Nah."

She walked over to our chair and wrapped herself in a towel. She was trying not to look at Wes, but I know she was aware of him as much as I was. I think she was making herself available for him, if he did want to talk or apologize.

"You keep looking at that guy," Jesse said. "Are you trying to make me jealous? Because he seems like a weenie."

"No. Absolutely not." But I was glad he was getting jealous. "That's Morgan's ex. And . . . I hate him."

"Enough said."

Jesse called out to Zito and started to swim toward him, but I noticed that as he did, he started kicking harder than he needed to. Then he and Zito began to wrestle in the water, trying to dunk each other, and Jesse kept angling his body to make sure his wild splashes were going in Wes's direction. Wes took one step back, and then another, and finally turned around and walked out.

Morgan, I think, was a little shocked. Shocked and disappointed that he hadn't tried to talk to her. I felt bad for her, actually. But if Wes was going to let a little spray of water stop him from making things right with Morgan, well then, he wasn't worth pining over. I really hoped she saw that.

Later, after everyone went home, the three of us went up to our hotel room. Elise's family had reserved a second room especially for us, with two double beds. I already assumed how the sleeping arrangements would go. Morgan and Elise in one bed, me in the other. Which was fine.

Elise yawned. She must have been exhausted. I glanced at the clock on the nightstand. It was 10 p.m. I felt bad that we hadn't made it up here earlier, got to spend more time together. I think we all felt the night closing in on us.

"Order anything you want from room service," Elise announced. Morgan and I glanced at the menu. It was all expensive. But maybe not to Elise's family, now that they had all that money. "Seriously. I want this to be the best night. Something we all remember forever."

So we ordered three French fries, a hamburger, two plates of chicken fingers, a club sandwich, three Cokes, and three ice cream sundaes.

"Look what else we have to drink," Elise said after she hung up the phone. She opened the mini-fridge and pulled out two bottles of champagne.

"Whoa!" I said.

"I made friends with one of the bartenders at the lobby bar, and he let me charge two bottles of champagne to the room, but he put them down on the receipts as steaks." I wondered why he'd do that, but she explained, "He used to live in Aberdeen."

We popped them both open. What began as a slightly awkward sleepover became us at twelve years old. Unguarded, silly, crazy. Drunk.

About twenty minutes later, there was a knock at the door. We quickly fell to a hushing heap on the bed.

Morgan whispered, "Oh, we're in trouble. I bet someone complained to the manager!"

"No, dummy!" I said. "It's the food we ordered!"

There were a few more knocks.

Morgan said, "Keeley! You open the door! Just in case it is the manager!"

I was still in my bathing suit and a hotel robe. "Why me?"

Meanwhile, Morgan was trying to wrestle my robe open so it would hang loosely over my bikini. "Because you are brave. Go be cute and get us out of trouble!"

"I don't want to!"

Elise snapped, "One of you open the door already." Where she'd been smiling and having fun a moment ago, now she seemed suddenly annoyed. Morgan and I both noticed.

I tried to bring things back to fun. I sauntered up to the door, and Morgan laughed in a gingerly way, but Elise didn't.

I opened the door, sticking my leg out first, as if I were a burlesque dancer. Morgan flopped down on the bed next to Elise and nudged her. But again, Elise didn't laugh. In fact, she wiped her eyes.

"Umm . . . hey," came a voice slow and unsure from the other side of the door. "I have your food."

It was the room service boy. He looked nervous. I said, "This is a special friendship night for Elise. She's moving to Florida, and we're going to miss her terribly."

She laughed dryly. "I doubt you will, Keeley."

The boy blushed. I wasn't sure what I had done wrong, but Elise was fuming. And drunk.

The three of us were quiet then, until he pushed the white cart in, lifted the silver caps from all our trays, and poured each of our Cokes from the glass bottle into a glass full of crushed ice, with a flourish.

He was taking forever, but I never wanted him to go. I knew as soon as he left, things were going to pop off. And they did. Right after the room door clicked closed.

"Can I get something off my chest?"

I nodded, but only because I didn't have any other choice.

"I think it's pretty crappy that you never told me yourself about what's been going on with your dad. Instead, I had to hear it from everyone else that he's trying to single-handedly save Aberdeen. Oh, wait, except for the one time you slipped and mentioned the rally in front of me and looked all guilty about it."

"Elise. Come on."

"If you had given me a heads-up if we had known that maybe Aberdeen was still going to be around, maybe it wouldn't have been so easy for my uncle to talk us into Florida. We could have waited. We could have built a new house here." She looked over at Morgan, and a tear ran down her face.

It stung, knowing what this was really about. It wasn't that I hadn't told her, it was about losing Morgan.

"Elise, I had no idea that what he was doing might actually work! Also, I didn't want to say anything because I didn't want to upset you." That was the honest truth. "And look. Who knows! If my dad is able to break this whole thing apart, maybe your family can figure out a way to stay." I dropped my head back and stared at the ceiling.

"Keeley, you know that's not going to happen! Why would you even say that to me!" Then she added, "It's like, you aren't even sad that I'm leaving."

"That's crazy."

"Is it? Because you seemed to be having such a great time tonight despite knowing I'm gone tomorrow."

"I was trying to have a good time *for* you."

"I don't want to have a good time, okay?" Elise dove onto the bed and sobbed. "And you made me feel like there was something wrong with me for that. Like I was being some kind of spoiled brat at my own party."

I looked at Morgan, my hands up. I did not want to fight with Elise. I went out of my way to avoid talking about this stuff with her. She was the one hell-bent on dragging it up. I wanted Morgan to defend me.

But Morgan just held Elise and patted her hair.

Even though I was right next to them, I sent Morgan a text. Should I go?

No. Definitely not. She's not mad at you.

I was glad she said that, but I still wrote back, Umm . . . yeah. I'm pretty sure she is.

She's upset that she's leaving. Just give her a minute.

But Elise cried herself to sleep, and then Morgan fell asleep too, holding Elise in her arms.

I stayed in the other bed, by myself, and watched the TV on mute until I passed out.

# 25

I woke up hoping that the tension from last night had disappeared as the champagne had worked its way out of our bloodstreams, or that Elise would be able to push it aside for the sake of our good-bye. I lifted my head off the pillow. Elise was already dressed and picking up things like her phone charger and bathing suit and shoving them inside a backpack. She kept passing our room service dining cart, full of the food we'd ordered but hadn't touched. And it was as if she made it a point to always keep her back to me.

Morgan was up and dressed too, watching Elise from the other bed. When she realized I was awake, she turned and gave a weak smile.

"Hey, Keeley. I think we're going to go grab breakfast." Morgan said it in a way that told me I wasn't welcome to join. Elise ducked into the bathroom, and Morgan mouthed *Sorry* and I shook my head, like *Don't worry about it.*

"You two go on ahead," I announced. "I'm not hungry." I tried to make it sound like there actually was an invite, and that it was my choice to stay behind. "I'll take a shower and meet you both in the lobby."

So that's what I did. I showered and got dressed for school and then ate a couple of cold French fries. I took a picture of the bathroom telephone, mounted to the wall next to the toilet, and sent it to Jesse with the caption `Hello? Nature, is that you calling? You've got great timing!` Then I took the elevator downstairs to the lobby.

Elise and Morgan weren't there, they were probably still eating, so I wandered into the gift shop. After looking at a selection of travel neck pillows, I started pulling some things together for Elise to take with her on the plane. I bought her a variety of sweet and salty snacks, all the new gossip magazines, a bottle of water, a neck pillow that looked to be made from the skin of a pink Muppet, and a bracelet that supposedly prevented motion sickness. I spent all the money in my wallet on her.

By the time I returned to the lobby, Elise and Morgan were sitting on the edge of a decorative fountain near the front desk. Elise was crying again, and the sound filled up the whole space. Her parents had just come down, and they were headed into the restaurant to have breakfast, her two brothers lagging quietly behind them. Their flight to Florida wasn't until later that afternoon.

"You should go," Elise said, though she gripped Morgan tighter. "You'll be late for school."

"Call me when you get to the airport, okay? I don't care what class I'm in. I'll pick up."

Elise nodded. "Okay."

Morgan pulled back and guided Elise's bangs behind her ear. "And we can video chat tonight, after you land."

Elise took a deep breath and closed her eyes, like she was

trying to gather all her strength to hold it together. "Well, I guess this is it," she said, her voice breaking. "Love you."

"Love you, too. And I'll talk to you in a few hours."

After another long, gripping hug, Morgan stepped out of the way and put a hand on my back.

It was my turn.

I reminded myself that even though Elise was angry with me, we were still friends. Maybe not as good friends as she and Morgan had come to be, but friends nonetheless. I would miss her. And I knew she would miss me too. We deserved a nice good-bye too.

"Got you a few things for your flight," I said, handing over two big plastic bags. And to my great relief, she smiled just a bit. As she dug around, I added, "There's some fun stuff in there. I got that grape gum you like. Four packs of it."

I leaned in to hug her and whispered, "I'm sorry," as she pulled away, and though I wasn't sure for what, that didn't stop me from saying it. I didn't want her to be mad at me. I didn't want her to leave like this, with us on bad terms.

"It's fine, Keeley," she said. Not exactly forgiveness, but close enough.

Our ride back to Aberdeen was relatively quiet. Morgan wasn't exactly crying, but every minute or so, a tear would roll down her cheek.

I leaned forward and held my finger over the radio button. "Want to play Guess That Song?"

She nodded and wiped her cheeks with her sleeve. "Okay. You go first."

I turned the radio dial, heard the song, and vaguely recognized it, but not enough to call it. I hammed it up, though, sang the lyrics I knew, mumbled and garbled the ones I didn't.

Things felt better when we got to school. Morgan and I had a nice long hug before we parted ways for first period. Jesse had left me a surprise in my locker. One of those stolen trophies. A 1986 tennis championship golden girl with her racquet held high. But he'd covered up the plaque with masking tape and had written *Miss Aberdeen, MVP.* A few kids even some of our teachers stopped me in the halls to say that their parents were behind Dad 100 percent.

In some ways, it felt like the worst was over. I had my best friend back all to myself, and the boy of my dreams, and there was a decent chance that we'd be able to save Aberdeen. I weirdly had a lot to be happy about.

I texted Morgan from honors science, where everyone in class was popping popcorn over a Bunsen burner because Mrs. Ambridge was the best. Want to go out for lunch? See if Mineo's is open?

She didn't write me back, even when I threw in My treat! but it was fine. I'd see her eventually in Nutrition. Nutrition was my only elective and, far and away, the easiest class on my schedule. In fact, I'd only taken it because Elise and Morgan wanted to and I wanted to have at least one class period with them besides lunch.

But Morgan wasn't there when Coach Dean took attendance.

I texted her again as soon as Coach Dean put on a movie. Where are you?

Halfway through the period, she wrote back.

Sorry. I just dropped Elise off at the airport.

Wait, what?

She texted me when we got to school, wanted to know if I could cut class, come back and drive her, so she wouldn't have to ride with her parents.

Why didn't you tell me? I totally would have gone with you!

She asked me to come alone. :(

I imagined it all. Morgan driving behind Elise's parents in their minivan. Both of them crying. They were squeezing all the friendship they could out of their last minutes together. And there wasn't anything left over for me.

The first five houses Levi and I cleared that afternoon were unremarkable. For Levi, it was business as usual. But these empty houses were starting to get to me.

Dad's protest rally had gone so well, and yet every block in town had a couple of red *X*s. If he did save Aberdeen, it was hard to imagine what it might look like. Would it be half empty? Would the people who left move back into their old houses? Or would new people from new places buy them?

Either way you sliced it, Aberdeen would never be the same town it had been.

When we walked through the front door of the sixth house, Levi looked around as if he had crossed into some alternate dimension.

"I was curious about this one," he said.

I couldn't muster curious if I tried. The place was nice enough, I guess. A small house, but with lots of windows, some questionable choices in wallpaper, a pretty stained-glass window above the front door. And thankfully, it was empty. No trash, no furniture, and thank God, no pictures left behind. I hated the ones where people left their pictures.

I sniffed the air. "Smells like cigarettes."

Levi sniffed too and then pulled his sweatshirt up over his nose. "I didn't know she smoked."

"Who?"

He raised an eyebrow. "Guess."

"Just tell me."

"Principal Bundy."

I straight-up gasped. "No way." I took a few steps in, searched the place with new eyes. Saw the divots in her living room carpet where her furniture must have been. Smelled a hint of cat food in the air. And then I spun around. "Wait, how can she be gone? This is our last week of school!"

Levi shrugged. "I guess the adjusters made her an offer she couldn't refuse."

I thought back. Usually I'd see Bundy strolling the halls at some point during the day. But I hadn't today. "So she bailed without telling anyone? Without saying good-bye to her students?" I felt like the wind had been knocked out of me. I'm not sure why. I hated Bundy. And it was totally validating to see that she was full of shit, her pretending to care about our school and about us.

But she was gone.

I'd probably never see her again.

I walked around her house like it was a crime scene, observing but not disturbing. I went upstairs into her bathroom, pulled opened the medicine cabinet with the tip of my finger. Empty, but for a few bobby pins. There was no shower curtain, but she'd left a little pink plastic razor on the side of the tub. I don't know why, but it was weird to think of her shaving her legs.

Levi came in to test the water. It was still on. "Annoying," he said. The bathroom was really small, so I had to squeeze by him to walk out.

I couldn't tell for sure which room was Bundy's bedroom, but the biggest one had mirrored closet doors and a large built-in bookshelf. The wallpaper was lighter from where a dresser had likely been. And there was a wall mount for a flat-screen TV bolted to the wall.

I thought about texting Morgan, but I hadn't heard from her after our exchange about Elise leaving. I'm not sure why I let that stop me, but it did.

I texted Jesse instead.

Guess where I am?

???

Bundy's house. Like . . . her actual house.

No way! Why?

She's gone. Left town.

ARE YOU KIDDING ME? What a bitch!

I grinned.

"Hey, I'm going down to the basement to flip the breakers," Levi said, ducking his head in. "Let me know if the lights pop on."

I quickly hid my phone. "Yup. Sure thing."

What's the address? Jesse texted.

I froze. I didn't want him to come. Not when I was with Levi, working.

Don't worry. I won't show up and get you fired. But I've got a killer idea. You're gonna love it.

I couldn't resist. I texted him the address.

Levi stomped up out of the basement. "She left all her utilities on. I kind of can't believe it."

"I can. She clearly doesn't care about anyone but herself. Actually, that is a blanket statement I'm going to throw on everyone who leaves Aberdeen. They are selfish jerks."

"You don't know why she had to leave, Keeley."

"She's our principal. Don't you think she should be here until the last day of school? She couldn't wait another few days? Come on."

Levi shrugged. "I'm just saying—"

"I can't believe you're defending her. You were all pissed off at me the other day because we lost Mock Congress. I didn't quit, remember? She kicked me off. She wasn't thinking about what was best for our team. And it all happened because you freaking tattled on me like a baby."

Levi's cheeks got red. "Yes, I did tell on you. We needed to practice, and you were making it into, like, a variety show. I was trying to get everyone back on track."

"By getting me thrown off the team."

"Look, I didn't know she was going to come in and do that. I felt really, really bad about it, okay? In fact, I was so upset, I basically couldn't get my head right before the competition. Instead of concentrating on what was going on, I was thinking about you on the bus by yourself, probably crying your eyes out. And I actually planned to apologize to you, too, but when I got back on the bus, it was like you couldn't have cared less."

"What are you talking about? Of course I was upset! I'd spent the whole year working toward that competition!"

"Well, you were acting all chummy chummy with the bus driver, laughing like you didn't care."

"For your information, I did cry, okay? I basically sobbed on that bus for two whole hours. But I wasn't going to show Bundy that."

"Well, how was I supposed to know? You were a bitch to me. And then you kept joking and laughing and so . . ." He shrugged. "I was like, *Forget this girl. She doesn't care, so why should I?*"

"But I did care. I did." I realized how clenched up I was. I closed my eyes and rubbed my temples. "Oh, whatever. None of it matters anyway. Look, can we please call it a day? I could really use a nap."

I opened my eyes and Levi was still looking at me, worried and concerned. He said, "Fine. Let me go get my work gloves."

I didn't know what Jesse had planned, and I felt kind of bad about doing it behind Levi's back. And maybe, if I hadn't already texted Jesse the address, I wouldn't have. But since I had, I unlocked a back window, one that was accessible from the concrete back steps, because what was done was done.

I decided to go straight to Morgan's house after work to make sure she and I were okay.

When I walked in, Mrs. Dorsey had her salon chair turned completely over. She was trying to remove the base, but she was having trouble getting some of the screws out. She was actually so focused, she didn't hear me come in. I worried that she might be disassembling the chair to pack it. I tried to sneak past her, but she said, "Damn!" and threw the screwdriver across the floor. Then she spotted me. "Jesus, Keeley!"

"Sorry. Do you need help?"

To my great relief, she said, "No. This chair's been bugging me forever. The lift always sticks and I figured since I only had one appointment today, I'd try to fix it myself." She wiped her forehead with her arm. "As you can see, I'm incredibly handy."

Morgan was upstairs on her bed watching her ceiling fan spin.

"Hey," I said. "Your mom looks like she's about to murder someone down there."

"Yeah. She's been in a crap mood all day. You know, she's barely had any clients since the flood. She's kind of freaking out about it."

Her room looked a lot neater. Elise's stuff was gone, and the old clothes and other things Morgan had out, spring cleaning or whatever she'd called it, were put away. It occurred to me that maybe she'd done that whole charade to make Elise feel better.

I climbed on her bed, into my spot, and looked at the rainbow sticker on the underside of her lampshade. It might take us a little while for things to feel normal again, now that Elise was gone. But I had faith that they would, eventually.

She sighed and smoothed out her comforter with her hand. "I hope this doesn't make me sound like a terrible person, but in a way, I'm kind of relieved. I feel like I've been saying good-bye to Elise for days now. It's been exhausting." She rolled on her side to face me. "But that's part of being a friend, isn't it? To be there for them when they need you, even if it's hard."

My phone buzzed.

Where've you been? Why haven't you liked my latest post? Hurry! I'm neeeeeeedy!

I pushed up onto my knees from my belly. "Oh, no."

"What? You're scaring me."

"Good. I'm scared too." But I was also excited. I loaded Jesse's new video. The cover frame was of Jesse dressed in a tuxedo. I held up my phone so Morgan could see it and pressed Play.

"Dear remaining students of Aberdeen High. I have something to ask of you." Out from behind his back came a rose. "Will you go to prom with me?" Jesse quickly put his fingers to his lips. "But *shhhh*. It's a Secret Prom . . . at Principal Bundy's house."

"Oh my God," I said.

"Oh my God," Morgan echoed. She squeezed my arm.

Jesse went on. "So, this might still be news to all of you, but . . . Principal Bundy has bailed on us. That's right, she's left Aberdeen for good. Kind of a bitch move, don't you think? I sure did, until she called me up and personally insisted that we use her old house to throw Aberdeen High one last party. Now, at first I thought about only inviting the remaining seniors, but now is not the time to be exclusive. Secret Prom is open to everyone still here. One last big blowout, on Saturday, the night after graduation." Then he gave out Principal Bundy's home address, told people to park on different streets, and that formal wear was mandatory. The last thing he said was "Spread the word. This message will self-destruct in twenty-four hours."

Morgan said, "If Levi sees it, he'll definitely tell his father. Don't you think?"

I put my hands over my mouth. "If Levi sees it, I'm getting fired." I let my hands down and then brought them back up again. "Oh God. You know what? *He* might be fired!"

My eyes traveled to the lower right corner of the screen. In under an hour, Jesse already had more than a hundred likes. He didn't even need twenty-four hours. By morning, everyone would have seen it.

"Keeley! You should call him and yell at him!"

"I guess . . . ," I said tentatively. "I've never called Jesse before. We only text." I hated how weird that sounded.

"Well, now's the perfect time," said Morgan. "He'll know you're serious."

It's one thing to build up the confidence to call a boy on the phone. It's another thing to do it with someone listening in. I felt, in that moment, what I imagined Morgan had felt with Wes, the time I was listening in when they broke up. But the difference there was that Jesse would never say something mean about Morgan. So I wasn't so much worried about that as I was that our relationship was somehow not what I thought it was. Because why was I learning about this prom the same way as everyone else, especially since I was the one who'd given him Bundy's address in the first place? I thought we were supposed to be partners in this. Cruise directors on this sinking ship.

I wondered if Jesse would even answer, or if he'd ignore the call, knowing I might be mad.

He picked up before the second ring.

Morgan pressed her head close to mine so she could hear.

"'Sup, Kee. What did you think?"

"Dude! You're going to get me in so much trouble!"

"What?" He sounded genuinely surprised. "With who? Hamrick?"

"Yes! I'm totally going to get fired because of you."

"He won't know you gave me the address."

Even though I didn't care *that* much, it was annoying that Jesse didn't think this was a bigger deal. "He's not stupid, Jesse. The timing is a little suspicious, don't you think? I mean, I'm in that house with him and then a couple of hours later, you announce Secret Prom at the same address."

Morgan gave me a thumbs-up.

Jesse took a deep breath. In that pause, I worried that maybe I was taking things too far. I didn't actually want to fight with Jesse. Especially not when our entire relationship was built upon the fact that we both wanted to have a good time. Did getting mad at him, especially over something as dumb as Levi Hamrick, jeopardize that?

"Your mad voice is very cute," he said, his own low and quiet and growly. I felt my heartbeat quicken. Morgan suffocated her squeal with her pillow. "Do you want me to cancel it?"

I thight about it for a millisecond. I didn't. Ever since the flood, Jesse had worked hard to make things fun, to keep people having fun. The times I spent with him were the only bright spots. They were the fuel to keep going, to have hope.

I didn't want to get Levi in trouble.

But I was touched Jesse would offer. I felt like it proved something about us that he'd do that for me.

"No, you don't have to do that. Just don't tell anyone I'm the one who gave you the address, okay? Not even Zito. And if Levi asks you himself, you can't throw me under the bus."

"That's fair. But before I agree to these terms, I need something from you."

My eyes got wide, and Morgan cuddled against me again. "What?"

"Will you go to prom with me? The last-ever prom in Aberdeen?"

I didn't want to correct him. Not because I wasn't still hopeful that my dad could stop this. But because if it was Aberdeen's last prom, that made it even more romantic.

I jumped around the room like it was one big trampoline.

"You still there, Keeley?"

Every cell in my body screamed *YES YES OH HELL YES.* But Morgan shook her head. She crawled away from me and grabbed a Sharpie marker and wrote on my palm, *TOO EASY!!!!!*

"Hello?"

"I, uh. I mean, is that it? That's your ask?" I laughed dismissively, all air through my nose. "Sorry. I would have expected something a bit more creative."

I waited for him to defend himself, but there was something suddenly funny-sounding about the air on the line. Quiet.

"Shit! He hung up on me!" I cried.

"Maybe he didn't hang up on purpose?"

Two seconds later, I got a text from him.

So you want creative, huh? Why don't you go look under your pillow?

My hands shaking, I turned my phone around to Morgan. I watched her lips move as she read, her eyes widening. We stared at each other for a second before Morgan dove across her bed and grabbed her keys from her nightstand. We slid our shoes half on our feet and flew out of the bedroom door, then hurled ourselves down the attic stairs.

Her mom was yelling, "Where are you two going?" but we didn't answer. We were too busy laughing. Morgan's mom had no idea what was going on, but she saw how joyous we were and joined in on the laughter too.

"I'm scared!" I screamed as Morgan peeled out of the driveway.

"Don't be scared, you dummy! This is it! This is what you've been waiting for!"

We tore across town, sped through the one blinking red light. My house had never felt so far away.

About three blocks before the turn for Hewitt Road, we got stuck at an intersection, forced to watch a lumbering parade of bulldozers being driven into town by men who didn't live here, who were in no hurry. We unrolled the windows and started screaming, "*Move move move!*" And Morgan laid down on her horn. They thought we were flirting.

"Screw it," Morgan said, and sped along the shoulder, a streak shooting past them.

We burst into my house, and Morgan followed me up the stairs. With every step, I added something to the mental list of embarrassing things Jesse could have seen in my room. Dirty underwear. A half-empty box of tampons. My teddy bear Rosebud, who since I'd found her in my attic had rejoined me in my bed.

We crashed into the room. Thankfully, it wasn't that messy. And it didn't look like he'd gone through my things.

I lifted the pillow off my bed.

He'd taken the art room supplies and made an old-school-looking valentine heart. It was all red glitter, on the heart and also on my bed. So much glitter that if it hadn't been sparkling, it would have looked like a big bloodstain from a crime scene. White letters on the heart said WILL YOU GO TO PROM WITH ME?

And stabbed straight through the heart was one of the school clock's golden hands. I recognized it right away.

Morgan's phone rang. It was Elise. I saw her name when Morgan checked the screen. "I'll call her back later," Morgan said, sliding her phone into her back pocket. Which, if I hadn't already been on top of the world, would definitely have tipped the scales.

# 26

---

---

As of Monday, the cafeteria was permanently closed. A sign covered the window on the door saying that all students, even freshmen, would be allowed off-campus for lunch until the school closed down on Friday. That's why it was weird when I heard laughter coming from inside it as I was on my way to the library.

I lifted up the sign and peered in. The cafeteria had been dismantled. Lunch tables folded down and pushed against the walls, chairs stacked in tall pillars, the cash register stations bare, the chip racks empty, the overhead fluorescent lights off.

Across the room and against the wall, one thing glowed like a night-light. The vending machine was still plugged in, a decent variety of snacks tucked in the metal coils. That's where I saw Jesse and Zito and two other guys on the soccer team going nuts on it, trying to pry the glass door open. Actually, Jesse was the only one doing that. The rest were cheering him on, or handing him things to use as tools. Like Zito. He must have found the metal spoon in the kitchen. Jesse tried using it like a crowbar, but it immediately bent in half, so he flung it over his shoulder and it hit the floor with a clang. Another guy was holding up a phone to record the antics, of course.

"Dude, hold the camera steady," Jesse said, cracking up as he took a few steps backward. Then he ran toward the vending machine and knocked into it with all his weight. The lights inside it flickered as it lifted onto two of its four legs. All the guys yelled, "Whoa!" and it probably would have fallen completely over if Zito hadn't been poised on the other side to steady it.

"Hey, Keeley!"

I turned and saw Levi hustling toward me from the end of the hallway. He had on dark jeans, a black-and-white-check button-up, the sleeves rolled up to his elbows, and his running sneakers. He was still carrying a hall pass even though no one checked them. "Do you not go to class anymore? I've been wandering around the school looking for you since the bell—"

We heard the boys running and knocking into the vending machine, tipping it up and then letting it rock back down. Then uproarious laughter.

I had a *gulp* feeling, as if I'd been caught smoking by my parents. I stepped in front of Levi to block his way into the cafeteria. "Don't look" was all I could think to say. Levi groaned and I tried to pull him down the hallway. "Forget them."

He gently eased me aside.

The boys didn't hear him come in. It wasn't until Levi flipped on the lights that they looked over. Jesse said, "What's up, Hamrick! You hungry?" And then they went right back to wrestling with the vending machine. Now Zito and another guy were rocking it hard from side to side.

Levi folded his arms across his chest. He wanted to stop them, but he didn't have any authority.

I think Jesse probably realized that too, because he didn't

seem to care. After a few more aggressive shakes, he ran off and came back with one of the cafeteria chairs. It was a plastic shell with four metal legs. He pushed the guys out of the way. "Here, we can use this to pry it open." He looked up at Levi and grinned. "No use letting these snacks go to waste."

I couldn't breathe. I stayed in the hallway, peeking just around the doorframe to watch but not be seen. With equal parts of my heart, I wished Jesse would stop, and I wished Levi would walk away.

Neither happened.

The door of the vending machine suddenly popped open, and you could tell by the sound that something inside it had broken. And the glass was now completely spiderwebbed with cracks. The guys really thought that was hilarious.

Jesse reached in, pulled out a handful of packets of Pop-Tarts from the coils, and flipped through them like a pack of cards. "Strawberry, strawberry, blueberry," he rattled off, tossing the ones he didn't want over his shoulder and onto the floor. "Oh yeah! Brown Sugar Cinnamon!" He tore into the wrapper with his teeth and spit the paper out. The rest of the boys grabbed for their own snacks.

I think Jesse was confused as to why Levi was still standing there, silently watching. "Sorry, man. I'm definitely calling dibs on Brown Sugar Cinnamon. But you can have any of the strawberry ones."

"I don't get it," Levi finally said. "You're out there marching on City Hall because you supposedly love this town so much, and today, you're breaking school property for laughs."

Jesse's smile faded. He cocked his head to the side. "Come on, dude. We're just fooling around."

I wanted to explain what I knew Jesse wouldn't. Or maybe even couldn't. That it was easier to shoot a stupid video, or plan a secret prom, than it was to think about what was really happening around us. I'm not saying what Jesse was doing was right. But I understood it.

Jesse saw me standing by the door. He seemed a little surprised, maybe because I hadn't made myself known. "Keeley! What do you want? Granola bar? Pretzel bites?"

Levi turned around. He wanted to see what I would say.

I tried to lighten the mood. "I can't even remember how many times this stupid thing cheated me over the years. I bet it seriously owes me thirty bucks' worth of snacks." I put my hand on Levi's back as I walked past him. "Go ahead. Have a Pop-Tart. It's on me." And then, to Jesse, I said, "You are crazy. Frosted Strawberry Pop-Tarts are the best Pop-Tarts." I leaned over and started picking them up off the floor. Along with the other wrappers and things that the guys had left there.

Jesse came over and grabbed me around the waist, lifting me up in his arms. "That's insane. Brown Sugar Cinnamon is like a cousin of Cinnabon. Frosted Strawberry is . . . practically healthy."

As Jesse and I continued to debate Pop-Tart flavors, Levi turned and walked out.

I ran to him, though I had to wriggle out of Jesse's arms to do it. "Hey. Wait. You never told me why were you looking for me." And then I whispered, "And I'll make them clean up. Don't worry."

Levi turned around. "It's not about that." He shrugged. "I wanted to give you the heads-up that the governor came into town this morning. He's making a big speech about the dam at the old mill building."

"What?" I whipped around. Jesse must have heard the shift in my voice, because he dropped what he was doing and hustled over. "When?"

Levi glanced at the clock behind me. "Now, probably. Like I said, I've been looking for you everywhere." It was that annoyed big brother tone he sometimes used with me.

Jesse had his car keys already out. "Come on. Let's go."

"Great. Now you two are cutting class?"

Jesse groaned, "Grow a pair, dude."

I tried calling my dad the entire drive over, but his phone went straight to voice mail. "Maybe this is a good announcement. Like, they're calling off the whole dam." Even as I said it, I knew how crazy it sounded.

Jesse leaned forward and looked at the sky though his windshield. "Maybe Ward gets struck by lightning. How awesome would that be?"

He was trying to make it better, I knew it. So I forced myself to laugh, even though I felt like I could puke.

The roads around the mill were blocked off to traffic. We ended up ditching Jesse's hatchback and running a few blocks to get there.

There, in the parking lot where we'd had the Slip 'N Slide party a little more than a week ago, stood Governor Ward. A low stage had been set up, with a podium and a microphone and a mound of ceremonial dirt. Someone to Ward's left passed him a fancy shovel with a beautifully oiled wooden handle and a brass blade that was as shiny as a trumpet horn. There weren't many people out here to see him besides a few who looked like they worked for the state in some capacity, drab suits, skirts and blazers, sensible shoes. Them and the press.

In the distance, I heard chanting. It had to be Dad.

As I followed their voices, I passed the reporter Shawn Wilcox. He was speaking into the camera. "We're coming to you live from Aberdeen, where we are awaiting a speech from Governor Ward regarding the Aberdeen Dam Project."

There was a little applause as the governor stepped forward. "Today, I am proud to announce that we are officially breaking ground on what will be the future home of Lake Aberdeen. In a matter of weeks, we've rewritten an environmental disaster into a story of conservation and preservation. Aided by our government, we signed very generous relocation deals with Aberdeen residents every single day. And, most importantly, we've begun taking the necessary steps to ensure that our river will safely flow through this commonwealth for many more generations to come." More applause. He lifted up his shovel.

Shawn Wilcox raised his microphone and shouted, "What do you say to the Reservoir Resistance protesters currently blocking the dump trucks from reaching the river? Do you feel you've provided them the answers they've asked for?"

Governor Ward paused. Then he waved a hand dismissively. "Of course, there are always people out there who want to exploit progress, capitalize on others' misfortune, turn a profit from a tragedy. Let me be clear to the remaining landowners who are holding out. I cannot allow your greed to put any citizens at risk for their lives and well-being. Part of why we must begin construction now is because the river typically reaches its lowest levels during the summer months, and that will provide us with the safest conditions for our workers. So we will continue in good faith, until we reach a point where stronger measures will have to be taken." He lifted his shovel again, scooped up a little dirt, and then let it slide off his shovel back onto the pile.

I spun around to look for Jesse. I'd lost sight of him in the crowd. But then I heard him scream out at the top of his lungs, "That's a fake hole! He's digging a fake hole, everyone!"

A few of the reporters chuckled. Governor Ward turned beet red.

I raced over to Jesse and pointed toward the driveway leading into the mill parking lot. The bulldozers I'd seen last night with Morgan were parked in a very long line along the road. Each one had a bored-looking driver inside, waiting, their diesel engines idling. Several other police officers were standing around, watching. And blocking them from entering was a human barrier, three or four people wide, several people deep, arms linked.

As we got closer, the chanting got louder.

"Damn the dam! Damn the dam! Damn the dam!"

It wasn't nearly as many people as had been at the rally, but I had to figure that was the point of Governor Ward calling his press conference out of the blue. He was hoping to catch my dad and his supporters flat-footed. Thank God he hadn't. Dad stood in the very front line of defense, my mom with him.

The sky was darkening. Though the wind was picking up, the sight warmed my heart.

"Dad!"

"Kee!" He hugged me. "How'd you find out?"

"A friend in school."

"Good. Word is spreading. Hopefully more people will make their way down. We've got Charlie and Sy over there making calls, telling folks to be here as quick as possible."

I turned to Jesse. "Is your mom around? Do you think she could come down?"

I saw him bite the inside of his cheek. "Um, I'm pretty sure she's working."

Dad was overjoyed. "They tried to pull a fast one on us, but Ward wasn't fast enough!"

"How did you find out, Dad?"

"Me," said Mrs. Dorsey, stepping forward. "One of my clients said she saw something going on down by the mills. I called your dad, told him he might want to check it out." I grabbed Mrs. Dorsey around the middle and hugged her tight.

Mom came over. "Keeley, why aren't you at school?"

"Because I want to be here supporting Dad."

She wasn't happy with that answer.

Shawn Wilcox, the reporter, came toward us. "Jim, this is terrific. Let me get you on camera answering a few questions, and then I'll take some video of you all standing here, okay?"

Dad nodded. "Let's do it." And Jesse and I quickly added ourselves to the human chain.

Shawn Wilcox pushed a hand through his hair. "Great. In three . . . two . . . And now I am with Jim Hewitt, leader of the Reservoir Resistance. What do you have to say about the governor's speech today? Any response to his charge that your movement is putting citizens at risk?"

"Well, obviously we disagree with that." Dad had to say it loud, because of the idling diesel engines puttering nearby. It looked like he was searching for more to say, but then he nodded for the next question.

"Do you believe it's safe to stay in Aberdeen with what scientists are now reporting about the instability of the land due to deforestation that occurred during the mill's heyday?"

Dad looked a little stunned at the pointed way he was being asked these questions. "Look, we want to know that Governor Ward has explored his other options before demolishing our homes. That's all we've asked for from the very beginning. And his office refuses to comment. What does that tell you?"

"Actually, the governor's office released findings today." Shawn Wilcox handed Dad a stack of paper, which Dad began to flip through. "Do you believe it's fair to ask the state to spend double the amount of money on this project to keep you in your home, when the residents of Aberdeen contribute the lowest tax income in the state?"

All the muscles in my stomach twisted up into one awful knot. Behind me, Jesse said, "Jeez."

My dad struggled for an answer. "I'm not going to comment on that until I've had a chance to go through this."

"So what's your plan now? Block the roads until you get an audience with the governor?"

"Yes. We'll have people standing here day and night until—"

At that there was a loud thunder crack and the air sizzled with electricity.

The wind kicked up and my hair whipped my cheeks.

Dad leaned in closer to the microphone and started over. "We will block this road until someone—"

After a flash of lightning, the rain came pouring down in

buckets and buckets. Everyone around ran for cover. Jesse grabbed ahold of me. "Come on, Keeley." But I pulled free.

"It's just rain!" Dad shouted. "Hold your positions!"

Dad tried to stand his ground, but the rain was driving sideways. After another crack of thunder, Mom rushed to his side and tried to pull him.

He shrugged free.

I know he didn't do it on purpose. It was 1,000 percent an accident. But Mom fell backward, her feet slipping out from under her. She hit the ground with a sickening thud, flat on her back, and it sent up a plume of muddy puddle water. She didn't move for a second, the rain pelting her face.

Dad wasn't even aware that she'd fallen. Not until he heard me scream out for her. Then he turned around and was shocked at what he'd done. The guys who worked with him on the repairs, Sy and the older guys, gave Dad stern looks. He shuffled forward to help Mom up, but it was too late. Mrs. Dorsey and I were already at her side. Mrs. Dorsey looked mad, madder than the time Morgan and I went through her underwear drawer and she found us dressed up in her sexy pajamas. Mrs. Dorsey tried to help Mom to her feet, but Mom refused to take her hand. Mine too.

"I'm fine, everyone. I'm fine," Mom said. But I could tell, when she finally did get to her feet, that she was standing stiffly, and she was trying to keep weight off her left leg.

Dad wasn't even looking at her. He was watching the dump trucks roll through the gates.

Shawn pulled his KPBC-issued windbreaker up over his head and said, "Let's go," to his cameraman. "We got enough."

Jesse and I didn't say anything to each other on our walk back to his car. Or the first few blocks that he drove. It wasn't until I saw him making a turn up the hill that I said, "Just take me back to school."

"Why?"

I didn't want to go home. "I'm supposed to work with Levi."

Jesse kept his eyes on the road. "Who cares about that? You know, you should quit that job. Especially now."

I knew what he meant. Especially now that things weren't looking good for Aberdeen.

# 27

I immediately regretted coming to work, because Levi was clearly still pissed off about what had happened between him and Jesse in the cafeteria. Normally, anytime we hit a downhill, Levi would stop pedaling his bike and let us coast. But that day, he pedaled every downhill, like he was trying to sweat the anger out.

I wasn't in the best mood either, for obvious reasons.

My phone rang twice but I didn't answer it either time. It was Morgan. I wanted to talk to her badly, but I couldn't and wouldn't in front of Levi. Anyway, she'd probably already gotten the story firsthand from Mrs. Dorsey. I imagined them sitting at their kitchen table gossiping, just like the night after Spring Formal. They had to know it was just an accident. Dad would never, ever lay a hand on my mom. But I also knew how it probably looked. Bad.

So until I knew exactly how to spin it, I was sending her to my voice mail.

Levi stopped his bike at the blinking red light on Main Street and set his feet down.

I said, "You realize you aren't a car, right?" When he didn't answer, I mumbled, "No, of course you do. Because if you were a car, you'd run this light like everyone else in town does."

"It's the law."

"Fine. Whatever."

I waited for him to start pedaling again, but he didn't. We stayed stopped in the middle of the road.

"So you and Jesse Ford . . . are what? Boyfriend and girlfriend?"

"I don't know. Sort of."

"I thought he was dating Victoria Dunkle."

I hadn't really thought about Victoria since kissing Jesse at his Slip 'N Slide party. And I liked it that way. So I said, sharply, "They were never dating."

"But weren't they together at Spring Formal? When I found you—" Levi stopped himself. He knew better now. "They were in the hallway together that night."

"Sure. They were in the hallway together. But that doesn't mean they were *together* together." I bounced my weight up and down on his pegs. "Anyway, she doesn't live here anymore, so . . ."

"So you're together, then," he said, pushing.

"Levi, I don't know, okay? We're just having fun. You should try it sometime."

"Fun like breaking a vending machine? Yeah, count me out."

That started him pedaling again.

Levi skidded to a stop in front of the Aberdeen Cemetery gates.

It was a relatively small graveyard, barely bigger than a football field, surrounded by a low iron fence and a slack chain that hung across the driveway. I hopped off Levi's bike and unhooked the chain so we could ride in.

Most of the headstones in the back of the cemetery were recent graves, but the ones you could see from the road were old white rectangles shaped like front teeth, jutting out of the over-grown grass at odd angles.

Levi pointed to a cottage. "That's the old caretaker's house. It's been abandoned for a while, so it should be quick." He made some notes on his clipboard as I climbed back onto his pegs. This was the address we'd skipped a few times already.

As we pedaled in, I saw HEWITT etched into stone again and again and again. These were my relatives. Some were a hundred and fifty years, two hundred years gone before I was born. I think I'd heard a story about each one of them, though, from my grandpa. He was the only relative I knew in this graveyard, only he didn't have a gravestone. On his deathbed, Grandpa had asked Dad to scatter his ashes around. He wanted to spend eternity with his family, but not be cold in the ground.

"Hey, do you know what they're going to do with the people buried here?"

Levi shrugged. "They'll move them."

"Move them where? Like to another graveyard nearby?"

"Keeley, I don't know."

"I have family in this cemetery, Levi. Don't be a jerk, okay?"

Levi braked suddenly, sending us into a full fishtail spin. If I hadn't been holding on to him tight, I would have fallen off. "My mother's buried here. So don't act like this means something to you, when you've only just thought of it now, okay?" He hit the *okay* in a sarcastic way, trying to mimic me.

I burned white hot. I badly wanted to tell Levi off. But I kept my mouth shut because he was right. I *had* just thought of it then, for the first time. And because a dead mom trumps dead extended family any day of the week.

He put his bike up on the kickstand. He did it so forcefully that it tipped over before he walked into the caretaker's cottage.

He stuck his head out the door a few seconds later. "Are you coming?"

I went inside and immediately sat on the stairs. The place was empty. There wasn't anything for me to do. With the clipboard in my lap, I concentrated on tearing off pieces of ugly-ass flowered wallpaper.

"Don't do that," Levi said, hitting the light switch above my head. The hallway light on the second floor flickered on and off. "You are a terrible worker, you know that? You barely do anything. In fact, you actually slow me down. After today, there are going to be a lot more houses to clear. If you can't keep up, then maybe you should just quit."

I glared at him. Could he be that dense? "You're lucky I showed up today. But I'm not going to quit. Especially now that I know I'm slowing you down. If you want me gone, you're going to have to fire me."

Levi dropped his head back and groaned. "All right, fine." He rubbed his hands fast over his peach fuzz. When he tipped his head back up, he said, "I wasn't going to ask you this, but—"

"Yeah, it was me. I gave Jesse Principal Bundy's address."

He looked so genuinely disappointed in me, I had to work on holding my mouth in an *I don't care* grin while he marched down into the basement. Each of his footsteps made the foyer light swing.

I wasn't sure what to do. I should have felt happy, but I didn't. I called out to him, "Look, I did give him the address, but I didn't know what he was going to do with it."

"I can't hear you!" he called back.

This was ridiculous. "Never mind," I said, getting up. "You know what? I'm going to go. I'll leave the clipboard on—"

"If you're saying something you want me to hear, you're going to have to come down," he called out from below the floorboards.

I went to the top of the basement stairs. "Do you want the clipboard? Or should I just leave it up here?"

"Why?"

"Because I'm going home."

He trudged back up the stairs and held out his hand. "You know, I'd be finished by now if it wasn't for you."

I handed the clipboard over. "I'm not a bad worker. I just hate my boss."

"That's great. That's just great. You know what? You're right. Clearly I am a bad boss. A good boss would have told my dad about your stupid Secret Prom thing."

Oh, crap. "Well . . . I hope you still won't say anything, because a lot of people are looking forward to it."

"Whatever. I could care less about a fake prom full of fake people."

I held myself rigid. "How are we fake?"

He opened his mouth and then thought better of it. "I don't want to get into this," he said, walking back down the basement stairs.

I followed him. "Come on. I want to know." Levi turned to me and rolled his eyes. "What's wrong with having a little fun?"

"Because not everything should be turned into a good time, okay?" He crossed the basement and crouched down at a piece of machinery, a furnace or something, and started messing with the valves. "I don't even know why I care. It's cool. Ditch out on work and leave me to do everything. Go to Principal Bundy's house and burn it down for all I care. Have a blast."

"It's not going to be like that," I told him. "We're trying to make the best of a bad situation. We're making lemonade out of lemons."

"Is that what you call it?" He chuckled. "Because I think you're trying to pretend it isn't happening."

I set my jaw. "Sorry to break it to you, Levi, but if anyone's doing that, it's you!"

"How's that exactly? Look at my job. I'm way more involved than anyone else at school."

"But you're walking around like a zombie, Levi. You go through these empty houses and it hardly registers with you that someone used to live there. You barely look at the stuff they've left behind, you just throw it in trash bags and set it on the curb. And you act the same way at school. I haven't seen you get sad once. Maybe it's because you have your sights set on the next phase. You're a—"

"Don't say it, Keeley."

*"A Guy Who's Going Places!"*

Levi curled his lip. "We're all going places. Everyone's leaving, Keeley. Not just me. I'm just being practical about it. You want to believe that your dad can stop this from happening, but trust me, he can't. The sooner you and your friends accept that, the better."

I waited for him to take it back. When he didn't, when he stalked over to the electric box, I turned around and left.

· · ·

Mom was still out seeing patients by the time I walked home. Dad stood in the driveway, his cane resting against the side of the garage. He had his table saw out and a beam set up across two horses. He was leaning over, pencil behind his ear, tape measure in his hand. The air smelled of freshly cut wood.

I wondered what he must be thinking. No one would think for a second that beginning the construction on the dam was anything but a huge step backward. Would Dad feel inspired to keep fighting? Or would he give up?

Usually Dad spent evenings outside, sharing a beer with the men who'd been helping him with repairs all day. Or holding court with neighbors who stopped by to pledge their support. But today, the only other person here was Mrs. Dorsey.

She held a pie in her hands, the crust golden brown and perfect, shiny fruit tar visible in the decorative slits. It had to be blueberry, Dad's favorite. Probably a thank-you for the work he'd done on her garage that very first day.

Neither of them noticed me coming up the front walk, and so before they did, I cut a diagonal across the yard to keep out of sight. Then I jogged around the back of our house and came up along the side of the garage.

"What would it hurt, to speak to the adjusters and just see what they offer?" She paused as Dad whirled up the saw and cut through another board, sending a spray of sawdust into the air. "You know, they might even be extra-generous with you, seeing as you're the leader of this whole thing."

Dad blew on the end of the board. "You're telling me I should give up."

Mrs. Dorsey shrugged. "They're starting work on the dam. What else can you do?"

Dad turned to face her. "We can hold strong. They can't move forward if we band together. They're not going to let us drown. Starting tomorrow morning, I'm going to call on every single person left in Aberdeen and ask them to sign a petition, promising not to speak with adjusters until our questions are answered by Governor Ward. If I can make everyone understand that we've got each other's back, then—"

"And you honestly think people are going to do that? You think people are going to wait until the water is up to their front doors? What's going to be left to save at that point?"

Mrs. Dorsey was a strong woman. Mom always said that about her, even before her divorce, but especially after. Dad was not used to having conversations like this. Mom took a completely different tack with him, gentle prodding, more supportive, less confrontational. But Mrs. Dorsey was coming at him hard.

"Have you talked to the adjusters?" I heard Dad's struggle to stay calm, the quiver underneath his voice.

She shook her head. "No. I haven't."

I let out a deep breath I didn't even know I was holding. I was pretty sure Morgan would have said something to me if her mother had talked to the adjusters, and I was glad to know my instincts were right. In a weird way, just that little piece made me feel better about everything.

"Well, I'm thankful for that, Annie. I know your support is keeping Jill strong. When she sees your name under ours at the top of the petition, I think it'll put her mind at ease."

Mrs. Dorsey's mouth pulled into a thin line. "I won't be

signing your petition, Jim, because I can't promise you that I won't eventually talk to the adjusters. As much as I'd love to stay in Aberdeen, and as much as I have Jill's back, I have to do what's best for me and Morgan."

"Well, you and I are in agreement on that. Everything I'm doing is for my family."

Mrs. Dorsey shook her head. "Come on. We all see how hard you're working. And I know for Jill, the one bright spot in this terrible mess has been watching you"—she paused, probably to choose her words carefully—"wake up."

Of course, I felt the same way. But there was a tinge to Mrs. Dorsey's words, a disappointment that there needed to be an *awakening* in the first place. Which was unfair. She didn't know what Dad had gone through with his accident. And no one was working harder than him now.

"Jill's taken on so much and given you the space you needed to deal with what happened. She could use someone to take care of her for a change. Imagine if you channeled all your efforts into her, helping her out around the house. Maybe take a part-time job somewhere."

"I'm sorry, Annie. Is this supposed to be a pep talk?" Dad laughed, like he was making a joke, except it was clear he wasn't kidding around.

She set the pie on his workbench. "I'm rooting for you, Jim. But know that there's not just one way to win." And she got into her car.

I wondered if Morgan knew what her mom was up to, coming over to talk to my dad like this.

Or if Mom did.

I hoped neither.

· · ·

We gathered around the television that night to watch the news. They'd aired a portion of the governor's speech and his ceremonial shoveling of dirt. They showed a bit of Dad's interview.

Then they cut to some interviews Shawn Wilcox had done with other residents of Aberdeen.

"Why would we want to live someplace unsafe?" said one neighbor.

Another grumbled that he'd been hired to help with the dam construction, his first paying job in years, and that Dad was trying to take that away from him.

Dad chafed. "That's not what I'm trying to do." He was defensive. And hurt.

Shawn Wilcox talked to one couple walking out of City Hall with signed paperwork. "Our offer was more than fair," they told him, and held up a document as proof. "And the money's being deposited directly into our account in days."

Dad said, "*Shit*," under his breath.

The final shots of the report were exactly what we'd feared. The rain, our human chain breaking apart. Mom trying to pull Dad to shelter and falling, all of the people there to support him scattering until there was no one left. The last shot was of Dad, Mom, and the other protesters seeking shelter underneath a tent for the workers. They looked like they were trapped, too many people crammed on a lifeboat. Like they were acting out the future storm, the next flood that everyone was so worried about.

"I really hoped he'd edit that part out," Dad said.

I had too.

Mom didn't say anything. She just stood up and walked out of the room.

# 28

---

---

Jesse picked me up for school. I tried to concentrate on the goodness of that small thing, of climbing into his car, of him only letting go of my hand to switch gears. Instead of looking out the window at the slow-moving train full of flatbed cars that carried huge pipes and concrete frames to drop off beside the river, I cataloged the things piled at my feet I was trying not to step on, like a paperback of *A Separate Peace* and a crushed box of animal crackers that had to be Julia's and a cheap pair of drugstore sunglasses with one mirrored lens missing. I memorized the color of the air freshener tree hanging from Jesse's rearview mirror, orange, and its scent, coconut.

I tried not to think about how, when Jesse beeped outside, Dad was also getting ready to leave, with a clipboard and pages of blank petition. Dad would be driving all over town today, hoping for signatures. I wondered what he'd look at, what he'd think about, to distract himself.

I tried not to think about the quilt and pillow he'd left on the couch, because he'd slept downstairs, not in the bed with Mom.

"Hey. Do you think your mom might sign our petition? It's basically a promise that she won't talk to the adjusters. Every name will help. My dad can stop by your house. Or maybe even drive out to Walmart, if she's working today."

Jesse nodded. "Yeah, sure. I don't see why not. I'll ask her."

Something had definitely shifted. I felt it as soon as I walked into school. Kids were giving me sad looks. Actually, they were sad looks for my father, delivered through me. I smiled, though, as if I didn't notice. I reminded everyone about Secret Prom on Saturday night. I teased them about how much fun it was going to be, all the surprises and fun things Jesse and I had in store for them. I whispered about Secret Prom at every possible opportunity.

It wasn't a complete lie. Jesse and I were going to Walmart to buy supplies later in the week. I knew he had ideas and I did too. Like paper corsages for the girls and boutonnieres for the boys. Or maybe a photo backdrop, with a round table and white tablecloth, and a pretty place setting, so people could take pictures sitting at it. So it would seem like a real prom.

There were only three days left of school and we were all, suddenly, seniors.

I was making a list of those things in homeroom when, for the first time, morning announcements included a reminder to report a non-Aberdeen mailing address to the guidance office when we had one, so they could send our records on to our new schools. And after that first bell, people started talking more openly about where they might go. Some kids thought they'd probably stay nearby, relocate to apartments or other houses in surrounding towns. But a lot seemed to think they might go far away, like Elise had. Different states. Whenever I'd walk by, those conversations got hushed or stopped altogether.

Since Bundy was already gone, school became even more of a joke. I didn't go to a single one of my classes that day. After homeroom, I just stuck with Morgan. I went to her study hall, I helped her clean out her locker.

Jesse sent me a text the period before lunch.

Yo. Opening Ceremonies of Aberdeen Gym Olympics start today during lunch. You and Morgan vs. me and Zito for the three-legged race. THERE WILL BE PRIZES!

I asked Morgan if she wanted to go but she shook her head. "Actually, I was thinking you and I could take a drive. The only thing is that I want to be back in time for English. Today's my last class with Ms. Runde and I don't want to miss it."

"Oh." I said. "Okay." Even though that didn't sound nearly as fun as Gym Olympics.

We got in her car and started driving with no specific destination. Basically up and down every single street that wasn't closed off to traffic, like we were garbagemen or something. It was surprisingly awkward, which I blamed on the larger circumstances. I did a lot of Secret Prom babbling to keep things from getting sad. And it ended up being a productive conversation. We decided that, instead of wasting money on new dresses, we'd wear something old of our mothers'. And we'd get someone to take a photo of us that we could give to them, after it was all over with and they couldn't ground us for lying.

"I'm almost positive I can fit into that dress she wore out to the car that day. The one from her Spring Fling," Morgan said.

"I bet my mom has her's in the attic. I'll check."

We decided to tell our parents we'd be sleeping at Debbie

Granger's house. Debbie was a girl we'd both known since kindergarten. We'd hide our prom clothes in our book bags, then change, and do our hair and makeup in Morgan's car.

"So have you and Jesse talked about what's going to happen after . . . whatever happens?"

"Not really," I said, breezy. "We're just enjoying the here and now." I tried matching how Elise would talk about the boys she dated, with a touch of indifference. It used to drive me crazy how little she cared about something that I so desperately wished that I could have. But Elise wasn't acting. She honestly didn't care. It wasn't that way for me. Not with Jesse.

"Is he going to college?"

"Yeah. Community college. That way, he can be around for his little sister, Julia."

"Well, that's awesome. If you get into Baird next year, you won't have to do the long-distance thing."

I nodded, even though that wasn't something Jesse and I had ever discussed. Our vibe was more *Let's make the most of our time here.* Which was fine when I had all the hope in the world that that day we'd have to leave Aberdeen would never come. But now, things were looking a bit less optimistic.

"Have you had sex with him?"

"What?" I practically screamed it.

"You heard me." She was looking at me intensely, scouring my face for some kind of clue.

"Morgan, if I had sex with Jesse Ford, I would call you immediately after. I might even text you during it, honestly, if I felt I could get away with it."

She seemed satisfied. "Do you want to lose your virginity

to him, though? If you did, the night of Secret Prom would be pretty epic."

I unrolled the window and laughed uncomfortably. "Umm, can we please change the subject?" It wasn't that I didn't think sometimes about what it would be like to be with Jesse. And it would definitely make for an epic story in the Book of Keeley. But we hadn't known each other that long. Not really. And the future was so fuzzy. As in, I wasn't sure if we had one.

I bit my lip. "Do you think he's expecting that to happen?"

"I don't know. I don't know anything about your relationship with him."

I felt all kinds of hot. "Wait. Is this why you wanted to take this drive? So you could ask me?"

Morgan adjusted her side mirror ever so slightly. "We haven't really talked about much lately."

"What do you mean? We talk every day."

"Yeah, but never about the meaty stuff. I feel like there's things you're not telling me."

I shrugged. "Not at all. I'm living the dream."

She still seemed frustrated with me. "It's not just the Jesse stuff. Like, for instance, we haven't talked about yesterday. How is your mom doing? Like, physically. I saw her fall on the news, poor thing."

I almost wanted to change the subject back to my sex life, but I forced myself to answer her question. After all, Morgan was my best friend. She was exactly the person I should talk to about this stuff. And I had Levi's stupid voice in my head, accusing me of pretending that bad things weren't happening. "It was an accident." When Morgan didn't immediately say *Oh yeah, of course,* I turned to face her. "It *was* an accident."

"Keeley, obviously!"

"What other meat would you like to discuss?"

"Okay. Well. Do you know what your dad's going to do now that the dam has started up? Has he talked at all about a backup plan? I was thinking that the adjusters might give him more money, since he's, like, the leader."

It was practically an echo. I realized then that Morgan must have known that her mom had come to talk with my dad. And I was now aware that anything I said would probably get back to her, too.

"He still has a lot of people supporting him. Our phone was seriously ringing off the hook last night. I mean, he's helped a lot of people get back into their homes, like you and your mom. They kind of owe him this, you know?"

I watched her to see how that landed. Morgan pressed her lips together. "Well, no matter how all this plays out, your mom has our full support." It took a second for me to notice how carefully Morgan had seemed to choose her words. "Hey, you want to see if Mineo's finally opened back up?"

Smugly, I settled into my seat. Now she was the one who wanted to change the subject. "Isn't it still closed?"

"One of my mom's clients said she saw people moving around inside there yesterday."

We couldn't pull up to Mineo's. That section of Main Street was closed to traffic. Actually, I don't think it had ever opened up since the initial flood. I remembered Mr. Viola saying how the town might purposely keep the roads closed. I hadn't noticed as much when I was working with Levi, because those barriers didn't apply to us. But now I did.

We parked and walked. I held up the caution tape for us both to shimmy under.

From across the street, I saw that the windows of Mineo's were dark. "Maybe they aren't doing lunch anymore? Just dinner?"

Morgan walked up to the door and pointed at a sign taped to the window. She read aloud, "'Thank you, Aberdeen, for your loyal service. Stay dry.'" Even though the doors had been padlocked shut, she still pulled on the handles. Hard. Then she flopped onto the curb. "I can't believe I'll never have a slice of Mineo's pizza again."

"Don't worry. It wasn't that good anyway."

I'd said it to be funny, to lighten the mood. But Morgan spun around and glared at me. "I don't know why you'd say something like that." She stood up and walked back to her car.

"I was kidding. And you know Mineo's sucks. Why are you acting like it's the best pizza in the world?"

"Because it's my pizza place, in my hometown, where I used to go eat lunch with my best friend. And now it's gone."

The pizza place was gone, the town might be too. Our friendship? I really hoped that was still intact.

On our way back to school, I casually said, "Hey. There was something I wanted to talk to you about."

"What?"

"Did you want to invite Wes to be your date to Secret Prom?"

She froze up. "Are you joking?"

"No. If this were a normal prom, you could bring someone from another school."

"I don't know. I mean, he didn't say two words to me at Elise's good-bye party."

"He clearly wanted to talk to you, though. That was obvious."

"You really think so?"

I tried not to be hurt over how easily she smiled for the rest of the ride back to school. Instead, I hoped I'd just fixed whatever was broken between us before the crack gave way.

# 29

Even before our little tiff at the graveyard, I had planned to blow off work with Levi to shop for prom stuff with Jesse. He wasn't going to be able to go until after dinner, which was fine. But taking the afternoon off would give me time to go home, shower, and make myself look extra cute.

So, after checking that the coast was clear of both teachers and Levi, I hit up my locker.

Inside I found a paycheck for all the work I'd done so far.

I guessed I was fired.

I didn't tell my mom that when I presented her with the check.

"This is terrific, Keeley. I know it doesn't seem like much, but a couple hundred dollars will cover your books for a semester."

"Can I have a little bit of money?" I asked her. "There are some, um, collections happening at school for an end-of-the-year party."

Mom gave me fifty dollars. Which was way more than I expected. I had planned to spend some of it on Secret Prom. I didn't want to think of it as a joke prom. It was going to be *my* prom. My prom with Jesse Ford.

. . .

I had dinner that night with just Mom, since Dad was out. "He's installing a new set of stairs to someone's house," she'd said. And I wondered what she knew about his petition, if he'd gotten many signatures today.

Mom cleared dishes and said she was going to take a quick nap. She'd pulled a double shift almost every day since the flood, and she devoted any free time left over to helping her patients deal with the aftermath. There were a bunch of seniors who had no local family around to help them. Some of these were people my mom had known her whole life. Old teachers from when she was a student at Aberdeen High, friends of her mom and dad, my grandma and grandpa. Mom helped them clean and pack, assisted in getting their paperwork in order, made them appointments with the adjusters.

I took a shower and then tried to find something cute to wear. Since it was finally starting to feel like spring, I went with a white sleeveless blouse with blue and yellow flowers and my favorite jeans, light blue with an authentic hole in the knee. Except I didn't find the jeans. I had put them into the laundry weeks ago but they hadn't made their way back into my drawer.

I peeked into Mom's bedroom, but it was empty.

When I went downstairs, I traced a circle through the living room and into the kitchen and craned my neck into the pantry.

It wasn't until I was in the living room again, leaning over the back of the couch toward the picture window to see if her car was still in our driveway, that I saw the top of her head bobbing up and down between the front cedar hedges.

I walked outside. She had a mat out for her knees, her garden tools, and a few empty plastic bags. I watched her carefully lift out a bulb with cupped hands, tendrils of roots cascading down like exposed veins. She placed it gently in a plastic bag.

"Mom?" It seemed like a crazy thing to be doing at night.

She looked startled, then, seeing it was me, sat back on her heels. "I thought you'd left."

"Do you remember washing my favorite jeans? The light blue ones?"

Her eyes went up to the sky, thinking. "I think so. Check the basket near the dryer. Actually, check the dryer itself. They might have been in the last load."

"What are you doing?"

"Your grandmother Jean gave me these freesia bulbs. Transplanted them from her garden to mine when your father and I were married."

I already knew that, of course. My mom always looked forward to when they would bloom white flowers in the summertime. She liked opening the front window and letting the smell into our living room.

"Why are you digging them out?"

She leaned forward, her hair hanging in her face. "Some of the girls at work were saying how all the rain was going to rot their garden bulbs." And then, either to remind me or shut me up, she nudged her chin back toward the house. "Check the dryer."

It was dark when Jesse picked me up about an hour later. I wondered if we might be going to Walmart alone, but Julia was with him.

"Sorry. My mom's still working. Which is good, she'll be able to give us her discount."

I ignored him. He didn't have anything to apologize for. Instead, I said, "Hey, Julia. You sure you don't want to stay in the front seat?" while she unbuckled, climbed over the middle console, and tumbled into the back.

"Nope."

"So, do you have a list?"

Jesse gave me the eye, like I was crazy. And then he held up his phone to show me a very detailed and organized list. Some of the stuff I expected. Plastic champagne flutes. Tea light candles. Other things were totally random.

"A kiddie pool?"

Jesse put his hands over Julia's ears and mouthed, *To keep all the beers on ice!*

"How much beer are you getting?"

Jesse wagged his eyebrows. "You only throw a party like this once in a lifetime! We gotta go all out!"

We had a blast going through the aisles together. Jesse pushed Julia in the cart. A few times he'd let go and send Julia flying toward a display of soup cans or books. Julia screamed so loud—not a scared scream, a happy, delighted squeal—and Jesse would grab the cart at the very last second and keep her from crashing. Most of the time, I hung off the front of the cart like a mermaid carving on a Viking ship.

"Oooh! Can we please get one of these for our dance floor?" I said when I found a portable disco ball. The box said it had four speeds and could be mounted on any wall. "We are having a dance floor, right?"

I noticed red creeping up Jesse's neck. His eyes narrowed to little slits. I had never, ever seen him angry before, not even on the soccer field when Aberdeen was getting their asses beat. It was so intense, so brooding. He didn't even hear my question. I stepped alongside him and tried to see what he was staring at over Julia's head.

His mother was talking to a man at the accessory counter. It was clear this guy wasn't just a customer, though. There was a familiarity, a flirtiness to them. His mother was leaning forward on her cash register, trying to slide a pair of hot-pink sunglasses onto his nose. The man kept turning his head at the very last second until she gave up. Then, while she pouted, he turned around and rested his back against the counter and twirled the display screen on her register around and around like a carousel.

Though Jesse had never told me anything about him, I knew this man was probably his father. Jesse didn't look like him as much as he did his mother, but they both had the same wide, mischievous grin.

I turned to him and whispered, "Are you okay?"

But Jesse was gone.

I looked left, then right, then left again.

"Where's my brother?" Julia asked.

"I'm not sure," I said, then pushed the cart down the end of the aisle and looked both ways. "Umm, I bet he probably went up to the register."

Jesse wasn't there, either. I texted him, but he didn't write back.

I wasn't sure what to do.

"Can we go see my mom now?"

"Maybe in a little bit."

Julia started kicking her feet. Not a full-on tantrum, but

her frustrations were clearly brewing. "Why are we just standing here?"

"Miss!" I looked up. A sales associate was flagging me toward her lane. "Excuse me, miss! This lane is open!"

"Come on, Julia. Help me put things on the belt, okay?"

As I watched the stuff get scanned and loaded into bags, and especially when I had to pay, I had pangs of regret. A lot of it was stupid junk. Like water guns and maracas and crap like that. Also, we were supposed to be getting his mom's employee discount. I actually had to put some stuff back to get it under fifty bucks.

I pushed Julia to the store entrance and lingered close to the automatic glass doors, so that if Jesse had slipped outside, he'd be able to see us.

"Ladies!"

Jesse came running from the side, where the fast-food nook was, three slushies in his hands. "Where have you guys been?"

I was annoyed with how flip he was. "Waiting for you. Where'd you go?"

"I thought you were following me." He looked at our cart. "Wait. You already checked out? I went running up and down all the lanes but I didn't see you."

I forced a smile. "Didn't you get my texts?"

He patted himself down. "Ugh. Left my phone in the car." Except I knew he had his phone with him. That was where he'd written his list.

"Do you want to go see your mom?" I said, knowing what his answer would be.

"Nah. It's fine. I walked over to her counter, thinking she could have you guys paged, but she's pretty busy."

We went back to his car and he clicked open the back hatch and loaded the stuff in. "I had to put back the disco ball and the piñata and the tiki lights. I didn't have enough cash."

"Oh, dang. I was going to use my mom's credit card. Don't worry. I'll bring cash for you tomorrow."

After making sure Julia was buckled up, he drove me home. The music was louder than it needed to be, maybe to keep me from talking. I watched him out of the corner of my eye, trying to see if he was okay. I had so many questions, things I wanted to ask him.

It bothered me that he so obviously was lying, but I also understood the impulse. Something difficult was happening here. Something intimate. And even though he was pushing me out of it, I still felt closer to him than I ever had, simply because I had been there. And the way he gripped my hand on the ride home, I knew he was happy I was with him.

We were getting closer. That was a good thing.

# 30

If Levi hadn't already fired me before he stuck my paycheck in my locker, I figured blowing off work on Wednesday would definitely have done the trick. But apparently I was wrong about that. He came by my locker right after homeroom. I was on the floor, cleaning it out. Tomorrow was graduation and the last day of school.

"Hey, Keeley."

I didn't look at him. I was still angry about what he'd said to me in the graveyard caretaker's house. "Hey, Levi."

"Umm, when you bailed on me in the middle of the work day, was that you officially quitting the job?"

"Pretty much. Was that check you stuffed in my locker yesterday a sign that I was fired?"

"Pretty much," he said sheepishly. "But here's the thing. I really need your help today." He explained that since the dam construction began, the pace of work had picked up significantly. "Okay, so you know how normally we have about six to eight houses to clear after school? Well, yesterday they wanted us to do twelve—and I only got through eight—and today they want us to do eighteen."

"Eighteen is totally impossible."

He crouched down. "I know. But maybe fifteen is possible, if we bust our humps?" He must have seen me frowning because he pleaded, "Just help me get caught up and then you can quit. Remember, you owe me. You needed a job, I gave you a job. And I haven't worked you hard at all. I've basically let you do nothing."

"I don't know," I said, keeping him dangling. I liked him begging me.

"What if I give you my pay too? You'll make double today."

Fifteen houses at twenty bucks a house was three hundred bucks for the day. And since I'd spent all my money yesterday at Walmart, I said, "Fine."

"I'll see you after school," he said quickly. And then walked away. I wondered why he'd made such a quick escape, but then Jesse came up.

"What'd Hamrick want?"

"For me to work today."

"Please, Keeley! Quit that stupid job already!"

"Think of it like this. So long as I stay on Levi's good side, there's no way he'll tell his dad about our Secret Prom."

Jesse nodded. "Good point. But after that, just quit, okay? We've only got so much time left. I don't want you blowing it with Hamrick."

I kissed him. "Promise."

I think I would still have been annoyed with Levi if I hadn't seen the work wearing on him. Not in the same way it wore on me, which was directly tied to my dad. But his own stress. He wanted to please his father. And he was worried about his graduation speech. He kept mumbling lines of it to himself. Whether or not he wanted to admit it, he had to have feelings about graduating. There was no way he was going to Secret Prom, so Friday would be the end of Aberdeen High for him.

So, for his sake, I tried to be a better worker. I bagged up people's discarded possessions faster. It wasn't even that hard, because I was less interested in the things I found. I had long since stopped counting points for weirdness. It was all trash, trash that was sinking my dad's efforts, and the faster I threw it away, the less it got to me.

"Hey, can I ask you a question about my speech?"

"Shoot."

"I'm between two different Albert Einstein quotes and I'm not sure which one is better." He pulled out a stack of note cards from his back pocket. His handwriting was very neat and precise, but there was a kidlike quality about it too, like someone practicing their letters. "Okay. Which do you find more inspirational?" He cleared his throat. "'*The important thing is not to stop questioning.*' Or '*Try not to become a man of success, but rather try to become a man of value.*' I'm kind of leaning toward that one."

"You want my honest opinion?"

He winced. "Umm, maybe not."

"I think both are boring as hell. Also hackneyed to the point of being completely devoid of meaning."

"Jesus, don't hold back or anything." He groaned. "I've been working all week on this thing."

"Why are you so stressed about this speech?"

"Because it's the culmination of everything I've worked for my entire high school career."

"So?"

He stared at me, slack-jawed. "So? Isn't it obvious how important that would make it?"

"Levi, listen. Our principal bailed, so has half the school. And here's the thing. No one's really going to be listening."

Levi frowned. "Gee, thanks a lot."

"What? Don't take it personal. Speeches are boring, Levi. I bet I could guess some of the other things you're going to say." I tapped my lip with my finger. "Do you make some kind of mention of how we've all grown so much since freshman year?"

His face flashed with shock. He pulled his hoodie over his head. "I don't want to play this game."

"Wait," I said, cracking up. "Do you also say how nervous and scared we all were to start high school?"

Levi broke into a jog and ran into a bathroom and closed the door. Through it, he grumbled, "Thanks a lot for your help. So glad I asked you."

"I'm not trying to make you mad. I'm trying to take the pressure off. There's a formula to these big-moment speeches, and you've clearly got it down. So don't worry about it. Take the night off. Do something fun."

He was quiet for a second. "Hey, I thought you said you checked this bathroom. The lights are still on."

"Forget it."

We finished the last house on our list as the sun was going down.

"Fifteen. That's a new record for us."

I shook the can of red spray paint. It felt too light, the little ball inside clanking hard against the sides. I made the *X* but the stream sputtered toward the end. I tried not to think about what that meant for my dad.

Levi started packing up. While he did, I texted Morgan. Just finishing up work. Do you want to hang?

I'm video chatting with Elise tonight. She's going to walk me around her new town.

I waited for her to invite me, but she didn't. Which, if I'm being completely honest, kind of pissed me off. Elise leaving was supposed to bring us closer together, but I'd never felt like we were farther apart.

Then again, maybe it was just the bummer of everything that had been happening that was bringing me down. And seeing Elise's new life would be a distraction for her like Jesse was for me.

Before I really thought it through, I asked Levi, "Umm, what are you doing now?"

"Going home and throwing my speech in the trash. Why?"

"Let's do something. You should have one last stupid adventure before you graduate, especially since you aren't going to Secret Prom."

"You're right about that."

I shook my head. "Levi, your problem is that you don't know how to have fun."

"I do too."

I folded my arms. "I dare you to have fun. Right now."

"What? Like *now* now?"

"Yes. Like . . . ready . . . set . . . Fun!" Levi stood there, staring blankly. "See. I was right."

"Quit it. I just don't know what's fun that we could do right now."

I pulled at his belt, his ring of keys. "You've basically got access to anywhere in town. Isn't there any place you want to go? Something you want to see?"

"No place that we're actually allowed to be."

My eyes went wide. "Now you're talking! Come on. Where?"

He dropped his head back. "I don't know. I guess, if I had to pick something, I'd pick, maybe . . . the movie theater."

We had a single-screen movie house in Aberdeen, down near the mill. They'd built it for the workers, and my grandpa said he used to go as a boy for a buck.

Aberdeen Cinema didn't exactly keep up with the times. The sound was pretty shitty and the seats totally uncomfortable. The popcorn was stale and too salty, and sometimes the fountain soda tasted weird and chemical-y. But we'd still go, especially on rainy days in the summertime, when there was really nothing else to do. My favorite was the week before Christmas, when the theater would play an old print of *It's a Wonderful Life* and let people in for free, so long as they brought a can or two for the town food bank.

But once Morgan got her license, we started going to the megaplex in Ridgewood, with stadium seating and Dolby sound and a counter full of different fancy flavored shakers you could put on your popcorn. I felt bad about that now, abandoning our hometown spot for the shinier, newer thing.

"Let's go."

"The workers started diverting the river, so the water's backed up down there now. "

"Well, if we can't get in, we can't get in. But let's at least try." He kicked something on the ground, a rock maybe. "I promise

I'll wear a hard hat and a reflective vest and a life preserver . . . whatever."

He climbed on his bike. "All right. But if anyone's down there, we have to go, okay? If my dad found out I was doing this, he'd kill me."

I nodded. "Absolutely."

It became a much bigger production than we'd thought. Levi took me on his bike. The street the theater was on was flooded, just like he said it would be. We couldn't even get close. I figured he'd just turn around, but instead he put down his kickstand near a shed. Opening the padlock, he pulled out a kayak and two life jackets.

"How'd you know this was here?" I asked.

"It's rescue stuff. For the construction site." He held up the life vest. "Come on," he said. "You promised."

There would be no getting in the front door of the theater. Water was halfway up the glass. But Levi paddled us around to the back, where it was all brick wall. With his paddle, he was able to pull down the ladder of a fire escape. And we both climbed up. The door on the first landing was locked, so we went up to the next one. We were at least three stories high at that point, but with the water below us, I told myself it wasn't as dangerous.

Still, my heart was pounding.

Levi was able to open that door. After clicking on his flashlight and shining the beam around, he let me go in.

A long hallway with old movie posters led to a tiny door. It opened into the projection room. There were two folding chairs there, along with a big metal block where the projector had sat. It was gone though.

There was a glass window that looked down on the theater. I cupped my hands to the window and tried to see in. Levi came and shined the flashlight down like a projector beam, and it caught the dust in the air. There was half a white screen, and only half the seats in the very back. Everything else was underwater.

"Good call," I said. "This might be the coolest thing I've ever seen."

Levi was quiet for a minute. "My mom and I watched every single Harry Potter movie here."

It made my heart hurt. "How did she die?"

"You don't know? I thought everyone did." I shook my head. "Car accident. It's why they put up that red blinking light."

Oh my God. I thought back to our conversation where I said everyone ran that light. I wanted to curl up into a ball and die.

"It's fine. It actually feels good, talking about her. My dad never does, so I really don't have a chance to much."

The flashlight whipped up to his face as Levi wiped his eyes on his sleeve. "Didn't think I was going to cry." I doubt he'd wanted me to see that, but he wasn't ashamed. With Levi what you saw was what you got.

I hadn't expected any of this. I only wanted Levi to have fun. But now, here he was, crying over his dead mom in front of me. I reached out and gave him a hug. I hugged him like Morgan had hugged Elise when she saw her destroyed house. Like a friend who just wants to be there for you. I didn't let myself think in that moment about the people I'd let down on that front lately. I just focused on being there for Levi, and tried to make that enough.

• • •

It seemed like every day, Mom came home from work with some weird artifact of another person's life. Something they couldn't bear to throw out but that it didn't make sense to take with them, and everything had a vintage sheen to it because almost all of her patients were older people. A set of crystal candlesticks that wouldn't look out of place on any grandmother's dining table. An old record player that came with its own carrying case. A framed collection of state quarters.

I remember holding up a comforter in a plastic bag. "This thing is brand-new. I can't believe someone just threw it away." I thought it would look good in my room. It was baby blue with these beautiful illustrations of different birds all over it, like pages from an Audubon Society field guide.

"Every Macy's in America has that for sale. But an afghan knit by their grandmother? That's what you can't replace."

"I guess."

At first, the stuff began to collect in odd places around our house. It snuck up on me. I'd be walking through the living room on my way upstairs when a thing would catch my eye. And I'd stop and think, *How long has that painting of a tropical sunset been there? That ceramic crane?*

Every item was presented to my mother as a gift with a story. How a certain thing was acquired, what it had meant to them, and how glad they were knowing they could pass it on to her. I knew that made it even harder for Mom to get rid of. It was like throwing away someone's memory. Even if they were trivial things, they had stories. That comforter, I learned, was bought for someone's college-age daughter who ended up dying of an overdose. After that, I couldn't have it on my bed. I put it back downstairs.

I didn't love the feeling of taking on this stuff, especially not when we hadn't made any plans of our own. It seemed like a bad omen. All our eggs were in this basket, saving Aberdeen. We didn't have a backup plan.

I should clarify that. We didn't have a backup plan that was shared with me.

I found out that afternoon, when I was hunting for an old dress of my mother's to wear to Secret Prom. I hadn't found anything in her bedroom closet, so I pulled down the attic ladder and started climbing up into the crawl space.

"Where are you going?"

"To the moon," I said.

She folded her arms. "What do you need up in the attic?"

"Why? Can I not go up there?"

"I just don't want you digging through everything and making a mess. If there is something specific you want, let me know and I'll grab it for you."

"I won't make a mess."

Mom looked annoyed, but what could she do? Forbid me to go?

I ransacked a few boxes of old clothes but found nothing fancy, nothing dressy inside. Then I checked the cedar closet. There was Mom's wedding dress, Dad's corduroy wedding suit. And then I spotted a pale pink dress. The top was strapless and fitted, the bottom was a short bubble skirt with crinoline underneath to make it extra poufy. It was the one she'd worn to Spring Formal. I recognized it from the pictures.

I pulled off my shirt and slid the dress on over my jeans. It mostly fit, except I had trouble getting the zipper up in the back.

Morgan would help me with that, or else safety-pin it. How cool, I thought, that Morgan and I would be wearing our moms' dresses.

Before I headed back downstairs, I picked up my copy of *A Wrinkle in Time* from the bookshelf. I wanted to finish rereading it. When I did, I noticed a white piece of paper tucked between two books on the shelf below. Everything on that shelf was old and yellowed, but the paper was crisp and bright white. It had been folded in threes. I opened it up.

It was an offer from the government adjusters for our home. Five hundred thousand dollars.

The two signature lines, with my mom's and dad's names printed under them, were blank.

I immediately imagined my mom at City Hall, helping one of her patients meet with an adjuster. And afterward, she'd linger until she could be sure no one else was around. Then she'd duck in and ask one, confidentially, what they might expect for a settlement.

If Dad found out, he'd never forgive her. If the people who were still supporting Dad found out, that'd be even worse. They'd never forgive him. He'd managed to get a page and a half of signatures. Not much, but it was still something. And there were still a few people in the balance, like Mrs. Dorsey and Jesse's mom, who hadn't signed but hadn't made any moves yet either.

Obviously, I wasn't going to tell anyone what I had found. But who else could? One of the adjusters? Mom? Mrs. Dorsey probably knew. Which meant Morgan did too. I really hoped my mom wasn't that stupid. But the fact that I was there, holding that offer in the first place, didn't give me much hope.

# 31

**Friday, May 27**
Extended Weekend Forecast: We are tracking a band of severe thunderstorms moving up from the south. Current models project Aberdeen County receiving significant rainfall beginning in 36–48 hours. Please stay tuned for further updates.

The graduation ceremony for the final senior class of Aberdeen High was held first thing in the morning. Underclassmen were excused for the day, our last day, but a lot of us showed up anyway.

Not Morgan. She'd decided that yesterday would be her last day. She said good-bye to all her teachers, took pictures of us in front of our lockers. I was surprised, especially considering the guilt trip she gave me over my supposed nonappreciation of Mineo's, but I wasn't about to call her out on it, since that fight was over and done with and things were okay between us again.

I remembered from years past that graduation tickets were a hot commodity. Each senior was allotted four, and in the days leading up to graduation, a lot of trading and wheeling and dealing went on to score extra tickets for grandparents or aunts and uncles.

Not this time.

The front three rows were filled with seniors, obviously. Behind them, there were maybe ten rows designated for family. And then the middle of the auditorium was empty, just a smattering of underclassmen until the very last rows. Some kids even had their feet up on the vacant chairs in front of them.

You couldn't really tell any of the seniors apart, because they had on the same hunter-green gowns and matching caps with gold tassels. Some people had decorated the very tops of their caps, which was a loosely embraced tradition. Usually they said SENIORS RULE and that sort of thing. There were a few of those here. But other kids had taken a somewhat more depressing view and wrote things like RIP ABERDEEN and I CAN'T SWIM.

Our high school band was basically dismantled, so a saxophonist, a trumpet player, and a flutist were the only ones onstage, and they played the processional march as loudly as they could, so it would fill the room.

I was pretty distracted. Secret Prom was tomorrow, and the forecast wasn't looking good.

Actually, it was looking terrible.

Supposedly another big storm was coming our way, and for the first time, there was talk of another potential flood. I turned myself into an amateur meteorologist. I was cross-referencing different forecasts, refreshing the radar apps on my phone.

The vice-principal introduced Levi as class valedictorian. Levi walked up and shook the vice-principal's hand, then took his place behind the podium. He had his stack of note cards with him, just as he had yesterday. He flipped nervously through them as if he'd discovered they were out of order or written in a different language.

"Hello," he eventually said. Too loud.

A few people snickered.

I watched Levi stare out at the crowd. He put his note cards down and then gripped the sides of the podium as if it were his seat on a roller coaster.

"So . . . I'm going places."

It took a second for some kids to make the connection to the article, I think. Of course, I got it right away. Jesse, too, because he spun around in his seat and gave me a wide-eyed look. Levi helpfully held a copy of it up for the people who didn't. "See," he said, tapping the headline. "It says right here. Levi Hamrick, *A Guy Who's Going Places!*"

He took a deep breath. "I have to say, I was pretty embarrassed when this came out. But honestly"—he shrugged—"that's who I wanted to be. I've been preparing to leave Aberdeen ever since . . ." He paused, and I was almost hoping he wouldn't say it. "Umm, ever since my mom died. And so when we got the news about the dam, I thought to myself, *Good. Now I won't have to drive through the intersection where my mom was killed ever again.*"

You could have heard a pin drop.

"But then yesterday, while I was out with a friend, I found myself thinking that once Aberdeen is gone, I'll never ever get to stand in a place where my mom and I were happy together. Even though I normally try not to look, I can see her everywhere if I want."

My phone buzzed. A text from Jesse. Wait. Are you his therapist?

And then another. Seriously though, wtf is this speech? Dead mother = major graduation downer.

I wrote back LOL, but if I actually had *laughed out loud*, it would have been that nervous kind. Not ha ha funny laughter.

Levi went on. His cap kept sliding down his forehead,

probably because his hair was freshly cut. "We've been told that all good things must come to an end. Even things that feel permanent. Stuff that maybe we take for granted. Like this town. Or for me, my mom. So how tightly *are* we supposed to hold on to stuff that we love? Really tightly? Or not at all? Should we be sad when they go away? Should we fight? Or is letting stuff we love go inevitable, like that old adage says?"

He paused. At first I thought it was a dramatic pause. But then I realized, no, Levi was waiting. Waiting for someone to tell him.

The entire crowd shifted uncomfortably in their seats, like a ship leaning to the side.

Jesse spun around and made a cuckoo face.

I could barely look at Levi. I had pushed him to go off his script. It definitely wasn't boring, but it wasn't exactly going well. He was just sort of standing there, rambling.

And God, oh no. I realized he was about to cry.

Sheriff Hamrick, who was only one row ahead of me, had his jaw set. But the veins in his forehead were bulging. He was not happy.

I had to do something.

I let my phone fall into my lap, cupped my hands, and started one of those slow golf claps. *Clap. Clap. Clap.* Nice and slow. Other people began to join in and speeded up. *Clap clap clap.* I stomped along with it too, and other people joined in. The room filled with thunder. *Clapclapclapclap.*

"Right, okay," Levi said, as if someone had told him to get offstage. He nodded and went back to his seat.

Then, after a few more speeches, it was diploma time.

When the vice-principal said Jesse's name, I whooped and

hollered. Jesse came across the stage with a snorkeling face mask and breathing tube in his mouth and flippers on his feet. And moved his arms like he was swimming. That got a good bit of applause, probably the most of everyone. He took his diploma, shook the vice-principal's hand, and went back to his seat.

Levi crossed the stage, and I clapped for him, too. I felt bad that it was so quiet. He looked shell-shocked from his speech. Vacant.

A heavy silence came over the entire room once all the diplomas were handed out. I think because we knew this was the end. Not just of their senior year, but of Aberdeen High.

The graduates stood up and filed past us. The band played them out, but it sounded more like a funeral march.

I got up, smoothed my skirt.

Everyone was hanging out on the front lawn, taking pictures, hugging teachers, crying. There were four huge Dumpsters parked along the bus lanes. Mayor Aversano was wasting no time.

I looked around and saw Jesse getting his picture taken with Julia. His mother was taking the photo with her phone, and Jesse had Julia perched up on his shoulder, as if she were a parrot. The man I had seen at the Walmart, Jesse's dad, was not there. Which was a relief.

I walked over slowly, hoping Jesse would see me before I got there. But he was too busy playing with Julia, running around the parking lot, trying to grab his diving mask back.

"Way to graduate," I said, and gave his arm a playful punch. "The swim gear was a nice touch."

"Thanks." He ducked and gave me a quick peck on the cheek before he went back to chasing Julia.

"This is my mask! I'm going to need it for our new swimming pool!"

I figured Julia was talking about the kiddie pool we had bought for Secret Prom. Jesse scooped her up and covered her mouth. Maybe because he was embarrassed that he hadn't paid me back yet? Then he said, "Keeley, what are you doing now? Let's go eat breakfast somewhere. And then I was thinking we go and shoot a video about *you know what*. Reiterate the instructions, make sure everyone knows it's going off tomorrow, rain or shine."

"Sure, okay. I don't think I have work until later." I pulled out my phone, thinking I should text Levi, but Jesse snatched it away.

Jesse rolled his eyes. "I bet Levi doesn't take off for graduation."

Julia broke free and Jesse chased her again. I found myself standing next to Jesse's mom.

"Hi, I'm Keeley." I waited for a flash of recognition. "Um, Jim Hewitt's daughter?" She looked blank. "The Reservoir Resistance."

Jesse's mom nodded, but she still looked confused. Or maybe she was just distracted. I wanted to ask her about the petition, not give her a hard sell, but maybe casually mention it, but Jesse was calling, "Keeley!" He gave the mask back to Julia and sent her running toward Jesse's mom. "Let's go!"

"Bye," I said shyly to Jesse's mom.

Jesse put his arm around me. I kept glancing back at the school. It was starting to sink in that this was it. Really it.

"I'm just going to say bye to Zito. Here's my keys."

"Oh. Okay."

Jesse took off. Zito was near his car with his family. Jesse came up and gave him a high five, hugged a woman I assumed was Zito's mom. He lifted her off the ground the same way he did to me sometimes. Zito's mom kicked her legs and squirmed.

I looked around and saw Levi standing a few feet away, next to Sheriff Hamrick. Levi smiled obligatorily as his dad took his picture with his phone. Then the two stood side by side, surveying the parking lot. A couple of teachers came up and patted Levi on the back. And also a couple of the AP nerds. But that was it.

I wanted to go over to him, tell him I liked his speech. And I totally would have, if not for Jesse crouching down, waiting for me to hop on his back so he could give me a piggyback ride to his car. A minute later, he was driving us out of our former high school parking lot for the last time.

As we pulled away I thought about the locket I'd passed up to buy with my Spring Formal dress. Sometimes I regretted it, but I wasn't sure what I would have fit in a locket anyway. There were suddenly a million memories I wanted to hold on to. I didn't want to let anything go.

I texted Levi after lunch. Hey where are you?

At the police station picking up today's paperwork.

Oh. Do you have a lot of houses to see?

Yeah.

Immediately after, he wrote, Sorry. I know that's not what you want to hear.

It's fine, I wrote. I can help you again if you want. You don't have to pay me double this time. Consider it a graduation present.

Okay, thanks.

He texted me the first address.

My stomach growled. I had done the dainty eating routine at the diner with Jesse. Can you maybe bring me something to eat? I mean, there are donuts at the police station, right? Cops and donuts, that's a thing, isn't it?

Unreal.

And then, a few seconds later, I got you a chocolate glazed.

Our first house of the day was in the flood zone. And the closer I got to the river, the more red *X*s I saw painted on front doors. There were mountains of garbage and furniture on every corner, some as high as the street signs. It was a little bit scary, actually. Like an apocalypse.

Levi was waiting on the curb, and as soon as he saw me walking toward him, he stood up and pushed the hood of his sweatshirt off his head.

"I forgot to tell you that I liked your speech," I said. "In case you were wondering."

"I'm glad *you* did."

"What do you mean?"

"My dad." He shook his head and handed me my chocolate donut. He'd put it in a Ziploc bag, along with a napkin. "I think he was looking forward to graduation more because it meant I was that much closer to leaving."

"Why do you say that? He's got to be proud of you."

"I know he's proud. But he's also, like, pushing me out the door. It was his idea that I do this precollege summer class. I told him it doesn't matter, it's not like I'm getting credit for it or anything. I'd rather stay here and help out. But he won't listen. He actually told me this morning, 'You want this to hurt as little as possible? Then you need to rip the Band-Aid off as fast as you can.'"

"Yeesh."

"I know."

And then, I think because neither of us knew what to say next, we turned our attention to the clipboard, checked the address on his paper against the one we were standing in front of. The sheet was full of addresses, people who were gone.

This particular house was more like a cottage. It was small and plain and utilitarian, closer to a garage than a home. It looked to have had a nice flower garden, at least before the flood. Now it was as if a tractor had plowed straight through the beds, tearing out the flowers, snapping wooden garden stakes in half, crushing the ceramic lawn ornaments.

A fallen elm had taken down half the front porch. Someone had put a chain saw to the limbs blocking the door. The front window was nailed over with plywood. Levi pushed the front door open wide. The living room stayed dark, because of the plywood, so we used flashlights.

The rooms were still full of everything, but nothing was where it belonged. Things had floated and bobbed to new places. We stepped through carefully. The brown carpet was still soggy like moss. Mud slicked the walls.

This was the first and only time I was afraid to be in one of these houses.

I leaned past Levi and glanced into the kitchen. There were stacks of canned goods on the table and a pile of dirty dishes in the sink. "Jeez," I said. "Did this guy take anything with him?"

"Hello?" Levi called out.

No one answered.

So we shrugged at each other and then got to work. Jesse flicked light switches while I turned the stove knobs in the kitchen and listened for a hiss.

"I think the gas is off," I called out.

"Okay. I'll check the lights in the back bedroom." He pointed at a room off the kitchen, where a bed was covered in blankets.

We were both looking when a body sat up.

I screamed and Levi instinctively put himself ahead of me.

"One minute," a man's voice grumbled.

Levi turned to me, eyes wide. "Go outside. I'm going to call my dad," he whispered.

Before I could, the man spoke again.

"I wasn't expecting guests." There was a phlegmy cough, the kind only an old person could achieve. "Let me get on some pants."

I laughed but Levi hushed me and said, "Thanks, sir! We'd appreciate that."

Fifteen minutes later, we cleared up the misunderstanding. Russell Dixon had not evacuated. There was apparently some confusion, as the adjusters had come to visit him a few days ago. They had made him an offer and then condemned his house, leaving him no real choice in the matter. But Mr. Dixon wasn't aware of that. He simply thanked the men for their time, but only so they'd get the hell off his property.

Mr. Dixon was one of the people who'd come to our house that first morning after the flood. And his was one of the names on my dad's petition.

When we explained the mistake, he looked so sad. "I feel like this is my fault. I was trying to be polite to these guys."

"It's not."

He sat across from us at his kitchen table, with his salt-white hair and a scruffy beard that helped fill out his hollow face. He had on a stained button-up shirt and pants that were too big for him. To me, he said, "Your daddy's been by here a few times, fixing stuff for me. He checks in on me, brings me groceries, and makes sure I'm okay. I'd been meaning to tell him they shut my power off, but I know he's real busy with other folks. I didn't want to bother him." He sighed. "I'd offer to make you kids some tea or something, but I don't have no water, neither. I'm on the well but the pump's electric."

Levi pulled me aside. "Mr. Dixon can't stay here. Especially not with this new storm coming. I just texted my dad."

I felt my lip curl. "Levi! Why'd you do that without talking to me first!"

Levi opened his mouth to defend himself. But thankfully he thought better of it.

I stepped outside and called Dad.

"Yeah, Kee. What's up?"

"Dad, I'm at Russell Dixon's place."

"Oh, no. Is everything okay?"

"Yeah. I mean, no. They've condemned his house. He didn't even know. And now I think the police are coming over to take him away."

"Damn."

"Dad, he can't stay here. And not just because of that. His house is like . . . falling down. He doesn't have water, electricity . . ."

I welled up, because it was just so sad. I wanted to ask him, *Did you know? Did you know things were this bad?*

Dad let out a sigh. "I'm on my way."

When I went back into the kitchen, Levi was sweeping the floor. I knew why. He didn't want to have a conversation with Mr. Dixon.

Mr. Dixon looked at me and said, "Please tell this boy to put that broom down. A little dirt ain't going to kill me and sweeping it up ain't going to save me, neither." He wasn't mad. He was smiling.

"He just wants to help." I said it even though, suddenly, none of what we were doing felt that way, no matter how Levi tried to spin it.

Mr. Dixon lifted a shaky hand and smoothed his hair. "Do you think they're going to make me go right now?"

Levi glanced at me. I pressed my lips together. I sure as hell wasn't going to break the news to Mr. Dixon. Quietly, Levi said, "Probably."

"Did you want us to help you pack anything up? We can put some clothes in a bag for you."

Mr. Dixon glanced around his house. It was almost too overwhelming. All of his possessions, everywhere.

"Well." He rubbed his chin. "I'd like to take some of these paintings, if I can." He pointed around. Some were hanging up on the walls, but others were piled on the floor. There were maybe forty paintings. And those were the ones I saw. Who knew how many were in other rooms. "My wife . . . she took up painting after she retired from the mill. And these remind me of the things we did together. She was good, wasn't she?" He got up. "I guess

I can't take them all. I don't even know where I'm going." He looked up at me. I couldn't tell if his eyes were watery, or just wet in that old man way. "Maybe you two could help me decide?"

I was so angry when we finally got outside. "They were going to condemn this house with him in it! Is this really the side you're on? Pushing people out of their homes like this?"

"Pushing him out? Keeley, this home isn't safe for a dog, never mind a person. How could your dad let him live like this in good conscience?"

"My dad is taking care of a lot of people, okay? And it wouldn't have to be all up to him if the governor wasn't such an asshole."

"Well, I hope your dad is doing a better job with the others than he is with Mr. Dixon."

I glared at him. How could he say that?

Our dads pulled up at exactly the same time.

My dad and Sheriff Hamrick were bumper to bumper.

"This isn't right," Dad started in.

"Now, hold on a second, Jim."

"Where are you going to take him?" Dad was shouting.

"Tonight? To a shelter. And then tomorrow he can talk with the adjusters again, maybe with someone to help him understand what's going on."

"You're damn right he will. I'll be with him this time." Dad scoffed. "All this for a stupid housing deal in the city. You know it. I know it."

Sheriff Hamrick put his hands behind his back. "I'm not going to say you're wrong, Jim. These plans have been in the works for a long time. And they won't let you stand in the way."

He tried to take a step forward. "Take care of your family. Do the right thing, before it's too late. Check the weather. You don't have much time."

Dad gripped the head of his cane so hard, his knuckles turned white. "What's that supposed to mean?"

"Your daughter is helping people. What are you doing? Who are you looking out for?"

Dad turned as dark as a storm cloud. And I did too. I wouldn't say my dad was a hero. Far from it. But he was trying to do the right thing.

I jumped in to defend him. Sheriff Hamrick might have had Levi under his thumb, but not me. "This job isn't about helping people. It's about pushing them out. And you know what, I never wanted it in the first place. I quit."

Levi's face fell, but I needed my dad to know I was behind him 100 percent.

If Dad was at all intimidated by Sheriff Hamrick, he didn't show it. He walked straight into Russell Dixon's house. I followed him, of course. I'd like to think that maybe Levi would have come with us, if not for his dad. But he didn't. Sheriff Hamrick put Levi's bike in the trunk of his squad car, and the two of them drove away.

---

## 32

**Saturday, May 28**

⚠ **EMERGENCY BROADCAST SYSTEM ALERT**: A Flash Flood Watch has been issued for Aberdeen County and Waterford City for the next 24 hours as we continue to track a developing storm. Rain is expected to begin this evening. Saturated areas will be particularly susceptible to heavy runoff and debris flows. Residents are being asked to monitor later forecasts and be prepared to take action should an upgrade to a Flash Flood Warning be deemed necessary.

---

I doubt anyone would have guessed I was heading to prom. I was disguised as a Normal Girl Attending a Sleepover Party—navy sweatshirt over a black-and-white-striped tank top, and dark-rinse skinny jeans, my hair in a ponytail, my skin clean and completely free of makeup. Inside the sleeping bag was Mom's old dress and a pair of nude patent leather heels that pinched like hell but that I would suffer through. I tucked my pillow under my arm.

Oh, and galoshes. I was back in my damn galoshes.

But strip off my clothes and I was a prom paper doll ready to be dressed. I'd triple-shaved my legs to make sure every inch was smooth. My feet were pumiced and lotioned, with toenails painted raspberry red. I'd dotted perfume along my collarbone. I had on my strapless bra and my cutest pair of underwear, a pale pink cotton bikini with a ruffled edge, because

Morgan had reminded me that Jesse and I would probably share a sleeping bag.

We hadn't done more than kiss. But I suddenly began to imagine the possibility of losing my virginity to Jesse Ford, the boy of my dreams, in my mean old principal's house, before our entire town slipped under water.

If the rain hadn't been pounding my window, none of it would have felt real.

But it was real, as real as poor Russell Dixon being escorted out of his home, as Sheriff Hamrick's warnings, as my waning hope that there would be a happy ending for Aberdeen.

The epicness of all those things combined turned something I wouldn't have considered into something I desperately needed. Because I knew sex with Jesse would overshadow all the terrible things that had happened. It would give me something good to cling to. That was the power of Jesse Ford. Being with him made everything else I was feeling inside disappear. And I needed that now, more than ever before.

So I decided it right then and there. Yes. If the chance to have sex with Jesse Ford at Secret Prom presented itself, I'd take it.

I sent him a quick text. Weirdly, I hadn't heard from him since he dropped me off yesterday afternoon.

Hey Prom Date. Guess what? The last 24 hours of my life have sucked so hard, it's not even funny. I don't even know where to start. Sigh. Anyway, I can't wait to see you tonight.

I held my phone for a few minutes after. And then I turned it off so I wouldn't have to invent a reason for why Jesse wasn't writing me back.

· · ·

Morgan was to pick me up at 8 p.m. I waited until 7:59 to go downstairs.

Mom was lying across the entire living room couch. I figured she was doing paperwork, but she was actually reading a book, something I hadn't seen her do in forever. It looked old. The dust jacket was flaking away in places, and the author photo on the back was dated, a woman in big shoulder pads and bigger hair.

Though I didn't say anything to her, Mom sat up and glanced at her wristwatch. "Oh no! I meant to only read a chapter or two! I have work to do." She rolled her neck in a circle. "Is your father still outside?"

I shrugged. He was supposedly working, though I didn't hear any tools, just his radio.

"Keeley. Is everything okay? You've barely said two words to me all week."

I turned and smiled my fake smile. "Yeah. Everything's okay."

"Good. Have fun tonight."

I watched her cross the room. She paused at Dad's dirty plate from lunch, still left on his computer desk. She looked as if she was about to pick it up, but then didn't. Which annoyed me. Dad was still working hard, harder than Mom even knew. And she decided now to be a bitch about him cleaning up after himself? I would never forgive her for meeting with the adjusters behind his back. In fact, I was starting to blame my waning hope on her. Maybe she'd compromised him, if the mayor and the governor knew she wanted to take the money and run.

I heard a car pull up and I grabbed my bag, barely shouted "Bye!" and rushed out. But it wasn't Morgan. It was another pickup truck. Charlie, and he had another man in the cab with him. Not Sy. Someone else. I sat down on the porch and watched as they parked and sprinted into Dad's open garage door bay. He was sitting on a folding chair, just watching the rain fall.

Morgan pulled up. I didn't even have to turn my head. I heard her music. Led Zeppelin, blasting. When I did, she smiled at me, played drums on her steering wheel. I hadn't seen her do that in forever. She was beaming a big smile, ear to ear.

"Can you turn that down a sec?" I said, tossing my stuff into the backseat and pulling my hood up over my head.

She laughed. "Okay, Grandma."

I was trying to hear what the men were talking about with Dad and took a few steps closer, but I still couldn't. Not with the rain and not with their voices hushed, quiet. I knew it was something not good by their body language. The two men shoved their hands in their pockets. Dad crossed his arms. Then he saw me, lingering nearby, and dropped his head.

"What's happening?" Morgan asked.

I could have gone over and asked, but honestly, I didn't want to know. I just wanted to get to prom, be with Jesse, and forget all my troubles.

"Oh, he's got something big cooking," I said.

"No kidding." She didn't sound skeptical, exactly. But she was watching Dad too.

"I don't know all the details. He's being super-secretive. But yeah. It's all good." I turned the music back up. "Let's go!"

On our way across town, Morgan got a text from Wes. Since the roads to Aberdeen were now closed to nonresidents, he'd had to sneak in through the woods. When we pulled up, he was standing on the side of the road in his boxers.

I reached across the car and beeped Morgan's horn before she could stop me.

Wes jumped. That actually put me in a good mood. "Whatcha doing, perv?" I probably should have started things off with him on a better note, but I knew teasing him would make me happy.

"My jeans were muddy and I didn't want to get Morgan's car messed up," he said, quickly stepping into a clean pair of navy pants and pulling them up.

"Aww, that's sweet," I said, mainly because Morgan looked nervous, and I didn't want her to think I was going to go at it with Wes all night long.

"That was actually kind of scary," he said, crawling into the backseat. "I think I walked over five miles." He leaned forward and gave Morgan a peck on the cheek. "Hi."

"Hi," she said shyly.

"I got you this," and he pulled out a beautiful corsage. It was all white and ivory blooms. As soon as he popped open the clamshell, the whole car filled up with the smell of freesia. "Sorry I didn't know what color dress you were wearing."

"Oh my gosh, you didn't have to do that."

As we drove, Wes got dressed up in the backseat, putting on the rest of his navy blue suit with a white shirt and black tie. He looked like a prep school advertisement. But I thought that was nice of him to do, to take it so seriously.

Just as Jesse's video had instructed, we parked a few blocks away from Principal Bundy's house. It was almost an unnecessary precaution because all but one of the houses had been cleared on that street, but Jesse wouldn't have known that. Wes stood on the sidewalk as we shimmied into our dresses and put on our makeup.

And that's when I noticed Morgan's dress. She hadn't worn her mother's clingy lace one, like we planned. She was wearing her dress from Spring Formal. The one she'd bought to wear to prom with Wes, before they'd broken up.

I couldn't believe she hadn't told me beforehand. I waited for her to say something about it to me now, but it didn't happen. Then I remembered that I had turned my phone off earlier. So maybe she had. It started to rain, so the three of us hurried toward the house, Morgan explaining to Wes about the night as we went.

"Basically, Keeley and her boyfriend set this whole thing up. It's amazing. I mean, can you believe it? A prom inside our old principal's house? This is like a movie."

I instantly forgave her for the dress betrayal, because I liked that she was bragging about me to Wes. And, honestly, it was a lot to be proud of. This was the kind of night that people would talk about their whole lives. If we were lucky enough to have a reunion one day, this would be the story everyone would relive, minute by minute. Plus, it made sense. She was still in love with Wes. Breaking up with him was never something she'd wanted to do. It was something she'd done for me, to prove how much our friendship meant.

Tonight, we could both be happy.

We walked into Principal Bundy's house through the back door. Jesse was leaning on the kitchen counter, looking at something on his phone. He was in a legit tuxedo and black Converse sneakers, and he looked amazing. I was about to say hi, but then some random girl, I think she was a freshman, jumped over the top of him, boobs pressed into his back, giggling like crazy, trying to see. Jesse kept pushing her away, shielding whatever he was looking at. They were so involved with each other, he didn't even notice us walking in.

But Morgan noticed. And she frowned. "Who's that all over your boyfriend?"

My stomach dropped. I wanted to turn around and walk straight back out the door, but instead I pretended not to hear her and pushed in front of Morgan and Wes so I would be the one leading the way.

"I'll go get you guys some beers," I announced like a hostess, once we'd made it to the living room. Morgan stared unblinking at me for a second or two before walking with Wes over to the corner and putting their stuff down.

I'd had a very different idea of what the night was going to be like. I knew Jesse had bought some jokey things, but there wasn't one element that was classy or nice. It was like a bad frat house. The kiddie pool that Jesse had said was to keep the booze cold was in the middle of Bundy's living room, only filled with bubble bath. Inside it were two soccer boys and a girl, in their underwear, very drunk.

Someone had stolen the picture of Bundy that hung in the high school foyer and leaned it against the wall. People were flicking bottle caps at it, then beer cans and bottles. My shoes crunched over the broken glass. They were already hurting my feet, but there would be no taking them off.

I found three beers in a cooler at the top of the stairs. When I turned around, Jesse grabbed me and kissed me. I could tell he'd been drinking. Not one or two beers, either, but then again, he'd been here all afternoon setting up. Maybe that was why he hadn't texted me back.

"Were you not going to say hi?"

"Hi," I said flatly.

"Hi," he mimicked back, pouty like me. Then he knocked into me, like we were both joking around. "You look hot in your mom's old dress. Is that weird to say?" He smothered me with a hug. It did feel good to be in his arms. "Where's Morgan?"

"She's in the living room. I'm about to deliver beers."

"I'll come with you."

I made sure to put on a smile as we approached.

"This was such an awesome idea," Morgan said. "Thanks for inviting underclassmen."

"Well, it would have been pretty empty if it were only seniors. Plus, you know, I'm sure Keeley wouldn't have had as much fun without you here."

He was trying. I softened a little.

But then his arm slipped off me. "Well, seems like you guys have found the alcohol already. Help yourselves. I'll be back. Got to make the rounds."

I wasn't surprised that Jesse was about to walk away. But I couldn't believe he wasn't going to take me with him.

I pulled on his tuxedo tails. "Hey, can we talk for a sec?" I was about to add something jokey, like *Don't worry . . . not about that slutty girl who was hanging on you two seconds ago . . .* but Jesse pulled himself free.

"Kee, I'm about to start a beer pong game in the dining room. Let me kick some ass and then I'll catch up with you."

Catch up with me?

I would have said something, but Wes and Morgan were only a couple of feet behind me. So I told Jesse, "Okay," with forced brightness.

I waited. And I waited. As I wriggled through the party, I ran into Jesse a few more times. I'd try to talk to him, start up a conversation, but he'd do something to get out of it, like do a dance move past me or clink beer bottles with me, then walk away.

The thing was, I didn't want to have some big conversation with him. I just wanted to tell him about what had happened with Russell Dixon, about the thing that had just happened with my dad, and get it out of me so I could move on. I knew he'd say the perfect thing to make me feel better, if he'd give me all of five minutes.

Meanwhile, Morgan and Wes were totally cozy. Though she'd been so excited for the party, they were just standing in the corner with each other, talking intensely. Catching up, I suppose. She was the only girl with a corsage on her wrist.

At some point, I even stopped trying to make eye contact with Jesse. I just kept drinking.

As I was finishing one beer, Jesse came over and placed another in my hands.

"Prom pics!" he yelled out to no one in particular.

Jesse pulled me in close under his arm, put his chin on my head.

"You two are the cutest," Morgan said, pulling out her phone.

After a couple of poses, I felt him start to drift away. This time, I had drunk enough that I wasn't going to let him go.

"Please don't blow me off again to go hang out with Zito or whoever."

"Zito? He's not here. He left town yesterday."

"What?"

He made a face. "You were there, Keeley. I said bye right after graduation."

I thought back. I did watch him bro-hug Zito and kiss Zito's mom, but the scene didn't register as a *good-bye* good-bye. "I thought you guys were best friends."

"We were friends, yeah. I mean, do guys have best friends?"

"I think they do." But I was starting to get nervous. If Jesse could be so over Zito, how quickly was he going to forget about me?

"Hey. Did you see the Bundy dart board upstairs? I set that up for you. Come on. Let's have a contest. Winner takes—"

"I want to talk to you. Didn't you get my text? I had a really terrible day." I don't think he heard me. He was too busy getting clapped on the back by two guys passing him on their way to the kitchen. "Jesse!"

"Sorry." Of course Jesse laughed. "I'm just trying to have a good time, Keeley. I mean, if you want to talk, we can talk. But, and I don't mean any disrespect, can't it wait until tomorrow, when we aren't in the middle of the most epic party ever?"

"No."

He shrugged with a little bit of annoyance. "All right, all right. Let me just deliver this beer to Denise."

I was simmering. I did not move out of his way. "Denise? Is that the girl who was hanging all over you in the kitchen when I walked in?" Even though I'd been drinking, my mouth felt so dry. I saw that Jesse had four beers in his hands. I downed the one I was holding, took one of his for myself, and swallowed a big swig.

"Yeah. Why are you acting so jealous?"

*Because you are supposed to be my date.*

*Because we've been kissing for weeks.*

*Because this was supposed to be me and you, together, till the end of Aberdeen.*

*Because I need you right now.*

"I'm not jealous. It's not like this is a real prom, anyway."

He pushed a laugh out of his nose. "Were you honestly expecting it to be one? Are you mad that I didn't pick you up in a limo? That my tux smells like mothballs because I bought it for five bucks from the thrift store? Sorry you feel let down. I did my best to have a fun night for everyone."

"Oh, I see. Maybe it was crazy for me to expect you to maybe, like, I don't know, want to spend time with me tonight? I mean, I did pay for this crap when you saw your dad at Walmart and freaked out."

His eyes cut straight through mine. "I told you I'd pay you back. And for your information, that wasn't my dad. That's Julia's dad."

I steadied myself against the wall. "Well, how was I to know that? You never said anything about how weird you acted that night."

"This is crazy," he said, trying to shake our entire conversation off. "You're my date tonight, no one else."

"Then why haven't you hung out with me at all?"

"Because I've been busy! I'm trying to make sure everyone has a good time." He ran his fingers through his hair, pulled on it a little bit. "And, if I'm going to be completely honest, I knew you'd be in a downer mood from the text you sent. I've been waiting for you to loosen up and have fun. I don't want to sit in a corner and have some sad talk, Keeley. And you shouldn't either. It's not the night for that." He was annoyed with me. Clearly. "Now, I'm going to play cards with some people. That's what these beers were for," he said. "But you go ahead and keep that one," nudging his chin to the one I'd taken from him. "Hopefully it'll put you in more a party mood."

As he walked away, I saw Morgan lingering at the doorway. She'd been watching our tiff. She knew I saw her, but I turned my back to her anyway and just started opening kitchen cabinets and drawers for something to do.

And then something caught my eye. It was a small square of paper taped to the refrigerator.

To Whom It May Concern:

When moving, my beloved cat, Freckles, escaped before I could get him into his cage. After much searching, I was not able to find him. He is microchipped and has a thin red collar. I have left word at all local animal shelters, but should he come back to the house while someone is here, would you please get in touch with me ASAP?

Below that, Bundy left her cell phone number and e-mail address.

I spun around to show it to Morgan, but she had already left the room.

Bundy was a monster, leaving Aberdeen without her cat. I felt self-righteous in the moment, or that's how it came across in my brain. Really, though, I was mad. And sad. And so wound up that I was about to explode.

I slipped a finger underneath the paper and carefully pulled it away from the fridge, so it wouldn't rip. I folded it in half and squeezed it tight. Then, while I walked upstairs, I dialed the number and put the phone to my ear.

It rang three times before Bundy picked up.

"Hello?"

I whispered back, "Hi."

Bundy spoke again. "Hello? Who is this?"

Then I said, "Meow," and hung up.

I started snapping pictures of the house, the chaos. The kids in the pool. The picture of her face with bottles thrown at it. I kept texting them to Bundy. One after another after another.

I was calling her again when I saw Morgan and Wes rounding the corner. I quickly hung up and rushed over to them. We went and got more beers together. I drank the next one fast. I was about to toss the bottle when Wes came up beside me.

"I was hoping to clear the air at some point."

"You don't have to do that." I went back to my phone and typed out another *meow* text.

Wes lowered his head. "I want to apologize for saying what I did. I didn't know you were listening."

"But you meant what you said. That I was obnoxious and not funny and that none of your friends like me."

Wes cocked his head back, surprised. "I was mad about what happened in the pharmacy."

"Wes, I was joking."

"Yeah, fine. You were joking. But it wasn't funny."

"Well, that's your opinion. To be honest, I don't think you have the greatest sense of humor." I put my beer bottle into the crook of my arm, opened up another text and typed *meow* over and over and over again.

Morgan grabbed me by the arm and pulled me aside. "Why aren't you just accepting his apology?"

"Because he's not sorry. He basically just said so himself."

"Well, maybe it's because he's still waiting for an apology from you."

"I mean, I guess I could apologize for the fact that he can't take a joke."

"That's not funny, Keeley."

"Come on, Morgan. You know I didn't mean to make him mad!"

She lifted her arms and let them fall back down to her side. "So what? You're never going to be okay with Wes?"

"He doesn't like me. I don't get how that's not a deal breaker for you."

Her eyes welled up. "Then why did you tell me to invite him?" Her voice was notably quieter.

I tried to find the right answer, but I was too drunk. "Honestly, I don't know. I was trying to make you happy, I guess. You were getting so annoyed with me the other day, when we were driving around town."

But instead of Morgan understanding, her face tensed. "I wasn't annoyed about Wes. I was annoyed with how you were acting. How you've been acting for the last few weeks."

I felt a fight building between us, getting bigger than either of us wanted it to. I quickly tried to take the heat out of things. I waved my phone around like a glow stick at a concert. "Wait. Hold on a second. I've got something so hilarious to show you."

Except she wasn't looking. Her head was turned toward Wes, who was now across the room, sitting glumly in a folding chair.

I grabbed her chin and forced her to look.

"Who are you texting?"

I cackled. "Bundy!"

Morgan took the phone out of my hands. I chugged the rest of my beer as she scrolled through my texts. "I don't get it."

"Bundy lost her cat before she bailed on Aberdeen. I'm basically torturing her." Morgan glanced up at me, utterly horrified. I let out a whopper of a sigh. "Oh, God. Let me guess. You don't think it's funny either?" I took my phone back. "Never mind."

She shook her head. "I know you're going through a lot right now. And you clearly don't want to talk to me about it. But you need to talk to someone. Because this . . . "—she pointed at my phone—"isn't you, Keeley."

"Come on! She's a horrible bitch, remember? She totally deserves this!" She was still frowning, so I put my phone away. "I'll show Jesse. I bet he'll think it's funny." Morgan turned to walk away from me. I had to pull her arm to make her stop. "I don't want to fight with you. Can't we go back to having fun?" I sounded so desperate. Just like Jesse had when he said the same thing to me earlier.

"I'd rather we just be real with each other."

I laughed dryly. "That doesn't sound fun at all."

Morgan folded her arms. "You're not going to want to hear this, but I'm going to say it anyway. I don't think Jesse is good for you. I thought he was the perfect match, but now I see that he's not. He's all the parts of you that are broken."

352 • SIOBHAN VIVIAN

"At least my boyfriend is nice. He doesn't make you feel like shit. He's trying to make people happy."

"Except for you. You've been trying to talk to him all night! I've watched you! He's totally avoiding you." She shook me off. "You know what? Forget it. We'll play pretend like we're twelve years old again. But just remember what you said in the car to me a few weeks ago. I always sucked at it."

And then she stalked away.

I wobbled in the opposite direction, trying to find the front door. I passed Jesse on my way. He was playing cards with his friends just like he'd said he would be. I called his name, but he either didn't hear me or pretended not to.

Once I made it outside, I pulled out my phone and, with shaking hands, texted Levi.

Hey. Can you come get me?

I honestly expected him to tell me to fuck off. It was pouring rain, buckets of it. It was what I deserved. But Levi texted back quickly. I'll be there in 15.

And while I was waiting outside, I heard a meow.

Under a bush was Freckles. He was wet and his fur was matted. I got down on my hands and knees and I could feel the mud soaking into my dress. "Here, Freckles. Here, Freckles," I whispered. Then I tried to grab him, because it was raining and thundering hard. But just as I got close enough to touch him, he hissed at me and then darted off.

Punctual as always, Levi came pedaling up on his bike. He barely came to a stop before I climbed on his pegs.

"Looks like you had a fun time," he said, peeling back the hood of his rain jacket.

"Please don't choose this moment to show me your sense of humor." I tried to maintain my balance, but as soon as Levi started pedaling, I nearly tipped us both over.

"Jeez, Keeley. How much did you drink? Can you even ride on my pegs?"

"Just get me out of here."

I gripped his shoulders so tight. Levi rode with one hand on his handlebars. The other he snaked around my back, so he could hold me.

Even with the rain, I heard my parents arguing from outside our house. They weren't expecting me home tonight, so they were freely going at it.

"Do you want me to come in with you?" Levi asked.

Creeping through the front yard, I looked back and whispered, "It's fine." And then I almost tripped.

"I'm not going to leave you out here."

"Just go!" I snuck up underneath the window. I didn't want him, of all people, hearing anything Dad might say.

He didn't want to. And he must have understood, because he said, "Look, I'll leave now, but I'm going to ride back here in ten minutes and if I don't see you upstairs with your bedroom light on, I'm staying with you until you're ready to go inside."

A lump filled my throat. "Thank you."

I crept up onto the porch, careful to miss the squeaky boards. And then I sat down with my back against the wall and shivered underneath the living room window. Mom's dress was ruined for sure. Also, everything else in my life.

Mom said sharply, "How do you see this playing out? Honestly?"

"You're asking what my end game is."

"Well, Mrs. Dorsey heard from Morgan, who heard from Keeley, that you have something big planned. So why can't you share it with me?"

I had started to sober up, but the rush of my stupid lie, one I'd told only a few hours ago to Morgan to make things seem okay, traveling back here and making it all worse, left me woozy.

"Because I can't! I just need you to trust me!"

I was surprised to hear him say that. So Dad did have a plan? Of course he did. I never should have doubted that.

"Please, Jim! Tell me what we're holding on for! You only have like, what, seven families signed onto your petition? They've already started work on the dam."

"They've started their *preliminary* work. I've done the research, okay? They're just diverting the water so they have a dry space to build. It's nothing that can't be undone. And if we hold on making deals, they can't legally move forward on the actual dam construction. Not without suing us for eminent domain or condemning our house, which they can't—"

"So it's a game of chicken. You're playing a game of chicken with our future." I wanted to throw up, and not from the beer, as Mom laughed a snotty laugh. "I've been supporting this family for the last two years, scraping by, working night and day to try and save up enough so that Keeley can go to Baird. I have nothing for dorms, nothing for books, she'll definitely have to work while she's there, but she won't have to take out a single loan. But if we got the kind of money I hear some people are getting, she could have her pick of schools. She could send out a hundred applications next year and pick the best school, not just the one we can afford right now. We could spend the rest of this summer taking family trips all over the country, touring colleges."

"Jill, you're hysterical."

Mom *was* hysterical. And God, my heart was breaking for both of them. I didn't want to be the reason they were fighting. "Of course I'm hysterical! We're about to get evacuated again! I know you care about Aberdeen, I know you care about what your family built here. But you can't care about that more than you care about us. You need to put us first, Jim."

Dad sounded like he was about to explode. "I have a plan. And holding out is part of that plan. What I can't do now is sign papers!"

Mom started pacing the floor. "We've got a chance here to do everything over. And I'm not going to let you ruin it for us." I held my breath. Would she tell him she had met with the adjusters?

No, she wouldn't. She'd say something worse.

"I have to take care of myself. And to do that, I have to put myself in the driver's seat."

"What are you saying?"

"I'm leaving."

I barely covered my mouth in time to muffle a gasp.

"Leaving what?"

"Aberdeen." Mom took a breath. "And you."

"Jill, wait a minute now, I—"

"You're not putting us first, and I can't participate in this charade any longer. When you are willing to think about us, instead of yourself, maybe there will still be a chance. But I can't say that for sure."

She walked out of the house, the screen slapping behind her. Walked right by me, not seeing me at all, and got in her car. I knew exactly where she'd be going.

To be with her best friend.

Dad followed her out to the road. He screamed after her, "Please, Jill! Just trust me! Just give me a little more time and you'll see!"

I got to my feet. Dad saw me as he walked back to our house. "Keeley, I . . ."

"It's fine, Dad. You don't have to explain." More than that, I didn't want him to.

I went inside and clung to the banister on my way upstairs. I turned on my bedroom light and stood in the window. Levi rode by as he'd promised. He didn't wave. He just kept pedaling.

## 33

**Sunday, May 29**

⚠ **EMERGENCY BROADCAST SYSTEM ALERT:** A Severe Thunderstorm Warning is currently in effect for Aberdeen County. Heavy precipitation is predicted beginning this evening and continuing for the next 24 hours. Stay tuned for further updates.

I woke up the next morning hung over as hell.

I hadn't heard from Jesse. Honestly, I didn't expect to.

But I was bummed to see that I'd slept through all of Morgan's Where are you? texts from last night. They'd started out concerned and eventually got irate, when she realized I'd left without saying good-bye. She'd sent things to me like I can't believe you and I'm so mad at you and Still mad, but text me so I know you're okay.

Sorry I missed your messages, I replied. Didn't mean to worry you. Sooooo hungover. Can barely remember what happened last night. Call me when you get a sec.

It was another lie. I remembered everything. The fight with Morgan, and Jesse, and then finding out that my parents were separating.

I needed my best friend.

I brought my phone into the shower with me. It rang as I was mid-shampoo. I squinted away the soap and checked the screen.

I didn't recognize the number, it wasn't one programmed into my contacts.

Principal Bundy.

I felt my entire body squeeze in on itself. I hit Ignore and hoped she wouldn't leave me a voice mail. But of course she did.

"Keeley. It's Teresa Bundy. Look. I don't care about the pictures you sent, I don't care about the house. But please call me back and let me know if you saw Freckles and if he looked"—her voice broke—"okay. Please, Keeley."

I was shaking. I set the phone down.

I got dressed and went downstairs. Mom had not come home, and Dad was on the couch, watching television. I sat quietly down next to him.

Mayor Aversano was on the steps of City Hall, flanked by Sheriff Hamrick and other officials. "I wish I had better news, but we're facing another storm," said Aversano. "And because of Aberdeen's already compromised state, we are anticipating very unsafe conditions, even more so than the storm earlier this month. We need to get as many people out as possible, and as quickly as possible."

I glanced at Dad.

Aversano continued. "Police and fire crews will be driving through neighborhoods today, directing people to leave, offering assistance. The adjusters will continue to be available to meet with residents, but at a new location outside of Aberdeen, which will be announced shortly. Many homes are likely to suffer serious damage from flooding. I would suggest leaving with all you can, under the assumption that there won't be much to come back to on Tuesday."

Dad shut off the TV. "Was this what Charlie and his friend came over to tell you last night?" I asked.

"Yes. And also that they were going to accept the offers being made to them."

"I bet Mom's at Mrs. Dorsey's. You should go get her, Dad." I suddenly wanted him to do all the things Mom had been saying. To channel his energy into taking care of us.

"I'm sure she'll be home soon. Anyway, I've got people on the way over. We need to discuss our next move."

Dad called an emergency meeting at our house. Where the first meeting had packed our living room, there were now plenty of seats. Maybe half of the people Dad had gotten to sign his petition to stay in Aberdeen showed up.

I hoped Dad would finally share his plan. The thing that would save us, the thing he'd been hinting at to Mom the night before.

"I can't sugarcoat it," Dad began. "This new evacuation puts us all in a tough spot. But not an impossible one."

Uneasy murmurs went through the room.

A voice said, "If we don't go in the next twenty-four hours, we'll be stuck here. I heard they're permanently closing the roads into town for any vehicles that aren't part of the construction efforts after this evacuation. Once someone leaves, you won't be able to come back in."

"You know what'll be next? The Internet."

"And the power. They'll shut that off."

Dad raised his hands to try and quiet the room. "Here's what I'm proposing. We're all going to pool our resources. I'm sure everyone's got a stocked pantry, and we'll keep each other fed. My house is on the highest ground. We can take cover here and—"

"What about my job? How am I going to get to work?"

"There will be ways. Get you through the woods and have someone pick you up on the other side . . ."

People looked around the room skeptically. One man actually said, "You're not making sense, Jim."

Bess raised her hand. "Jim, I don't know what you've heard, but a few of my neighbors told me what they got in settlements. They might not be speaking truthfully, but it sounded generous. Maybe we should cut our losses."

I'd never seen Dad looked so desperate. "But you all signed my petition. You promised me you wouldn't make a deal."

Bess stood up and placed a hand on Dad's shoulder. "We're sad to see Aberdeen go, but our lives will go on. They have to."

The others nodded like they agreed. All except for my dad.

I sat there with my arms folded, thinking, *How is this going to last?* even though I knew the answer. It wouldn't. It was already over.

I still hadn't heard anything from Morgan and I was getting nervous. She didn't even respond to a series of sad frowny-face pictures I'd taken of myself.

I was starting to panic. I had screwed up so monumentally last night. Everything I had tried to use to make things better— everything from Jesse to those awful texts I'd sent to Bundy— could have cost me her friendship. If I lost Morgan, I would be truly devastated.

Mom arrived home later that afternoon. I wanted to ask about Morgan, when she came home this morning, had she said anything about me, but I didn't have the chance.

"Where's your father?"

It hurt to say, "He's sleeping." I left out what he'd said to me when he walked up the stairs after everyone had left our house. Which was "Let Sheriff Hamrick drag me out."

She nodded, like things were affirmed. She handed me a box. I figured she was going to ask me to start packing, but by the way she looked when she lifted it, I knew there was already stuff inside.

I opened the flap.

It was my dress from Spring Formal. Or it used to be. Now it was a rag, a wrinkled mess, because I'd balled it up after the dance, shoved it under Morgan's bed, and forgotten about it.

"Keeley."

"Mom, let me explain. I—"

"I've never owned something so nice." She held the dress up to the light. "I imagined you'd wear this in college sometime. Maybe to a special party. Or an interview. Or a conference."

She got up and went to the kitchen. I followed her.

"Mom, please."

She leaned forward at the sink, rubbing her temples. "Keeley, I don't know how else to say this except to just come out with it." She stood up straight and turned to face me. "I put a deposit down on an apartment this morning. It's between here and Baird. I'm packing up my stuff today and I want you to do the same."

"But what about Dad?"

"I can't worry about him anymore."

"How could you say that? He's been trying so hard for us." I knew that in fighting for Dad, I was fighting for myself, too.

"Keeley, I'm the one who's been here, day after day, for the last two years, trying hard for us. Not him."

"So what? He can't make up for it now?"

I desperately, desperately wanted her to say yes. But she said,

"I'm going to stay at Annie's tonight. We're having a little good-bye sleepover and they could use the help packing up."

"They're leaving too. Where?"

"Honey. You should talk to Morgan."

I was trying to. But Morgan wouldn't take my calls.

I took my box upstairs. Inside it was every last possession I'd left at Morgan's house. A pair of Christmas pajamas I hadn't seen in months. My copy of *Mockingjay*, which I'd loaned her but she'd avoided reading because I said it was a letdown. She was returning everything that made us friends.

I kicked the box into my closet.

If Morgan wouldn't take my calls, I'd have to do something else to get her attention. Something big, before it was too late.

## 34

**Sunday, May 29**
⚠ **EMERGENCY BROADCAST SYSTEM ALERT**: As of 1:00 PM, Governor Ward has issued an evacuation order for Aberdeen County. All residents are being asked to relocate in advance of the coming storm system. Please stay tuned for additional information.

---

I knew there was only one person who could help me get back into Morgan's good graces. Jesse Ford. So I borrowed Dad's pickup truck and drove over.

There was a moving van outside his house. I tried to make sense of the timeline. We'd just gotten the evacuation order. So why was Jesse already packed?

And then it all made sense. His caginess about his mom signing our petition. The way he'd avoided me at Secret Prom.

Jesse was coming through the front door with a box in his hand. He looked embarrassed. Julia came running up to me, squeezing me at the legs.

"You were just going to leave." My chest was closing in on itself.

"Ahh, Keeley. I was going to tell you last night. When the time was right."

He might have believed that, but I knew better. The way he was pushing me off all night, the way he didn't want to be close to me. It was because he didn't want to tell me the truth. He was leaving.

He tried to hug me but I scooted out from under his arms. "I would not have left without telling you. I would not."

I wiped my eyes. "Your mom was never considering supporting us, was she?"

He sighed and tipped his head back. "I mean, I told her about it. But my mom has a crap job at Walmart. We live in a trailer. And Julia's dad is a piece of shit who's always lurking around. This is going to be good for us."

These things were true. I knew they were. "Do you know where you're going?"

"About an hour away. Sharpsburgh. Not far." He finally looked at me. "I hope we can still be friends."

Maybe Jesse was easy for me to forgive because we were so alike. And I did know, deep down, that he was a good guy. But Morgan had been right. Jesse and I weren't good for each other. I was as broken as he was. We were never fully honest with each other, not completely. And so the loss of him was strangely muted. Especially when stacked up against what was happening with me and Morgan.

"I hope so too. Because as of this moment, you're basically the only one I have."

"Wait. Why? Did something happen between you and Morgan?"

I wrapped my arms around myself. "I need your help. I need to come up with something big to get Morgan to forgive me. I really, really screwed up bad with her last night." I felt my lip tremble. "Actually, no. That's not even true. I've had a lot of little screwups, little breaks. I tried to ignore them, hoping they'd go away. And now everything is in pieces."

Jesse tried hugging me again and this time I let him. "Don't

worry, Keeley. We can fix this. Everything can be fixed." I nodded, rubbing tears all over his shirt, because it had to be true. "Of
course I'll help you. What's the plan? What are you thinking?"

"I need to prove to her how much she means to me. That
what we have is worth saving."

"Hmm. Try this. If you close your eyes and think of the best
time in your friendship, when everything was as perfect as can be,
what do you think of?"

And that's when it hit me.

I drove us to Viola's.

The whole time, he was looking at me.

"What?"

"You caught me off-guard before, Keeley. Showing up at my
house like that. I . . . I just want to make sure you know that I'm
honestly going to miss you." He sounded genuine. And genuinely
surprised.

I couldn't believe I was almost going to have sex with him.
"Never mind that now, okay?"

I parked and ran for the door. It was padlocked closed, an X
already spray-painted on the door.

I cupped my hands to the glass and peered inside. There
wasn't much to see. Bare shelves, the empty cash register stands. I
ran down the sidewalk, looked inside another window. But near
the booth where Mr. Viola used to watch over things, just as it
had always been, was the sticker machine.

I started to kick at the glass door.

Jesse came up behind me, scooped me around the waist, and
pulled me away. "Whoa, whoa. Wait a second. What are you up to?"

I bit my lip. "I need that sticker machine."

He laughed, until he realized I wasn't joking. And then he said, "Okay."

In that moment, I was grateful not to be with Levi. I would have had to explain things, I would have had to corrupt him to do it for me. I didn't have to betray him on this.

Jesse ran around the building, casing the area. I was hoping some side door would be unlocked. But when he came back, he had a brick in his hands.

"Step back."

To his credit, Jesse never asked me to record it. It would have made a crazy video for sure. Us smashing the glass, dragging that sticker machine out, loading it in the back of the truck. When I told Jesse I needed him, he simply came through. It made me feel better about everything. I loved him for a reason. And hopefully, I'd be able to come through for Morgan, and she'd remember the same thing about me.

We took the machine to Jesse's house. He tried for nearly an hour to pop it open. "How is this stupid thing harder to get into than a vending machine?"

I used all the quarters from the console in my dad's truck. And when that ran out, Jesse broke open a glass jar where he'd been saving change for years. We did it assembly line style. Jesse loaded the two quarters, I pushed in the metal latch, and Julia pulled out the white cardboard sleeve and checked to see if we'd hit double unicorn jackpot.

"I was right," Jesse said. "Boys don't have these kinds of friendships." He sniffed his fingers. "Eww. Change is so gross.

Everything in the world should cost at least a dollar."

Sticker after sticker came out of the machine sandwiched between white cardboard. None of them were the one I wanted. And then, eventually, I pushed in two quarters and nothing came out. I tried again. Nothing.

"This is false advertising," Jesse complained. "They have to have the damn double unicorn there!"

Jesse turned around and crawled over to Julia, searching through all the discarded stickers on the floor, in case we'd missed it somehow. I took a more drastic approach. I stood up and stomped on the display glass with my foot. It took three times before it shattered it into a spider web of broken glass. And then I started pulling at the shards, not even caring that my fingertips were getting sliced and diced.

"Keeley, whoa! Wait a second!"

He eased me aside. With gentle hands, he carefully removed the broken glass, and then the display page with the double unicorn sticker. With a scissor, he cut out the shape with a surgeon's precision. "Put a little tape on that and she should stick to whatever you want just fine."

"Thank you." I was still shaking, I was so nervous. "I could have never done that as good as you did."

"I hope it works," he said. "Hell, if I didn't want to make out with you right now, *I'd* be your best friend."

"I got to go," I said. I hugged him. "Good-bye, Jesse."

He was slow to let me go, even though I was pulling away. "This isn't good-bye," he warned me. "I'm not leaving until tomorrow. You'll know when it's good-bye."

# 35

I drove over to Morgan's house with my sleepover bag packed, as if this were a normal weekend night, as if she had invited me over.

My mom and Mrs. Dorsey were at the kitchen table. They didn't hear me come in and both of them spun toward me guiltily. Both had big glasses of wine.

They had been packing up Mrs. Dorsey's kitchen, wrapping her glasses in newspaper. Not the mismatched stuff, like random pint glasses with different beer names on them, or the cups Morgan and I had collected from McDonald's when we were kids. She was only taking the good stuff. But the job was only half finished.

Mom had on one of Mrs. Dorsey's black salon capes, and her hair was slick to her scalp with dye the color of melted chocolate. Underneath, she was wearing a pair of my pajama pants. Mrs. Dorsey was in her nightgown and slippers, and she held a little cup of dye in her hand and a paintbrush in the other.

"Mom?"

"Surprise!" she said, tipping a full wineglass to her lips. Then she burst out laughing so hard she almost blew the wine straight out of the glass.

"What are you doing?"

"Getting a makeover. And don't make that face. You always tease me about dyeing my hair!"

I wasn't the only one. The three of us used to harp on her every birthday—me, Morgan, and Mrs. Dorsey. Mom had long ago decided to let her hair go gray naturally. She argued that she wasn't good at "lady stuff" and she'd never be able to keep up with the maintenance, even though her best friend was a hairdresser.

Mrs. Dorsey said, "Morgan's out, Keeley. Should I text her, tell her you're here?"

I started to cry. I was jealous that Mom and Mrs. Hewitt were having the sleepover night I wanted to have with Morgan. Their friendship would last no matter where they went. And ours was already falling apart, before Morgan even left Aberdeen.

Mrs. Dorsey rushed forward and gave me a big hug. "Sweetie, it's okay. You're here. That counts for a lot in my book."

"Don't text her. I'll just wait. I can help you pack."

I kept myself busy for the next two hours, and boxed up their living room and carried their stuff to the U-Haul parked out front.

And then I heard a car outside. I rushed to the window. Morgan pulled into the driveway. I could tell from how her hair was fixed, and her dress, that she'd been with Wes.

I went out the front door and met her in the driveway. She looked surprised to see me. And, unfortunately, not exactly happy.

"Hi."

"Hey."

And she walked right past me, in through the back door. I followed her, I had no other choice.

We came into the kitchen to the sound of giggles. Mom's hair was back to her original color, the color I had only ever seen in photographs. Ginger ale. She looked happy. And even though I knew Mrs. Dorsey'd had a hand in whatever had gone on between my mom and my dad, I couldn't bring myself to hate her. If anything, I envied her. She'd been able to do with Dad what I never could with Wes. I wasn't willing to tolerate Wes, but Mrs. Dorsey had supported my dad for as long as she could, solely to make my mom happy.

"I look young!" my mom said. "Don't I look young?"

Morgan and I made faces at each other like, *Oh God*, like a friendship reflex. That was the only time that night we still felt like friends. And it was fleeting. She passed me on her way through the door and headed upstairs. I followed.

Her room was all packed up.

"So, you're leaving."

I heard her swallow from across the room. "Yeah. Did they tell you where?"

"No. They wanted to, but I thought I should hear it from you." I sat down on her bed. "Will it be close?"

"Near my mom's sister. Mom is opening up her own beauty shop. I'm really happy for her, too. I wasn't when she first told me. But I am now."

Mayfield. That was the name of the town. I went there one summer with Morgan's family. It was a six-hour drive away.

"That's so far."

She nodded.

"I'm sorry about how I acted last night. I will apologize to Wes. I want to make it up to you. I want us to still be friends."

"Do you?"

"Of course I do!"

"Because I feel like ever since high school started, things have been different between us. You've held me at arm's length for a while now. And maybe I should have said something earlier to you. But after the way you were acting at Secret Prom, and that stuff you did to Bundy, I feel like I don't know who you are." She dropped her chin to her chest and stared at her floor. "Maybe this is just the way it goes sometimes. Friends grow apart, and it can be long and painful to disentangle from each other. But with Aberdeen going under, it doesn't have to be that way for us. It can just end. A clean break. No hard feelings."

"Please don't say that, okay? That's crazy. You sound completely crazy right now."

"You've always been there for me. Always. You were there when my dad left, you were there when I was sad about Wes. But I don't feel close to you anymore. A friendship is a give-and-take. I feel like I only get this jokey version of you. I'm looking at our friendship and thinking, *Can we even survive a move?* I want to believe we have a future, Keeley. But right now, I just don't see it."

It was the perfect opening. I pulled out the double unicorn sticker and presented it to her in my cupped hands like the special, magical thing it was.

"Oh my God," Morgan gasped. "Is that what I think it is?"

"Yup," I said, coyly. I smiled, but Morgan didn't see it. She'd already turned her back on me.

"I can't believe you actually thought a stupid sticker was going to fix this."

• • •

I didn't leave, and Morgan didn't tell me to go. I don't think either of us could bear the thought of having to explain to our moms that our friendship was over. I never fell asleep that night. I'm not sure if Morgan did either, which almost makes what I did worse.

Sometime in the middle of the night, I got up and quietly went through her moving boxes, looking for that sticker book. I didn't want her to have it, not when she was so willing to let me go. But I couldn't find it.

And then I realized why. Because she'd already thrown it away.

I crept back into the bed we were sharing and shut my eyes until morning.

## 36

**Monday, May 30**
⚠️ **EMERGENCY BROADCAST SYSTEM ALERT:** A Flood Warning is now in effect for Aberdeen County. A Severe Storm Warning is also in effect. Heavy rains will continue intermittently throughout the day, with the heaviest band reaching Aberdeen County after 7:00 PM. All residents are asked to seek shelter immediately. Stay tuned for further updates and instructions.

Mom drove us both home as Morgan and her mom loaded the last of their things into the U-Haul. She knew things had gone badly—that must have been why she didn't ask me what happened.

I helped her get her things into the car.

"I'm going to stay and help Dad. He's going to need it. I don't think he's packed anything."

"I know this is hard for you, Keeley. It's hard for me, too. But we have to let Dad be in charge of Dad. We can't save him, just like he can't save us. Do you understand?" I nodded. "I want you with me by this afternoon, Keeley. Before the worst of the rain gets here."

I hugged her and kissed her good-bye. Then I went inside our house, and instead of helping Dad like I'd promised, I lay in bed just like him.

My phone rang an hour later. I checked it, thinking it might be Jesse, but it was Bundy. This time I picked up.

"Keeley! Thank goodness you answered! They won't let me in to get him!" She was frantic.

"Freckles looked fine. He was under the front bushes. I tried to grab him—"

"He ran away. Of course. He's a very skittish cat. Can you please try again? He loves to chase string. Or a shoelace. Bring something like that with you. I bet you can grab him."

"I'll try." I might as well try to make things right with someone.

"Thank you for being decent enough to answer. I wasn't sure if you would be."

And then, *click.*

I spent the rest of the afternoon at Bundy's house trying to get Freckles out from underneath her porch. The cat was a monster, it didn't trust me at all, I guess for good reason. After an hour cooing at it and waving a damn shoelace around like a white surrender flag, I basically backed it into a corner. The thing hissed and bit my hand, but I managed to wrestle it into a cardboard box I'd brought with me.

Got him. We're leaving sometime this afternoon. I'll let you know when and we can figure out a place to meet.

Thank you, Keeley. Thank you so very much.

I wanted saving Freckles to make me feel better, but it barely lifted me up at all.

I was walking home with him under my arm when Levi came along. He wasn't on his bike, he was in a car.

"So you do have your license after all."

He reached across and opened the door. "Climb in."

I did, and the box in my lap mewed.

"Should I ask?" he said.

"Don't. Just know that in this box is the one thing I've done right."

He stared at me. "That can't be true," he said, and then smiled. "I'm glad you're okay, Keeley. And I'm glad I get to see you before everyone takes off for good."

"I'm anything but okay," I told him. "But thank you. I'm glad too."

"Do you want me to take you home?"

I didn't. Because I knew that this might very well be the last time I saw Levi Hamrick. "You're working?" He nodded. "Can I ride along with you?"

"Sure. I don't know how long I'll be out here. They're going to call us in eventually. But so long as I am, you can stay with me."

An hour later, we pulled up to Morgan's house.

I'd seen it on his clipboard. Her address. And once I did, I spent every second thinking, *Can I do it?* I settled on that I *should* do it. I should go inside and see it for the last time. Otherwise my last memory in that house would be so horrible. It would be that sleepover where we couldn't look at each other.

I peered in the front door. I'd hardly ever used it, except for last night. The front door was for the mailman. Or a stranger. Levi stepped past me and opened it.

I took a shaky step backward, as if I might get sucked inside against my will. It was a big step, and I sort of fell backward, down one step lower.

Levi looked confused.

"Are you not coming in?"

I turned away from him and sat down on the stairs. "No."

"Keeley—"

"I can't," I said. I still wouldn't look at him, but I know my voice told him everything.

"Okay. I'll be out as soon as I can."

I kept my eyes pinned on the house across the street. Another dark, empty one. Where Morgan's neighbor lived, with all the dogs. They'd bark constantly. But it was quiet today.

My phone vibrated, but I didn't fish it out of my pocket. Not the second time either.

But I did grab it at the third.

Want

To

Dance?

I wrote back, Not really, Jesse.

But we might not have the chance again, he wrote. And then, I'm in the gym.

I didn't want to go. But for whatever reason, I couldn't say so.

I'm kind of busy.

And then Jesse wrote, Let me give you the good-bye you deserve.

I heard Levi call for me from inside the house. "Keeley? Hey, Keeley? I need your help a minute."

If Levi didn't know then, he knew by the time he came out looking for me why I didn't answer. I was gone.

# 37

**Monday, May 30**

⚠ **EMERGENCY BROADCAST SYSTEM ALERT:** A Severe Storm Watch is currently in effect for Aberdeen County. Expect heavy rainfall this afternoon, with flooding overnight and into Tuesday. Emergency workers who are not considered essential, along with all remaining residents, are advised to seek safe shelter immediately.

I stood at the parking lot entrance for a few minutes before I moved a muscle. The lot had turned into a strange and terrifying beach in the days since graduation, with dunes of demolition rubble rising out of the water every few feet, some as tall as me. I couldn't see beyond the mounds, but I knew I was staring at my former high school.

The workers had made a hasty retreat because of the coming storm. All their construction equipment was parked up the street behind me, where the elevation was slightly higher. I wondered if they'd come back and clean this mess up. Maybe, maybe not.

Actually, probably not. They'd only come back for the things they valued, the construction equipment, their vehicles and tools. A school that had been around for generations wasn't worth anything to them. Soon there wouldn't be anyone left in Aberdeen who cared.

I called out for Jesse. Even though I hadn't wanted to stay

at Morgan's, I was majorly regretting coming to meet him here. I didn't want to see this, how quickly something that was such a seemingly permanent part of my life, a place where I spent most of the last three years, could so quickly be reduced to piles of garbage.

I was about to yell for Jesse again but then snapped my mouth shut. If either of us was caught here, we'd be arrested, no doubt about it. I bet the mayor or maybe even the governor might try to use it as leverage against my dad. Like, they might threaten to press charges, give me a permanent record, screw up my chances for college, if he didn't sign a deal. I knew there wasn't much hope for him saving Aberdeen, but I definitely didn't want it to fall apart because of something stupid I'd done.

Even though he didn't answer, Jesse had clearly heard me calling out for him, because my phone suddenly buzzed in my hand.

Shhh. Just meet me in the gym already.

There's still a gym? I wrote back. And then, when he didn't respond, I typed, Come on. This is crazy.

Jesse didn't reply to that text either, basically leaving me no choice. I trudged forward and scrambled over one after another of those rubble hills, chunks of plaster or wood or brick or metal shifting under my galoshes, sharp things poking into my palms, my feet splashing down into the water when I reached the other side. At the top of each hill I'd catch a glimpse of our battered school. It hadn't been completely destroyed, not yet anyway. The science and English wings were gone, the main entrance, too. But half of the building was still standing, the entire right side, plus the gym.

After I made it across the parking lot, I walked alongside the building toward the gym. Every classroom was dark and every window had its panes busted out. All the doors I passed had been spray-painted with red *X*s and stripped of their locks. Knowing that the electricity had been turned off didn't make things feel safer.

The gym door had been propped open with a couple of loose bricks. This let in enough light to see. Otherwise, it would've been pitch black.

I peeked into the doorway but didn't see Jesse. My heart was pounding.

The bleachers were ripped from the walls, the basketball nets cut down, the banners removed, the cage lights missing from dangling wires. There was easily three inches of water on the floor.

Taking a small step in, I whispered, "Jesse! Let's just say goodbye like normal people."

Again, he didn't answer. But music began to play. Quietly, from a phone speaker.

A slow song, complete with saxophone.

And then Jesse stepped out of the shadows and into the wedge of light.

He was in the same outfit from Spring Formal. Not the wrestling singlet, but a pressed shirt and tie and slacks. He was remarkably clean, while I was covered in dirt and water from crossing the parking lot, so he must have changed when he got here. His blond hair curled behind his ears. He looked just as gorgeous as he had that night.

"What are you doing?" I said, the back of my neck prickling, because I already knew.

"There's a few things I need to say to you, Keeley." He held out his hand, beckoning to me to come closer.

"Jesse, we shouldn't be here," I said, splashing toward him. "Please? Can we please go talk somewhere else?" I took his outstretched hand and tried pulling him to the door, but he stayed rooted. He turned his palm and cupped my hand in his like he was about to propose. "Jesse—"

He smiled shyly. "You brought up how shitty I'd acted at Spring Formal, and I realized that I never explained myself. What I was thinking."

"Don't worry about it. Everything's fine now. You and I, we're good. We're cool."

He took a deep breath and exhaled it. He was worried about what he was going to tell me. Nervous. "Do you remember what you said to me when we were slow dancing?"

I forced a swallow. Inside my brain, my voice sounded like the last repeat of an echo before it fades to silence.

*I'm in love with you, Jesse Ford.*

The memory had me burning bright in the dark. I felt the urge to defend myself because I *had* been joking when I told Jesse I loved him. But I also couldn't deny the truth underneath my joke, so I kept my mouth shut.

"We'd had so much fun that night. Our whole running-through-the-rain thing? I have never done something so epically cool with a girl before. In fact, as soon as we got into the gym, I couldn't wait for the stupid dance to be over so you and I could go hook up. I even told Zito and those guys they needed to find another ride home because—"

I shook my head. "So I wasn't crazy. You did want to kiss me at Spring Formal."

"Wasn't it obvious?"

"Jesse! One second, we were slow dancing and everything felt so perfect, and the next, it was like you couldn't get away from me fast enough. Then, when I found you in the hallway with Victoria . . ." I'd pushed down just how much that had hurt me after we first kissed a couple of days later. But saying it out loud to him, finally, made me remember. "Can you blame me for thinking I'd gotten it wrong?"

He gave my hand a squeeze. "Look. I think even you can admit that it was a heavy thing to say in the moment. And I don't typically do *heavy* with my relationships. In fact, I avoid it. For me, it's like, once a girl gets too attached, that's the time to disconnect. Otherwise, it's going to be all hurt feelings and anger and drama. That's why I grabbed Victoria. I felt like I needed to defuse the situation fast."

"Did you kiss Victoria in the hallway that night?"

Jesse shamefully dropped his head. He had. I'd been hoping he hadn't but he totally, totally had. "I didn't want to hurt you."

"So you thought making out with some other girl would let me down gently?" I pulled my hand free. I felt myself getting heated, and I didn't want to be. My heart was already feeling way too fragile.

"I liked you, too, okay? But I did what I thought was best to manage your expectations. And then when the whole Lake Aberdeen craziness started, I thought, What's the harm, if we're all saying good-bye in a few weeks? Why not live in the moment?"

"This is stupid, Jesse. Let's please not talk about this anymore. I can't handle another crappy good-bye."

"That's the thing, though." He wet his lips. "I can't stand here and tell you I would have fallen for you if this had been a normal school year." He took one step closer to me, and then another. "But I did fall for you, Keeley. And now I don't want to let you go. I don't want to say good-bye."

I was trembling. I tried making a joke to cover it up. "I already knew that, Jesse," I said, slapping his arm. "You couldn't even tell me your mom had signed a deal with the adjusters!"

Jesse didn't laugh. He didn't even crack a smile. "Because I didn't want to ruin our last days together. I wanted to spend every minute with you and I wanted every one of those minutes to be good."

His intensity caught me completely off-guard. "But you are leaving, Jesse. And I don't know where I'm going and—"

"None of that matters. We can figure something out. Keeley, my closest friends don't even know me as well as you do. I've never talked about my family to anyone before, not even Zito. What we have . . . it's not like any other relationship in my life."

I wanted to remind him that he'd actually never willingly talked about his family stuff with me. In fact, we hadn't had a single discussion about them. But I figured his feelings were so bottled up inside him that even the littlest release felt like a dam bursting. I understood that, more than anyone else could.

He went on. "We're the same in so many ways. That's why you came to me for help yesterday. Because you knew I'd get exactly what you were trying to do with Morgan." He brushed a piece of hair out of my face. "I know we can make this work."

"Make what work?"

"I want to be with you, Keeley. I don't want to lose you." There was something different about his voice. It was stripped of the bravado. Of the humor. It was weirdly small.

"Jesse . . ."

"Just think about it." He pulled me closer so I had to look up to see his face. "There's no reason why we can't have fun together every single day, from today forward," he said, brightening. "We don't have to walk away from Aberdeen feeling sad. I know things are screwed up in your life. Whatever happened with Morgan, stuff happening with your family. You and I can be the silver linings of this super-shitty cloud."

I tried to hold on to Jesse's words. I let my head fall onto his chest. He was warm. And his heart was beating so fast. "This was everything I wanted you to say to me the night of Secret Prom."

"I know I screwed that up, Keeley, but trust me, I already had these feelings for you. I was just freaking out about losing you. I didn't want to tell you I was leaving, I didn't want to go, I just wanted to have a good night with you. That's why I acted like such an idiot."

I'd never stopped to think about what life with Jesse would be like somewhere outside Aberdeen. I didn't dare let myself. He was an almost mythic part of my adolescence, someone so larger-than-life, he almost didn't seem real.

"Being with you was something I never, ever imagined," I said. "And having your attention made me feel, I don't know, like a stronger, better version of myself. But . . ." Jesse's smile began to fade, and it was heartbreaking, but I forced myself to keep talking. "But I don't want someone I can just have a good time with."

"You don't."

I shook my head. "Sometimes I'm going to be sad."

"Well, then, I'll know exactly how to make it better!"

"You can't always make it better."

"I don't get it. You told me you loved me the first night but now you don't want to be with me? Because you want to be sad sometimes?" He said, "Huh?" like he didn't understand, but I knew he did. Because no one looked sadder than Jesse in that moment.

I didn't know how to say it, because I was realizing the truth in that moment for the first time. How I had needed Jesse because I thought he was the way for me to repair the rift in my friendship with Morgan. I'd needed Jesse because I didn't want to think about life without Aberdeen. But I didn't have Morgan anymore, and Aberdeen was lost too. Jesse just didn't matter to me in the same way now.

"I'm sorry."

Jesse blinked. "Wow." He exhaled long and slow. "I don't want to sound like a jerk, but I don't think there was one part of me that thought you'd turn me down." After laughing a bit, he undid a few buttons on his shirt and fanned his neck. "That doesn't make me sound like a jerk, does it?"

"No, Jesse."

"I don't believe you, but for the sake of my ego, I'll pretend that I do."

"When's your family leaving?"

"In a couple hours." He shoved his hands into his pockets. "What about you and your dad?"

"I'm not sure. I'm kind of waiting for him to tell me."

"Do me a favor then and text me when you're headed out, so I know you're okay." He wrapped me in a hug. And there was something about how hard he squeezed me that told me that, though he was sad, he was also relieved. Because Jesse was still

Jesse. So it didn't even catch me off-guard when, before letting me go, he swayed me back and forth as the slow song playing on his phone reached a sax solo crescendo. Then he twirled me around and dipped me, and the two of us were laughing.

It was almost too perfect that Jesse, in that moment, defaulted to the joke. It really was easier that way. It also immediately validated my choice to let him go, because I suddenly wasn't interested in easy anymore.

# 38

⚠️ **EMERGENCY BROADCAST SYSTEM ALERT:** Significant flooding has been reported throughout Aberdeen County. Residents are advised to seek safe shelter immediately. Stay tuned for further updates.

I texted Levi. Hey, is your dad home?

No. There's all kinds of stuff happening at City Hall. Press conferences and things. Turned it into a command center. Why? Where'd you go? Are you safe? Also you left that satanic cat in my car and it keeps hissing at me.

I didn't answer any of his questions. I just went straight over to his house.

Levi answered the door in a pair of plaid pajama pants and a police academy T-shirt. I think he'd just showered, because he smelled so good.

He brought me into the house. I was surprised to see that not much packing had been done. But of course Levi's dad would be one of the last to go. He'd be in charge of things after the rest of us were gone.

"I'm sorry I left you today."

"Whatever, I guess I should have expected it. Seriously though. Whose cat is that? It scratched the crap out of my arm."

I held my breath for a moment, unsure. "You're a good guy,

Levi. I know I'm an idiot sometimes, but you know I care for you, right? I want to make sure you know that before I go."

"Are you okay?"

I shook my head. "No. I'm not."

Levi stepped forward, and he touched my hair. "Keeley."

I had never heard my name so softly. Except for one other time. When Levi found me in the hallway. I felt from him what I'd felt from him then, only magnified a million times. A warmth, a caring. A comfort. He was seeing me at my lowest, my most vulnerable. And it was okay.

His gaze slowly lowered to the floor and his cheeks turned pink. "You're looking at me like you want to kiss me."

Was that what I wanted? Truly? Or was this another cover for my feelings, for the hurt I was feeling over Morgan? My heart was beating a mile a minute, and I don't remember moving, but the space between Levi and me started to close up.

Even though I wasn't sure of anything, I knew I could tell Levi everything. Because I was my most me with him. I'd once felt that way about Jesse, but it turns out that was because we were broken in the same way.

I wanted to talk and I wanted to kiss Levi and I wanted to start completely over and it all was a jumble in my brain that I couldn't untangle in time.

Headlights bounced across the wall.

Levi jerked his head around. "Shit. My dad's home. You have to hide."

"You're not allowed to have girls over?"

"No, I'm not allowed to have *you* over."

He opened a nearby door and guided me into a dark room. "I'll let you know when the coast is clear. Just stay hidden." He held on to my hand longer than he should have, because he didn't want to let go.

It took a minute for my eyes to adjust. And then I saw the big desk and the papers. This was Sheriff Hamrick's home office.

I started looking around quietly. For what, I wasn't sure. On his desk were a mess of papers, and one framed photograph of Levi, Sheriff Hamrick, and Levi's mother. I stared at it. His mother was beautiful. Tall and graceful. Levi and his father were smiling toward the camera. But Mrs. Hamrick had her head tossed back, her mouth cracked wide open, midlaugh.

Next to the photo was a half-drunk bottle of gin.

I turned around and saw a huge poster-size printout tacked on the wall. It was a survey of Aberdeen. All of the houses that would be wiped away. All of them marked with a red *X*.

Except for one on Hewitt Road.

We were it.

The sheriff walked in the front door, and heard Levi speak to him. Their voices were low and mumbly, but I wasn't really listening anyway. I was staring at that map.

At the graveyard.

It was marked REMOVAL OF HEADSTONES.

But what about the bodies?

I wasn't sure, but I had a feeling that if there was any hope for us, for Aberdeen, for putting my family back together, it was on this map.

I quickly pulled out the pushpins and rolled up the paper as quietly as I could. Then I snuck out the window.

# 39

---

**Monday, May 30**
⚠ **EMERGENCY BROADCAST SYSTEM ALERT:** Dam construction is being temporarily halted until further notice, due to dangerous flooding conditions. Stay tuned for further updates.

---

Rain pounded the windows. We spread out the plans on our kitchen table. Dad rubbed his unshaven face for a few quiet minutes. He was in a chair and I was leaning over his shoulder.

"I mean, I'm not sure," I said again. "But every one of our relatives is in that cemetery, Dad. And that goes for most people here. This is going to be a big story, whether or not anyone has signed deals. At the very least, this could buy us some more time. Shift the conversation back to what's right and what's wrong."

"You did good, Keeley," Dad said. His hand rested on mine and gave it a squeeze.

My phone buzzed in my pocket but I ignored it. "So what's the plan? Should we call that reporter guy? Shawn? I know you think he screwed you over in his last story, but this is too juicy—"

Dad stood up. "I'm going straight to the governor."

"Oh." I was surprised. It seemed to make more sense to get the story out first, but Dad was already hustling to change into a clean shirt. I didn't want to slow his inertia. "He's down at City

Hall. I think Mayor Aversano's there too. And Sheriff Hamrick. They've got a whole command center set up."

We got into his truck and headed over to City Hall. The streets were practically deserted, but a few residents were still packing up their cars and heading out. My phone buzzed a few more times. I knew they were texts from Levi. I was afraid to open them but I forced myself.

Where'd you go?

Are you still here?

My dad left again. Can you sneak back over?

There's something I need to tell you. And I don't know how much time we have left.

His last text made me think he still wasn't aware of what I'd done. We'd be heading into this showdown with the element of surprise in our favor, which was good. But also, Levi would know soon, which made me feel sick. Because we'd had that *almost* moment. In an alternate universe, his dad would never have come home, I would never have found the paper, and we would have kissed. I steeled myself—this was better. This would save my dad, my family, maybe even the town. If things worked out, then it would all have been worth it.

We parked right in front of City Hall, blocking a fire hydrant. A few news trucks were lined up across the street. Probably preparing for their nightly live broadcasts. They saw my dad, recognized him, and turned their heads as we raced up the steps.

A policeman stopped us just past the main doors. He looked very surprised to see us. "Whoa there, Jim. Where do you think you're going?"

A few wooden chairs lined the hall. Dad backed away from

the officer and took a seat on one, a smug smile on his face. He leaned his cane against the wall. "Tell the governor I need to see him. Now." He folded his arms.

Something about that smile made me uneasy. The thing we were holding was proof for sure, but it wasn't something to gloat about. Especially because of where it had come from and what I'd risked to get it. I wanted to tell Dad to take it down a notch, but I couldn't with the police officer standing in front of us, looking at Dad like he was crazy. He unclipped the radio clipped to his chest and radioed for Sheriff Hamrick to come out.

A minute later, the sheriff stepped out from behind a closed door. "What's this all about, Jim?" He sounded tired. "You know people are busy back there."

Dad laughed. He held up the tube of paper. "Look familiar?" Sheriff Hamrick stared, his brow furrowing. "It should. My daughter had the good sense to sneak it out of your house tonight."

I saw it hit him. Sheriff Hamrick looked at me with such disappointment and anger, it made the hairs stand up on my arms.

"That's stolen property," Sheriff Hamrick said.

"This is my golden ticket."

I turned to Dad, confused. "Dad . . ."

With that, Sheriff Hamrick spun on his heel and disappeared into another office farther down the hall.

"Dad, you shouldn't instigate them." My voice felt tight inside my throat.

"I know what I'm doing, Keeley," he said, and he leaned forward to see down the hall. "I want you to wait out here."

"No. No way."

Finally he faced me. "Keeley, listen. You are waiting out here."

A door opened down the hall. There, hanging half out of the doorframe, was Governor Ward. His suit was rumpled. "All right. Let's talk, Mr. Hewitt."

Dad stood up. I followed him. He turned and shot me a look. "Dad, I'm coming with you!"

He opened his mouth to say no, but Governor Ward spoke first. "Let her hear this, Hewitt. She stole the damn thing for you. Shouldn't she know what's really going on?"

Something in Dad's face shifted. The bravado in him tipped out a little and spilled on the floor. But after hearing that, I was definitely going into that room whether he wanted me to or not. I stepped past him and walked into the office first.

Mayor Aversano was on an uncomfortable-looking couch. Sheriff Hamrick was standing in the corner of the room, talking intensely on his cell phone. As I walked in, he gave me the meanest look, mumbled something quietly into the phone, and then quickly ended the call.

Not thirty seconds later, I felt my pocket buzz. And my heart sank all the way down to my toes.

"I'll make this quick," Dad started. "What we have here is proof that you have not made plans to move the bodies in the graveyard. If you double your opening offer, I'll give up the movement and fade away quietly. If you don't . . . well, I'm going to walk this right back across the street and let the reporters have a go at it."

Dad set a piece of paper on the desk. It was the adjusters' offer I had found in our attic, five hundred thousand dollars. I'd thought my mom spoke to them behind Dad's back. Only he was the one who'd gone.

But when?

Why?

I leaned closer to the table and saw the date. It was Wednesday, May 25. The day after dam construction began.

Dad had been willing to leave then. But I guess not at that price. He wanted more.

And now he was practically blackmailing the governor into giving him a million-dollar payout? When he was letting someone like Russell Dixon live in squalor?

My pocket buzzed again. I felt like I was going to be sick.

The governor laughed and eased into the chair behind the desk. "Here's the thing, Hewitt. I'm not afraid of you. I'm not afraid of this story. I can say it was a mistake. The graveyard won't be flooded until the last stage of the project. We have time to do whatever we want. You are the one who is out of time. Out of leverage. All your supporters have made deals. So it's no longer in our interest to pay you to be quiet. Because no one is listening to you anymore." Dad was still as stone. "And our opening offer, which I still believe was generous"—he took the paper and crumpled it into a wad—"is null and void." He spread his palms out on the desk. "I will offer you half of our bid. That's two hundred and fifty thousand dollars, under the condition that you leave Aberdeen tonight. And that is only because your daughter is standing here with you. I feel for her, and your wife, who clearly didn't know the game you were trying to play."

Dad cleared his throat. "What you're doing to this town is wrong. You know it and I know it."

"More wrong than you manipulating your neighbors to stand by your side to earn yourself a bigger payday?"

It all started to make sense, especially when I thought back to the fight we'd had outside Mr. Dixon's house. When Sheriff Hamrick had said to my dad, "Your daughter is helping people." He knew then that my dad wasn't doing it for the town. He was doing it for himself.

Dad was trying to look tough, but I knew by the way he was gripping his cane that he was feeling anything but. "And what if I don't agree to your offer?"

The governor shrugged. "I guess you could try waiting out this storm. But you might not have a home to come back to. In that case, we'd be forced to condemn this site and—"

"Okay. Wait a second here. Just wait one second here, please. I get it. You want to punish me for being a pain in the ass. And maybe that's what I'm due. So yes. I'll agree to take a cut. I will. But let's say three hundred thousand dollars. Remember, I'm losing a home and a business, and from what I understand, those people were given more than—"

"What business?" Aversano said from the couch. "You haven't worked in years."

Dad turned so he was only facing Governor Ward. I watched his heartbeat in his neck. "Three hundred thousand dollars and I'll sign whatever I need to sign and you'll never see me or my family again." As if to prove it, Dad picked a pen out of the pen cup on the desk and clicked it.

The governor leaned backward, as far as the chair would go. "Two hundred thousand dollars. You held your cards too long, Jim."

The mayor picked some dead leaves out of a potted plant. "We know your wife is gone. You aren't going to win her back empty-handed. You're not going to look like the hero then."

Dad met my eyes, just briefly. I'd never seen him look sadder, not even in the hospital after his accident. And then, with his head down, he said, "Deal."

I couldn't be in the room any longer. Before I walked out, I walked up to the desk where Governor Ward sat. "But you will do it, right? You will move the bodies?" I looked pleadingly at Sheriff Hamrick.

"Of course," Mayor Aversano said from the couch. "Clearly, this was an oversight. Thank you for bringing it to our attention."

I stumbled out into the hall. I was covered in sweat, my T-shirt sticking to me.

With a shaking hand, I checked my phone for the texts Levi had sent to me while we were in the room.

You are the most selfish person I've ever met.

I will NEVER forgive you for this.

Tears rolled over my cheeks as I tucked my phone into my back pocket. I heard the main doors open down the hall. There was Levi, coming in from the rain. He peeled off his raincoat and set it down on a chair. The police officer stepped aside and let him into the hallway, no questions asked. Levi ran a few feet before he saw me. But once he did, he skidded to a stop.

"Levi, I—"

"Don't. Don't even, Keeley. I'm not here for you. I need to talk to my dad. He's going to kill me."

The hallway was narrow and Levi was waiting for me to step out of his way before he'd get any closer. But I started walking toward him instead, trembling. "Please. Let me explain."

"There's nothing to explain. You completely betrayed me."

I felt light-headed, and I put a hand out to the wall in case I fainted. It was too hot and too bright. "That's not what I wanted."

He couldn't have looked less convinced. "If you really cared about me and my feelings, you would have talked to me about what you found instead of stealing it. We could have gone to my dad together and asked him what was happening. Instead you stole from my house and went straight to your dad."

"I was trying to do the right thing."

He laughed snidely. "The right thing for you, maybe. And your dad. You wanted to win, that's all. You wanted to win and you felt completely fine with screwing me over to do it."

It was not lost on me, even in that moment, the irony. That my father had done the same thing to me, only moments ago. He'd held whatever his true plans were close to his chest. It was just how my mom had said. He wasn't putting us first. And I hadn't put Levi first. Both of us had been dishonest with the people we supposedly cared about. And now it was blowing up in our faces.

"I wanted to force them to do the right thing for your mom and everyone else who's buried in that cemetery. Yes, of course that would help my dad. But it would help other people too."

But instead of understanding me, seeing it from my side, Levi bared his teeth. "I shared stuff with you. Stuff about my mom that I haven't talked about with anyone. You wouldn't even have thought about that graveyard if it weren't for me."

"I care about you, Levi. I care about you so much. That's what I came to your house to tell you today." He closed his eyes and dropped his head back and I knew he was thinking about it, how we'd almost kissed. I wanted to go back to that moment and do everything differently.

"The worst part is that, if you had asked me, I probably would have told you to go ahead, take the stupid paper." Hearing Levi say it, I knew it was true. He would have. My breath caught in my chest. "I've done everything you've asked of me ever since all this stuff went down. I feel like I earned that from you. The trust. But you cut me out, Keeley. So for the last time, stop pretending like this was for me. It wasn't."

And that's when I knew there was nothing I could say to Levi that would make it better.

Because there was nothing my dad could say to me.

And yet, I still tried.

"My dad . . . this whole thing wasn't what I thought. He wasn't trying to save Aberdeen for the right reasons. Or maybe he was in the beginning, but not anymore. I don't even know, to be honest. If I had known that, I . . ." At that point, I was sobbing. "I didn't mean to hurt anyone. I made a mistake, but I thought it was the right thing to do."

He shook his head. "It's doesn't matter. It's over. And you've actually helped me. I'm glad Aberdeen is going under, because I know for sure I'll never have to see you again." He edged past me.

About an hour later, Dad walked out of the office, his face wan. He had a piece of paper in his hand. He didn't look at me and I didn't look at him. We got into his truck and were escorted by two police cars back to our house. One of them handed me a purring Freckles. He'd been taken out of the cardboard box and put into a proper kitty kennel with a soft towel, probably by sweet Levi. By then, the rain was coming down harder than hard, the streets were flooded worse than that night we were all brought into the gym. Another officer gave us a handful of cardboard boxes to fill up, but in the time it had taken him to bring them from the trunk of his car up to our house, they'd gone pulpy and were collapsing. But he didn't seem to care.

"You've got thirty minutes."

I didn't even know what I was shoving in there. I was crying so hard. Dad came into my room to help me, but I screamed at him to get out.

Thirty minutes later, we got back into Dad's truck. The police cars followed us again, all the way out to the highway. When we reached the Aberdeen town limits, they slowly peeled away. With Freckles's kennel on my lap, I turned around in my seat and watched my hometown disappear in a mix of rain and tears.

"I thought things would work out differently," Dad said quietly.

And though I was so mad at him, I had to nod. I had to give him at least that.

It broke my heart. Because he wasn't a bad person. Just like I wasn't a bad person. So how did we both screw up so badly?

## 40

**Tuesday, October 11**
Sunshine, breezy, high of 45°F

I was five months into my new life when I learned that the dam had been completed. It struck me as slightly anticlimactic, only because water had continued to slide over Aberdeen all throughout construction. You could see it happening from the lookout on the other side of the river, which I visited sometimes. But now that things were finished, it would happen quickly. A complete overtaking. Some said a few days, others predicted a few hours.

Welcome to Lake Aberdeen.

Governor Ward planned a huge celebration. There'd be a parade, carnival rides and food trucks, and fireworks at night, and the Ridgewood High School Marching Band would play during the ribbon-cutting ceremony. That was the reason why I heard about it before a single poster or banner went up. Governor Ward's invitation was the top story of morning announcements.

I say *top story* because now that I was a senior at Ridgewood High School, morning announcements were an actual news program beamed from the school's television studio to the flat-screen televisions in every single classroom. Everyone in my homeroom knew I was from Aberdeen, and they all discreetly glanced over to see if I was, I don't know, going to cry or something? Well, I didn't cry. I kept my face in my AP trig textbook and pretended to be too absorbed to have heard anything. There were a handful of other former Aberdeen residents who now went to Ridgewood. I bet they acted the same way. We were all friendly, but I wouldn't say we were friends. They were better about starting new lives for themselves than I was. They made new friends, aligned themselves with new groups. If they missed their old lives at all, I couldn't tell.

Mom had moved us to Ridgewood about a week before my senior year started. She'd signed a lease on a different apartment close to Baird, and she and I had been living there for almost a month, but when she heard from another nurse that half a duplex in Ridgewood was going to come up for rent because the occupant had died, she broke that lease and signed a new one. Actually, she didn't have to break the lease. Dad took it over.

So she and I lived on the ugliest street in Ridgewood, where the houses were old and small and none of them had front lawns. The first rental had been nicer and less expensive, but Mom felt that the opportunity for me to have a senior year at one of the best public schools in the state was too good to pass up. Luckily, I didn't have to repack anything because I'd never bothered unpacking in the first place.

Mom settled into our new place right away. And though it didn't feel like home, not to me anyway, she had done a lot to make the place cozy. Little by little, she replaced the cast-off stuff she'd gathered from her departing patients with things of her own choosing. A chenille throw found on sale at Marshalls to replace someone's hand-knit afghan. Other things she made, like a white canvas cover for our old couch, and pillows with goldenrod flowers and periwinkle stripes. I wondered if that was what my life would be as time passed, memories replaced with new experiences.

Mom could have completely refurnished the apartment all at once with the settlement money Dad had given her, but she was trying not to spend a dime of that. She and Dad agreed it should be college money for me, so I wouldn't have to go to Baird if I didn't want to.

I had actually decided to apply to a few other schools that I never would have considered if not for the college fair my new high school put on. I went to the fair because I had nothing else to do, but I ended up talking to a few admissions counselors. My life was now a weird blank slate, and I could insert myself anywhere pretty easily. I had no best friend to leave behind, no boyfriend suggesting I stay close, no cozy bedroom in my childhood home pulling at my heartstrings. It was all gone. But the upside of that was that, even though Ridgewood's curriculum was infinitely harder than anything at Aberdeen High, I was killing it. I had nothing else to do but study and do homework.

When I came home from school that day, Mom was on the linoleum floor, her back up against the fridge, our kitchen phone pressed to her ear. "Okay, well, I should probably go. Keeley just walked in from school. Oh, wait, just hold on a second, Annie." Mom cupped her hand over the receiver and whispered to me, "Do you want me to see if Morgan can come to the phone?"

She asked this every time.

Though I always wanted to say yes, I never did. If Morgan wanted to speak to me, she would. She knew my number. More than that, she knew I was trying to get in touch. I had to wait for her to forgive me, if she ever would.

I'd lost count of how many times I'd reached out to her since the day she left Aberdeen. At first, I would leave her these long rambling messages. I'd talk to her as if she were on the other end of the line, instead of sending my call straight to her voice mail. But now, months later, I'd keep it short and sweet, not much more than "Miss you, Morgan."

Elise and I were still in touch. She texted me totally out of the blue, near the middle of September. She wanted to know how I was doing, if I had made any new friends, stuff like that. It was more than I deserved, and I immediately wondered if Elise was acting as an intermediary for Morgan. But then, I realized, no. Elise was just that terrific a person.

She was liking Florida, especially the boys, who were perpetually tan. She loved living in a place that was more diverse. "You should really think about going away for college. You need to be meeting different types of people, seeing that the world is a bigger place. And, I mean, the food alone, Keeley, oh my God. I'm obsessed with Cuban food. I don't know that I could stomach one of Saint Ann's bland old casseroles again."

It was weird. I'd always thought Elise and I were friends, but it wasn't until after she left that we actually got close. There was more room for us now that we didn't have Morgan's attention to compete for.

I hadn't heard from Levi, either, but that was a different story. He was at college now, far away from Aberdeen. He wasn't online at all and he'd changed his cell number.

But I thought of him, especially as the weather changed. I imagined what he might be doing, wondered if he liked college, if he would join a fraternity. He probably wouldn't join a jock one, but maybe an academic one. He might have met someone.

Someone kinder and nicer than me, who wouldn't screw him over the way I had.

Mom stood up to hang up the phone and then spontaneously hugged me tight. I knew it hurt her that I was hurting, and she hated that there was nothing she could do to fix it.

"Did you hear about the dam being completed?" I asked.

"Yes. Your dad mentioned it today when he called."

Dad had taken a job at one of those big-box hardware stores. They made him a greeter, in the front of the store, and let him sit on a stool. He knew a little about everything, so they thought that'd be the place where he could help the most people. With his first paycheck, he came and asked Mom out on a date. She said yes. Now they did a weekly dinner and a movie, early enough so he could drive her back to our duplex so she could do some paperwork. It was another thing that gave me hope. My mom really loved my dad, and vice versa. They were working on their relationship. I just wanted the same chance.

"We're going for dinner tonight, if you'd like to join us."

I shook my head. "Bring me back something."

When Mom and Dad left on their date, I decided to finally unpack my boxes. If Aberdeen was going to be no more, what was I hiding from?

As soon as I opened the first box, I realized what had kept me from doing it. The thing is, it's hard to know for sure what's worth saving and what to throw away when you only have thirty minutes to sort through everything you own, and you weren't given nearly enough cardboard boxes, and you're sobbing your eyes out. I knew I'd made mistakes. I'd thrown away stuff I wished I had kept. I'd held on to plenty of things I should have thrown away. And I didn't want to confront them. It was easier to hide than to deal, because I knew there was no going back and fixing things.

And yet, I couldn't bring myself to throw that sticker away. Not when it was the only piece of Morgan I had left.

I was tossing a stack of old spiral notebooks when a worksheet fluttered to the ground. It was from my junior high health class. A diagram of the pituitary gland nestled just below the ear in a human head.

Obviously, in and of itself, the diagram didn't mean crap. I promise I have no particular affinity for the pituitary gland. The doodles I'd added with my colored pencils were what took my breath away. The long hair and brown eyes and pink lips on the head to make it look like me. Jesse Ford's initials inside a droplet of hormone being secreted into my bloodstream. I'd even turned the droplet into a heart shape.

It was proof that I truly had loved Jesse Ford forever, or at least since the sixth grade, which I believe is the first time you can really love a boy in a way that feels possible, not like playing pretend. And, for a brief moment, he realized that he loved me, too. But by then, I was a different person. I couldn't say a *better* person, but someone who couldn't ignore their shortcomings.

Still, I hesitated to throw the paper away, because how many girls can say they got what they always wished for?

I took a picture and texted it to Jesse. Julia and his mother had settled about an hour away, near his grandmother. And now that Julia was taken care of, Jesse had decided to move to California. Los Angeles, actually. He was taking improv acting classes. He'd even booked a commercial for a car. It was all about a bunch of college kids turning off the highway and cruising through the desert to find the perfect place to watch a meteor shower. He didn't have a speaking part, but he was the driver. It was great casting. Or, maybe because I knew him, I could actually believe he'd do something as crazy as that.

This is the best thing I've ever seen, he wrote back. And then, Miss you.

I missed Jesse, too. Just not in the way he was hoping. As someone I had chosen to let go of, rather than someone who'd let me go. That made all the difference.

When Dad and Mom came home, I was in the living room watching television. I'd made it through three boxes. There were two more, but I was exhausted.

Mom had brought me back a slice of cake. When she went into the kitchen to get me a fork, I asked Dad, "Did you hear about the dam being finished?"

"Yeah. Guys at the store were talking about it. Wondering if I was going to go and make a scene." I felt my mom pause in the doorway. But Dad leaned back, easy. "I told them they were crazy. I have a lot of fight left in me, but now I'm fighting for the right things."

"I'm thinking of going," I said. "See who I might run into."

My mom frowned. She sat down on the couch and rubbed my head. "Oh, Keeley. I don't want you to get your hopes up. I know Morgan won't be there," she said. "Annie's working and she said Morgan's really involved with her new church group and they're going apple picking somewhere." She looked like she wanted to say more, but she didn't, and I was glad of it. We were both hoping that one day Morgan and I would patch things up and I'd be able to hear all the details about her new life straight from her.

But it sucked to know that, because it was exactly what I'd been hoping. That I might see Morgan. That maybe this was my test, to see if I had the courage to come and face what I had lost head-on.

The possibility of our reconciling was feeling more and more remote. My throat closed up and I started to cry. "Mom, did you ever have a fight like this with Mrs. Dorsey? This bad?"

Mom had tears in her eyes too. She wiped mine away with her thumbs and then her own. "No. We never have. But that's not to say we haven't had our fights. Believe me, we have. We've had to reinvent our friendship a hundred different times."

"I don't know how to fix this."

"You need to start caring for yourself, Keeley. What's done is done. I know you want to take back whatever happened, but you can't. But you still need to put one foot in front of the other and find a way to keep going."

Dad reached down to the coffee table and pressed the power button on the remote. The TV flashed and then went dark. Then he turned to face me on the couch. "I want to tell you something, Keeley."

Mom took this as a cue and went back to the kitchen. I heard her fiddling with stuff. Dad and I had never had a conversation about what had happened the night we left Aberdeen. "Your mother and I are both so proud of you. You've come to this new place, you're doing terrific in school, but I know you're missing your friends." He took a deep breath. "I made so many mistakes.

But more than anything, I regret that I involved you in them."

"It wasn't all you, Dad. I was screwing up plenty on my own."
I let my head fall on his shoulder. "But thank you for saying that."

"It was addictive. To be seen by you and your mother, not
to mention people in town, as someone who could lead them.
Someone they wanted to listen to. I felt so much shame for the
way I acted after my accident, so sorry for myself. And I was really
desperate to right those wrongs. I wanted to believe that if you
and your mother saw me that way, maybe that was really who
I was. I hid from the truth, which was that I had a family who
needed me long before all this mess began. Not to be a hero, but
to be there every day, for them. So that's what I'm trying to do
now. Just show up as who I really am and hope that's enough."

I understood, of course. It was exactly why my big sticker
move hadn't worked. Morgan didn't need a big gesture. She
needed me to be a better friend. Instead of fixing the problems, I
deflected and distracted.

Wiping my eyes, I decided I would still go to the dam celebration, even knowing that Morgan wouldn't be there. If she never
wanted to forgive me, I had to be okay with that. But I'd never
forgive myself if I didn't take my last chance to see the place where
we became friends, before that disappeared forever too.

# 41

The day Governor Ward dedicated the dam to the former residents of Aberdeen couldn't have been more gorgeous. Bright sun, blue sky, chirping birds, turning leaves reflecting their fire in the water. As promised, there were food trucks and carnival rides parked along the shore of the new lakefront park. What had been there before? It was hard to tell and I don't think many people cared. They were more concerned with staking out a place for their lawn chairs to see the fireworks that would be set off from atop the dam come sundown. Though it felt wrong, I bought myself a caramel apple. The whole vibe was celebratory, but for me it was like throwing a party at a funeral.

After today, there would be no reason for anyone to come back. Even if we didn't patch things up, at least I could get essential news about Morgan from my mom. But Levi? I knew he'd be gone from my life forever.

I stuffed my hands deep into the pockets of my cardigan and walked around, hoping to see a familiar face. There were a few. A teacher here, a former classmate there. But I can't say I felt much seeing them, even the ones who stopped to hug me, who asked how I was doing. One girl told me that Secret Prom would always be her very best memory of life in Aberdeen. I told them I was fine, everything was great. And when they asked me about Morgan, how she was doing, I straight-up lied. I couldn't tell them the truth. How badly I'd screwed everything up in those final days.

Had anything changed?

Maybe what Morgan had said was true. Was I so emotionally closed off that I couldn't feel anything?

No. That wasn't the case. Because I had all the feelings when I spotted Sheriff Hamrick, standing near a coffee cart, talking to other officers. Some of them wore uniforms from other towns.

I froze and watched for a few minutes, hoping I might see Levi. But of course he wasn't there. His college was something like ten hours away.

I approached the sheriff carefully. I had nothing to lose.

"Hello, Sheriff Hamrick."

He glanced at me and looked away. "Hello, Keeley."

One of the other officers snickered. "Your dad here?"

I ignored him. "I wanted to ask you how Levi is doing."

"He's terrific." Sheriff Hamrick tipped his coffee cup to his lips and took a sip. "He's really taken to school. I don't even think he's planning to come home for Thanksgiving." And then, as if it struck him that he should be polite, he added, "Thanks for asking."

I waited for more. I wanted so much more. But that was all Sheriff Hamrick was going to give me. He had already turned so his back was to me.

"Well, please tell him I said hello, okay?"

Sheriff Hamrick nodded. I knew he wouldn't say it. He had no reason to. He didn't want any part of Aberdeen holding his son back. Not his dead mother and especially not me. That was his M.O. from the very beginning. And maybe Levi was better off.

All I could do was hope Levi understood why I'd stolen that map from his father's office. That even though I'd had my dad's back in that moment, I was thinking of him, too.

I made my way over to the new operations building, where I found Governor Ward mid-speech, gesturing toward the long plank of concrete floating atop the river in the far distance. He was boasting about the special "mini-museum" he'd commissioned, a room dedicated to the history of Aberdeen curated by an actual professor of history at the city university and generously funded by the developers of his now-revived waterfront development deal.

Gag me, please.

I hung toward the back of his crowd and looked out at the water. There was nothing familiar to see from this angle. We were upstream, across the river from what had been the north end of Aberdeen, about a half mile away from where the old mill used to be. And you couldn't see much besides the water.

After Governor Ward snipped a silk ribbon to polite applause from the crowd, the Ridgewood High School band kicked into a muted version of our national anthem. People turned and dispersed.

I stood there for a second as the realization hit me.

This was it.

The end.

Really, truly, the end.

The dam held back the water, but everything inside me was breaching the wall. I turned away and hustled, beating everyone back to the riverbank.

I'd picked the wrong guy.

I'd lost my best friend.

And now I wouldn't even have my hometown to go to again.

I had so many regrets. So many. I should have been a better friend. I should have been honest with Levi, let him in.

But maybe I'd done one thing right.

If Governor Ward had kept his promise, it would have made stealing the plans worth it. I'd believed him when he said he would. But the governor was also a shady guy. Clearly. Our former mayor was now an executive at the waterfront redevelopment corporation. I hadn't ever heard anything about those graves, where they were supposedly being moved to. There was no way for me to check.

I walked down to the water. There were kids playing there, their faces painted like different animals. A game of tag was in progress. They used me as a block. A girl with tiger cheeks was after a boy with bird feathers. He darted behind a shed and she ran for him, pounding the ground in a circle.

The shed, it hit me, looked exactly like the one Levi had opened when he and I paddled out to the Aberdeen movie theater.

What if I could prove to Levi that he did matter to me? He'd pretended not to care what happened to his mom's grave, but I knew deep down that was bullcrap. Self-preserving bullcrap, which I was the queen of.

I had to see if Governor Ward had kept his word, even though I'd already lost everything.

The graveyard was on a hill. There was a chance the water hadn't covered it yet. I could see if it had been dug up. It he kept his word, it would be a field of holes.

I had to try.

While the little kids stopped and stared, I opened up the shed and dragged out a kayak from the racks inside. Then I climbed in and pushed off from the water's edge. I pulled my hair back into a ponytail, lifted up a paddle, and started to row furiously from the shore.

Police were all around the festivities, likely hoping to stave off any last-minute protests, but no one seemed to be on the water. At least not in the direction I was paddling in—away from the dam and toward what I hoped was Aberdeen.

It had to have taken an hour. Maybe two. I heard the band still playing in the distance, but I was far out of sight of anyone who might be onshore. I floated by a few houses that hadn't been torn down. I looked up to the hill, hoping to see my house, but I couldn't. It was too misty.

I was suddenly faced with this sense of doubt. If I did find out that the bodies hadn't been moved, what would I tell Levi? Should I lie, to protect him?

It didn't matter. I just needed to do it. To free whatever it was.

I paddled harder.

I thought I might be close to the cemetery when I saw another kayak off in the distance. I was caught. I tried to paddle hard away, but by that time, my arms were barely functioning and the effort was pathetic.

The kayak closed the distance on me fast. I knew it was fruitless. I threw my arms up in the air, like, *Arrest me*. And then I saw.

It was Levi. I think he was almost as shocked to see me as I was to see him.

"Keeley, what the hell are you doing here?"

He looked tired. He'd let his hair grow in some. Not much, but long enough for it to be matted from bedhead. It was a soft, velvety shade of brown.

"Levi! I was coming to make sure they'd done the right thing." Our kayaks drifted slowly toward each other. It was so quiet. Just Levi and me, floating on top of what had been our home.

"What are you doing out here?" I asked him. "Does your dad know you're back? I just talked to him, I asked him about you."

"No. He has no clue. I had no plans to be here, actually. But last night, I don't know. I got in the car and started driving. Ten hours later . . . I made it." He shook his head. I think he was still in shock. "I came here for you, Keeley. I just didn't think you'd be here."

"I don't understand." How could Levi be here for me and also think I wouldn't be here?

He took a deep breath. "I was so mad at you when you stole that map from my dad, I purposely didn't tell you something very important."

"What?"

"When I was in Morgan's house, I saw that she had left something for you."

"Oh my God . . ." I remembered Levi asking me to come inside and see something. "What? What was it?"

"It was an envelope with your name on it."

Probably with a good-bye letter, a list of the reasons why she didn't want to be my friend anymore. But even if that was it, it would give me some closure. "Did you read it? What did it say?"

"No. I left it all where I found it. In the middle of the floor. I was going to tell you about it when you came over that night.

But then everything happened and . . . it was a way for me to hurt you back."

"Well . . . It's probably gone now."

"There's still a chance. Before I left town, I checked to see if you found it. When I saw it still on the floor, I stuck it inside a Ziploc bag and taped it to one of the blades of her ceiling fan."

"Are you serious?"

"Yeah. I didn't really want to get involved, but I figured that would buy you more time."

"Except I didn't know there was anything to find, Levi! I haven't talked to Morgan once, not once."

"I was afraid of that," he said shamefully. "That's why I came."

Our kayaks began to float away from each other, so Levi leaned forward and grabbed the nose of my kayak and pulled it so we were bobbing side by side. "Even though I hate what you did, I can't pretend that I'm someone who could live with that on my conscience. That's not who I am. I know how much Morgan means to you. So I drove all night. I thought I'd at least try and get that letter for you." His eyes fell. "But I've been out here paddling around for hours now, looking. I'm pretty sure her house has gone under."

Tears slipped from my eyes. "Thank you. Thank you for trying. That's more than I deserved, Levi."

He asked me, "Why are you here?"

"I wanted to make sure Governor Ward kept his promise and moved the bodies. Except I can't find the graveyard. I have no idea what part of town we're floating over." But the truth was, I couldn't look away from Levi.

"He did," Levi said. "My dad made sure of that." His head

dropped ever so slightly to the side. "But I don't think he would have if it not for you."

We bobbed up and down in our kayaks. We were completely adrift. But eventually we'd have to go.

"Keeley, why are you crying?"

"Because I've lost Morgan, I've lost Aberdeen. I don't want to lose you."

"Every time I thought about you, Keeley, I felt sad."

Hearing that broke my heart.

"But now that you're here, sad is the furthest thing from what I feel. I don't want to let you go either. Not if I don't have to."

Levi leaned across his kayak, and I leaned too. He kissed me. I wrapped my arms around his neck and kissed him back.

I think we would have kissed each other forever if we hadn't been interrupted. But someone shouted, "Put your hands up!"

We both turned and looked. Three police boats were motoring toward us. Sherriff Hamrick was in one of them and he looked madder than mad.

Levi took my hand in his. I knew he wasn't going to let me go. Not in the way that mattered. And I wouldn't either.

And then I see it taped to the fan. Just as Levi said it would be. An envelope inside a Ziploc bag.

"Someone went through a heck of a lot of effort to leave this for you," he says, rubbing his chin. "A couple hours later and we'd have been too late."

"It was Levi," I say, my cheeks burning.

"My son did this?"

I nod. "And I'll be forever grateful that he did. Because if I ever had a chance at finding closure, it's right there."

Sheriff Hamrick clicks his flashlight off, and for a few seconds, he doesn't say anything. Meanwhile, I try to figure out how the heck I'm going to get it.

Then the boat begins to rock, as Sheriff Hamrick jimmies the attic window open, and when he does, a rush of water pours into Morgan's bedroom. He puts on a life vest and swims inside. I grab the flashlight and aim the beam steady on the fan so he can see. Bobbing in the water, he carefully cuts down the package with a knife and swims it back to me between his teeth.

"I hope this helps you," he says, as he climbs back into the boat. And then he angles himself as he dries off, to give me some privacy.

Dear Keeley,

You probably won't ever get this letter. That's fine. I'm not sure you're ready to hear what I have to say anyway. But I need to get this out before leaving Aberdeen for good. So here goes . . .

I was awake last night when you climbed out of my bed. I heard you rummaging through my stuff. I knew you wouldn't find what you were after. The sticker book, obviously. I'd already thrown it away.

It wasn't even hard to do, because that's all it was, Keeley. Just a sticker book.

The double unicorn . . . I still can't believe you found one. And there was a second, when you showed it to me, where I wished that it would magically fix everything.

Only I knew it wouldn't, because of Wes. Keeping his presents didn't make losing him any easier. Ignoring that I missed him didn't make it hurt any less. Pretending I wasn't in love with him didn't make him disappear from my heart.

You've been going through a lot, too. I know that. With Jesse and with your family. You couldn't talk to me, or you didn't want to. Either way, I felt guilty for not being the best friend you needed. And also that I needed people other than you.

Last night I said that I want to believe we have a future,
but that it's hard to see it now. We've both got things we
need to let go of . . . hurt and bad feelings and this idea
that the way our friendship used to be is the only way
it ever could be. Throwing that sticker book away was a
step in the right direction. Our friendship wasn't working
anymore and I don't want to hold on to the past. The past
is bringing us down.

You need to take those steps too, Keeley. To figure
out who you are outside of our friendship, away from
Aberdeen.

The next time I see you, it will be someplace else. I think
that's good. It'll be easier for us to make new memories.
Because even though it's hard to see the future right now,
it's harder for me to imagine that you won't be in it. I just
need a little time. And so do you.

Love,

Morgan

I'm crying when I look up from her letter.

Not because our sticker book is gone forever. Or for all the
things lost underneath the water. My tears are ones of relief,
because I can finally see the new beginnings all around me.

# Acknowledgments

Zareen Jaffery is the kind of editor who answers brainstorm texts after midnight, who always finds more time in the schedule, who shares her own personal anecdotes knowing you'll steal them for the perfect plot device, who'll drop everything to read pages you're unsure about, even on the weekends. In other words, there is no better editor in the business than Zareen Jaffery and I am infinitely grateful to be working with her.

I am also lucky to have found a home for this book with the terrific team at Simon & Schuster, all-stars including but not limited to Justin Chanda, Anne Zafian, Chrissy Noh, Katy Hershberger, Mekisha Telfer, and designer Lucy Cummins, who created my beautiful cover.

My agent, Emily van Beek of Folio Junior, thank you for being my fiercest advocate long before I had a book to fight for.

Jenny Han is my best friend and first reader, the Danny to my Kenickie.

Much love to friends who read and gave invaluable input— Adele Griffin, Jill Dembowski, Brenna Heaps, Emmy Widener, Morgan Matson, Lynn Weingarten, and Brenna Vivian.

Thanks to Dan Silianoff for the dam knowledge and Mark Flaherty for the legalese. And to Ashley Andrykovitch, for the painting that started it all.

Lastly, to Nick Caruso, Irene Vivian, Harry Vivian, Asiya Jaleel, Kristen Cibak and Molly Boswell Caruso, thank you for keeping my real life in order while I was busy making up an imaginary one.